DEATH
MESSAGE

Kate London graduated from Cambridge University and moved to Paris where she trained in theatre. In 2006 Kate joined the Metropolitan Police Service. She finished her career working as part of a Major Investigation Team on SC&O1 – the Metropolitan Police Service's Homicide Command. She resigned from the MPS in August 2014. Her debut novel *Post Mortem* was published by Corvus in 2015.

Also by Kate London

Post Mortem

DEATH MESSAGE

KATE LONDON

CORVUS

For my sisters, Ann and Felicity

Through the sharp hawthorn blows the cold wind.

Shakespeare, *King Lear*

PROLOGUE

October 1987

The great storm of 1987 was the before and after of Claire Mills' life. More than twenty years later, she still woke in the middle of the night with a sudden ice-cold alarm that had her sitting up and seeing with luminous clarity those uprooted trees and crushed vehicles. The terror in her heart in the lonely hours of the morning was always the same: that the smaller traces of disaster in her life that she had chosen to ignore for so long had, on the morning after the storm, been emphatically written on the landscape, crying out for her to notice them at last. Among the many, many reproaches she made to herself was this one: she had failed to pay attention to portents.

She had known her daughter had secrets.

She had known too that her husband was having an affair, but whenever she had thought of his all-too-obvious infidelity – and she admitted to herself now that she had strived *not* to think of it – her sideways-glancing decision had always been to ignore it. It would blow over. His affair had perhaps not been the cause of what happened, but it was another symptom of her wilful somnambulism. She had been too attached to her becalmed life. She had kept a tidy house. She had loved her central heating and fitted carpets, the newly installed Everest windows.

When daylight came, it offered the consolations of reason. The storm had, perhaps, facilitated in some way what followed, but it had surely been no supernatural harbinger. Still, each year, whenever the days shortened into autumn, she faced alone her belief that her own wilful blindness had brought such disaster on her.

Those trees, those upturned roots.

In the warm confines of number 14 Eccleshall Drive, the evening of 15 October 1987 had held no surprises, no deviations from the normal. Alone in her sitting room, Claire had watched the late-evening weather forecast. Michael Fish – bald pate, thin-framed glasses – stood confidently in front of his isobars. 'Earlier on today,' he said, 'a woman rang the BBC and said there was a hurricane on the way.' He gave a little chuckle: it was easier after all in the 1980s to dismiss the fears of women. 'Don't worry,' he said with a smile. 'No hurricane is on its way.'

So England went to bed. This was a newly minted country. An Iron Lady had put the Great back into Britain. This was not a nation that was frightened of wind.

Claire stirred herself from her seat in front of the television. Her husband, Ben, sat alone in the dining room, his head bent beneath the overhead lamp as he studied for his yachtmaster's certificate, not considering the ships that would break their moorings in the night. She got up and pushed the button on the television. In the kitchen, she boiled the kettle, filled a hot-water bottle, and then, in her slippered feet, walked steadily up the stairs to her daughter, who was sitting at her desk doing her homework. She lifted back the duvet of her daughter's single bed and placed the bottle on the mattress.

'Lights off now, Tania.'

It was in the early hours that Claire became aware of a constant banging, as if horses were galloping on hard floors above her. Still asleep, she couldn't place it. What was happening? Was it an argument? Was someone throwing chimney pots from the roof? Gradually it drew her towards the surface of consciousness. There was a continuous wailing glissando, as if the atmospheric layers high above the bay window of her bedroom were being played like a saw. The house, she realized, now fully awake, was moving, actually moving, leaning and creaking. She reached out to her husband, said, 'Ben, Ben,' but he rolled away from her, groaned, pulled the covers over himself. She swung her feet out of bed and into the pink flip-flop slippers that waited for her beside the bed. She pulled on her dressing gown and went downstairs.

Tania was already there, standing in the front room in silky ivory pyjamas and bare feet. The storm was howling outside, banging and crashing, but she seemed to have found her own little pool of silence. The light switches were empty of power and she was standing in the half-light shed by the window. Claire felt blessed by this suddenly intimate image of her daughter. Usually Tania had that teenage awkwardness that distrusts or is ashamed of its beauty, that hunches over and avoids the gaze of others, but here, thinking herself unobserved, she stood gracefully, with a timeless poise like one of Degas' dancers. Her hair, tied into several long plaits as preparation for her latest silly hairstyle, fell down her slender back. Her weight was on one hip, the other foot arched, with the toes turned under as if carrying some memory of primary-school ballet classes. Claire had always loved her daughter's long, thin feet, felt she had known the hard little heels even before Tania was born. They had made corners through her taut pregnant stomach, as if she was concealing little anvils inside her belly.

She joined her daughter at the window and they stood side by side and watched the lime tree in the garden opposite as it bowed constantly like a courtier desperate to please the wind. The noise was incessant, wailing, banging. Lights were on in other houses in the street. Faces stared from other windows.

Tania said quietly, 'I *love* it, Mum. I love it.'

'You're not frightened?'

Tania, mesmerized by the travails of the tree opposite, did not answer immediately. A flowerpot had fallen from a first-floor window and crashed into the street. A solitary uprooted geranium lay on the pavement. A bin, taking the opportunity to escape its usual drab destiny, rolled down the road.

Tania said, 'It's scary, but it's fab too. Like *The Wizard of Oz*. I've always liked the first bit the best, the black-and-white bit. How the house turns in the twister and the cow blows past the window, and the two men rowing in a boat raise their hats to Dorothy. The Cowardly Lion and the Tin Man are there already in their overalls. And the Wizard himself, with his horse-drawn caravan—'

Claire interrupted, doing her best Professor Marvel. 'Better get under cover, Sylvester, there's a storm blowing up, a whopper.'

Tania laughed, and Claire sneaked her arm around her daughter's narrow waist, hugging her to her. Tania was too old for that usually, but somehow the storm had made an exception.

'Oh yes. I loved it too. That howling wind and the galloping horses and the trees outside the window, just like now.'

The harsh bell of the phone woke them in the morning from their resumed sleep. Tania was too quick for her mother, hammering down the stairs and scooping up the receiver. Claire rolled onto her back and rubbed her exhausted eyes. Ben had already left without saying goodbye, but the bed still carried his whiskery male smell and the warm indentation of his sleeping form. Ignoring destruction, he had set out to weave through the blocked streets in his new Audi. He was proud of that car. It was brand new. Gold-coloured.

Claire called down to her daughter. 'What is it?'

Tania's feet running lightly up the stairs. Suddenly she was in a hurry, but she popped her head round the bedroom door.

'Oh, just Katherine, Mum. School's cancelled for today. There's trees everywhere apparently. We're going to meet up.'

Katherine: Tania's best friend. Since primary school they'd been inseparable. When Katherine had started playing the violin, Tania had insisted on learning too. Katherine was from a musical family, but from the start everyone said it was Tania who had real talent. Claire's heart filled to bursting when she saw the two girls walking down the street together in their school uniforms, their violin cases swinging by their legs. They hadn't been getting on so well recently – perhaps it was because Tania's playing seemed to be irrevocably pulling ahead of her friend's – but still, Claire could tell that this was one of those friendships that would last. She could see them at each other's weddings.

She made her way downstairs and set to work clearing up her husband's breakfast things. She needed to get a move on. There'd been no call from Mrs Hitchens, the woman whose child she minded. She must be trying to get in to work too. Claire turned on the radio. From upstairs came a loud pounding and a female voice filled with longing. She recognized the song. 'River Deep Mountain High.'

She called upstairs. 'Tania, turn it down, I'm trying to listen to the radio.'

Train lines are closed, and thousands have been left without power . . .

Through the ceiling came the wall of sound that was pure Phil Spector. Fancy Tania getting into that stuff. She was twenty years too late, surely. The music built, cavernous, with a rhythm that wrenched at Claire's heart and seemed to insist she tap her feet and click her fingers. She switched the radio off and called up again, trying to compete with the music.

'Tania, do you want porridge or an egg?'

She climbed the stairs. Tania was in her bedroom, swinging her hips from side to side, and doing that punk jumping-about thing that her generation were all doing. Her back was turned. She was admiring her moves in the mirror.

Claire moved in behind her. After a slightly sceptical pause, she began to swing her own hips. She raised her arms and moved her hands from side to side.

'This is how you do it.'

Tania cringed. 'Oh Mum.'

'Don't be mean. I was young once too.'

The sound was building again, irresistible. A pounding rhythm that she couldn't seem to ever catch up with. Tina Turner breaking your heart. Claire put her hands above her head, turned them from the wrists in flamboyant 1960s circles, swung her hips. It was a long time since she'd danced, but she used to love it before Tania was born, before she was married.

Tania laughed and joined in, moving in synch with her mother.

The memory is very strong, and nearly twenty-seven years later, Claire Mills conjures it: Tania, wearing her big colourful glass earrings and blue sparkly eyeshadow. The music has stopped leaving them both breathless. Tania has lost the grace of last night and recovered her adolescent awkwardness. Her skirt's too short. Her hair is out of its plaits and has frizzed out. There's a smell of hairspray. Her school timetable is pinned to the mirror. Claire will miss her when she goes to university. Not long now. Just three years. At this moment, she is so beautiful that Claire could squeeze her until she could breathe no more. She says, 'Darling, you look lovely.'

'Thank you, Mum.'

She doesn't want to spoil the moment. But still, you have to bring them up properly. It's part of loving them.

'Just that skirt . . .'

Tania wrinkles her nose. 'What?'

Claire kisses her daughter on her head. 'Well, just maybe a tiny bit short. Up to you.'

From downstairs, the smell of burning.

'Oh Christ, the toast.' And Claire runs down the stairs and opens the windows, fanning the smoke outside with a tea towel.

Five minutes later: Tania in the kitchen doorway. Denim jacket, drainpipe jeans, two strings of necklaces, orange lipstick, school bag slung over her shoulder, violin case in her hand.

'I'm off, Mum.'

'You haven't had any breakfast.'

'It's OK, I don't want any.'

Outside the kitchen window, Mrs Hitchens draws up in her new Sierra. Fancy her trying to get in to work on a day like this! If it were Claire, she would have jumped at the opportunity to spend the day with her child. But even though the school has closed, Tania is still going out. She's going to revise with her best friend, hang out, listen to records.

'But you've got to eat, Tania.'

Sitting alone in her bed, Claire sees it as if it is the present. Mrs Hitchens unloads her toddler and his day bag from the car. Tania passes, kisses Claire on the cheek. 'It's OK, I'll be fine.'

She opens the front door, Claire stands just behind her in the hall. The lilac tree from the garden opposite is lying across the road. It's a shame. She loved that tree, particularly in June, when the street smelled of blossom. Mrs Hitchens is walking up the path with little Simon's hand in hers.

'You going to Katherine's, Tania? What time will you be home?'

Tania kisses her again.

'I dunno, about six.'

Then Mrs Hitchens blocks Claire's view of her daughter as she walks along the path and away down the street.

And alone in her bed, Claire remembers *The Wizard of Oz*: Professor Marvel in his horse-drawn caravan. He looks into a crystal ball and persuades Dorothy to go home to Aunt Em and Hunk and Hickory and Zeke, and as Dorothy runs away into the storm he says:

'Poor little kid. I hope she gets home all right.'

PART ONE

1

Wednesday 9 July 2014

A crow – glistening black and iridescent – was jumping about on the flat roof. A small, slim woman stood beside him, smoking. Detective Sergeant Sarah Collins wore polished black Oxford brogues and a grey trouser suit that in recent months had become slightly too roomy around the waist. Her hair was short, her hands tidy, the nails neatly filed but unpolished. From a distance, the simple neutrality of her appearance might have made her seem younger than her years, but close up, the mark of experience on her face aged her somewhere in her mid-thirties. It was a simple face – square-jawed, even-featured – that didn't look as though it easily broke into a smile but a seriousness and intelligence in the eyes softened any hint of severity.

Sarah extinguished her cigarette and threw the crow one of the nuts she had brought for him. How silly: tears were suddenly rolling down her face. She couldn't help but think that it said something truly ridiculous about your life when you were sad about saying goodbye to a crow. She pulled the back of her hand across her face, turned away from the bird and looked towards the river.

A cruiser was moving slowly upstream full of sedentary tourists, the sightseers of the megacity skating upon the river's surface as shallowly as water boatmen. Sarah knew too much about the Thames. She could no longer see it as a place for pleasure cruises. Nor was it any more to her a river of history and literature. Not Elizabeth I making her way downstream on a gilded barge. Not even Dickens' river of fog and industry, of docks and cranes, toerags, mudlarks and stevedores eking out a living from its dirty but profitable shores. No, policing had made the Thames an impersonal place, a place of physics. The grey-brown canalized river was an inexorable tidal sweep, a mass of cold and filthy water in relentless laminar flow. She knew how young men set off pissed and high-spirited from one bank only to find themselves suddenly in the grip of a current that was accelerating powerfully, sweeping them downstream as small and irrelevant as Poohsticks. She knew how bodies snagged like refuse on the clean-up cages. Unbidden, it entered her mind that perhaps it was those in despair who knew the river best, who came to it as if on pilgrimage with their weighted rucksacks and cast themselves upon its indifference.

For three years, attached to the Directorate of Specialist Investigations, Sarah had had this view of the Thames from the flat roof outside her office window. Deaths in contact with police had been her bailiwick. At the start of her posting it had seemed clear that her job was to contradict the river, to assert the importance of each little life, however small it might be in the scale of the universe. Recently, though, this conviction had threatened to slip away from her, as though her voice were only snatched up and dissipated by the river's indifferent roar.

She'd joined the directorate with a certain defiance. After all, investigating the police wasn't a job every officer wanted. Perhaps that was what had attracted her. It was an arena that demanded pure impartiality, an ideal of investigation at its purest. It had been a badge of honour for her to be fearless, impervious to opinion. It was as if she had believed she could put her hand in the fire time and time again and never be scorched.

Well, she'd been wrong.

It was six months since her former colleague, Detective Constable Steve Bradshaw, had let her know exactly what he thought of her, and it had hurt. She'd admired him as a detective and thought of him as a friend. 'No wonder you're so fucking lonely,' he'd told her at the end of their last investigation together. He'd gone further, rubbed it in, said he felt sorry for her. He'd told her to get herself a fucking dog.

Ever since the close of that investigation into the deaths of Hadley Matthews, a male police officer, and Farah Mehenni, a teenage immigrant girl, who had fallen to their deaths from a tower block Sarah felt she had been treading water, trying not to get swept away, knowing she had to move on.

She cleared her throat and turned back to Sid, the crow, who was waiting for her, his head cocked, his eye bright and beady, his beak as hard as galvanized rubber. Crows were cleverer than dogs, she'd read, adaptable. 'You be good,' she said, and clamped her jaw shut against any more tears.

All detectives have moments of burnout, she told herself. It's just the nature of the job.

That morning, she'd picked up an unmarked car from her new team in Hendon. She was making a positive move. She was going on promotion to be a detective inspector on Homicide. She knew the unofficial calls would have gone out as soon as her application was in, checking up on her, finding a way to stymie her move if the words spoken into the phone were sufficiently bad. But clearly the words had been good. The boss had said they were happy with her, and he must have meant it.

She hung up the bag of bird food and ducked under the open window into her office, determined to put her stuff into the car quickly and leave without a backward glance. But Jez, one of her detective constables, was waiting awkwardly for her, shifting his weight from foot to foot, making her think of that stupid crow. There was that bloody painful boiled egg in her throat again, the heat behind the eyes. They must have that red, swollen look. It must be obvious.

She was saved by a flash of humour. How could she not smile at Jez's flash gold cufflinks, the high-collared white shirt stretched tightly over his no doubt gym-primed chest, the rather nice leather satchel that had probably cost too much. He was young, good-looking. He tried too hard. He'd been supportive, kind to her when she was at her most lonely. She'd come to like him.

She said, 'I'd better get a move on.'

There was a pause.

'I got you something.' Blushing, he pulled a flat package out of the bag. He might have guessed how suddenly close to tears she was because he added, 'Don't worry, Sarah. Open it later.'

She nodded. All her stuff was packed away into the blue plastic crate that stood on her desk.

He said, 'Can I carry that down to the car for you?'

She shook her head. She wouldn't risk speaking.

He said, 'I'll look after Sid.'

She reached out for a piece of paper, took her pen from her inside jacket pocket and wrote, *Thanks, Jez.*

He put his hand on hers. 'No worries. I'll catch you later. They're lucky to have you. Homicide will be a bit of a break after this, more straightforward.'

Sarah barely noticed the roads she was driving except when they were suddenly peopled by memories from her years of policing. Fulham Palace Road, outside the florist: a posh guy, face-down stone drunk in the street. She'd been at the very beginning of her service, still in uniform. When they'd got him upright, he'd swayed towards her, breathing fumes of vomit, and told her she looked *adorable in that hat*. She switched lanes, pulled round the Broadway. Hammersmith nick on her left, two police horses waiting for the gates, their tails switching. She had remembered the

Shepherd's Bush Road as launderettes and tatty takeaways, but it was being repainted in a tasteful muted palette that seemed aimed at suggesting country houses rather than Zone 2 Central London. If you had to be rich even to live on a main road, where on earth were the poor going to go? Shepherd's Bush itself, reassuringly unsalvageable – a brief memory of rowdy Australians outside the Walkabout – then, on the island of scrubby green encircled by choked traffic, the echo of a crying girl with broken fingernails and a bruise to her cheek.

Back on autopilot as she headed north-east, her thoughts returned to their usual obsession: the investigation into the deaths of PC Hadley Matthews and Farah Mehenni.

It had been her last full investigation at the DSI: the one that had made her look around for a new posting. She and Steve Bradshaw had been practically first on scene and found them both smashed against the concrete but still warm from the life that had left them.

Outwardly the investigation had been a success. Inwardly it was anything but. She felt she'd carry it with her all her career. She thought of the pretty young police constable, Lizzie Griffiths, who'd been on the roof when Hadley and Farah fell and who had run away, going missing for days before she and Steve could locate and interview her. She remembered with more discomfort Lizzie's boss, Inspector Kieran Shaw. If anyone had to pay it should have been him. She couldn't pinpoint the feeling that slid uncomfortably inside her: dissatisfaction, frustration, anger – yes, anger certainly. Guilt, maybe. Self-doubt. Certainly a darkness. She checked herself. She needed to stop herself circling around these thoughts, stuck in the same place she'd been for months.

She focused back on the road, the here and now. It was just the nature of a detective's job: some things stayed with you. Some things couldn't be resolved. You had to accept that. She was doing that. She was moving on.

She was threading her way through residential streets of 1930s semis, Victorian terraces, slowing for speed bumps and winding through the maze of closures that tried to prevent drivers using them as rat runs. Her years as a detective had made her as knowledgeable about cut-throughs as a London black-cab driver. Here, by an arcade of shops, her first homicide as a detective constable. The victim had made it across the street to bleed out in front of his mother as she ran downstairs from her flat above the off-licence. The murderer had been only seventeen, imagining he was in a movie when he killed the other boy over a bag of weed.

Like a homing pigeon she accelerated along the A41 and then turned left down past the big-money residential developments that were forcing their way upwards like big-money Redwoods. She swung into the entrance to the Peel Centre, passed the security check – the civilians at the gate as usual never in any particular hurry – and pulled round under the concrete portico that framed the entrance to the site.

For a moment she stood on the parade ground, allowing the site to seep into her bones, all her love and hatred for the place, acclimatizing herself to the open space, onto which a light drizzle was falling from a grey sky. Ranged around were low-rise buildings, with white concrete and green fascia, brick-clad columns, strip windows and a skyline of long flat roofs.

Hendon: less famous than New Scotland Yard, but to many who worked for it the secret heart of the Met. The business of dealing with the public, with victims, witnesses, families, suspects: that was all done elsewhere. Hendon was a back office, a place where you wouldn't be bothered by someone who didn't know how things worked in the police world of abandoned children, violence and madness. Until recently everyone had trained here and passed out on this parade ground in ranks of shiny shoes, polished buttons and white gloves and it was a place you returned to throughout your service, a place where things were going on but that kept itself to itself. It was going to be a fresh start in an old location.

Carrying her blue plastic crate up the floating treads of the murder block, Sarah snuck into her new office and pulled the door shut.

Her new boss, DCI James Fedden, had told her she would be taking on a job straight away, and sure enough, three storage boxes were waiting on the desk. Operation Egremont: the disappearance of Tania Mills, a teenage girl, back in 1987.

She put her crate on the floor and ran her fingers over the top of the first box. She wanted to open it and start reading, but she should wait until she could work systematically.

Quickly she began setting up her base camp, sorting her stuff into drawers – bags of nuts for those nights when everything was shut and you weren't getting home, a box of cereal for early warrants, a toothbrush, toothpaste, soap and a towel. She threw her shoulder harness with cuffs and asp into a bottom drawer, got out her legal Blackstones and lined them up on the shelves, set up her coffee machine on the windowsill. Then, with no ceremony, she opened the present from Jez. It was a framed picture of Sid, bearing the handwritten legend *Illegitimi non carborundum*. It was a nice thought. She hung it on the wall, next to a picture of her dog. They made her smile. Other people had children. She had a dog and a crow.

There was a light knock and then the door was pushed open. Detective Inspector Peter Stokes' face was hidden by the two large storage boxes he had in his arms.

'Where do you want them?' he said.

Sarah cleared a path. 'Oh, just stick them on the floor.'

He placed them by the window, stood up, scratched the back of his head, looked out towards the parade ground. He'd done his thirty years. This was his final shift and she was his replacement. It was his office she was moving into. He turned, offered his hand.

'Welcome to Homicide, Sarah. Thanks for taking on Egremont.'

'Yes, thanks. No problem.'

He was a career detective, grey around the temples, no longer excited about anything. Tall, a bit sweaty and overweight in a baggy suit and an undistinguished tie. Sarah didn't know him well, but she assumed he could never have been much interested in rank: just got hooked on solving crimes. He seemed reluctant to leave, and that wasn't really surprising. It couldn't be easy handing back your warrant card and trying to retrieve as a much older person what it had been like to be a civilian.

The boxes he had brought in were of dark mottled cardboard: better quality than the stuff issued nowadays. The spines, facing towards her, carried printed Op Egremont labels that were peeling away.

She put her hands on her hips. 'I'm just about to get to grips with it, actually. Is there anything you need to tell me about it?'

He shook his head and mirrored her body language. It was as if they were pulling up their shirt sleeves to start work together.

'Nothing that springs to mind. Ring me when you've read through it. If you've got any questions, that is.'

Sarah smiled sympathetically, and after a pause, he smiled too. 'You don't *have* to ring me, of course,' he said.

'No, it's useful to know you wouldn't mind. Thank you.'

'The boss sends his apologies, by the way.'

'That's fine. He emailed. Thailand, isn't it?'

'That's right. Daughter's getting married.' Stokes went over to the desk, put his hands on the first box. 'Do you mind?'

'Of course not.'

He opened the box, took out the top item and handed it to Sarah. 'Here she is.'

It was the Missing poster for Tania Mills. It had that elusive something that marked it as the past – a stiffness in the paper perhaps, or the sheen of a time when the Met outsourced such matters to a printing company, a dark, less sharp typeface, the smell of something stored too long in a box.

The poster bore a black-and-white black-bordered photograph of the missing girl, looking evenly at the camera. She was in her school uniform, with a too-fat diagonally striped tie and her hair in long plaits. Awkward, but pretty. The hotline number was for a London code long gone, superseded numerous times by the growth of the city and the changing nature of telecoms.

Stokes folded his arms across his chest. 'To be honest, she's been haunting me for nearly thirty years. I first worked the job as a young DC. I'm really hoping this new lead goes somewhere. Part of me wants to follow it up myself, of course. If you can solve it, I'll buy you a case of champagne. That's a promise. I'm a man of my word.'

Sarah wanted to offer some intelligent consolation. She put the poster back in the box, taking a moment before she spoke.

'Surely it's the fate of every serious detective to carry unfinished business into retirement? I've already got jobs that bug me and I've still got nearly twenty years to do.' She smiled. 'Not that I'm claiming to be serious myself.'

He shrugged, still looking at the poster. 'I've got to let it go. I know that.'

'What's your feeling? Are you sure she was murdered?'

'Well . . .' Gently, he put the lid back on the box. 'Her disappearance was so totally out of character.' He opened his hands as if he were a magician with a disappearing trick. 'And to never make contact again, never? Not in all this time?'

'It does seem the most plausible explanation. But she could have had some sort of accident. Simply be dead, not murdered.'

'Yes. That's true. But still, no body.'

There was a silence. Then Sarah said, 'And the family can't stop hoping?'

'Don't really know about Dad – he doesn't want updates unless it's really necessary. Does everything over the phone. Finds it too painful to meet. As for Mum – she's definitely got the candle lit at the window. Thinks it's a betrayal to give up on Tania coming home.'

Sarah exhaled. Of course that was the case: hope was the last act of fidelity.

'Have you told them about this latest line of inquiry?'

He shook his head. 'I've told Dad but I'm leaving Mum to you, I'm afraid. I can't stand to go through all that with her again. The hope, then the disappointment. We've had so much crap information over the years.'

'They're not together?'

'Separated about twelve months after the disappearance. It's often the way. I got into the habit of seeing Mum about once a year. We have a coffee. I tell her we never give up.'

'Can't be easy for you.'

'No, it isn't.' He rubbed his right eyebrow with his index finger. 'Still, hardly as difficult for me as for the family.' He threw his hands out in sudden frustration. 'Problem always was, no body! No physical evidence. No opportunity for a helpful DNA hit because the technology's so much better now and the bastards didn't know then that they hadn't better leave anything of themselves behind.' There was a brief silence. Then it seemed that Stokes couldn't stop himself. 'The job throws money at the cases that capture the public's attention, but nobody's interested in properly resourcing an obscure investigation into a fifteen-year-old girl who went missing more than twenty years ago.'

But it was normal, Sarah thought. How could the job possibly fund all of these missing people and lost causes? She checked her pessimism. She didn't know yet whether it was a lost cause or not.

And a new lead surely meant there would be some money on the table to investigate. It was her professional responsibility to hope.

Stokes, as if he was remembering to make small talk, glanced at the photo of the shiny black crow with the particularly beady eye. 'Who's that?'

Sarah smiled. 'Oh that. That's Sid – a former colleague.'

'He didn't fancy Homicide, then?'

'No, he was a strictly Special Investigations kind of a corvid. They promised me they'd feed him.'

He tapped the photo of the spaniel. 'And this little chap?'

'That's Daisy. I've only just got her. Don't know what I was thinking.'

'Looks like a nice dog.'

'She is. A lot of fun.'

'What do you do with her when you're on duty?'

'I've got a dog walker. She goes there full time when I've got a push on.'

Stokes nodded. 'I remember when we used to be able to bring our dogs into work. CID nights there always used to be some mutt or other lying under a desk. Just one more thing we're not allowed any more. Oh well, times change.'

For the first time Sarah felt his gaze focusing on her with the necessarily cool regard of a detective. It was an unconscious habit all the good ones had – to bring their professional attention to bear on non-professional matters.

He said, 'You live alone, then?'

'None of your business.'

She had tried for a bit of cheek in her voice but it wasn't a style that came easily to her. Stokes had heard only her defensiveness.

'Sorry,' he said quickly. 'Didn't mean to intrude.'

'No, not at all, no worries. Only joking. Yes, I live alone.'

She opened the Op Egremont box, removed the Missing poster,

found some Blu Tack in her drawer and stuck the poster on the wall directly above her computer.

Stokes nodded. 'Nice gesture. Thanks.'

'No problem.'

She thought she had been giving him a clear message that the conversation was over, but perhaps his detective gaze had seen a trait in her that evoked sympathy because he now said, 'Listen, Sarah. Don't worry too much about Egremont. I never got round to it. Not properly. It's just not possible. Once we pick up a live job, you'll be too busy. You have to find a bit of space for down time.'

She tried to brush him off. 'Don't worry. I'll only do what I can.'

But he wasn't having it and interrupted. 'This job can eat you alive.'

She offered her hand. 'I'll see you at the Crown later on.'

He enclosed her smaller hand in his two and smiled. 'Look, this job, Tania Mills. I know you'll give it a good go. I'm grateful. But don't worry. I'm also realistic.'

'Hey,' she said. 'It's OK. I get it.'

He released her hand. 'Sorry. I've got two daughters. Sometimes I need to be told to back off.'

'That's OK. But still, back off.' She smiled.

He said, 'You'll like it here. And I'm sure you'll do well. I've heard about you on the grapevine. I'd have liked to have worked with you. I admire someone who's a bit bloody-minded.'

The door shut. Sarah slipped a capsule into the coffee machine, got out her reading glasses.

The disappearance of Tania Mills was an investigation that had long gone cold, but now, after all these years, there was a new lead. Erdem Sadiq, a prisoner on remand at Thameside, claimed to know what had happened. Sarah had wanted to interview the informant herself to get a measure of his evidence, but the DCI had told her it was too late for that.

'We've already booked the interview. HMP will never let us change the officers at this stage. Don't worry. I'm sending someone good: Lee Coutts. You'll like him. He's keen as mustard. Reminds me of myself as a young man. Anyway, don't get too excited. The snout's a sex offender – he's got his own reasons for talking to us. This is something just to get you started. Work it slow time. Live investigations have to come first.'

Fedden hadn't been encouraging, but he was right to be dubious about any information Erdem Sadiq might provide. Sadiq had a strong incentive to talk: if he gave evidence that led to a charge, he could expect time off his own sentence.

Sarah lifted the initial investigation summary out of the box. It was typewritten and bore Tippex corrections. The past felt so distant, so different, that it was hard to believe that she herself had been alive in 1987, throwing her satchel over her shoulder and walking to school with her older sister. As she began to read she reached back through the gap of time to that other girl who had walked out of her own front door on the morning after the storm, and disappeared.

Situation report: Operation Egremont
Victim: Tania Mills
Date of disappearance: 16 October 1987

Summary
Tania Mills left her home on 16 October 1987 at approximately 0900 hours. Tania's school was closed due to the storm. Tania told her mother, Claire Mills, that she was going to see a friend, Katherine Herringham, to revise for her O levels. Tania frequently studied outside

the home. Her parents had thought she would pursue a musical career but recently she had decided instead to study modern languages. Tania was known to walk to her friend's through a local park. Katherine reported that Tania never turned up but that she hadn't been worried because Tania often changed her plans.

Tania's disappearance was reported at 1930 hours. Her mother, Claire Mills, told police she had expected her daughter home by 1800 hours but had not initially been concerned. Tania was fifteen, almost an adult. Claire had thought there was an innocent explanation for her delay in returning home.

By the time Tania's father, Benedict Mills, returned home Claire was anxious. Benedict Mills drove to Ellerby police station and reported his daughter missing at the front counter.

Immediate action
Borough officers made an initial search of the park and surrounding area. The work was hampered by darkness and storm damage, including many fallen trees. Tania's friends were contacted at their home addresses. None reported seeing Tania at all on 16 October. The following morning the investigation was taken on by the local CID. The park was cordoned off and an extensive search undertaken. A pair of jeans that had belonged to Tania were found. No other evidence was recovered. Robert McCarthy, the local park keeper, was arrested but subsequently eliminated from the inquiry. There was no sign of fighting or damage in any area of the park. No one reported seeing anything unusual. Tania's school, Hachett's, had reopened. Teachers and pupils were

spoken to. An appeal was made in the local paper, the **Ellerby Gazette**, and on BBC London and Capital Radio...

The initial investigation and the subsequent reviews had generated hundreds of statements. And the files contained other things – exhibit lists, school reports, photographs. Sarah read for three hours. Still she felt she had only just started. She needed to get to know Tania, to reach out to her through the silent years. This wasn't mere sentiment. It was her task as a detective to concentrate hard on every detail until the victim she had never met became a breathing person, revived for the sole purpose of rolling the film. It might be something hidden that unlocked what had happened – a criminal activity, a secret friendship perhaps – or it could be just a random detail. The victim made a detour to buy cigarettes or left the party early or left the party late.

Sarah was more dependent than usual on witnesses. In 1987, there had been fewer opportunities to intrude. Fewer cameras. No helpful internet browsing. No teenager's phone accessed hourly to check her texts, update her status and tell an investigator where she was and who was important to her. She hoped the detectives had known their job: to cast their net widely and to encourage people to feel safe to speak.

Finally she stood up, rubbed her face, clasped her hands behind her neck and stretched backwards.

She was irritated by the investigation's constantly repeated refrain that conjured a good girl – doing well at school, a talented musician – and very little else. Where were Tania's misdemeanours? Where were the bits that made her a teenager – the untidiness, the day bunked off school, the secret smoking? Where, crucially, was the anomalous detail that might offer a fresh line of inquiry?

The only bit of grit that hadn't passed through the sieve was an out-of-character shoplifting incident in Selfridges, six months before

Tania disappeared. Tania had been arrested. Nothing had come of it. It wasn't much but it might be worth probing. One other thing had drawn her attention. On the morning of her disappearance, Tania had secretly changed out of her jeans and into a short skirt. It was the last time police had evidence of her alive. Perhaps that moment too could stand some re-examination.

It was late afternoon and the other officers from her new team were already leaving, going straight to Peter Stokes' leaving drinks. Still, she told herself, she could squeeze in a quick visit before that.

She made a phone call, shut down her computer, pulled on her jacket.

Sarah knocked at the front door of the house Tania had left nearly thirty years ago. She'd called ahead and driven the twenty minutes or so west to the nice suburban neighbourhood, the tree-lined residential streets.

The door opened. Claire Mills was in her late sixties and still trim. The first impression was of one of those well-turned-out women who can't leave the house without foundation and lipstick. Neatly bobbed ash-grey hair. A blue brocaded jacket over a matching knee-length dress. Around her neck a Liberty-print scarf. It was the briefest of impressions. Tania's mother quickly turned into the hall and guided Sarah inside, leaving her alone in the front room while she made tea. Still, despite the bright colours of the scarf, the smart clothes and the well-cut hair, Sarah had immediately recognized the immobility in Claire's expression, the certain fixedness around her mouth and eyes: it was the imprint of settled grief shared by so many of the otherwise very different next-of-kins she had encountered. This woman's life had been suspended in 1987. All her other activities gave only an illusion of movement around an unbending grief.

The front room – and it was a front room, not a sitting room – was a shrine.

One wall was covered with a Danish-style shelving system entirely devoted to the missing girl. A framed newspaper cutting of Tania with other girls all lined up holding a ball and wearing medals: *U14s net prize in school netball competition.* A Grade 8 certificate for violin, *with distinction*. Photographs in frames. Tania standing on a stage playing her violin in front of an orchestra. Tania – pinafore dress, white tights – curtseying by a piano and handing flowers to Princess Diana. Tania at the beach, a toddler with bucket and spade. Again at the beach, an older Tania – tiny breasts just budding – wearing a sailor one-piece with a white fringe around the hips and sporting red plastic heart-shaped sunglasses. There were objects too. A teddy bear. A small glass horse. The school music prize for 1986: a treble-clef music trophy.

Standing in the silent room, a thought suddenly came: Claire was holding the line but one day she would be gone too. All this memorabilia would become like a family video in a cardboard box of miscellanea in a junk shop that no one is interested in possessing, and the desire to find Tania would be silenced too.

The door to the hallway opened and Claire entered, carrying a tray with two china cups, a small teapot, a sugar bowl and milk jug, a plate of biscuits. She put the tray on the circular coffee table and smoothed down her dress with both hands before sitting.

'Ben wouldn't let me put photos up. He finds it easier than me to let go of things that cause him unhappiness. When he left I really let rip.'

Sarah mustered a smile and moved towards a chair. 'I hope you don't mind me looking.'

'Not at all.'

She accepted the offered cup of tea. 'They are lovely photos.'

'Thank you.'

'She was a violinist?'

'Oh yes, very good. Grade 8 by the age of fourteen. With distinction. Everyone said she could play professionally.'

She'd trotted it out like an incantation. How many times had she said that since Tania had gone? 'But she'd decided not to study the violin at college?'

'Well yes, that's right. I was pleased in a way. It's very competitive. The better you get, the better everyone else is. Makes girls anxious. And all that practising! I thought she'd have more of a life if she kept it as a hobby.'

Sarah nodded, picked up the cue. 'Was she a particularly anxious girl?'

Claire frowned, a tiny indentation between her brows. 'Not particularly, no.'

'You must miss her terribly.'

'Every day.'

'Would you tell me about her?'

Claire smiled – pleased, Sarah understood, to have the opportunity to say the words. 'She was a lovely girl, absolutely lovely. Beautiful, talented, kind.'

Sarah nodded. 'I want to ask you about something . . .'

Claire smiled again. 'Ask whatever you like.'

'Well, the morning she disappeared . . . she changed her clothing. After she'd left home, I mean.'

Claire shook her head in mock despair as though she was talking about a girl who had just that minute walked out of the room.

'Teenagers! I'd said to her I thought her skirt was too short and she changed into jeans – only to please me, it turns out, because as soon as she was out of the house she changed back into the skirt.'

'You don't know anything more about it than that?'

Claire tilted her head, narrowed her eyes. 'No,' she said. 'Why, should I? An arrest was made but they told me it was a mistake. Is there more to know?'

Sarah smiled. 'No, not at all. I'm just new to the case and trying to get a better picture.'

There was a constrained smile. 'That's all right.'

Sarah paused. 'There's one other thing I wanted to ask you about . . . I hope you don't mind.'

'Please.'

'There was a shoplifting incident, about six months before Tania went missing.'

Claire frowned again. 'Oh, *that*. That was nothing! She'd gone into town, to Selfridges. She was at that age, you know? Beginning to experiment with how she dressed?'

'Mmm. So what happened?'

'She tried on a leather belt and left the shop without realizing she was still wearing it. Silly girl. Anyway, the officers accepted her account. Nothing came of it.' After a moment's pause, Claire added, 'Do you mind me asking why you want to know about that?'

'Like I say, I'm trying to get a feel for the case, for Tania. It's just so out of character.'

'Yes, though it isn't really, because she hadn't actually stolen anything.'

'No. So, Selfridges, central London. That's quite a way from here.'

'Yes, but you know these girls . . . they've been raised in the city. They're so confident with the trains and those department stores . . . they can try clothes, make-up, perfume.'

'Was she with a friend?'

'I don't think so. On her own.' There was a pause. Then Claire said, 'If you think it might be relevant, you could ask my ex-husband. He went down to central London when she was arrested.'

'Yes, I might do that.'

Claire's mouth was tense. 'He doesn't want to talk about her, does he? Moving on. New family, all that.'

'I've not met him yet.'

After an angry pause: 'It was less than twelve months before he moved in with her. The first one, I mean. He's on his third wife now. Nothing stops him.'

'I see.'

'I've wondered if they were already together – before Tania disappeared, I mean.'

'And what do you think?'

'I think they must have been, yes.'

'But you don't know for sure?'

'Not for sure.'

Claire looked down and stretched her fingers out.

Sarah said, 'I'm sorry to ask you this stuff.'

'No, no, no. It's *fine*. Don't feel you have to treat me with kid gloves. Anything, anything at all that might help.' She met Sarah's eyes. 'Biscuit?'

Among the Duchy Originals on the flowery china plate were Penguins in their shiny wrappers. Penguins splashing in water, penguins canoeing and skateboarding. Sarah leaned forward and chose a surfing Penguin. Claire took one too. They compared biscuits without comment. Claire's penguin was skiing. They both smiled as they unwrapped them.

Sarah said, 'Mind if I dunk?'

Claire put her own biscuit in her coffee. 'Dunk away.'

The melted chocolate was over-sweet and brought memories of a plate of biscuits waiting on the kitchen table when Sarah came home from school.

Claire said, 'They used to have shiny aluminium foil wrappers and the penguins were black and white. You can't get those any more.'

'You always keep a pack in the house.'

Claire nodded and Sarah knew better than to complete the thought.

For when she comes back.

Claire's voice carried a hint of protest. 'Sometimes missing people are found alive, even years afterwards. Jaycee Dugard, Natascha Kampush, Elizabeth Smart . . .'

She stopped speaking but Sarah's imagination had already leaped unbidden to those girls, imprisoned, raped, but – finally – returned to their families. It was a poisoned dilemma. If you prayed Tania was still alive, then what were you praying for?

Claire was speaking again in a rush of words. 'I know! I know how I must look to you. My silly Penguin biscuits! But if you *knew*. How I wish I could turn the clock back, stop her going out that door . . . ?

Sarah felt the tears come to her own eyes. She reached forward impulsively and put her hand on Claire's knee. 'You can't imagine how happy it would make me to be able to find her for you.'

Claire looked directly into Sarah's face. She nodded as if in surprised recognition of something she hadn't expected to find there.

'Thank you. Yes, I can see that. Thank you for that. Yes. Thank you.'

Sarah could hardly hear the words. She had, she felt, momentarily ceded control of herself. It wasn't professional. She had lost the thread of why she was here, what she could offer. She sat back into her chair and into her mind came an unwelcome thought. *This already means too much to me.* There was another pause. Then Claire said, 'Why don't you tell me about this new line of inquiry you've got?'

———

Afterwards Sarah stood in the park just along the street from Tania's house. The sky was gunmetal grey and the park was luminous with the strangely bright light that sometimes precedes showers. Perhaps she was doing it on purpose – making herself late for Peter Stokes' farewell drinks – but no, she dismissed the thought. There'd still be time to pop in for a quick one.

She began to walk the route Tania's school friends had said she normally took. The path wound downhill through trees. On the left was a children's playground with horses on springs and a flying fox – new things. Sarah tried to picture how it had been on the morning Tania disappeared. She had seen the photographs: the uprooted trees, scattered branches, the turned earth.

Further down was the park keeper's hut: a small building, shut up. Timber walls: planks layered vertically, green with lichen. Dirty floral curtains at a small square window. A padlock on the door. It was a ghost building. In 1987 this had been the fief of the investigation's main suspect, Robert McCarthy. Sarah had read the account of his arrest more than once.

When police entered the park that first evening, Robert was there in the dusk: a slightly portly man who, at the age of thirty-five, was still dressed by his mother in cardigans and trousers with braces. He'd hung around. With a certain slackness around the mouth and that something about him that missed the point, he hadn't matched the emotional state of the others looking for the lost girl. He'd got on people's nerves.

The following day, when the park continued to be the focus of the police search, Robert was there again, bothering people, asking too many questions. He was the park keeper but no one seemed clear how he'd got the job. The park was only a small area of land and there was no real need for a full-time keeper. He was only paid an honorarium organized, it turned out, through the local church. Robert and his mother Pauline had been regular churchgoers. One of the more switched-on uniformed constables asked him for a cup of coffee.

Robert was honoured to have a big policeman in full uniform sitting in his hut. He gave the constable the best chair – the chair, he said, usually reserved for his mother – and made him a cup of instant coffee on his Calor Gas camping stove. PC Lawrence complimented Robert on how nice he kept everything. There was a big white plastic bottle for water, a little blue plastic bowl for washing up, a clean tea towel hanging on a hook. Some Matchbox cars were displayed on a shelf. There was also a folded pair of girl's jeans on the table and Lawrence asked whose they were.

'Tania's.'

'Tania's?' Then, after a pause, 'How come you've got her jeans then?'

'Because she came in here to change.'

'To change?'

'Yes.'

'And why've you kept them?'

'She forgot them. I want to give them back to her.'

The copper wrote in his statement that he had wanted to liaise with the investigators before taking any action but he had also not wanted to leave Robert in his hut where there might be more evidence that could be destroyed. So he nicked him. He used handcuffs because, although he was compliant, Robert was quite a big man.

Claire Mills was spoken to by detectives within the hour. She identified the jeans as the ones Tania had been wearing when she'd left home the previous morning.

Robert seemed quite happy in custody. He chatted with the police officers who gave him tea and biscuits. Pauline, his mum, came down and they were allowed a private word in one of the interview rooms. Pauline explained to Robert that the police just needed to find out everything they could. They would ask him some questions and he should tell the truth. Then everything would be sorted out. Robert didn't need a lawyer because he hadn't done anything wrong.

But Robert's mood began to deteriorate when his mother was no longer allowed to act as his appropriate adult. As she had provided an alibi for him for the whole of the previous day, she was part of the evidential chain and couldn't be involved in the interviewing process. Then a neighbour said she had cut Pauline's hair in the afternoon and Pauline's reliability as a witness was blown. She was arrested for perverting the cause of justice.

Robert saw his mother being booked in at the custody desk. It wasn't clear to Sarah whether this had been done on purpose as a way of pressuring him. It had been a different time. Police had not been so aware of the dangerous suggestibility of vulnerable suspects. Robert told the interviewing officer he didn't understand what was happening. He had always liked policemen. Many of his Matchbox cars were police cars.

A search of the hut turned up a photograph of Tania and Robert. Robert's possession of the photograph was put to him in interview. He answered that he had the photograph because he loved Tania. She was special, not like the other girls: always friendly.

The interview was suspended. A warrant of further detention was obtained to enable further questioning. Detectives executed a warrant on Robert's house. They found a collection of porn magazines under his bed. The local vicar, Reverend Byers, came down at Pauline's request and acted as Robert's new appropriate adult. The interviewing officers put it bluntly to Robert in interview that he had murdered Tania. Robert put his head in his hands and wept. There were so many tears that they had to get a cloth to wipe the table. Detective Constable Clarke asked Robert if he was crying because he felt guilty about what he had done. Robert replied that he didn't feel guilty: he was crying because Tania was dead.

Clarke asked how Robert knew she was dead. Robert didn't reply, only wept inconsolably.

Where had he hidden the body?

Robert started rocking with his eyes closed and his hands over his ears.

Robert was returned to his cell. The officers told the Reverend Byers they wanted to review the evidence, see if they had enough for charging.

The jailer brought a cup of tea to Robert's cell and caught him masturbating. The jailer told him he should be ashamed. Tania dead and Robert was wanking? What kind of a monster was he? Perhaps the officer's comments were understandable: he was only a young man and feelings were running high. There were posters of Tania everywhere. A press conference had been held earlier that day and the officer had seen it: Tania's father frozen-faced, her mother sobbing, unable to get her words out. In any case, all hell broke loose. Robert tried to punch the jailer and then had to be restrained to stop him banging his own head on the cell floor. Even on a constant watch with a sympathetic female officer sitting next to him and a male officer standing at the door just in case, Robert kept weeping and rocking. The Reverend Byers asked to speak with the superintendent. He insisted his views be recorded. He entered them himself on the custody record in a beautiful italic long hand.

Robert, an adult with special educational needs, has been in detention for more than three days.

Robert has been masturbating in his cell. This is inappropriate but indicates his state of mind. I have known Robert for about eight years and have never seen behaviour like this. His mental condition is clearly deteriorating under pressure. He is confused and distressed.

The evidence against Robert appears to be as follows. He had a photo of Tania and a pair of her jeans in his workplace – for which he has given an explanation – and some pornographic magazines at his home.

Questions remain unanswered. If Robert has killed Tania then how – with an IQ so low he can only read comic books – has he managed to conceal her body so effectively and in such a short period of time? How has he destroyed any evidence of violence on himself or elsewhere?

It is suggested that Robert's distress is evidence of his guilt.

My view is that Robert wept in interview not because he knew Tania was dead but because he misunderstood the detective constable who accused him of murder. To a person with learning difficulties the accusation amounted to a perhaps unintentional misrepresentation of the evidence. Robert thought the police knew that Tania was dead.

Robert has told detectives that Tania was kind to him. She was unusual in taking the time to talk to him. Quite understandably, Robert loves Tania, and so, when he believed she was dead, he wept.

I am concerned that opportunities may be lost by this focus on Robert McCarthy. The police do not know what has happened to Tania. No body has been found. She may still be alive.

The reverend's comments had clearly given pause for thought. Robert was bailed with conditions to report to the police station daily. The newspaper reported only that a local man was helping police with their inquiries: Robert's name wasn't given. Still, everyone in the neighbourhood knew who he was. Eventually he was released from bail and the charge against his mother for perverting was also dropped on compassionate grounds. The investigation into Tania's disappearance continued. But Tania was never found and no one was ever charged for her murder. The cloud of 'no smoke without fire' that hovered over Robert never lifted.

Robert's hut was graffitied with the words 'nonce' and 'pervert'. A brick was thrown through Pauline's front window. Robert couldn't go back to working in the park. For a while he and his mother lived in the rectory. It was a big, cold nineteenth-century building. Reverend Byers said there was plenty of room for everybody. Then Pauline managed to sell her place and they moved away. Robert had been no more than collateral damage in an investigation that was never solved and never closed.

Sarah walked back up through the park. Time had passed. The young replacement trees that had been planted then were tall now.

An opportunity had been missed. If he hadn't been a suspect then Robert had been a witness. He'd said Tania had changed in his hut. He was the last person the police knew of who had seen Tania alive.

Sarah slid into her car and smoked with the door open. That was it for the day. She ought to nip over quickly and share a drink with her new team.

She closed her eyes and leaned back in her seat and thought of her own sister's death in a collision so long ago: the earth turned around the fresh grave and how, impervious to the clay that soiled her best skirt and clogged her shoes, she had knelt and found a fossil, the shale splitting open in her hands perfectly, like hooks and eyes suddenly releasing to reveal the imprint of a fern millennia dead.

She opened her eyes and turned the key in the car's ignition. She considered once more driving over for the retirement drinks for Peter Stokes. She saw in her imagination a bunch of officers at the bar, buying shots, ribbing each other. They all knew each other, had experienced the push of working murders together more than once and had now been drinking for a few hours. It would be painful to try to find her place. Anyway, she told herself as she pulled away from the kerb, out here she was already part of the way home. Did she really want to travel in the wrong direction? It didn't matter missing it. There'd be plenty of others.

After five minutes she stopped at a Turkish all-night supermarket on one of the outlying streets that took her through the sprawl of London and into its leafier outskirts. From the darkness of the street the shop was brightly lit. Huge bunches of coriander and mint outside the door. Inside, a big screen showing multiple CCTV cameras. A dark-haired young man stood behind the counter. There was evidently still enough of London in this shop for it to be useful to look as if you might be handy with a broom handle, should anyone want to chance his arm.

Sarah nodded hello and moved round the shop with a metal basket, throwing in tinned vine leaves, some salad – good tomatoes here – a plastic package of meat as a naughty treat for Daisy. Standing at the back by the cold dairy fridge, she caught sight of someone she recognized but couldn't place. There was a flutter of excitement that she tried to stifle. She lingered, standing back in the aisle, flicking through her mental card index. The woman's back was turned but there was something very familiar and somehow cheerful about the tight jeans around the plump bottom, the dark curly hair. Then in an instant she realized who it was. She turned and walked quickly towards the till.

Caroline Wilson: the former maths teacher of Farah Mehenni. Sarah had interviewed Caroline as part of her last inquiry at the DSI.

She'd liked Caroline the moment she'd set eyes on her standing on a table in her classroom, sticking a drawing pin into a poster. She'd been so sweet, so precarious on the wobbly table, a bit shameless too, her bum showing above the line of her jeans because her arms were raised. The feeling hadn't been mutual, not to begin with anyway. Caroline had quizzed Sarah quite hard on the investigation and Sarah had liked that too. She'd liked that Caroline had cared so much about her dead pupil and had wanted to see right done by her. By the end she'd felt that Caroline trusted her, believed that she'd do her best for Farah. Now that the case had been closed with no tangible result and no one called to account, Caroline was the last person Sarah wanted to bump into.

The man at the till began scanning her items and placing them in a blue carrier bag. *Hurry up,* she wanted to say.

There was a tap on her shoulder. 'Detective Sergeant Collins?'

There was that wide, kind face that Sarah remembered so well, the smile lines at the eyes.

'It is you, isn't it?' Caroline said.

That was breaking the rules: calling her out in a public place when she was on her own and off duty. She nodded at the man behind the counter, who had also clocked her now. Hastily passing him a twenty-pound note and with no more than a glance over her shoulder, she said, 'Sarah Collins, yes.'

The shopkeeper handed over her change. She turned to leave but Caroline was still standing there, obviously expecting a chat. There was an awkward pause. Caroline smiled again. 'I'm Caroline. Do you remember?'

'Yes.'

Caroline either didn't notice or ignored the deliberate rudeness of the monosyllable.

'I was Farah's teacher, yes?'

'Yes, I remember.'

And she did remember the interview with her in the classroom. Farah had been a quiet girl, Caroline had said, and good at maths.

She remembered something else too: Caroline's girlfriend arriving at the end of the interview. Patti: that was her name.

Caroline smiled again, and it seemed a genuine smile, with no reserve, no hidden disapproval. 'You didn't find anyone responsible in the end?'

It would be so much easier to face someone who was unfriendly, who blamed her as she blamed herself for the outcome of the investigation.

'I can't really discuss it.'

'But it's public, and that's what the inquest found, isn't it? Misadventure.' She'd said it so kindly, as if she was trying to understand. 'I looked it up. An accident, a mishap, no evil intent.'

Why did she have to spell it out? Sarah got her car keys out of her pocket. Perhaps that would be clue enough. 'That's right. If you'll excuse me.'

'What about that officer that went missing . . . PC Lizzie Griffiths? What about her? Why did she run away?'

'I can't discuss it. If you followed the inquest, you'll have read her account.'

There was a pause, and in that pause there was just the hint of that smile at Caroline's lips, the crease at the edges of her eyes. Then she said, 'You always this tense?'

Sarah returned her gaze steadily. 'When I'm off duty in a supermarket and being put on the spot, yes, I am.'

Caroline reached out, put her hand on Sarah's shoulder. 'I'm sorry. I'm sure you did your best.'

Sarah flushed with emotion at Caroline's unexpected kindness. What made it so hard was that Caroline was someone she would have liked to talk to. But she couldn't talk to anyone. She couldn't risk it. Anyone might speak to the press. How could she possibly trust her? She imagined the officers from her new team – by now, no doubt, laughing together at their war stories. She felt pathetic standing here alone with her blue carrier bag full of tinned vine leaves and the processed meat for the dog.

Caroline was speaking. 'Are you OK?'

Sarah nodded. She really needed to leave.

'I could buy you a drink, maybe? I won't talk about the investigation, not if you don't want me to.'

'Another time perhaps.' Then, after a pause, 'How's Patti?'

The smile was suddenly quite broad now. She could see Caroline's evenly spaced white teeth. 'You remembered her name.'

'I'm a cop. It's my job to remember people.'

Caroline laughed as if she didn't believe a word of it. 'OK. Whatever. Look, ring me if you want to. Patti's away. She's gone to family in St Lucia.' She turned to the man behind the counter. 'Oi, nosy. Have you got a pen and paper?'

Sarah drove almost blindly away from the shop, threading her way through suburbia, thinking compulsively of PC Lizzie Griffiths, who had run away and disappeared for days. She remembered Lizzie's evidence to the inquest – how her memory of what had happened on the roof of the tower block had come back to her only in fits and starts. An expert witness had testified that Griffiths – who had witnessed her colleague PC Matthews and the girl, Farah, fall to their deaths – had been suffering from PTSD.

Griffiths told the court she had no idea why she'd run and Sarah, watching, had felt the court's heart go out to the pretty young woman standing giving evidence in her uniform. She was so young, so pale, so vulnerable. She'd gone to the roof of Portland Tower, risked her life to save the five-year-old boy that Farah had abducted. Everyone had felt for Lizzie Griffiths. But Sarah had *known* she was withholding evidence, that there was more to it than that. She just couldn't prove it. The inquest hadn't criticized Griffiths and it would only be a matter of days before the results of the internal disciplinary inquiry into her actions would announce its findings. Sarah was no longer part of that. It was no longer any of her business, thank God.

She pulled into her drive. It was a small detached house that she could never have afforded if she hadn't been lucky enough to put a deposit down fifteen years ago. Then the mortgage had seemed impossible; now it was a snip. The house had probably trebled in value. Putting her key in her front door, she could hear scratching and whining. As she pushed her way in, the dog snaked around her, blocking her entrance, its young spine in a supple curve, ears back, tail wagging low, paws up on Sarah's suit trousers, panting, reaching up to lick her.

Sarah laughed. 'All right, all right, Daisy.'

She was late home. She should have asked the dog walker to keep Daisy longer. She picked the spaniel up and nuzzled her ears with her nose. Daisy was light, lively, her ribs wriggling beneath her skin as she strained to lick Sarah's face. She should never have got the dog. With the hours she worked, she wasn't in any position to have a pet. Her own mother had gently counselled against it, but she'd been so low when she'd seen the litter advertised in a newsagent's window, and the dog had been so sweet.

Sarah moved through to the kitchen. There was a pool of wee on the floor. She couldn't bring herself to reprimand Daisy. The dog in any case knew she had done something wrong. She was doing her penitent face, ears back. Opening the back door and putting her outside, Sarah said, with no conviction, 'Yes, you are a naughty dog.'

She cleaned the floor and then opened the plastic wrapping on the slices of meat. Hearing the scrape of her bowl against the stone floor, Daisy rocketed back in from the garden. Sarah watched, feeling guilty, as the dog wolfed the meat down.

She slipped on her wellies. Although it was fully dark, she reached down the dog's lead and set out in the darkness to walk the steep track behind her house.

2

It was nearly midnight. The estate was lit by pools of orange tungsten light that softened out into darkness. Mark Brannon pulled his hood up and walked across the central grassed area, passing by the small rubber-surfaced toddlers' playground. In this dispossessed space a group of boys were turning bored circles on pushbikes. One of them stretched out his hand as he cycled past to slap Mark's outstretched palm. Mark looked to his right and saw with approval that a sweatshirt had been thrown over the CCTV camera that covered the area.

Mark's days of cycling around in the early hours drug-dealing were more than ten years past him. He'd moved on, was driving for one of the local crime families now. He had the don't-mess-with-me look. Although he was no more than five foot eight tall, he was big-chested, muscular and walked like a fighter. He wore jeans, brown chukkas, a denim jacket with a hoody underneath. He made his way along the concrete walkway, took his shoes off outside the front door and slipped his key into the lock. He eased the door quietly shut behind him and padded into the sitting room in his socks.

Georgie was asleep with the dog on the sofa. The dog raised her head slightly and waved her tail cautiously. He'd found her a couple of years previously in a cardboard box on the street with the rest of her litter. She'd been no more than a ball of fluff with eyes as pale blue as his own. He'd tucked her under his arm and taken her round to his cousin Marley's. Marley shampooed the dog, used the hairdryer, tied a ribbon round her neck. She got a box specially from Paperchase and he'd popped the puppy inside and presented her to Georgie and his daughter. He could still remember Skye's screams of delight when she opened the box. A puppy! He could see the mixture of love and slight irritation on Georgie's face. He should have asked her before he got a dog. Skye had been given the job of naming the puppy and she'd chosen Candy. It was also of course a name for heroin. He'd taken some flak off the boys for that! The dog had started small but just kept getting bigger. There was something slender in her frame and narrow in her head that suggested greyhound, or saluki maybe, but the fur was all wrong for that – fluffy, brown and black.

He squeezed next to Candy on the edge of the sofa and tried to stretch out. He'd been drinking for hours. After he'd argued with Georgie, he'd gone to Marley's. It was important to go out when he felt like that, and Marley and him, they went way back, right back to the beginning when it was just the two of them against the world. He could trust her. She'd got his back. Good old Marley. When even Marley had had enough of listening to him, he'd moved on. He'd walked to a friend's, had a few joints, a line or two of coke. He'd finished up with a bottle of whisky by himself in the park.

The television was on, the sound low. The screen lit Georgie's face with changing white light. It was one of those reality programmes about houses. The house had a view of the beach. The surf rolled in and the presenter walked slowly along the sand. The dad wanted to make a new life in Australia. The mum wanted to stay in Halifax. The family had difficult decisions to make. Mark pulled a roll-up from his pocket and lit it. He got up and walked to his daughter's bedroom.

Although she was seven, Skye still slept with the blue canvas night light that rotated and threw pictures of the moon and stars.

Her face was peaceful. Her hands rested over the covers of her princess quilt. She was a mini-me version of her mother: slender limbs, long straight blonde hair. He squatted by the side of the bed and watched her, put his hand above her mouth, feeling the almost imperceptible rise and fall of her warm breath. The room smelled of clean child, of laundry and shampoo. God, he loved his family so much he thought his heart would burst. That was what made him so angry.

He went back into the sitting room. He moved around the flat, stood in the kitchen. It was all open-plan, but the main room was an L shape with the dining and kitchen area in the bottom stroke of the letter. He saw the perfect order of the kitchen. She'd been cleaning while he'd been out. No dishes on the side. Her shelf of knick-knacks rearranged and polished up. How could she be so heartless? He hadn't been able to think of anyone but her all night. He'd practically made himself sick with it. But Georgie? She didn't even wake up when he got in. He flicked ash into the kitchen sink.

He stood behind the sofa, tapping his foot on the floor. The programme was still playing. He reached for the remote control from the sofa arm, turned the volume up to maximum until the presenter sounded like a crazy person, shouting about a mezzanine. At last Georgie stirred, raised her head, bleary-eyed.

'Shh, Mark. Skye's sleeping.'

Christ, if only she could be kind!

'Is that all you've got to say to me?'

Candy, catching his tone, lifted her head and growled softly. Georgie was getting up, unfolding her long limbs. She was in loose pink pyjama bottoms and a sleeveless T-shirt, bare feet, as supple as willow. She moved to the television and flicked the off switch.

'Not waking the kid. Is that all you care about?'

Georgie rubbed her eyes. She was so fucking beautiful and sexy.

'Where've you been, Mark?'

He moved around the sofa towards her.

'Never mind that.'

'I'm pleased to see you. I'm pleased you're back.'

But the words were ruined by the tense little frown that had tightened between her eyebrows. Why couldn't she just love him completely, like he loved her? His family, it was everything to him. Who was it put the food on the table while she stayed at home lighting joss sticks?

He grabbed her, one hand on her bottom, the other between her legs. She put her hand on the back of his neck, moved her mouth against his. But he could feel that the action was half-hearted. He stopped, pushed her away. 'What's the matter with you?'

'Nothing.'

'You had your boyfriend round here? Can't do it twice in a night, is that it?'

'I've been here with Skye all night.'

He took her phone out of his jacket pocket, threw it on the floor. 'I want you to unlock that. I want to see your texts.'

She laughed – as if she thought that would make him believe her!

'Fucking funny, is it?'

He pushed her in the middle of her chest. She stepped backwards, had to steady herself. The dog growled again.

'I love you, Mark, you know I do.'

He pushed her again, then heard the light tap of the dog's paws on the laminate floor as it trotted towards him, growling softly. 'What the fuck?' He grabbed the dog by its collar and dragged it into the kitchen. That fucking dog, it owed him its life! Was that how it repaid his kindness?

'Don't you fucking growl at me!'

Georgie watched, the heels of her hands under her chin, her palms spread across her cheeks. 'Please don't hurt Candy.'

'What do you think I am? Some kind of fucking MONSTER?'

He'd raised his voice and the bloody dog started barking. He picked up a chair to threaten it and then, when the dog snarled, he hit it with the chair. There was a yelping whine, then a whimpering. The dog crawled under the table.

He stormed back to Georgie, grabbed her by her T-shirt.

'You happy now? Is it fucking funny now? Look what you've made me do. You happy I've hurt the dog?'

She shook her head.

'I fucking love that dog.'

'Mark, please.'

All she fucking needed to do was to be nice.

His daughter's bedroom door opened. She stood on the threshold, looking at him. He said, 'Go back in your room, Skye. Right now.'

Georgie turned to her daughter. 'That's right, Skye. Go back to bed.'

The door closed. He said, 'Happy now? Happy now? Happy now?' She didn't reply so he asked her again. 'HAPPY NOW? ARE YOU HAPPY NOW?'

She shook her head just once. If she could only say something kind! That was all he wanted.

'I love that dog, you bitch.'

'I love the dog too, Mark. We all love the dog.'

He slapped her across the face, hard. 'You fucking bitch. You've made me hurt the fucking dog. Don't you dare tell me you love the dog.'

She wiped the side of her mouth.

And after that he couldn't remember exactly what happened.

3

Lizzie Griffiths parked her 2008 Golf in one of the off-street police bays and placed on the dashboard the letter from the detective inspector authorizing her to leave it there.

Caenwood was a busy police station on the edge of central London: a big square 1960s building with steel-framed windows, high walls around the yard and CCTV cameras facing the street. Lizzie got out of her car and tried swiping her warrant card in the side door that led to the yard. The light flashed red: clearly the card hadn't been activated yet. She hesitated. It was her first proper full day back at work and it didn't help with her trepidation that it wasn't turning out to be easy getting into her new nick.

She'd dressed up to give herself courage – new dark wool suit, sky-blue silk blouse, soft navy court shoes – but all she'd achieved was to feel as if she were playing a part. Why ever had she worn heels? She was a runner, never comfortable when her feet weren't flat on the ground. She was slim and athletic – she wore the clothes well – but she felt exposed, overdressed rather than brave. The wind was cold and her hands were already chilled. She tried to put them in her jacket pockets, which, she discovered only now, weren't cut.

The street was lined with parked police cars, white forensic vans. A group of plain-clothes officers emerged from the gate, carrying stab vests, and piled cheerfully into one of the cars. Lizzie felt it: that police rhythm she had been away from for months. It held her there, caught between two opposing forces, one telling her to go inside, to be part of it all again, the other telling her to run away, just as she had fled impulsively after Farah and Hadley had fallen to their deaths. She saw that moment: the wind whipping across the roof of the tower block, Hadley and Farah on the edge, blue sky and clouds behind them. Lizzie knew how badly wrong things could go.

She went into the station office. People were seated around the perimeter. A woman wearing a lanyard and talking on her phone. Three spotty boys in unlaced trainers. A red-faced vagrant who was probably responsible for the stale smell that filled the room held a cat on a piece of string.

At the counter, a man in a deerstalker hat and dog-tooth jacket was talking loudly at the station officer. Before Lizzie could show her ID, he'd turned crossly to her and asked, 'Would you mind waiting your turn?' She smiled apologetically and flashed her warrant card at the young female station officer who barely glanced at Lizzie as she reached below the counter and pressed a button.

The hallway was darkly utilitarian, with a black plastic floor and no windows. Posters on the walls carried exhortations to meet targets or dress smartly. *Don't fail the Victims Charter!* A cleaner was moving slowly down the stairs, swiping them with a filthy mop. Although she'd been there only once before when she'd met her new detective inspector, Lizzie knew the way to her new office. She moved up the stairs and turned left along the corridor. She'd been accepted on the training scheme for detectives and had been posted to a borough domestic violence unit. It was all part of the new start she was supposed to be making after the deaths at Portland Tower.

The disciplinary board had gone through its process. They'd sought a misconduct finding for her absence without leave, but her barrister had successfully argued that she'd been suffering post-traumatic stress when she disappeared. Afterwards the chief superintendent had called her in for a meeting. Privately, he said, some people thought she should have had a commendation for her bravery in saving the life of the five-year-old boy, and for trying so hard to save Farah. He'd shrugged – she'd understand that in the circumstances it hadn't been possible. Still, they didn't want to lose her. They wanted to integrate her back into work. She needed a new start: a new role, a different nick far from all the officers who had known Hadley.

She'd known everyone at her old station. Here everyone who passed her was a stranger. More than ever, she felt the absence of Hadley. Nearly thirty years in the job, he would have known exactly how to deport himself in a foreign nick. Briefly she felt his big bear arm around her as she walked down the corridor in her ridiculous shoes.

No one looked up when she stepped inside the large open-plan office. The detective inspector's office to her right was empty. She cast her eyes around. The desks were pushed together in banks of six or so, most of which had no one sitting at them. Their surfaces were dirty, crowded with heaps of files tied together with treasury tags, overflowing plastic in-trays, discarded free newspapers. Photos of suspects were on the walls, some fenced in with thick bars drawn in marker pen. Whiteboards carried the names of officers and their shift patterns. Some names had cut-outs sellotaped next to them: Shaggy Rogers from Scooby Doo, Bret Maverick, Foxy Brown, Jessica Rabbit. Directly in front of her, a computer had a notice stuck to the screen, the typeface bold and large: *This dinosaur is a SHIT dinosaur.*

In the far corner, an officer had looked up from his screen and was smiling at her, beckoning her over with his index finger. He was brown-eyed, mid-thirties, good-looking but scruffy. His hair looked like he'd just dried it with a towel. He was wearing an unremarkable blue shirt and a maroon V-neck jumper that had gone a bit bobbly.

'Are you the new girl?'

Lizzie felt herself colouring. 'Yes, Lizzie.'

He beamed and rubbed his hands together. 'Manna from heaven!' He stepped from behind the desk and she saw that his grey trouser bottoms were tucked into his socks. He followed her eyes and smiled. 'Oh, that? Carpet fleas. We're infested.'

Immediately her ankles were itching. She reached down and tucked her trousers into her pop socks.

The man giggled. 'Oh, you're channelling Audrey Hepburn!'

Lizzie giggled too. She was feeling better. He smiled and offered his hand. His grip was warm and surprisingly strong. 'Ash Attalah. I'm your skipper.' He sat again and glanced at his screen, then back at Lizzie. '*Acting* skipper, that is. I'm actually just a DC like you.'

'Well, I'm just a *training* DC.'

'Frankly, my dear, who gives a damn? We're taking on water quicker than we can bail it out. All hands welcome. Talking of which, we've got one in the bin. I've no one on duty except you and eight new crime reports to screen. Will you be OK to deal?'

'Yeah, of course.'

Lizzie flicked the mouse on the computer in front of her. It made a whirring sound like a spaceship taking off.

'Where's the inspector? I ought to say hello.'

'Bridget? She's practically *never* here. Which, don't get me wrong, is no bad thing.' He passed her a paper folder. 'Here's the handover from the arresting officers. Your first prisoner's a nasty fucker, so congratulations. Good to start with a worthy subject.'

Custody was heaving. Officers queued for the desk and leaned against the wall making small talk with their prisoners and the solicitors. At the desk, a lone female sergeant was booking in a handcuffed prisoner who leaned over, hanging his neck between his shoulders like a worn-out vulture waiting around in the desert heat for something to die. Entirely new to the nick and to her role as a detective, Lizzie nevertheless felt the usual police obligation to look as though she knew what she was doing. She checked the custody screen whiteboard and found her way down the corridor to Male 3.

She slid the wicket down and looked through the Perspex at her prisoner.

Mark Brannon was lying on his back on the plastic mattress, eyes open, jeans unzipped, his right hand resting comfortably on his stomach, his left arm flung out by his side. He made no response to the opening of the wicket, so Lizzie slid down the Perspex pane and said, 'Mark.' He stirred, fastening his jeans without embarrassment and swinging his legs over to the floor to come slowly to standing. He wore a blue and white striped football shirt and a grey hoody. He shambled towards the door, rubbing the stubble of his shaved head with his right hand. He had small hands with short fingers and round short nails. Although he wasn't tall he was evidently strong, and had the look about him of a man who would punch first and ask questions later.

He put his face against the opening and Lizzie leaned back from his breath. A sour smell came off him, but he had film-star pale blue eyes – shadowed, startling. They wouldn't look out of place gazing at the horizon in a cowboy movie.

'All right to wash my face?'

Lizzie stood beside him at the end of the windowless corridor as he squeezed pink liquid soap from the dispenser onto his open palm. He bent over the sink and splashed his face and head, drawing his fingers up the back of his neck and over his scalp.

She said, 'QPR, is it?'

He didn't reply, bending over the tap and swilling out his mouth.

Lizzie half sang, *'We hate you, Chelsea, yes we do.'*

Brannon unravelled ample quantities of the ribbon of blue paper towel from the plastic dispenser on the wall. He dried his hands and face and said quietly, 'I can't stand that stuff. Idiotic.'

Lizzie shrugged. 'Sorry. Just making conversation.'

Brannon considered her. 'Don't I know you?'

'I doubt it. I'm new to this ground.'

'No, I've definitely seen you somewhere before.' His eyes narrowed as he sought to place her. 'What did you say your name was?'

'Lizzie.'

'Lizzie what?'

No avoiding it then. 'Lizzie Griffiths.'

'Now then, *Lizzie Griffiths*, be a sweetheart. Can I ring my missus? I just want to make sure my little girl's all right.'

'Let's see how the interview goes. Your solicitor is waiting for your consultation.'

Twenty minutes later, they were in interview. The solicitor's head was bent over his notepad, revealing hair that straggled thinly over a sun-spotted pate. Brannon leaned back in the chair opposite Lizzie, his legs stretched out straight in front of him, his arms folded across his chest. The room smelled of him – alcohol and the stale odour of a man who had slept in his clothes.

'Mark – can I call you Mark?'

'No comment.'

'OK. Do you understand the caution or do you need it explained?'

'No comment.'

She glanced at the solicitor but he didn't even look up.

'You've got legal representation. We'll move on. Did you say "Hello, cunts" to the officers?'

This provoked a smile. Lizzie could see them clearly in her imagination, those two uniformed officers reaching the end of their night duty, meeting Brannon outside his flat. Apparently he'd been eating cheese on toast and smoking.

'For the tape – Mr Brannon is smiling.'

'No comment.'

'Did you slap Georgina Teel in the face?'

'No comment.'

'Did you then grab her by the hair and call her a "fucking two-timing little bitch"?'

'No comment.'

'Did you push her in the chest, and when she fell, did you sit on her chest and call her a "fucking whore"?'

'No comment.'

'Did you spit in her face?'

'No comment.'

'Did you drag her by her legs into the kitchen?'

'No comment.'

'Did you lie on the couch and instruct Georgina to make you some cheese on toast?'

'No comment.'

'Where was your daughter when this was happening?'

'No comment.'

'Where was Skye, Mark?'

He looked at her, clearly angry for the first time. His mouth was tight, his jaw clenched.

'Where was Skye?'

'No comment. No comment. No fucking comment.'

Lizzie glanced at her watch. She should cover defences. Defences? She trawled her mental back-catalogue of excuses and lies. What possible defence could there be?

'Is Georgina Teel making this account up?'

He studied her face. 'Has she given a statement, then?'

Look at him: wrong-footing her. Lizzie hesitated. The brief paragraph in the domestic violence report booklet hardly justified the word 'statement', although it was, at least, signed. The account was a messy three-line scribble written in a failing black biro that alternated between blotching and fading. The handwriting fell off the page, was crossed out and misspelled, probably scrawled in a pressing hurry. But more concerning to Lizzie than the statement's paucity was the complication of telling Brannon that his partner had given evidence against him. Who wanted to add to the risk that already dogged Georgina Teel by admitting that?

The solicitor looked up. He had bags under his eyes and the whites were threaded with blood vessels.

'If there is a statement then you'll have to disclose it if you come to charge.'

'We have a brief statement, yes.'

Brannon leaned forward. 'What does she say?'

'I shan't be answering any more questions on this. You are not interviewing me.'

His solicitor lifted his hand slowly. His jacket cuffs were worn. There wasn't much enthusiasm in the gesture, but still, fair play to him, he was doing his job.

'If you want to draw any sort of inference from this interview, you need to provide me with sufficient disclosure to advise my client.'

Lizzie thought of this unknown Georgina Teel being dragged along the floor and then making Mark Brannon the slice of toasted cheese he had been eating when the police arrived.

'Georgina says you assaulted her last night, Mark. That should be sufficient disclosure for you to be able to tell me whether she's telling the truth or making it up.'

Brannon leaned back and closed his arms across his chest. 'No comment.'

'Any reason she would make it up? Any mental illness, any resentment, any jealousy perhaps?'

She was tempted to add, *because after all you're a nice guy, quite a catch.*

'No comment.'

'What about self-defence? Did she attack you and you were just defending yourself?'

Brannon turned to his solicitor, who spoke just loudly enough for the tape.

'I remind you of my earlier advice.'

Brannon paused and rocked back in his chair, a parody of a man making a decision.

'No comment, then.'

It turned out to be a struggle simply to get Brannon back into his cell. First she had to queue to sign him back. Then he asked for another consultation with his solicitor.

The female custody sergeant – glamorous with highlighted blonde hair, dyed dark eyelashes and a seen-it-all attitude – eyed Lizzie with irritation as if it were she who was asking for the consultation.

'You'll need to facilitate that.'

Lizzie tried to protest. 'Sarge, I've got to write the report for the prosecutor . . .'

The sergeant's mouth had set into a thoroughly pissed-off line. 'No, *Detective*. He's your prisoner. I can't spare a detention officer.'

So Lizzie stood in her uncomfortable heels, leaning back against the wall and watching while Brannon and his brief talked behind a closed glass door. All this effort for what? A suspended sentence? A community order? Her phone buzzed. It was from Kieran, a text. 👍?

He was due back in London tonight ready for an early shift the following day. The plan was to take Lizzie out for a meal, celebrate her first day back at work. She tapped in a response – an echo of his emoticon – and then deleted it. Here she was again: hesitating but not in the end, she suspected, refusing to meet.

Kieran Shaw had been her inspector when Hadley and Farah died. Even before their deaths, it had been a mess: Kieran was married and had a daughter. After the deaths, when Lizzie had been bewildered, he had taken control, been very clear – too clear perhaps – what she should do. He'd stuck by her, put himself on the line, accompanied her to the misconduct hearing. But when it was all over he had had little patience for her abiding unease. It was time to move on. No amount of introspection would bring Hadley or Farah back.

Her thoughts were interrupted. Ash had slipped in beside her and was now leaning next to her facing the consultation room, watching Brannon and his brief talking. Lizzie closed her phone and slipped it into her pocket.

'That brief's taking his time, isn't he?' Ash said. 'They're not paid by the hour any more.'

'He's not the duty brief.'

'No?'

'Brannon's got friends. Looks like they're looking after him.'

'Interesting.'

There was a silence. Then Ash said, 'A little bird told me the nasty custody sergeant is being mean to the pretty new detective.'

In spite of herself, Lizzie laughed.

Ash said, 'Brannon's partner Georgina has rung. She needs to speak to you.'

'But I'm stuck here!'

'I've had a word, and the very nice detention officer Hussain is going to help us out. When you go past Sergeant Hitchin, make sure to say thank you. You don't want her to take against you. She can be more vengeful than Anne Boleyn.'

Lizzie stared at the board in the inspector's office. It was marked up with all the borough's cars' registration marks, next to the names and mobile numbers of the officers who had taken them out scrawled in wipeable marker. There wasn't a single car available. She didn't feel confident to do the rounds of the offices asking people if they would give up their car. Her own Golf was downstairs; she'd take that. She shouldn't really use her own car on duty but taking public transport would add more than an hour to a day that already looked as though it was stretching out into evening.

By car, Georgina's flat was only fifteen minutes from the nick: straight along the main shopping street with its independent cinema and gastro pub, then quickly off into the poorer, rougher side streets. Lizzie parked in a metred bay directly outside the block, made her way up the stairs and along the external walkway. Just by the landing someone had drawn a hopscotch in blue chalk. A pink girl's bicycle with tassled handlebars leaned against the wall just beyond the front door. *tasselled*

Georgina was slim and tall in tight pale jeans. She had long blonde hair, enhanced with some highlights and straightening. She wore a sleeveless white T-shirt that showed her small breasts and thin arms. She led Lizzie into the narrow hallway. It was too warm. Heat belched out of radiators turned up full.

'Do you mind taking your shoes off?'

'No, not at all. In fact I couldn't be happier.'

Squatting down to place her shoes on the shoe rack, Lizzie noticed Georgina's long and beautifully kept feet; her painted toenails. On the inside of her ankle was a tattoo of a lotus flower. She stood up, feeling a bit foolish in her pop socks.

Entering the sitting room through the frosted door at the end of the hallway, she saw a seven-year-old girl sitting at the table. Her mum was visible in her: long legs in pink pedal pushers, long bare arms, a narrow chest in a white T-shirt with a cupcake on the front. Two blonde plaits fell forward onto her shoulders. Her sock-clad toes were curled over the spindles of the wooden chair and her head was bent in concentration over a loom as she weaved colourful rubber bands.

Another woman of Georgina's age was sitting to the right, on a white sofa behind a glass coffee table. The room was darker there, and Lizzie couldn't see her properly.

Georgina said, 'Be a good girl, Skye. Go and finish that in your room. I need to talk to this lady.'

'But I need the table.'

'You can watch a DVD later. Now do as I tell you. Go to your room. I won't tell you twice.'

Skye gave Lizzie a brief but winning smile. She collected her loom and pot of rubber bands and disappeared into her bedroom. Georgina walked towards the kitchen.

'Cup of tea?'

'Yes, please.'

The woman on the sofa spoke up. 'I'll make it, Georgie.'

'Ah, thanks.'

The woman looked at Lizzie, and Lizzie smiled. 'Hi, I'm Lizzie.'

The woman didn't smile back. 'Yeah, I know who you are.'

She was probably late twenties, light coffee-coloured skin and frizzy golden hair, the side of her nose pierced, a sporty cropped top showing a hard brown stomach with a navel pierced by a bar and jewel. She disappeared off to the kitchen area and Lizzie noticed, for the first time, a dog sitting there in a basket with a blue cast on its front right leg.

She sat down at the table. 'What's happened to the dog, then?'

Georgina shrugged and sat opposite. 'Broke her leg, didn't she? Stupid thing. Ran out. Got hit by a car.'

Lizzie's eyes flicked around the flat. 'You keep this place immaculate.'

'I'm a bit OCD. Comes from my mum.'

'Your mum's the same?'

Georgina laughed. 'God, no. The opposite.'

For the first time Lizzie spotted the bruise beneath Georgina's eye. It had been skilfully masked by foundation. The other woman brought a tray over with the tea and a plate of biscuits. The cups were china, with saucers. The woman sat down as if she were an accepted part of whatever was going on.

Lizzie said to Georgina, 'Has anyone photographed that bruise?'

Georgina's right hand went fleetingly to her face, but the other woman interrupted before she could answer.

'Look, we might as well get to the point. Georgie rang me this morning in tears. She can't go through with it.'

Lizzie turned to her. 'I'm sorry, I don't know who you are.'

'I'm a friend of Georgie's.'

Lizzie moistened her lips. 'OK.' She turned to Georgina. 'Is this true?'

Georgina's eyes flickered towards the woman, and then back to Lizzie. 'Yes.'

The friend interrupted. 'Mark's Skye's father. They're a family.'

'Could you tell me your name, perhaps?'

'Why should I?'

'Maybe I need to talk to Georgina on her own.'

'But I'm here to support her.'

Support her: the phrase claimed the high ground and demoted Lizzie, as though her role was to harm Georgina.

'Georgina, do you mind talking to me without your friend?'

The friend interrupted again. 'Why is that necessary?'

Lizzie looked straight at her, making no attempt to disguise her hostility. 'Because this is a legal matter and you won't even give me your name. I'm going to be taking a statement from Georgina.'

'But I'm here to support her!'

'So you've said.' Lizzie looked at the table, composed herself. She spoke kindly, concentrating entirely on Georgina. 'Georgina, do you need your friend to stay?'

The friend said, 'I can stay, Georgie, if you need me.'

Georgina shook her head. 'No, it's OK. I'll be OK.'

'You sure, darling?'

'Yeah, I'll be fine.'

'All right. I'm on my phone. Any time.'

There was some bundling around. The anonymous friend put her head into Skye's bedroom to say goodbye, bustled out, pulling her zip-up jacket around her as if to say she was not at all impressed with Lizzie Griffiths.

There was a moment's silence after the door had shut. Then Lizzie said, 'Why don't you tell me what's going on.'

Georgina pressed her hands against her eyes. She seemed incapable of speech. Lizzie waited.

'He says he loves me . . .'

'He's not allowed to contact you, not even through another person.'

'He didn't. Marley just came round, off her own bat.'

'Marley?'

'The girl who was just here. The one you kicked out. He'd called her from the station. She just wanted to tell me how upset he was.'

'Hang on, Georgina . . .'

'He says he's sorry! He loves me. He loves Skye. He wants to change. Make a fresh start.'

Lizzie looked at her tea and thought twice. It crossed her mind that Marley might well have spat in it. She put the cup back on the saucer.

'Do you believe him when he says he'll change?'

'I don't know.' She wiped the corner of her left eye.

'He shouldn't be contacting you at all.'

'He just wants me to give him a chance.'

'But what if you don't, hey? What if you said no more second chances? What if you said enough is enough?'

Georgina didn't reply.

'Hasn't he made promises like this before?'

'You don't get it. I can't leave him.'

'Why not? Are you frightened of him?'

'Marley said you'd be like this.'

There was a pause. 'Marley? Is she a friend or relative of Mark's?'

'That's got nothing to do with it.'

Lizzie nodded. 'OK.'

'She said you'd try to pressure me. Said you wouldn't understand.'

The door to Skye's room opened and both women immediately stopped speaking and looked towards the girl, who was standing in the doorway holding a loom band in her outstretched hand. For the first time Lizzie spotted that her nails were varnished with flowers and butterflies.

'I made this for you, Mum.'

It was pink and blue and purple. Lizzie said, 'That's lovely. You made it all by yourself?'

Skye took a step forward. 'I can make one for you too.'

'I'd like that.'

Georgina got up and took it from her. 'All right, Skye. I've told you to stay in your room.'

Skye pulled a face at Lizzie but retreated. Georgina slipped the band over her wrist. There was one there already. Lizzie met Georgina's eyes and her police knowledge crowded in: the harm a man can do.

Georgina said, 'Do you have children?'

'No.'

'You got a boyfriend, though?'

Lizzie shrugged. Could Kieran really be described as a boyfriend?

Georgina was giving her a misplaced smile of complicity.

'Men are from Mars, isn't it?' she said.

Lizzie smiled uncertainly. 'Yeah, I s'pose so.'

'You've not seen it, but Mark's very loving.'

Lizzie's heart suddenly went out to Georgina: her tidy flat, her Buddha in the hallway, her beautiful feet, her obedient little girl.

'It's a pattern,' she said. 'Don't you see?'

'He's only like that when he's drunk! He's going to stop drinking. He's promised. He said that to Marley. He said he knows he's got to stop drinking.'

Lizzie remembered the report of Brannon's first recorded assault: a GBH on a shopkeeper who had tried to stop him stealing from his corner shop. Brannon had been fifteen at the time. It seemed he'd been enraged at the idea of anyone stopping him doing what he wanted. He'd called the shopkeeper a Paki, knocked him backwards with a blow to the forehead from a drinks can he'd taken from one of the shelves. Then he'd broken his collarbone by stamping on him. He had taken nothing when he left the shop. He'd been assaulting people ever since.

Lizzie said, 'Why don't you take a step back? Give Mark a chance to prove he can stop drinking. When he comes out, you can have a little break, maybe?'

'If I say yes, does that mean you'll drop it?'

'Georgina . . .'

Georgina raised her voice. 'You won't, will you?'

The door to the bedroom opened again and Skye was standing there with another loom band.

'Skye, I told you to stay in your room!'

Skye's face was pulled tight. 'But I made this for Lizzie. She asked me.'

'You didn't. You never had time to make another one. Go in your room!'

Skye's expression crumpled. She started to cry.

Suddenly there was an absence of sway in this usually governed place. Georgina's head was in her hands. Skye seemed stranded in the middle of the room, as if she were a small figure alone on a beach, about to be cut off by the tide. Lizzie got up, stepped towards her.

'That's lovely, thank you . . .' She took the loom band and rested it in her palm. 'It's great.' She slipped it on her wrist and twisted her hand from side to side. 'I'll treasure it.'

She glanced at Georgina. She was sitting with her elbows on the table and her face pressed into her hands. Lizzie turned back to Skye, bending to eye level and putting a gentle hand on her upper arm.

'Your mum will be fine in a minute. She just needs a moment to talk to me. Will you be all right to wait in your room? Not much longer now.'

Skye nodded.

'Hang on a moment . . .' Lizzie stepped towards the table and took the plate of biscuits. 'Why don't you have a couple?'

The bedroom door shut again. Lizzie sat and waited. Georgina blew her nose.

'You're a natural,' she said.

'What?'

'With Skye.'

Lizzie laughed. 'Dunno about that.'

Georgina smiled sceptically. 'Have to get you babysitting.'

'She's a sweet girl.' Lizzie showed off her wrist. 'Anyway, I will treasure the loom band. I've never had one before.'

They both smiled. It was funny and nice; they both felt it.

Georgina said, 'Skye's worried sick. I can't do that to her, split us up. You've got to understand that. Mark, he just needs to stop drinking.'

'But what about if you . . . took a short break?'

Georgina's eyes darted about. 'I can't, don't you see?'

'You need to think about Skye.'

A sudden fierceness. 'I'm *always* thinking about Skye. I always put my daughter first. What are you saying?'

She'd said the wrong thing. Of course she had. 'Georgina . . .'

'Skye *loves* her dad. And he *worships* her.'

The wrong thing, but still.

'It's not good for her to be around violence.'

'He'll go on a programme.'

'So take a break while he does that. She shouldn't have to see her father hurting her mother.'

'Are you threatening me?'

'What do you mean? I'm just concerned.'

'*Concerned?* I hate that word! I know what you lot are like. Always think you know best. Leaving Mark? You've no idea! Skye's fine.' She looked around at her impeccable flat. 'Do you see anything to worry about?'

'Of course I don't. This place is lovely.'

'I don't want the social coming round.'

Everything she had said had made things worse.

Lizzie suddenly remembered her colleague Hadley, his bulk squashed into a tiny wooden chair, a tortoise balanced on the flat of his hand. It had been a miserable little flat. The eldest boy had smashed some stuff up. The exhausted mother, raising four children on her own for far too long, still didn't want her son arrested. Hadley had kicked the boy out and then sat talking, waiting to ensure he didn't return too quickly. He'd had his own tortoise when he was a child, he claimed. *They can be a devil to find.* The woman had relaxed, smiled. Hadley had had that way about him. Still, nobody could ever have accused him of overestimating his effectiveness.

Some people just can't be helped. Never forget: we're the police, not the bloody social workers, thank the Lord.

Another memory came: the indelible freeze frames of a post-mortem. Cosmina, a woman she had briefly known, reduced to meat and bone and gristle. The whine of the Stryker saw and the smell of burning.

Lizzie looked around the room: the tidy shelves, the sweet dog, the framed picture of Skye with her dad at a skating rink. Well, she'd tried. She had. Now she would follow protocol. She opened her bag and took out the statement papers that she had placed neatly in a plastic folder. She popped her ballpoint.

'If you're absolutely sure you don't want to give evidence, I'll take a withdrawal statement and inform the prosecution service. They'll make the decision, not me.'

'Do that then.'

She began filling in details. 'It doesn't necessarily mean they won't prosecute him . . .'

'But it makes it unlikely, doesn't it?'

Lizzie checked her phone for the date. 'Less likely. They can summons you, or go ahead without your evidence.' She filled in Georgina's name. 'OK, what do you want to say?'

Georgina's face was tense. 'What you say to them will make a difference, won't it?'

Lizzie shrugged.

Georgina insisted. 'What are you going to tell them?'

Lizzie knew exactly what she would write on her report to the prosecutor: Brannon represented a continuing and significant threat to Georgina. Skye too was at risk. Brannon should be charged and a summons was needed to compel Georgina to give evidence.

She said, 'I'm a police officer. It's my job to look after the criminal aspects of this. Why don't you let me refer you to a domestic violence charity, someone who can talk this through with you, someone who isn't part of this process?'

Georgina wasn't misled. She shook her head. 'And why don't you tell me what you are going to say to them?'

'I haven't decided yet. I'm going to think about it.'

'Well, have a think about little Skye before you write anything down.'

'I am thinking about Skye.'

'A girl needs her father.'

It was already four when Lizzie headed back to the office. She hadn't eaten since breakfast. She pulled over and ran into M&S and stood in a dream state in front of a bright fridge full of harissa chicken and king prawn salads. She picked up a risotto and then put it back, unconvinced. Her phone buzzed: it was Kieran. She'd text him to say she was probably going to be late off, but when she glanced at her screen she saw he was the one blowing her out.

Sorry, parent–teacher meeting. Forgot. I'll be with you, but late.

Who knew what was really making him late? She'd learned not to ask. She pocketed her phone, pulled a potato and spinach curry from the shelf and succumbed to the temptation of a chocolate bar as she queued to pay.

Ash was still in the office, glued to the screen. She threw her bag on the table and he looked up.

'How'd it go?'

'Withdrawal statement.'

'Fuck.'

'Yep.'

'You'll still have to get charging advice.'

'Yes, I know.' She got the curry out of her bag. 'Where's the microwave?'

Ash glanced at the ready meal and raised his eyebrows. 'Oh, looking after number one, are we?'

'Sorry. Didn't think you'd still be here.'

'Bloody offered to help out with a prisoner, didn't I?'

'Any good?'

'Pah! Stupid bugger's thrown a duvet at his missus.' His phone buzzed. 'That must be Mr Slumberdown ready for me right now.' He pocketed his phone and sauntered out of the office.

The shadows were lengthening on the buildings opposite the office windows. The lawyer at the other end of the phone sounded Welsh. Lizzie imagined him with his cup of coffee and his never-ending list of case summaries that all needed clicking and reading and deciding. Did he have a Rayburn and a view of the sun setting over the valleys? Was there a Labrador sleeping at his feet? Perhaps he was in pyjamas. Perhaps naked. Perhaps he was a centaur. Who bloody knew?

'First thing, officer, is she going to go to court?'

'She gave an initial statement, but now she's withdrawn.'

'OK, leave it with me . . . Come back to me in twenty minutes. While you're waiting, can you submit a risk assessment, please? I want to know what the protection issues are.'

Lizzie set the timer on her phone and put a large piece of paper on the keyboard: *On phone to CPS! Please do not disconnect.*

She sat at her desk and entered Brannon's name and date of birth into the intelligence programme. The machine sorted and loaded reports from the various police indices – crime reports, calls to police, notifications to social services.

Seven-year-old Skye had achieved her first police reference number while she still moved in the ultrasound ocean of heartbeats and budding limbs. Police had been called by a neighbour, who reported sounds of a violent argument. Shouting was heard, and banging. Georgina, visibly pregnant, refused to let the officers enter.

Mark, standing behind her in the hallway, furiously demanded to know which neighbour had called them.

Lizzie clicked on the next one: a report from the local Accident and Emergency. Georgina in hospital with bruising to her arms. The doctor believed the injuries were non-accidental. Georgina said she'd got them when Mark had stopped her falling downstairs. The doctor noted that Skye, then two years old, was very clingy to her mother.

Lizzie typed quickly.

A mug of tea appeared by her left hand. Lizzie looked up. Ash was standing next to her, offering the biscuit tin at a tilt.

'Custard cream, Detective?'

She shook her head. 'No thanks. How come you're not in interview?'

'John Grisham had some more queries about the duvet. I tried to suggest it wasn't *Twelve Angry Men*, but to no avail. They're back in consultation.'

He picked up the headset and dangled it threateningly over the phone. Lizzie shook her head. 'Don't wind me up.'

Ash tutted. 'Storm alert. New girl already losing plot.' He put the headset back on the desk. 'What's the panic?'

'No panic,' she said, pressing send on her email and taking a digestive. 'The brief needed a risk assessment.'

'And what did you decide? Is Brannon a proper threat to life or merely a common or garden arsehole?'

'I think he's both.'

The timer on Lizzie's phone sounded. She picked up the headset and unlocked the mute button. 'PC Griffiths here.'

'Yes, officer. I'm just reading your risk assessment. I think we'll charge him.'

Lizzie turned the key in the lock and opened the heavy door. Brannon was lying on the bed, looking at the ceiling. He moved to sitting and smiled: a nice smile that had regret in it.

'Look, I'm sorry how I was earlier.'

She shrugged.

'I'm a bit of a wanker, OK? Only when I've been on the piss.'

He was more likeable after a few hours' sleeping it off. Sadder, more human, with those piercing blue eyes that suggested a distant horizon.

'Yeah, it's all right.'

'What's happening?'

'I've got two charges of common assault for you.'

'Don't mess about, do you?'

She shrugged. 'Do you want legal representation?'

He shook his head, already standing up to go to the custody desk. 'No, let's just get on with it.'

They had to queue for the sergeant and sat side by side on the bench. There was a text from Kieran. Lizzie turned her back and read it. He'd be in London shortly. She texted back.

Prisoner. Finished in 30. Can you pick me up?

Brannon leaned over her. 'Meeting someone?'

Lizzie closed her phone.

He said, 'Mind my own, is it?'

'I guess.'

He looked at her and played air guitar, humming along. 'Name the tune?' he said.

It had come into her head instantly. '*I bet you look good on the dancefloor.*'

She nodded. 'Yeah, all right. That's enough.'

He rubbed the top of his head, back and forth. 'Look, Lizzie – it is Lizzie, isn't it? I know you think I'm an arsehole, but I do really love her, you know.'

'Uh huh.'

There was another silence. Then he broke it again. 'I love little Skye too.'

Lizzie looked at the custody sergeant – an impeccably uniformed man with greying hair and skin so black it almost shone. He was dealing with a lot of evidence, methodically scanning the seal numbers into the custody programme. There were hard drives, phones, a baseball bat . . . It was taking an age. She really didn't like having to spend time with Brannon. He'd started again.

'I couldn't love her more.' He smiled self-deprecatingly. 'I'm a bit of a cunt when I've had a drink.'

'You'd better not say any more. You're still under caution. I'll have to write it down.'

'Yeah, but I want you to understand. I'm not a bad man. I've a good heart. I *love* Georgie. I love my family.'

'OK.'

'OK?'

Lizzie turned to him. 'I dunno, Mark. What do you want me to say?'

Hallelujah! The officers were clearing the evidence bags and the custody sergeant pinged an imaginary bell on the desk. 'Next.'

The charges were straightforward. The problems began when Brannon realized that Lizzie was applying to remand him.

He turned to her. 'Oh fucking *come on*. You're joking! I've been in here all day. I want to go home to my daughter.'

The sergeant intervened, stretching his hand out. 'Talk to me, not the officer. I'm the one who decides.'

Brannon frowned, never taking his eyes off Lizzie.

'Why don't you like me?'

'It's not personal, really.'

'It's my fucking missus! And my daughter. I live for them.'

A couple of officers came over and stood next to Lizzie. One of them put a hand on Brannon's shoulder. 'Come on, mate. Calm down.'

Brannon shrugged him off. 'I'm not your mate. Fuck off.'

The sergeant glanced at the two officers. 'I'm granting PC Griffiths' application for a remand—'

Brannon banged the custody desk with his fist. 'I'm not going to fucking hurt Georgie. I love her.'

'You two, can you help PC Griffiths put Mr Brannon back in his cell.'

Brannon walked quickly, head down. Lizzie followed behind the male officers, who escorted him into the cell and shut the door. Brannon was shouting. 'I want a cup of tea.'

She opened the wicket but left the Perspex shut. Brannon was standing right by the opening.

'You've never made a mistake?'

When she didn't answer immediately, he said, 'Well?'

'Course I've made mistakes. We all do.'

He didn't answer, just stared at her. She smiled nervously. 'I'll get you that cup of tea. You take sugar?'

'But you've been allowed to move on?'

Moving on? Well, she was trying to. 'Look, I've got to go. Do you want that tea or not?'

He stepped back from the wicket. 'Two sugars.'

She stood in the cramped little room next to the Styrofoam boxes of reheat meals and the shelves of evidence bags and weapons tubes. She checked the tea wasn't scalding in case he threw it at her, stirred the sugar in with the plastic stirrer. When she opened the wicket, Brannon was still standing there. She passed him the tea carefully, standing back. But he seemed relaxed now, calmer.

'Thanks, love.'

'No probs.'

She went to shut the wicket and he said, 'Can I just ask you something?'

She felt a twist of irritation. She'd told Kieran thirty minutes. 'I'm in a bit of a hurry . . .'

'Do you believe in giving people a second chance?'

She smiled. 'What a question to ask a police officer!'

'What do you mean by that? You're a person, aren't you? What makes you so different from the rest of us?'

'Nothing. Just that, well, you know that's not part of my job. Forgiveness and understanding, that stuff. I'm in the investigating and charging part of things.'

'Yeah, but you think people can change, yeah? As a person, I mean, you think that?'

She thought of Georgina. She hoped to God Brannon *could* change, but she wasn't convinced. 'Honestly? I don't know.'

'You *don't know*?'

She shrugged. 'I'm only a police officer.' He seemed very worked up again. 'Do you need a smoke? I'll ask one of the detention officers if they've got time to take you out.'

His Paul Newman eyes narrowed and his jaw clenched. He nodded as if he understood her well enough.

'You're a clever little cunt, aren't you?'

Something stopped her closing the wicket. Suddenly he had all her concentration.

'A hypocritical little cunt too.'

She could feel the heat coming off him.

'Quite happy for the second chance, aren't you, when it's *you* taking it. Don't kid yourself. I know who the fuck you are, PC Lizzie Griffiths. You're that copper that let that girl fall off the roof.'

———

Ash had already gone when she got back to the office. There was a note on her desk: Toodle pip!

Lizzie's phone rang: Kieran was waiting for her downstairs. After her encounter with Brannon all her misgivings about Kieran had evaporated. She pressed send on the charging file, grabbed her bag and ran down the stairs in her heels. The Land Rover was parked in the street and the lights flashed for her. She couldn't see him clearly in the darkness of the interior, just the outline of his face turned to her in deep shadow. He flashed the lights at her again and she was filled with warmth. He was smiling.

4

Sarah was running late. It was today that Detective Constable Lee Coutts was interviewing Erdem Sadiq, the grass who said he had information on Tania's disappearance. Sarah had stayed late in the office to brief Lee before he left for the prison, but Lee – late twenties, glossy-haired and shiny-suited – hadn't given the impression of being particularly interested in what she had to say. Still, the boss had said he was a good officer. Perhaps she hadn't needed to interfere.

She dumped the job car in a residents' bay and ran up the stairs to the flat. The safety chain was on and a man peered at her through the narrow gap between door and frame. Sarah saw stubbly wide grey cheeks, big ears, hair in his nostrils, pale blue eyes. She showed her warrant card and gave the code.

'Lotus Cortina.'

The man unhinged the safety chain. He was short and dumpy, dressed in dark trousers with braces and a white buttoned shirt with the sleeves rolled up. A little behind him stood a loafing, loose-limbed, white bloke wearing a blue beanie hat from which curls escaped – Ewan, Robert's social worker, Sarah assumed.

'Welcome to my home,' Robert said grandly, welcoming her in with a sweeping gesture.

Ewan smiled at Sarah to go ahead and they stepped inside, Robert shuffling behind them into the living space. The room carried a sour smell of bristles and old wool cloth and Palmolive soap.

All around the room, on shelves and in cabinets, in boxes piled up neatly on the floor, were hundreds of toy vehicles – lorries, sports cars, pick-ups, ambulances, mobile homes, fire engines, police cars, several car transporters, a bomb disposal van, camper vans, three snow ploughs, lined up side by side.

Sarah walked over to a collection of liveried police cars: Austins, a Mini Cooper van, a Daimler, a Ford Granada and a Capri.

'Can I pick one up, Robert?'

'Yes.'

She picked up a BMW with white livery, a red stripe along the middle panel and a T bar on the roof. It had the satisfying weight and detail of the old die-cast metal toys.

Robert said, 'That's a BMW E28 528i from 1987. Hampshire Constabulary were using them.'

Ewan was standing behind Robert and he shook his head vigorously. Clearly it wasn't easy to stop Robert once he got started. It made Sarah smile in spite of herself. She put the miniature BMW back on its shelf and said, 'Actually, Robert, I'm here to talk about Tania.'

Robert's hands dropped to his sides. He looked like an old soldier repeating rank and number.

'They asked me all about it on the day. I only saw Tania when she came into the hut to change into her skirt.'

Sarah had read the transcripts of the interviews. Robert had been adamant. He'd been in the park all day but he'd seen Tania only briefly, first thing in the morning when she'd asked to use his hut. The problem was that the interviewers had seen him only as a suspect. All they'd been interested in was breaking down his account and getting a charge. They hadn't asked the other questions, the questions that might have led somewhere unknown.

'Robert, can I sit down?'

He nodded. She took her place on the hard settee.

'Do you want to sit too?'

He sat next to her. She noticed his shoes – black orthopaedic-type lace-ups, polished to a shine. Ewan moved over to the kitchenette. He began filling the kettle.

'Do you remember that morning, Robert? The day that Tania went missing?'

'Yes.'

She tried to prompt him into fluidity. 'There'd been a storm.'

'Yes.'

'Tell me about Tania.'

'She asked to change.'

'How was she? Was she in a good mood?'

He shook his head. 'I can't remember.'

It was even harder than Sarah had thought it would be to get Robert to talk. She wasn't sure whether that was down to memory or reluctance. She said, 'Did your mum tell you not to talk about it?'

Robert nodded.

'I wish your mum was here. I would say sorry to her for what happened.'

'Mum's dead.'

'I know, Robert. I'm sorry.'

''Sall right.'

There was a pause. Then Sarah said, 'I'm not trying to trick you. I don't think you hurt Tania. I think you were her friend. I know it upsets you to talk about it, but you see, you are very important. You might remember some little detail that would help me to find her. Her mum is still waiting for her to come home. I'm sure you want us to find out what happened.'

Robert scratched his nose. He looked across at Ewan, who was still standing at the sink. Ewan nodded. 'If you can help, Robert, I think you should.'

Robert looked down at his feet and lifted his shiny toecaps a couple of times. Then he spoke.

'It was the morning. All those trees, fallen down. Tania run up. She was excited, in a hurry. Said could she use my hut to change.'

'OK.'

'I waited outside. She come out of the hut in a skirt. I said did she want a cup of tea but she said no thank you and ran off. I went into the hut. Her jeans were on the floor. She'd left them there. The legs were pulled out the wrong way. I put them right, folded them. I was going to give them back to her.'

'You didn't see her again?'

He shook his head. 'No.'

'Tell me about the rest of the day. Did you stay in the park?'

Sarah let him talk.

He had been worried about the trees. There were branches everywhere, some hanging off. Dangerous. He had taken his big shears and his stepladder. It was hard work – climbing the stepladder with no one to steady it. Children whose schools were closed were playing.

Sarah imagined the busy park in 1987. Even though she had lived through it, the past still had a patina, almost as if it were a pastiche: big haircuts, the police in tunics, the Berlin Wall still standing. It was hard to believe in the reality of it all now, the real desires and actions, the fact that it had once had been the present, with outcomes that could have been different.

Robert had made himself tea, eaten his sandwiches. He'd walked the park, all its little side paths, its hidden places. He'd talked to the dog walkers, the mothers waiting by the swings. To help with conversation his mother had taught him the names of the flowers in the beds: yellow potentilla, white phlox, busy Lizzies in such bright colours he could not bear to be near them. His favourite thing was to stand by the main road and watch the cars.

There was nothing in Robert's account that suggested to Sarah anything other than a lively park on the day after the storm. It was a small area and even if there had been a place, a quiet corner, where something could have happened, surely it wouldn't have been possible to get a body out without a disturbance or someone seeing something? The following day the park had been thoroughly searched and there'd been an appeal for witnesses, but no one had come forward.

Sarah said, 'You had a photo of Tania in your hut.'

'Still got it.'

'I thought the police seized it.'

'The reverend made them give it back.'

'Is it here?'

He shuffled over to a chest of drawers. He found it easily. The image had the broad white frame of a Polaroid and was in a bad condition. The colours were dissolving, getting closer to each other in hue. The image itself was limned over as if by a grey wash. Still, beneath this veneer the trace of a younger Robert remained, a huge smile on his face and his arm around Tania.

'What a lovely picture. You're both smiling. You liked each other.'

Robert looked down towards his shoes.

'Who took the picture, Robert?'

'No one.'

'There must have been someone behind the camera. Who was that?'

'Tania took it.'

'How could she take it? She's in it.'

'She had one of those things. I don't know what they call it. Makes a sound.'

'She had a camera with a timer?'

Robert shrugged. 'Maybe.'

They took a break. Ewan made everyone more tea, handed out chocolate digestives.

'Let's go back,' Sarah said. 'Right back to the beginning of your friendship. How did you first come to speak to Tania?'

'I heard shouting.'

'Shouting?'

'Yes. I was worried. I hurried over. They were arguing.'

'Who was arguing?'

'Tania and a man.'

'When was that?'

'It was a sunny day. The park didn't have so many people in it.'

'OK.'

'Tania was in her school uniform and the man saw me and he stepped back from her.'

'What did he look like, the man?'

'Tall.'

'How tall?'

Robert shook his head. 'Don't know.'

'Taller than you?'

'Maybe.'

'Taller than Ewan?'

Robert smiled broadly. 'No!'

Sarah hid her disappointment. There was nothing distinctive about the man's height.

'Anything else?'

'No.'

'Black, white?'

'White.'

'How old?'

'Older than Tania.'

'What you'd call an adult, a grown-up?'

'Yes, a grown-up.'

A white male adult, possibly a bit taller than average height, possibly not. Great.

They were arguing the first time Robert saw them, but when he had appeared around the hedge, they had stopped. The man had said, 'Oh bloody hell', and stepped back from Tania.

'How was Tania, Robert?'

'What do you mean?'

'Was she happy, sad, calm, angry?'

'She was crying.'

'Crying?'

'Yes. But she stopped when she saw me. She said, "It's all right."'

After that Robert had become friends with Tania. Sometimes she stopped and talked to him in his hut or paused with him in the evening light. He had seen Tania and the man together from time to time.

'Why did you never tell the police this?'

'They never asked.'

'Is that the only reason?'

Robert looked across at Ewan, who nodded encouragement.

'Tania told me never to tell anyone. She was my friend.'

'OK. So you saw Tania walking home through the park with this man?'

'No.'

'No?'

'It was always after he dropped her off.'

'Oh, he dropped her off?'

'At the far side of the park. Sometimes he would stay with her in the park for a bit, but she would always walk home on her own.'

'He had a car?'

'Yes.'

'Do you remember it?'

'Of course. It was a green Series III XJ6 Jaguar.'

———

Sarah pulled into the parade ground at Hendon and called her new boss. She hadn't been updated yet on what information Lee had gleaned from his visit to Erdem Sadiq at HMP Thameside.

'Let's have coffee in the canteen,' Fedden said. 'I'll come down to you. I'm the fat guy in the blue suit.'

The white sky was slowly losing its brilliance and the parade ground was emptying of cars. Most people's working day was either already over or ending. Sarah pushed the seat back and waited, thinking about this meeting and how much she wanted it to go well. Some senior officers had elusive reputations, but Fedden was not one of them. As soon as she'd got her posting, a sense of him had arrived quickly at her door. 'Fedden?' they'd said, smiling at her and narrowing their eyes as if not convinced this was a good idea. Been in the job forever. Likes a result. Bit of a hard nut. He had a famous turn, apparently: singing 'It's Not Unusual' at boozy work dos. He had a nickname too, of course: the Bulldozer.

She wondered what Fedden had heard about her and what her nickname was.

He was exiting the murder block – Sarah recognized him easily enough from his own description. She got out of the car and he waddled towards her across the parade ground.

She offered her hand. 'James.'

His hand was small, with short stubby fingers. 'Everyone calls me Jim, please.'

They began to move towards the canteen, Sarah checking her pace to accommodate the DCI's breathlessness.

'Good holiday?' she asked.

'You've heard the joke? Once in a lifetime. I'm never bloody doing that again.' He wheezed when he laughed and showed small gappy teeth in a wide mouth. 'No, it was great, but I don't know what's wrong with Chipping Norton for a wedding. Damn sight cheaper, too.'

The canteen was virtually deserted, but a group of specialist search officers were queuing in front of the only available counter. It offered sugar food – coffees, paninis, chocolate brownies and flapjacks wrapped in cellophane. Fedden and Sarah stood slightly back.

'So, our informant gave us a suspect,' Fedden said, rubbing his hands together.

Upbeat, Sarah thought, that was the ticket: men like Fedden liked enthusiasm. 'That's good.'

The lady who was serving – grey-haired, tidy and patiently conformist in her neat blue uniform – glanced at Sarah and smiled. 'What can I get you, dear?'

'An espresso, please. What will you have, Jim?'

He pulled out his warrant card. 'It's on me. My usual, love. I'm having a flapjack. They're really good, you should try one. Give us two, please.'

They moved towards an unoccupied table by a window that looked out over the parade ground. The silver birches that were part of the police memorial glowed like white bones in the fading light.

Fedden threw his capacious jacket over the back of a chair. 'So this Erdem Sadiq chap says he knows who did it: Andrew Walker.' He unwrapped the flapjack on his plate and took a bite. 'I'm the last person to believe a grass, but I have to admit, the intel on Walker is good. Registered sex offender, so there's evidence he may have these tendencies. Lived locally to Tania Mills in 1987.'

'How did Sadiq say he got the information?'

'They were cellmates. Walker told Sadiq he did it when they were sharing wank fantasies.'

'That'll be interesting if Sadiq has to give evidence in court.'

Fedden threw his head back and laughed. 'Can you imagine the cross-examination?'

Sarah said, "'So Mr Sadiq, you were masturbating . . .'"

Fedden snorted with laughter. He controlled himself, wiped his forehead with a paper napkin. 'Anyway, we've got enough to nick Walker. I've tasked Lee to get a Section 8 warrant.'

'Sorry, I've missed all this. Lee hasn't sworn it already?'

She wished immediately that she'd phrased that differently. The boss clearly wished she had too: there was a pulse of movement as his jaw tensed momentarily. Then he smiled.

'He has. This afternoon . . . I'd have talked it through with you, but you were out on inquiries.' He finished the flapjack and slugged some coffee. 'I'm very keen to put the bad guys away . . .'

'Me too.'

'Great! Let's crack on.'

'But you said yourself, we've got to be sceptical. Sadiq's got his own reasons for talking to us. He's got previous for sexual assault on a thirteen-year-old and he's up for sharing extreme images of children. Without a letter from us for the judge, he's looking at a long sentence . . .'

'Yes, but he's not just made this stuff up. Walker lived in the area at the right time. How did Sadiq know that?'

'I agree, the information's definitely worth following up. But I'd prefer the softly softly approach. We need to do more research. Perhaps we could just delay the warrant?'

'You know these guys, they always keep stuff, trophies. If Walker hears we're sniffing around, he's going to destroy anything he's got. We'll execute the warrant tomorrow. Lee's organized a search team. Walker's a continuing threat to women.'

It crossed Sarah's mind that perhaps *threat to women* was what Fedden thought she wanted to hear.

He was still talking. 'Lee can assist in interview . . .'

Sarah felt a sudden splash of heat across her neck and face. She had just caught sight of DC Steve Bradshaw entering the canteen, car keys in hand, with a bunch of other male detectives. He still had that reassuring look about him: the worn brown paper-bag face, the unassuming clothes, the soft brown shoes. The boss had seen him too, because he raised his hand in enthusiastic greeting. It was only as he turned towards them that Steve clocked Sarah. It came to her in a rush – as undoubtedly it had to him – how she'd thought of him as a friend and how all along he had been silently disagreeing with her. At the end of the Portland Tower investigation, he'd told her he'd joined the job to put the proper bad guys away, and that as far as he was concerned PC Lizzie Griffiths – young and inexperienced – just didn't pass muster. That was before he'd told Sarah to get a dog.

Steve was shaking Fedden's hand. 'Boss.' Then he nodded to her – 'Sarah' – and she nodded back. 'Steve.'

Fedden said, 'You two know each other?'

It was clear this was *a good thing*. Steve said, 'We were at the DSI together.'

'And you've both had enough of that! Bloody understandable. Impossible job. I saw they've issued a press release about that Portland Tower job.'

Sarah and Steve briefly caught each other's eye. Sarah had known this news was coming, but it still caught her off guard. Steve tossed his car keys and glanced towards the men he had come in with, all now seated around a far table. 'Anyway, sorry, I've got to go . . .'

'That's all right, quite understand.'

Steve turned to Sarah with a nod. 'Sarah.'

'Nice to bump into you, Steve. Just one thing.'

'Yes?'

She smiled. 'I took your advice.'

He tilted his head. 'What advice was that?'

'I got a dog.'

Briefly there was a little frown between his eyebrows, but it quickly dissipated. A smile passed uncertainly across his eyes. 'Oh. Good. What sort of dog is it?'

Sarah smiled. 'A spaniel. Daisy.'

Fedden looked between them, confused.

Steve lingered for a moment, as if on the edge of saying something. Then he glanced at Fedden and threw his keys again. 'Well, gotta go. Catch you later.'

There was a pause as he walked away. Fedden said, 'Bloody good detective.'

'He is, yes.'

Fedden nodded towards the untouched flapjack on Sarah's plate. 'You not eating that?'

'No.'

'Do you mind?'

'Be my guest.' She pushed the plate over. 'If I may . . .'

He was chewing, and only nodded in reply.

'The Tania Mills job. I need to develop some background on the victim.'

He swallowed. 'I'd like to help but I can't give you what I haven't got.'

'Just one officer –'

'I've got three jobs going to court. I've just lost two seconded to child protection. One DC off with stress. We're catching a murder every on-call nowadays. Honestly, we're strained enough with live jobs.'

'The moment we put Walker's door in, this is a live job.'

Fedden leaned back in his chair and loosened his tie. He slipped it over his head and placed it on the table.

'Look, do an appeal for information on Walker. Ask for witnesses, anyone who knew him. That might dig up a bit more background, find any links to Tania.'

'I'm worried about that. He's a sex offender.'

'So what?'

'We'd be putting him on offer.'

'Would we? Why should anyone know where he's living? In any case, we're only interested in what he was up to *then*. If you're really worried, use a photo from the time and don't name him. You know: *Anyone who has memories of this man . . .* We can justify it. As I said, he's a threat to women.'

When Sarah didn't answer Fedden wiped his forehead with the paper napkin. 'You're still not happy?'

She tried to conceal any discomfort that might be leaking onto her face. 'No, it's OK.'

Fedden rubbed his pink bottom lip with his index finger. 'Sarah. I have to tell you that you came here with a rep for being a bit difficult.'

Her skin was prickling. 'I'm sorry to hear that.'

'I do my best to run a happy ship. Everyone's welcome aboard but I'm the bloody captain.'

Sarah mustered a smile and a salute. 'Aye, aye, Captain.'

Fedden leaned back, folded his arms across his chest. 'No flapjack and you're not drinking your coffee. What's bloody wrong with you?'

'I've got a coffee machine in the office. I've got something I need to do before I go off.'

He nodded and softened. 'I like a grafter. I've heard good things about you too, Sarah.'

'Glad to hear that.'

He started to move his chair back to stand. 'So, are we done?'

'If you could give me just one officer for a couple of days, even.'

'Fuck. You're like a bloody dog at a bone!'

'One of my best qualities.'

In spite of himself, he laughed. 'OK, bloody hell. Let me run something past you. There's a girl in the office, works . . . what are we supposed to call it nowadays? Oh yes, reduced hours. Part-time, anyway.'

Sarah knew exactly who he was suggesting. She'd heard the rumours: lazy, unmotivated, not a proper cop.

'It's not Elaine, is it?'

'You've heard about her, then?'

She shrugged innocently.

'They didn't call her Fat Elaine, did they?'

'They did. You're not selling her to me.'

'Well, I'm fat, so don't hold that against her. You can have her right now, with no other commitments, straight off the bat. How about it?'

'The fact that you're offering her to me lock, stock and barrel after all you've said about having no one available suggests you don't think she'll be much of a loss to the team's strength.'

'Oh come on. Give her a few days to see if she can prove the team wrong. If she's useless, I promise to think of someone else.'

'But then at least you'll have the evidence to get rid of her.'

He opened his hands and shrugged. 'Only if she's not up to it.'

Someone had left an *Evening Standard* on top of one of the bins in the stairwell of the murder block. Sarah scooped it up and made her way up the stairs and along the corridor. The daylight had dimmed, and as she walked, she triggered the movement cells and the fluorescent lights flickered on. She popped her head into the incident room. Elaine was sitting alone at her terminal, inputting data. She looked up and Sarah said, 'Can you join me as soon as you've got a moment?'

She put a capsule into her coffee maker.

The newspaper was folded at the relevant page and Sarah read the headline.

FEMALE POLICE CONSTABLE CLEARED
OVER PORTLAND TOWER DEATHS

The Independent Police Complaints Commission has today asked for a review into whether body-worn cameras should be made compulsory for all police officers. The policing watchdog made the recommendation after announcing that PC Lizzie Griffiths, who was present at the deaths of PC Hadley Matthews and a teenage girl, Farah Mehenni, will face no disciplinary action.

PC Matthews and Miss Mehenni both fell from a London high-rise . . .

Sarah skipped to the end, the obligatory quotes, the inevitable dissatisfaction.

Younes Mehenni, the father of the dead girl, said he was bitter about the investigation. In a statement issued through his solicitor he said, 'This isn't justice. The British police have protected each other and covered up evidence of their corruption.'

But a spokesman for the Police Federation said, 'Following the tragic events at Portland Tower, both a criminal and police investigation have shown no evidence of wrongdoing on the part of PC Lizzie Griffiths or her commanding officer at the time, Inspector Kieran Shaw. At the hearing Professor Millar gave evidence that Lizzie Griffiths has suffered severe Post Traumatic Stress as a result of witnessing the tragic deaths of her colleague PC Hadley Matthews and Farah Mehenni. She asks to now be left in peace to continue her career.'

Sarah folded the newspaper shut. So that was that. Due process had run its course. She had no reason to reproach herself. Work: that was the thing.

She sat and scanned through her notes from the interview with Robert McCarthy.

At first it was difficult, and then, suddenly, she had lost herself in the new investigation, reaching out to Tania, imagining her running to Robert's hut in the park and changing into her skirt in such a hurry that she left her jeans behind on the floor.

Her thoughts turned to the man in the park, the man Robert had said Tania used to meet. He was impossible to trace on description: white, older than Tania, indeterminately tall. But he had driven a green Series III XJ6 Jaguar.

She googled it: saw a long sedan with alloy wheels, a sloping bonnet and chrome grille. It was a car that managed to be simultaneously both flash and conservative. The car of a man who had been doing OK and was pleased for people to know it.

She picked up the phone and rang the intelligence task force.

A high-pitched estuarial female voice at the end of the line told her that Series III XJ6 Jaguars had had a production run of 400,732 vehicles. 'Stand by . . .' After a pause, she explained exactly what that meant. 'That's the population of Stoke-on-Trent, or Oxford and Swindon combined.'

'Did you look that statistic up specially, or did you know it already?'

'Don't be snarky. Just don't want you to expect us to work miracles.'

There was a pause. Then the woman relented. 'You got anything to narrow it down? Any sort of VRM, even partial?'

'Nothing.'

'It's historic data. You'd have to go to the DVLA, but there'll be lots of green ones.'

'British racing green?'

'That's right. They all loved it.'

'OK, thanks for your help.'

'Not a problem.'

Poor Tania. An older man with a low-slung Jag in British racing green – a cliché that couldn't easily be traced. Perhaps Andrew Walker had had a Jag – but that would be just too lucky. She couldn't even hope for that sort of luck.

Jag Man then: it seemed that Tania had had secrets. If she was dead – as she probably was – then perhaps it had been those secrets that had killed her.

Sarah certainly didn't blame her. What fifteen-year-old doesn't harbour secrets? She remembered her own teenage years, how she would notice some of the girls in particular, crave their company, find herself drawn to them. How she would try to hide her feelings.

She'd gone on a few dates with boys. Seen *Robocop* with one who had sneaked his arm around her and tried to kiss her on the mouth. She remembered other awkward fumblings at teenage parties: a boy undoing her bra, a clinch in the back of a car. It had felt – how could she phrase it – not *quite right*, unmotivated, like being on a geography field trip in an uninteresting country where you don't really like the food.

Girls had been different, the opposite in fact. She had revelled secretly in their sweet beauty, their brand-new breasts in their school shirts, the charm of their strong calves when they played hockey on the sports fields, the neat V of their legs.

Then there had been Jessie Adams, a school friend: awkwardly thin, clever. She smoked cigarettes behind the bus stop, drove a car before anyone else and gave the other drivers the finger. Jessie: chaotic, wild, sleeping with too many boys. Adorable Jessie. Sarah watched her slyly, helped her out with her homework, covered her tracks for her when she bunked off school, tried to ingratiate herself without Jessie noticing how hard she was trying.

One summer's afternoon, they climbed a tree together and spread themselves out on its broad boughs. Jessie talked about her father's small-town affairs, her mother's depression. Sarah, lying on the horse chestnut's generous limb, watched the light filtering through the leaves in flickering splodges, settling and moving over the fine blonde hair on Jessie's legs and arms. Jessie could have talked about shopping lists or the bus timetable: Sarah would have been happy. She had been in a half-dream of heat; her hand running down the ladder of Jessie's ribs was no more than a gesture away . . .

A tap at the door and Elaine stepped into the room. 'You needed to talk to me?'

Sarah slipped her chair back, rubbed her hand across her face. 'Can I get you a coffee? I've got my own machine. It's good.'

'I'm all right, thanks. What's this about?'

Sarah thought of all the things she could say but discounted them. There was no way to proceed other than factually, without emotion.

'I need some help with Operation Egremont.'

A suspicious look flickered across Elaine's face. 'Why are you telling *me* this?'

'I need to trace a person of interest. I want you to contact the victim's school friends—'

'I'm sorry. I'm not free for your inquiries. I work in the incident room.'

Sarah took a breath, but she couldn't stop herself.

'You are a police officer, a *detective*. The Met has provided you with specialist training. The boss has released you to work on Egremont. Is that a problem?'

Elaine knew she couldn't refuse. Her eyes moved shrewdly across Sarah's face. 'I haven't got a problem with working on Egremont . . .'

'OK.'

'But can you tell me, will this be outside my rostered hours? I have a negotiated shift pattern. I have family responsibilities. My husband's in the job too. I have to work around him.'

Sarah sighed. It was so bloody tiresome!

'How does your shift pattern work?'

'I do short days, five days a week. I work this late turn to cover my husband's early turn. No weekends.'

No weekends?

'Does that suit you?'

'No. Short days are shit. It was the best I could get.'

'I wouldn't be complaining out loud. It's a lot better than I have.'

Elaine pursed her lips: not impressed.

'I'm not even going to get into this. You can think what you like.' She shut her mouth so hard that her jaw stiffened. Clearly she intended to stop but couldn't. 'And don't expect me to feel sorry for *you* either. If you choose not to fight for a life outside the job, then that's your decision.' She looked at Sarah coldly. 'In any case, mostly I find that the people who stay working late on their own haven't got much to go home to.'

Sarah felt her face go stiff at Elaine's rudeness. She tried to ignore the anger that was coursing through her.

'Over the next week, organize your own shift pattern. I don't care how you do it but I need you to do the work. Have as much overtime as you need. But I need to see results if you do incur.

Elaine started to get up, but Sarah began to speak again and she sat back down, a lifeless simulacrum of obedience.

'I'll email you a summary of actions before I go out. Main thing I want you to do is to talk to Tania's friends about any possible boyfriends and to try and trace a man in a green Jaguar. Tania had a best friend, Katherine Herringham. She had arranged to meet her the morning she disappeared. She'd be the first person to speak to.'

Elaine left a silence before she spoke. 'Are we done then?'

Sarah nodded. 'Yes, we're done.'

The door shut. Sarah closed her eyes. She was pleased to be alone. She was awash with feelings. Ashamed too at how she had spoken to Elaine using the brutal language of command. It had been retaliatory, of course. Only now was she allowing what Elaine had said to her to sink in. *People who stay working late on their own haven't got much to go home to.* It was true. She wasn't in any hurry to get home. The only responsibility she had was Daisy, and she was with the dog walker.

The *Evening Standard* was still open on the desk. Sarah reached into her bag and found the piece of paper on which Caroline had scribbled her number in the mini market. She dialled impulsively. The call was answered quickly and immediately Sarah regretted making it. She spoke in a rush.

'Hi, yes, sorry to bother you. It's Sarah here . . .'

The voice was throaty, playful. 'Sarah?'

'Detective Inspector Sarah Collins. I worked on—'

There was that teasing again. 'Yes, I know who you are! I didn't know you'd become an inspector.'

'I just wanted to say . . . Look, you've probably seen the news now. No disciplinary . . .'

'Yes, I saw it.'

'I'm sorry I didn't tell you yesterday. But I couldn't. I hope you understand.'

There was a pause before Caroline spoke. 'You sound more upset than me.'

'No!' That had come out too loud. Sarah toned it down. 'No, no, not at all, I'm not. It's just that . . . I know how much you cared about Farah and that you'd hoped, maybe, for a different result.'

'Look, why don't we meet? We could talk about it properly. We could get together, eat something. How about it?'

'No. That is to say, I'd love to. But I can't. It's not really a good idea to socialize with witnesses.'

And that was a true thing to say, and reasonable. They ended the conversation.

5

Lizzie Griffiths' mood was changing as subtly as ink spreading in water. Kieran, his hand on the small of her back, had become still but did not move, his eyes firmly shut as if he must concentrate on some flavour that was fading. He opened his eyes slowly and looked at her. 'Lizzie,' he said and smiled and rolled away onto his back. He stretched out his arms and legs.

Lizzie looked up at the ceiling. 'I have to renounce you.'

Kieran smiled. 'Renounce me?'

She wiped her eyes with the back of her hand. 'Yes. I must.'

'I've not been renounced before. Where did you get that from?'

She smiled and dismissed her own seriousness. 'It's *Jane Eyre*. I did it for A level.'

He rolled up and sat on the edge of the bed, pulled on his boxers. 'Too highbrow for me, I'm afraid. Anyway, you'll have to renounce me later. We need to get a move on.'

He moved around the room, rolling deodorant, pulling on jeans. Lizzie watched him. There was that police officer's tan from below the shirt line, and the rose tattoo on his bicep. It was an unashamed cliché and yet it was beautiful: a fairy-tale rose. That was Kieran: he could grasp the good things without shame. Perhaps when she had tired of the tattoo, she would have tired of him.

There was a latency about his body, a suggestion of power and some sort of hidden clarity about himself that she felt she lacked. She wanted to wrap herself up in it. His jeans fell down his stomach, just below his navel. Even though they had only just finished, she could begin again. Still there remained a moment between them that she couldn't erase. It was after Hadley and Farah had died. She'd been on the run and – for all the talk, all the emotion – they'd stood together alone in a field and he'd winnowed it down to the most essential matter of survival. *Don't think you can drag me down with you, because you can't.* She'd had a piece of wood in her hands that she'd been stripping away, and she'd tasted bark and misery in her mouth.

He turned and looked at her again with a kind smile. 'You're really sad.'

She shrugged. It had only been a moment, after all, and things had been desperate. There were other, better moments that surely outweighed it. When the initial investigation was over and they'd decided she should face no charges, she'd become ill. Signed off sick, she'd spent months living alone in a friend's caravan on the out-of-season English coast. Kieran had been worried, even his unassailable confidence shaken by her fragility. The brief chill between them was long gone. He'd been all concern, had found the time to be with her. She'd felt his warmth. It was real, just as real as that moment of coldness. He knew how to do this – the looking-after bit. He'd visited her, taken her out for meals in empty seaside cafés, sitting at laminated tables drinking cocoa and walking down the beach with her in the brisk, salty wind.

Now they were in a new phase. After the misconduct hearing, the Kieran–Lizzie relationship internal press release appeared to be headlined *Lizzie is moving on!* They didn't talk about it, perhaps because they knew that if they dipped below the headline, they might still not agree.

Kieran threw her one of his T-shirts and pulled her change of shirt out of her bag.

'I'll iron this for you.'

Moving across the hallway to the bathroom, she heard the sounds of 1970s soul, a twanging guitar, a soulful voice, a funky beat. She couldn't recognize the song at first, then realized it was Marvin Gaye. '*Let's Get It On.*' She looked to her right into the sitting room. Kieran was facing her, doing soul moves in front of the ironing board, stepping from side to side, holding the iron in his right hand but stretching his free arm out and moving it across his body. He danced well and with humour. She shouldn't be so serious! He flicked the iron off at the wall and beckoned her over in time to the music.

She smiled in spite of herself and turned away from him.

She stood in the shower with her eyes closed, the warm water sluicing over her. She dried herself, brushed her teeth.

This was Kieran's London flat, ostensibly just a place he crashed when he was on duty. His wife and daughter were in some little country place near Lewes. He'd taken the framed photograph of his daughter down from the wall, but Lizzie knew it was hidden away somewhere, easily recovered and hung back up. There was probably one of his wife too. But it wasn't only that he was married: secrets were his temperament, as much a part of him as rugby or fishing were a part of other men. He had returned to that other world, the covert world that he had been deployed to before he took promotion and was – briefly – her inspector on a uniformed response team. He didn't tell her anything about his new deployment. He was someone who could never share himself entirely. She suspected he would always need secret places, more than one phone.

She emerged from the bathroom. The ironing board had gone. Her shirt was hanging from the door lintel. Otis Redding now – 'These Arms Of Mine'. Kieran's eyes were closed, his arms folded round his body and he was dancing as if with himself. He opened one eye and beckoned her over.

She said, 'We'll be late.'

He wagged his index finger in teasing disagreement. That was Kieran: the moment, the moment. She turned to grab a quick coffee from the kitchen, but he put his arms around her and moved her from side to side in time with him.

'I'll be late.'

He kissed her, whispering into her neck. 'You can be five minutes late. I'll drive you.'

She turned to him and danced close, leaning into him, inhaling him.

She climbed into the Land Rover Discovery. He turned the engine over and told her to look inside the glove compartment. There was a copy of the previous day's newspaper.

'Page two,' he said, indicating and pulling away.

She turned to the article that reported the IPCC's findings.

She asks to now be left in peace to continue her career.

Left in peace. Whoever had come up with that bloody ridiculous phrase?

'You're out of the woods,' Kieran said, glancing at her. There he was again; didn't want to hear her doubts and equivocations.

'Look, I'm not free tonight,' he said. 'But Wednesday you're working a late turn. Pack a bag and I'll pick you up from work.'

They pulled up outside her new nick and he did something he had never done before: when he leaned over to kiss her, he said, 'It's a pain in the neck, but I think I love you.'

She stepped down from the Land Rover and he drove away, leaving her with the sudden loneliness of the pavement. It wasn't fair for him to say I love you. The phrase claimed its own echo and she had wanted to say it. *I love you too.* But how could she offer herself up to him like that? He probably couldn't meet her tonight because he was going home to his wife and daughter.

Her phone rang. It was Ash. 'Sorry, darling. It's Brannon. Urgent application to dismiss. You need to get to court on the hurry-up.'

All the job cars were already taken. She raced over on the tube, completed the fifteen-minute walk to the court in just ten, her step hovering on the edge of a run. She swore she'd never wear heels again. Her jacket felt tight across the shoulders. She wanted to take it off but worried about the pools of sweat that must have formed under her arms and down her back.

It was a new court to her and there was no one at the reception desk. She followed one of the gowned barristers as he walked quickly through the marbled atrium. Outside the numbered courts, people waited. Through a locked door she could see people queuing for a photocopier. She showed her warrant card and entered the offices of the Crown Prosecution Service.

The desks were piled high with files. Defence briefs lingered, irritating the prosecutors with jibes, goading and complaining about not receiving the information they required. Why was everything so last-minute? One of the clerks pointed out a small, thin man – early sixties, dandruff on his gowned shoulders – as the prosecutor tasked with fighting Brannon's application to dismiss. He was bent over a page, wig beside him on the desk, reading intently as if in some sort of bizarre Olympic sprint sport. His right hand, holding a fountain pen, twitched as if it wished to advance ahead of his eyes.

Lizzie moved over and stood beside him. He didn't speak or look up. If anything, his concentration increased.

She said, 'Um, Lizzie Griffiths, I'm the officer in the case for Brannon. It's the application to dismiss?'

He didn't even glance at her.

'Court Five. It may be a while before you're needed. You've time to grab a coffee.'

'Anything you need to know? You've seen his previous?'

'It's all here. I'm reading it now.'

'Can you tell me anything about his grounds for dismissal?'

'I'm sorry, no.'

'I just wanted to say—'

'I'm pushed for time.'

'Yes . . . that in spite of the victim's reluctance, I really think we should proceed.'

The lawyer darted a piercing look at her. He had clever dark beads instead of eyes.

'One other thing, before you go and get that coffee. Please don't talk to the victim if she's in court.'

The sharp warning look he had given her had only been momentary. He buried his head back in the case file.

Lizzie said, 'Why's that?'

The prosecutor's head didn't move but she could see he wasn't reading. He wanted her to go away.

'I can't discuss it. You can be expected to be called to give evidence. Wait outside the court until you are requested.'

Outside the court? Why outside?

He put his elbows on the desk and both hands to his temples as if to close out all distractions. She lingered for a moment, uncertain, then drifted away into the communal areas of the court. Georgina was there with Skye and her friend Marley. They looked at her with an intensity that was unsettling and she remembered she wasn't supposed to have any contact with Georgina. She walked away to the canteen on the first floor.

She stood at the window and looked out over the street, where building works were in progress, a crane's arm swinging a heavy concrete block into place. The court tannoy sounded.

PC Griffiths to Court Five, please. PC Griffiths to Court Five.

Lizzie followed the usher, a plump woman in a black gown, towards the witness stand. She stepped into the box, rested her hands on the shelf in front of her and took the oath. Marley, she noticed, was in the public gallery. Brannon, in the dock, gave her one of his aggressive, winning smiles.

The judge – a thin white woman with baggy eyes and a big nose – leaned forward. 'We have something a little unusual before us today. It's taken me quite a long time to decide how we should proceed.'

'Ma'am.'

'My concern is that you should not be intimidated by what follows, do you see?'

A stupid phrase came into Lizzie's head. *I attend upon your honour.* She almost laughed. In her nervousness she was in danger of falling into some kind of cod court protocol. Still, you couldn't say, *Sorry, I don't get you* to a judge. She couldn't think of an answer so she didn't say anything, just waited.

The judge smiled. 'Of course you don't see. I haven't explained yet. It seems the victim has been moved to make certain serious allegations against you . . .'

Allegations?

Lizzie's heart was suddenly hammering.

'As the accused is currently remanded on this matter, I feel it incumbent to hear these accusations promptly. However, I am mindful of your own circumstances. Ideally, you would have been afforded legal advice.'

Legal advice?

'In a moment, the barrister who acts on behalf of the accused will examine you. He will begin that examination with the caution and advise you that, should you wish to stop to seek legal advice, then that is your right. That's not just form. If at *any point* during this examination you consider that you do require representation, I want you to turn to me and request that I stop proceedings.'

Lizzie took a deep breath.

'OK.' Then she added as an afterthought, 'Your honour.' She blushed, put her hands on her legs to calm herself.

'Are you ready to begin?'

'Yes, ma'am.'

As she turned her head to face the defending barrister, Lizzie closed her eyes briefly so that she would not see, even for an instant, Brannon's grinning face. She would not look at him, or at Marley with her spiteful stare, but she did glance at the prosecutor. His hands were resting on the desk and he appeared to be gazing down steadfastly at them. Whatever it was, she couldn't expect any help from him. She was on her own.

The defending barrister, a blowsy, hearty woman in her fifties who kept rearranging her gown as if she couldn't quite work out how to settle it on her large breasts, began.

'Police Constable Griffiths, you don't have to say anything but it may harm your defence if you do not mention now anything which you later rely on in court. Anything you do say may be given in evidence. You have a right to legal advice and we can stop these proceedings for you to seek that advice. Do you understand the caution?'

'Yes.'

The woman adjusted her gown.

'Officer, last year you were implicated in the deaths of two people, PC Hadley Matthews and Farah Mehenni, who fell to their deaths from a tower block in London.'

A flush of heat passed through Lizzie. She wanted to get out of the box, yes, and insist on this legal advice the judge had offered, but somehow she was trapped here, imprisoned by form, her job, by herself. If she stopped the trial everyone would know. There would be a big kerfuffle, rumours spreading through her colleagues like wind over grass. She wouldn't be able to bear all those terrible hushed conversations behind closed police doors, the sudden silence when she stepped into a room, the fear and anxiety that would haunt her once more. She knew too that in all the heat and light, the prosecution against Brannon would be lost to the suddenly more compelling question of whether she was in some way guilty of misconduct.

'Would you answer the question, please?'

'Could you repeat it?'

'Last year you were implicated—'

'No.'

'No?'

'No, no, I wasn't. I was not *implicated* in their deaths. I was present at their deaths but there was no finding of misconduct against me.'

The barrister shuffled her papers.

'OK, so not implicated. Shall we say *involved*, then?'

'No, let's not. I was not involved either.'

'You were there?'

'I was there.'

'And how did it come about that you were there—'

The judge interrupted. 'Counsel, I can't see what relevance this line of questioning has to the matter before us . . .'

'Your honour, I am just trying to establish that this officer's record is not unblemished.'

'If I may say, counsel, you are not establishing that. In fact you are establishing the opposite.' She turned to Lizzie, a firm hand offered to a woman who was struggling in quicksand. 'Officer, to complete this line of questioning. Do you have any disciplinary or criminal findings against you?'

'No, your honour.'

Lizzie's nose was stinging and she could feel a painful heat behind her eyes. She was overcome by a memory, that last irremediable sight of Hadley and Farah before they fell, both framed by the intense blue of the sky behind them. She had been cleared of misconduct, yes, but that didn't mean she didn't feel responsible. She rubbed the back of her neck, took a sip of water.

She glimpsed Brannon and his tormenting grin. He'd managed to turn the tables on her.

The judge spoke. 'Officer, are you able to continue?'

Lizzie felt her feet on the ground, the cheap veneered wood of the lectern under her hands.

'Yes, ma'am.'

'Counsel, if you would resume.'

'Officer, the complainant in this matter, Miss Georgina Teel, has told the court that you have put undue pressure on her to give evidence against the defendant, her partner, Mr Brannon.'

'Has she?'

'In the manner of all those war films, officer, I am the one asking the questions. However, we'll make an exception today. Yes, indeed she has.'

The barrister smiled at her own joke. She was probably quite fun when she had a big glass of red wine in her hand. But Lizzie remembered Kieran standing by a stream while she stripped the bark from a piece of birch and her mouth filled with earth. *If you learn only one thing then let it be this: never give the bastards anything.* Maybe he'd not been so cold after all. Maybe he'd just been right.

She looked at Brannon, tasted the pungent smell of alcohol and male sweat that had come off him the morning after he had assaulted Georgina. Now Georgina had made an allegation against the very person who had tried to help her.

Die then, Georgina. Go ahead and die.

She had almost said it out loud.

'You understand that this is a serious allegation, officer?'

'Oh yes. Serious, but baseless.'

'Baseless?'

'Entirely.'

'We'll just go over the detail. Mr Brannon says that when he was in custody he tried to talk to you about his love for his family but you were dismissive. What would you say your attitude was?'

'It is not my business to have a view about Mr Brannon's feelings for his family. They don't affect the investigation one way or the other.'

'Answer the question, please. Mr Brannon says you were rude. How would you describe your demeanour?'

'Professional.'

'Mr Brannon says he got the distinct impression that you were not treating this investigation professionally. That it had become personal for you. That you in fact personally disliked him.'

The judge interrupted. 'Is there a question coming any time soon, counsel?'

'Yes, your honour, immediately. PC Griffiths, how would you describe your attitude to Mr Brannon?'

'Professional.'

That word, professional: it was becoming, Lizzie realized with a bitter smile, her own version of no comment.

'Professional?'

'Yes.'

The judge clicked her biro open and shut on the desk impatiently. 'A word you might be minded to take to heart, counsel. Have we covered this now?'

'We have indeed, ma'am. Apologies. And what was your attitude towards Georgina, officer?'

Lizzie remembered Brannon's cheerful recitation of no comment. She turned her hands outwards in a gesture of bemusement, smiled broadly at Brannon and said, 'Well, I'd have to say, it was professional.'

Then she remembered that she was still wearing Skye's loom band on her wrist.

'Georgina says you pressured her. You wouldn't allow her friend Marley to remain with her.'

'Marley would not provide me with her details. I did not know what her relationship was to the defendant or the complainant. I had the impression that if anyone was putting pressure on Georgina it was Marley, and of course the defendant himself, Mr Brannon.'

'Marley was there to support her friend. Did you offer the complainant any alternative when you excluded her? Ms Teel is a vulnerable young woman, as you must be aware.'

'She is vulnerable, yes.'

'Answer the question. Did you offer any alternative to Marley?'

'No. I took a withdrawal statement from the complainant and I asked her whether she would like me to refer her to a domestic violence agency, someone disconnected from the investigation who could talk to her in confidence.'

'And why did you do that?'

'She was distressed.'

'Oh, she *was* distressed.'

'Of course she was. She didn't want to break up her family. She said her partner, Mr Brannon, was only violent when he was drunk.'

The judge intervened. 'Police Constable Griffiths, I must stop you. We are not here to examine the evidence in this matter, only the admission of that evidence. Your last comment was, in any case, hearsay.'

'I'm sorry, your honour.'

The defending barrister shrugged her slipping gown back onto her shoulders and scanned her notes. 'So you admit Georgina was distressed?'

'I can't see why that is an admission.'

'I'll explain then. Georgina was distressed and you didn't stop to consider how this might affect her evidence? That perhaps she needed independent support when she was talking to police.'

'I was only taking a withdrawal statement.'

'But you were trying to persuade her to give evidence.'

'But not trying to persuade her to give evidence that would be untruthful.'

'And Ms Teel's daughter, Skye, was with her.'

'At times. Most of the time she was in her room.'

'Did you suggest that Miss Teel needed to consider Skye when she decided whether or not to give evidence against her partner?'

The questions had come so quickly. Lizzie hadn't been able to think or to follow the direction of the barrister's questions. Suddenly she grasped the nature of the accusation: that she had threatened Georgina over the custody of Skye in order to force her to give evidence against Brannon. That was why the judge had offered her legal representation. If substantiated, it was a criminal offence. What was the legislation? Would it be intimidation of a witness . . . perverting the course of justice, maybe. The ground had shifted. She, not Brannon, was the person in danger in this courtroom. She tried to remember the detail of the conversation she had had with Georgina. Skye had given her the loom band. They had both relaxed, that was it. And then she had said . . . she had said . . . what *exactly*?

'Officer?'

Lizzie looked up. The prosecution barrister was watching her intently. Never lie: that was something she had learned. Never, ever lie. 'I made a general comment. It wasn't about her giving evidence. I said she needed to consider the welfare of her daughter. Skye had been crying, you see. That was what prompted it.'

'Go on.'

'I was speaking generally. I said it was not good for Skye to be around violence . . .' The judge was making a note. Lizzie felt the matter slipping away from her. 'I was speaking generally. We have a duty of care to victims of domestic violence and to children.'

'Did you go on to talk about social services?'

'I did not.'

'You didn't? Really?'

The danger of even the slightest misrepresentation was etched on Lizzie's heart: put yourself before everything, even a successful prosecution. Tell the truth. Tell the truth. Let all else burn, but tell the truth.

'Georgina did.'

'Georgina did? Could you tell me about that?'

'She said something like she had had enough of social workers coming round. That Skye was fine.'

'Did you understand that to imply she was frightened that Skye might be taken into care if she did not give evidence against Mr Brannon?'

Lizzie remembered how she had suddenly softened towards Georgina, had liked her and feared for her. It had been weakness, she saw that now.

'I didn't understand that, no. It didn't occur to me. It's difficult of course. You see someone's personal circumstances . . .'

She stopped, lost for words, suddenly on the brink of tears.

'Go on.'

But she couldn't, because she was elsewhere.

She was sitting with Hadley in that single mother's house with the son pulling on his coat and storming out of the door and Hadley holding a tortoise on the palm of his hand. He said he had had one as a child and Lizzie hadn't known whether that was the truth or whether he'd been saying it only to comfort the distressed mother. Now that he was dead she would never be able to ask him. She smiled. How silly! Why ever did it matter so much? She imagined him laughing at her in the courtroom. You total numpty! Shaming the uniform! He'd been able to laugh at just about anything. She thought, *I can't do this job.* She was lost, totally lost. She didn't even know where she was.

'Officer?'

She put a hand on the lectern to steady herself.

The judge intervened. 'Are you ill? Will you be all right to continue, PC Griffiths? Do you need a break?'

From somewhere out of the darkness she found the thread of what she had been saying and she held on to it and allowed it to lead her out of the woods.

'Yes, ma'am. I'm all right, thank you. You have to *stay professional*, that's it, that's what I wanted to say. A colleague of mine, I remember, he said that to me once, "We are the police, not the social workers." I think he meant by that that we can't afford to become too involved. Our job is different, and for a reason. And so although I was afraid for Ms Teel and her daughter, I stopped trying to advise her and I took the withdrawal statement.'

The defence counsel resumed. 'Did you then write a report to the Crown Prosecution Service recommending that the prosecution continue and that the court issue a summons for the complainant?'

'I did, yes.'

'Did you consider how your comments about her daughter might affect Georgina's evidence?'

Lizzie shook her head. 'No.'

'Thank you, Police Constable Griffiths. No further questions, your honour.'

Lizzie stood outside Court 5. It was as if she was filled with scalding water, as though her skin was blistering from beneath its surface. She wanted to find somewhere less public, but the CPS room would be no sanctuary and she didn't want to sit in the cramped police room and face the other officers with their bags of evidence. Georgina, who was sitting at the far end of the waiting area with Skye, glanced at her. Lizzie walked towards the stairs. The cafeteria was closing up, but she managed to grab a bottle of water. She closed her eyes, waiting for the heat inside her to subside.

When she went back down to the waiting area, Brannon was leaving the courtroom with his barrister.

It was over, then. The case had been dismissed. He'd won. She wondered if there would be any repercussions for her. She couldn't walk any further towards the CPS office without bumping directly into Brannon, so she stood and watched from the entrance foyer as he went up to Georgina and, after a moment's hesitation, they hugged. Then he scooped up Skye and squeezed his daughter tightly, his hand around the back of her head. He put her down, pinched her cheeks until she squirmed, prodded her in the stomach. 'Dad!' He turned and kissed Marley on the cheek, squeezed her hand. He shook the defence barrister's hand warmly.

Anyone looking from a distance would be pleased for them. This was a happy story: a celebration, a family reunited, a miscarriage of justice averted.

Family: was there anything at that moment more uncomfortable? Lizzie thought of Kieran and his wife and child and decided never, ever to have children herself.

The congratulations were subsiding, the barrister making her goodbyes and walking away, pulling her gown about her shoulders. The little family gathered itself together and began to leave the court. The happy group was going to walk right past her. It was too late for Lizzie to turn away without losing face.

Marley spoke, her features twisted with triumph. 'Why don't you catch some proper criminals?'

Brannon said, 'Better luck next time.'

Georgina looked steadfastly down, holding Skye's hand. Lizzie wanted to say only one thing to her, something that she couldn't say, didn't say.

Next time, don't call police.

Lizzie sat on the top deck of the bus, on the front seat. Her impression was of splashes of the life below as the bus swung and moved forward, stopped and turned, surged and halted. Fruit stalls, the roofs of bus stops, a pram with a baby kicking, a bicycle wobbling precariously between the bus and the pavement.

The prosecutor had been slightly bored, impatient even, when he'd talked it through with her after she'd made her way back to the Crown Prosecution office. It was all fine, he'd said, his eyes drifting sideways to the pile of papers he needed to read for his next case. The judge had made it perfectly clear: Lizzie had no case to answer in terms of interfering with the witness. Nevertheless, her honour had ruled that Georgina's fear of having her child taken away made her evidence unreliable. That was why the case had been dismissed. Brannon hadn't even had to give evidence.

What Lizzie discovered unfolding within herself came as a blinding revelation: she was heartily sick of it all. Why had she put herself in this position for people she didn't even know?

She tried to make her thoughts stand still, to look at her situation and consider what she wanted. She was twenty-six and it filled her with terror. Her life was sliding away and she couldn't seem to grasp it. This bloody job!

She had tried to help Georgina.

She wanted to get off the bus and run until she could run no longer. As soon as she got home, she told herself, she would put on her running shoes. There was a freedom unlike any other in the fall of foot on ground, the rhythm of the heart and the breath. She had competed as a schoolgirl for her county, completed the 10,000 metres in thirty-six minutes. She had stopped running competitively because chasing the possibility that that time suggested meant running all the joy out of her favourite thing, straining and hurting herself to cut minutes from her time. Now policing felt like that too. It had been fun! She had enjoyed it. It was difficult to believe that now. She'd imagined an exciting future: solving murders, going undercover, maybe preventing terror attacks. Now, the reality of it was . . . Her thoughts stumbled. What was it? Shitty jobs, shitty lives, people you couldn't help.

And, occasionally, disaster. Hadley dead. Farah dead.

She had decided to carry on. She would survive it all by being a good cop. Now, sitting on the bus, she felt that to be impossible. It wasn't nine to five; it wasn't even eight till ten. It was like rearranging the pattern of your nerves until you became someone so different that you had lost the thread of who you once were. It was like her life would become a pair of running shoes run to shit.

She walked quickly to the police station, weaving ruthlessly through the slow-moving people, the charity chuggers, the newspaper stand, the on-street florist, a group of young men walking four abreast.

She went straight to the detective inspector's office but she wasn't there. She didn't know what to do with her momentum. Ash was sitting at his desk. He looked up, smiled.

'Hello, gorgeous.'

'Oh fuck it, Ash.'

'What?'

She took her warrant card out of her pocket, handed it across the desk, feeling stupid and hopeless.

'I just don't want this any more and I can't find the boss to give it to. Will you take it?'

He reached across the table. 'Of course I will, darling.' He opened it up, glanced at the picture with a smile and then peered in the inside pocket, behind the crest. 'You've left your Caffè Nero loyalty card in there. And ten quid. Don't you want to keep those?'

Lizzie sat down. She rubbed her forehead. Ash tapped the desk with his middle finger for a minute.

Then he said, 'I *agree* with you. Young thing like you, I think you *should* leave the job. In fact I think *everyone* should leave the job. How glorious would that be?'

Lizzie couldn't speak. She tried instead for a smile. Ash laughed at her efforts.

'Oh dear.' His eyes narrowed sympathetically. 'In all honesty, would you say right now's a good moment to take a decision?'

She shook her head. He offered her the warrant card. 'Take that back for now. Give it a day or so, see how you feel.'

Lizzie, feeling embarrassed, put it back in her inside pocket. Still, perhaps she had needed that melodramatic impulse to make the change she needed to make. Now she was back in the same place.

Ash said, 'To be honest, I'm not terribly good at intense. How about we bunk off and get an ice cream instead? There's a pretty boy works in there – should cheer us both up.'

'No, but thanks. I think I'll just finish up and go home.'

Lizzie nailed the Brannon report shut, as Ash had advised her to, updating why the prosecution hadn't gone ahead, making a referral to a domestic violence agency and emailing the detective inspector about her concerns. Bang on time she booked off duty, scooped up her bag and made her way down to the street.

Brannon was standing on the pavement outside the station, smoking. He smirked. She would have to pass him and she hesitated. He rocked on his feet and smiled happily. 'Hello, Lizzie.'

She nodded, 'Mark.'

She'd only had permission to leave her car in the off-street bay for a day, but it was waiting for her safe and sound, her little blue Golf. She flicked her key and the lights flashed. She moved past Brannon, her back prickling. She got into the car, resisted the urge to lock the doors, threw her bag on the passenger seat, reversed out into traffic. What was he doing there? His phone had been seized as part of the investigation – perhaps, now that the case had been dismissed, he was going into the nick to pick it up. Threading through the back streets and over the speed bumps, she began to let it drop. Someone like Brannon probably spent a lot of time going in and out of his local nick. If he wasn't there on his own behalf, it would be for one of his friends. In all likelihood, if she continued working out of Caenwood, she would encounter him frequently. He was one of those types who would always come again.

6

The front garden was paved over and held only plastic wheelie bins. Sarah opened the picket gate, and like a big blue caterpillar, a carrier-load of officers, all in blue babygros, moved silently past her into place. The bloke at the front was a lump: seven foot possibly, and broad across the shoulders. He carried the heavy red enforcer as though it was as light as an empty briefcase and moved towards the door with a surprisingly graceful confidence. He cradled the enforcer, his elbow crooked, looked over his shoulder to check for readiness. The sergeant counted a silent one-two-three with his fingers.

The big red key swung forward and the door splintered and gave way at one attempt.

They bundled up the stairs, shouting.

'Police, police, police!'

With Lee holding the premises search book and the warrant, Sarah followed slowly behind the public order officers, who were taking control and probably already thinking of a job well done and a table full of fried food and hot coffee. Sarah's work was just beginning.

It was a one-room flat in a partitioned Victorian house. Greasy washing-up was drying on a calcified stainless-steel draining board. The door to the bathroom was ajar and a smell of urine drifted. The curtains were nicotine-stained. On the table by the bed was a full ashtray, overflowing with dog-ends. Andrew Walker, sitting on the bed, drew his open hand down his face and yawned. He was wearing a vest and boxers, had long, thinning hair, a domed forehead, loose arms that showed prominent blue veins.

He said, 'Can I smoke?'

Everyone looked at Sarah, and she nodded. 'Yes.'

As Andrew was lighting up, his hands shaking, Lee stepped forward.

'I'm arresting you for the murder of Tania Mills in October 1987. My grounds are that we have information that you have confessed to this murder . . .'

Sarah, glancing around the room, saw an unusually large number of framed black-and-white photographs on the walls. A picture of an old lady eating an ice cream on a slatted bench. A wide-angle shot of kids skipping in an alleyway. They were the work, she guessed, of a keen amateur photographer.

One of the public order officers nodded towards a shelf that held about three decent old-fashioned film cameras.

'Likes taking pictures.'

'Typical pervert,' the sergeant added.

'Can we seize all the cameras and film, please,' Sarah said.

Andrew, making no reaction to the proceedings, offered his hands to the cuffs without protest. He held the cigarette in his mouth and closed one eye against the smoke.

Ellersby police station had replaced the old early-twentieth-century nick where Tania's father had first reported her missing. Built during the Blair years of plenty, it dominated the road: tinted glass, blue-and-white fascia, an impressive round office tower on the left.

In the interview room, Sarah's phone buzzed. She checked her screen. It was a voicemail from her father. Without listening, she knew what it would be about. In less than ten days it would be her sister's memorial service. Would she be able to make it? She switched her phone off, returned it to her pocket. She placed her pen on the desk beside her notebook, took a breath, composed herself, prepared herself to concentrate.

'I'm sorry about that. Please, go on.'

Walker, now wearing a light blue cotton shirt, frayed at the collar, and blue trousers, sat impassively. There was nothing particularly distinguishing about him – only his sharp nose perhaps, his pale skin – but a stench of solitude haunted him. His solicitor – Derek Holt: a wiry, quick-moving, besuited little man with a northern accent – read out his prepared statement.

'My name is Andrew Walker and this is my response to the allegation that I murdered Tania Mills in 1987.

'I am released on licence and I attend the sex offenders' treatment programme at HMP Ripon. This programme is only open to men who have admitted their offences and want to change their lives.

'I like girls' underwear, that's my thing. I don't want to touch people or to hurt them. I'm not violent. I only want to look.

'I imagine girls opening their legs and showing me their pants. I fantasize that they want to do this. I have these thoughts constantly. I can't talk to a woman or stand next to her without imagining what pants she is wearing.

'When I worked in an office I was forever dropping my pen on the floor by women's desks. I practically invented the selfie stick. One of the times I was arrested I had dressed up as a cleaner in a sports centre and taped a camera onto a mop handle. I put it under the door of a woman's changing cubicle. I go to the swimming baths and swim a lot underwater with goggles on. I've got very good at holding my breath. Ridiculous, isn't it? Who could blame me for thinking that what I did wasn't harmful?

'But four years ago I realized I had to control myself. I'm going to talk about it so that you understand how it happened.

'I just came across them: two girls sunbathing in a secluded part of the park. They had pulled up their skirts to tan their legs. As I walked past, I could see their pants just above the line of their skirts. God help me, it was the sexiest thing I had ever seen. There was a men's toilet nearby and I locked myself into the cubicle and tried to get them out of my system. But it didn't work. I kept thinking about them lying there, chatting and showing their pants. It felt like an emergency.

'I went back and one of the girls had gone. The other one had pulled her skirt down. She was lying on her side reading a book.

'There's an iron gate that leads into a little nature reserve. There's a bench in there and I sat and waited, almost hoping the girl would choose a different way out of the park. When she walked past it felt like fate. I got up, tried to make it look as though I just happened to be leaving the park at the same time as her. She quickened her pace but I caught hold of her upper arm and said, "You have to come with me."

'I took her behind a fallen tree trunk. I'd never felt anything so compelling. I told her to lie still and pull her skirt up.

'She did what I asked. If we hadn't been interrupted I would have done what I needed to and let her go. But I was interrupted. There was a black Labrador and the girl shouted out. The dog started barking. I got up and started running. A man grabbed hold of my shoulder and pulled me backwards. He called me a dirty pervert and punched me in the face. I managed to start running again. My nose was bleeding. A helicopter was circling above. I hid in a ditch. I could hear people tramping through the undergrowth and a police radio. A dog was coming closer, panting. I could see it through the brambles and nettles: an Alsatian barking furiously. A woman's voice shouted, "If you don't comply I will release the dog."

'Except for the arrest, no one spoke to me while we waited for transport. My nose was broken and it hurt like hell. One of the male police officers spat on the ground. I thought, if I could just have finished, I would have let her go and then they would have known I wasn't violent. I never got the chance to show that.

'They released the photograph of me the police took in custody. I looked like every sex monster you've ever seen. The detective chief inspector said I was one of the most vile and depraved individuals he had come across. They repeated that in all the papers and news reports. *The most vile and depraved.* He said the man who punched me was a hero. He might have saved a life. But that was a lie. I'd never have hurt her. I'd only wanted to see her pants.

'Still, I recognized that I'd crossed a line. I began to accept I had to do something, so I signed up to the programme at Ripon.

'I've spent a lot of time wondering why I'm like this. Maybe there's something chemical, or some event in my childhood, something I could understand and change. But my counsellor at HMP Ripon told me that worrying about reasons is a waste of time. This is how I am. It's permanent and I have to control it. So I do my best. I live at my designated address. I take the drugs they prescribe. I keep all my appointments. But it's a hard way to live. Now you say I've killed someone. It makes me wonder. What's the point? Can I ever make a life for myself?

'When I was on remand, I shared a cell with Erdem Sadiq, and I've worked out that he must be your snitch.

'I hadn't been convicted yet so I wasn't on the programme. We were on lockdown for up to twenty-three hours a day. Erdem is a sex offender too. We kept each other company by talking about what we'd like to do. There was a lot of time to make things up and we were bored. Masturbating is one way to stop being bored. It's a relief as well to have someone you can talk to. These are private thoughts that you daren't share with anyone. Sharing makes you feel better – it feels normal: you're not the only one.

'I didn't have to think hard to make up stuff about Tania. She'd lived only a few streets away from me when I was a young man. When she disappeared, her face was all over the newspaper. I could remember her walking down the road, waiting for the bus. I began to fantasize about what I had done with her.

'I talked to Erdem about this. I never said I'd killed her, just that she had agreed to me seeing her pants. She'd liked it. It had turned her on. Maybe the charge I was up on made him think that I'd not only looked at her pants: I'd murdered her. But I didn't kill Tania. I never even met her. Look at my criminal record. How would I have killed Tania in 1987 and then not harmed anyone since then?

'Erdem was on remand for possession of images of young girls. They were top grade – girls doing things even most adult women wouldn't. I don't know what he's done this time but I listened to what he wants to do. If he has actually done any of that stuff he'll be looking at some serious time. In those situations a man starts casting around, looking for ways out.

'He must have started to think how he could use the fact that I'd fantasized about Tania. I imagine you guys helped too. Talked him up, did you? Some of you lot, you're brilliant at that. Made him feel good about himself – he had some dirty pictures but he wasn't like me? I get it, because that's what everyone's like. Everyone – and I mean everyone – uses the bad guys to put a distance between themselves and their own dirty thoughts. But don't kid yourself. Erdem is as deceitful and concealed about his life as I ever was.

'Erdem's using me and he's using you. I'm a lonely man who's cursed by an obsession, but I never harmed Tania.'

They took a break. In a side room, Sarah began drawing up a map of the things she needed to ask Walker. She tuned out Lee's comments about the 'sick monster' they had just interviewed. It was like pervert bingo; soon she would have a full house of epithets. She understood Lee was angry and disturbed, but it was a distraction having to appear to listen to him. She wished she could have interviewed Erdem Sadiq herself, had an opportunity to weigh his evidence. Finally she said, 'I'm sorry, but I'm trying to concentrate.'

Lee, taking another stick of gum out, said, 'Just one question. Do you think he did it?'

'I don't know.'

'You know these creeps are the best liars you'll ever meet. It's part of their job description.'

'Yes, I know that.' Lee didn't seem satisfied. 'Is there anything else?'

'Just that it's usually the most obvious person.'

She looked at him. 'Don't you trust me?'

Lee led Walker through Sarah's list of questions. Dates, times, locations. He was a good interviewer: assiduous on the detail. Walker said he couldn't remember that far back. He didn't know what he was doing on the day after the great storm in 1987.

Sarah said, 'You can't remember the day after the storm? It was such a memorable day. A bit like 9/11. One of those days everyone remembers.'

'Well, I don't remember it.'

She made a note, moved on. 'Looking's your thing, not touching?'

'That's right.'

'You and Erdem were only fantasizing?'

'Yes.'

'Why did you need to fantasize about a real girl?'

'I'm only interested in real girls. She came into my thoughts. I didn't ask her to do that.'

'It was just a coincidence that you were fantasizing about a girl who had gone missing?'

He held Sarah's gaze. 'Perhaps because she was missing I associated her with dirty things. I fantasized that she was a dirty girl who'd like to show me her pants.'

She allowed herself to think, asked the simple question.

'Did you have a car in 1987?'

'Yes. A Mini. A red one. It was old. V reg.'

She made a note.

'Do you fantasize about other missing girls? Murdered girls?'

'No.'

'When did you start fantasizing about Tania?'

'Why?'

That was the first time he had answered her questions with a question. Something there had bothered him, something she couldn't put a finger on. She waited for a line of inquiry that would help her, but it didn't come. She returned to the simple question that had troubled him.

'Never mind why. When was the first time you fantasized about Tania?'

'I can't remember.'

'Before or after she disappeared?'

'After.'

'How long after?'

'I don't remember.'

'What prompted it?'

'I don't know. The photos of her in the paper maybe. All that stuff on the television.'

Instantly Sarah thought of that appeal Tania's parents had made: her frozen-faced father, her mother unable to get her words out. Some involuntary gesture must have revealed her reaction to Walker's words because he was studying her with a sly expression. Her emotion had pulled her into his account. Perhaps that was the first step towards believing it. Perhaps he had become skilled even at using people's disgust against them.

'You say you never met Tania?'

'Never.'

'Never spoke to her?'

'No.'

'Sure about that?'

'I've told you.'

Sarah chewed her pen. 'What did you tell Erdem you had done with Tania?'

His hands flipped outwards. 'The usual stuff. Like I've already told you.'

'Come on, you know I'm going to need the detail.'

He inhaled as though bored. 'She'd agreed to come to my house. She lay on her stomach with her legs open. I could see her pants. She let me stand there and wank over her.'

'How many times?'

'Once. It was that same fantasy, over and over.'

She thought about that: *that same fantasy, over and over*. 'Why were you so obsessed?'

'I don't know.'

'And did you ever tell Erdem you'd killed her?'

'Never. If he's told you that, he's made it up.'

They bailed Walker. What else could they do? They had no evidence against him except the word of another sex offender.

The A40 was evenly busy, the cars driving too close in the urban routine of slowing and speeding for the yellow Gatso cameras. The flyover swept Sarah down into the queuing traffic of central London. She filtered off into the outer circle of Regent's Park. She pulled over by the zoo and took a moment, breathing in the smell of grass and watching the giraffes from the pavement. She loved that they were here, improbably, right in the heart of London, and she hoped to find in their quirky grace some solace after the glimpse she had just had of Andrew Walker's mind. She smiled, charmed by their lopsided but surprisingly elegant walk – as if they were getting it wrong but succeeding anyway. She would have liked to put a hand on their warm sides, maybe place her cheek against a patterned flank.

Reluctantly she got back into the car and turned the engine over.

Her thoughts turned involuntarily to long-lost Jessie. She'd been so in love, so silent about her secret wishes. Once, during the school holidays, Jessie had telephoned.

'Quick! Come over. Mum's out all day.'

They'd wandered the large clean rooms of Jessie's mother's mock-Tudor house like cub-free lionesses set free on the savannah. Jessie had taken Sarah up the stairs to her mother's bedroom and Sarah had stood shyly hopeful, feeling the white deep-pile carpet beneath her socks.

Jessie had smiled and said in the voice of the Queen, 'Shall we? Do you dare?'

Momentarily Sarah had been on the brink of a gesture that would have been undeniable, a hand reached out to draw Jessie's face towards her for a kiss. Only just in time did she grasp the real meaning of Jessie's question. Her neck and cheeks burned, scalded by the only-just-avoided shame of the mistake. Recovering quickly and without giving it enough thought she said, 'Yes, OK. Why not?'

There was a boy: *his* name was lost now to Sarah's memory. She remembered only how much Jessie had fancied him and how the boy had hinted at trying a threesome.

He had a motorbike and arrived in minutes, roaring up the drive. Through the rippled glass of the front door Sarah saw his vulnerability as clearly as her own. Before he had even got off the bike he had removed his helmet and roughed up his hair. He kicked the bike over onto its stand, strode up to the house as if in a terrible hurry. What a disappointment that he had to be there, but he was incidental. What bliss it was to finally be on the crisp cotton sheets of Jessie's mum's bed with Jessie.

Jessie had worn, Sarah remembered, a fine white cotton lace bra over her small breasts, and matching lace pants. Sarah's hands roamed over her bottom, her stomach, down between her legs. She nibbled at her neck, up towards her ear. Jessie turned and began to kiss her.

And then the boy ruined it – that poor, foolish, annoying, jealous boy. How ridiculous that he should have been jealous when it was Sarah who was pretending, Sarah who was hiding.

'You're not paying me any attention!' he suddenly protested, getting up and stomping angrily away from the bed, pulling on his underpants in adolescent fury, all pimples and red face, almost falling over himself in his hurry to get his trousers on.

Jessie sat up, tried to console him. She walked over, pressed her beautiful body against him. He put his hand on the small of her back. She kissed him. It was abundantly clear where her real interests lay. Silently heartbroken, Sarah made her excuses and slipped down the stairs unprevented, barely noticed even.

A few days later, she tried tentatively to work the conversation round to what had happened, hinting as casually as she could that perhaps they might try it again.

'God no, Sarah! I might start liking it too much.'

Too much?

It was painful, but at least things were becoming clearer. She had recognized what had happened for what it was: a faltering first step. Maybe not Jessie, but there would be others. She would be less desperate, more discerning, less dissembling. There would be no boys next time. And no girls that wanted boys either.

But then something happened that she could never have imagined. Her sister Susie's boyfriend, Patrick, the one everyone liked, had driven his car into a tree. Susie was gone forever, and everything had changed.

The drive had passed by unseen. Sarah swung in past security and, parked in the shadow of the building, she paused to listen to her father's voicemail. She quickly drafted a text. She didn't want to risk him picking up.

So sorry, Dad. This year I am not going to be able to make it to Susie's memorial service. I just can't free the day up. I will be thinking of you and Mum. Much love, Sarah.

She hesitated, then pressed send. She took her bag from the car, swiped her way into the murder block.

Everyone else from her team was long gone, hurried home for their extended rest days before the on-call began, but from along the corridor she could hear voices and see lights coming from open doors of the neighbouring team. They must have caught a job. She fumbled in her bag for the key to her office. She would just take an hour to review Tania's file and update it with the results of the interview. She opened the door, rubbed her eyes, flicked the light on. There was a buff folder on the desk. A Post-it note from Fat Elaine was stuck on the top: *Richard Stephenson, Tania's violin teacher. Married at the time. Now divorced. Drove a green Jaguar.*

She opened the file. At the time of Tania's disappearance, Stephenson had been teaching at her school, Hatchett's. The headmaster at the time was now deceased, but Elaine had managed to contact the former deputy head, who'd remembered the car. Sarah logged on to her computer and emailed Elaine.

Well done on finding Stephenson. Please conduct further research – schools he worked at, orchestras he directed, reasons for leaving – and submit request to other forces for any intelligence, crime reports.

As she read over her email, she wondered whether she had enough to justify such intrusive investigations. Elaine had done basic intelligence checks. Stephenson had no criminal record. There were no crime reports relating to him within the Metropolitan Police District. There were no complaints, no 'intelligence only' rumours even.

She thought too about the workload she was about to dump on Elaine and how she would resent it. She finished her email brightly.

Thanks for all the work! I know it's a lot. I appreciate it!

She pressed send, then immediately wondered whether perhaps she hadn't been a bit heavy on the exclamation marks. Elaine didn't strike her as the kind of person who'd be a fan of enthusiastic punctuation.

She had twelve unread emails in her inbox. One was from the boss, headed *Andrew Walker appeal for info: suggested draft*. She clicked on it.

Detectives announce a £40,000 reward to help solve the 1987 disappearance of Tania Mills . . .

Here was the bit that really bothered her.

DCI Fedden wishes to draw the public's attention to photographs of this man [Sarah: attach] who lived in the area at the time of Tania's disappearance. Anyone knowing or encountering him during this time is asked to contact the incident room number below.

Fedden was making her move far too fast. It was too early to release this kind of thing. They needed to be dominating the information, not wandering around with the lights off. Certainly they shouldn't be encouraging every idiot with a grudge to come forward. But she knew Fedden wouldn't be gainsaid, so she sent him a quick reply, aiming for an upbeat tone in spite of her misgivings.

Fine by me. Thanks for running it past me. Sarah.

She needed to try to get ahead with her own inquiries. She emailed the school secretary at Tania's old school, Hatchett's, asking to visit on the morning of the first day of the on-call. She could squeeze in the inquiry before her official tour of duty started in the afternoon. Now she needed to go off duty for her rest days. When the on-call began, the team would have to respond to any murder within London. The hours could be punishing.

She logged off, locked her office door and made her way downstairs, pausing in the shelter of the building to smoke a cigarette.

Evening light was falling across the empty parade ground, the heat of the day bleeding from the tarmac. The office windows were all dark except for the offices adjacent to her own, which glowed orange. The neighbouring homicide team would be working through the night. She loved Hendon when it was like this – all the impurities, all the irrelevancies burnt off by the lateness of the hour. Anyone on duty here now had real police work to do, and Hendon had become fully itself: a secret and purposeful place that only the cops really knew.

She leaned back against the wall and reached out to Tania, her mind running over her knowledge of her, watching the musical teenager with the long hair running off to the park that morning. She saw the photograph Robert had shown her. Behind the grey wash, the desaturating colours, Robert and Tania stood together in the shade of a tree, his arm around her shoulders, both smiling, both apparently happy.

And then, with her contemplation of that photograph, a possible line of inquiry became suddenly, blindingly obvious. How could she not have thought of it before?

She stubbed out her cigarette and ran back up the stairs to her office. She logged on, took the exhibit book from the warrant on Walker's flat out of her desk drawer, ran her finger down the entries, carefully checking each relevant item's description against a Google search on the internet. She scribbled the reference SBB/23 C3427680 on a piece of paper, found the keys for the exhibit cages and made her way downstairs.

The strip lighting flickered into life. The basement was sealed grey concrete, windowless and airless. Apart from a constant low electric hum, the room was silent. Rows of sealed chain-link cages secured into the concrete were filled with floor-to-ceiling shelving units. She walked along the central aisle, past rows of stacked blue plastic crates that held the dried bloody clothing, phones, letters, children's toys and the other human detritus that had turned out to have unforeseen life as material evidence in the capital's murders and manslaughters.

At the end of the aisle she unlocked one of the cages and sat on the floor next to the shelf that had been put aside for Egremont. Here were the recent seizures from the warrant on Walker's flat. She looked through the boxes until she located the correct one. She lifted it off the shelf and sorted through it until she found SBB/23. Taking the exhibit with her, she locked the cage and made her way back upstairs. She sent Elaine an email.

I've got SBB/23 from the warrant on Walker's flat locked in my drawer. Please submit it for a speedy fingerprint and DNA comparison against Tania. Inquiries are active – urgent submission. Ask them to check the workings, particularly the film feed, for prints.

PART TWO

7

Wednesday 16 July 2014

Sarah unclipped Daisy's harness from the seat belt. The dog immediately jumped down from the car and ran up the drive. Mrs Edwards, a plump woman in blue housecoat and slippers, was already standing at the doorway. The dog began jumping, and Mrs Edwards bent down and scooped her up, stroking her behind the ears.

Sarah took out the dog's bed, treats, toys and food and walked up the drive with them in her arms. An envelope with cash in it was tucked into the dog bed. Mrs Edwards didn't like to talk about money.

'Thanks for taking her so early.'

'Not to worry, dear. We love Daisy here.' She nuzzled the dog. 'You just text me and let me know when you're picking her up. If I don't hear from you, I'll assume it's the end of your on-call. Poor little thing, she'll miss you.'

But looking at the dog in Mrs Edwards' arms, that was hard to credit.

Sarah was at the office by eight. Her request to Tania's old school had been forwarded to a Dr Gower who had emailed providing his mobile number. He had a fancy title, she noted – 'Director Of External Relations' – and signed his emails using all his initials: PhD, MA (Oxon), PGCE. She rang and explained her request. Gower apologized: he couldn't meet before ten thirty.

Sarah hesitated. The appointment was later than she would have wished. Still she reckoned she could squeeze it in before her official tour of duty started. She had breakfast, booked out a car and headed west.

Set in a quiet neighbourhood of Victorian houses, the earliest of the school's buildings was a Gothic whimsy: patterned brickwork, a steep slate roof with diminishing tiles and a little tower complete with lancet and rose windows. She'd googled the place. Hachett's had been a direct-grant grammar that had gone independent in 1980. Ranked outstanding by Ofsted, the school was now competing right up there against the top girls' schools.

The original building must surely have been listed, but somehow the governors had got permission for a modernist glass and steel extension that jutted out of the side and rested on two round pale stone pillars, sheltering an area of the playground from wind and rain. The addition spoke loudly of both privilege and ambition – a pretence at boldness that any fool would know was really super-smart and fantastically expensive.

Gower met her at the front door. He was about thirty-five, with prematurely silvered hair. There was a lot of smartness going on – polished shoes, crisp shirt, soft grey tie, a modest line of matching handkerchief showing in the jacket pocket. He insisted on a tour. 'Give you an idea of the place.'

The school spelled out a haphazard map of decades of shifting architectural styles – a 1950s flat red-brick building with external stairways, a 1970s block with a cantilevered roof. Beyond the buildings, sports fields stretched away. Athletics was in progress: girls practising the relay, pelting up the track. 'Fucking hell, Tabitha!' carried on the warm breeze, followed by the blast of a whistle. It was only two days before the end of term and Sarah imagined the long summer holidays stretching out before these young women.

Gower turned back towards the school buildings. A group of girls passed, wearing good-quality blazers and with nicely cut hair and an affected lethargy in their demeanour. One wore trousers and a hijab. It was all reassuringly diverse and contemporary.

'You had a chance to glance through Mr Stephenson's records?'

'I did, but there's not much to tell you. He joined the school in 1985 and left in early 1988 with excellent references. Music thrived under him. They hosted events, went to Salzburg. There's nothing to suggest any problem whatsoever.'

'Can I take a copy of those records?'

'I'll have to talk to the head. There may be data protection issues.'

'What about your records of the girls who attended the school at the time? Do you have an alumni society?'

'Could you perhaps tell me more about your investigation? It might help us come to a decision about sharing information.'

Sarah observed that remark with some scepticism. Gower struck her as someone who would be very alive to the dangers of historic scandal for a school like Hatchett's. But she checked herself. He did have a point – was she really going to start a firestorm of rumour on the sole basis that Mr Stephenson had once driven a green Jaguar?

'Not at this stage,' she said.

'I'll take you to our archive,' Dr Gower offered. 'It's open to everyone. You'll find some photos of the orchestra, that sort of thing.'

He led her through the entrance hall – geometric floor tiles, a cabinet with polished trophies, oil paintings of former heads on the walls – to a narrow wooden staircase that spiralled upwards. This was the old heart of the school and Sarah imagined it as it had been, before it was smartened up: the worn dusty treads, the banister spindles in need of a lick of paint, the creak of stairs. On the left were small music rooms with arched windows that showed sky and clouds. Through a glass panel she watched a plump girl in blue skirt and white cotton shirt scraping away at a violin. It was certainly possible to picture a hasty, furtive act here. Gower, perhaps anticipating Sarah's imaginings, mentioned quietly that the practice rooms were a recent conversion. Twenty-seven years ago, this had been a classroom of girls seated in rows with heads bent over maths and Latin.

At the end of the passage was the old staffroom, which had been converted into the archive. There were leather-bound albums with dates on the spines.

She leafed through 1987: sports days, snaps of girls completing their Duke of Edinburgh awards in cagoules and waterproof trousers. The orchestra in a local hall: white blouses and dark skirts. She peered into the frame and spotted Tania, a small figure, playing first violin. Here, a few pages on, a local newspaper report: *Hatchett's pulls up its sleeves.* Sarah fished out her glasses to read the small print. There were photos of storm damage, a description of a tree-planting initiative in Morville Park: *sponsored by the local council and funded in part by performances by the Hatchett's school orchestra.* Smudged newsprint: a black-and-white image of a man sitting on an uprooted tree – *Mr Stephenson, Hatchett's head of music* – girls standing in front of him holding bare-rooted trees and spades.

Sarah could understand why Hatchett's would be pleased to have an association with Morville Park. It was the hunting ground of Tudor princes, the website said, and so very different from the little neighbourhood suburban park from which Tania had disappeared. She googled the journey time and persuaded herself she could still make it. The on-call would last seven days and she might not have another chance for a while if they picked up a job. But the lanes filtered from three to one and the traffic slowed to virtually stationary. A woman wearing a long skirt and a colourful headscarf walked along the queue, a plastic bucket of roses tucked under her left arm.

Sarah took a side road and wove in the direction of an office and staff yard marked on the park's website. She parked by a railing with a locked five-bar gate and an open pedestrian entrance on the side.

The path was wooded. A sudden fall of rain had moistened the air and sent drops splashing off the broad leaves, releasing the scent of the earth.

It was further than she had thought before she spotted the wardens' green hut. By the side, a small locked area with a mini tractor and a couple of service vehicles. She knocked on the door, then tried it. It opened onto a rest area – a table and chairs, a small fridge, a toaster. There was a door through to another room, a toilet perhaps, or a changing area. A dreadlocked white man wearing headphones was sitting at the table, eating toast. He was tall and lean, in a green fleece and matching parachute trousers. Sarah showed her warrant card. He removed his headphones and offered his hand.

'I'm Tom. Come in. Want a cuppa?'

'No thanks. It's just a quick enquiry – I wondered if you kept any records of the replanting after the 1987 storm?'

'Harry's the guy you need to talk to.'

'Harry?'

'Harry Medcalfe. Knows everything about this place, and I mean *everything*. Worked here more than thirty years. He's retired now but we still see quite a lot of him.'

Tom leaned to one side, pulled a mobile phone with a cracked screen out of his back pocket. 'Here's his number,' he said, offering her the phone. She fished her glasses out of her bag. 'That's really helpful, thank you.' But as she unlocked her own phone to record the number, she saw that the screen was showing no bars. She ran outside and found a signal.

It wasn't too bad – the boss had left a voicemail only two minutes earlier – but still she had to calm herself. They'd picked up a job.

Tom drove her down the track in one of the electric service vehicles, bumping recklessly over potholes and tooting his horn while she called Fedden and tried to sound as though she had everything under control. She put on her blues and twos and made the twelve miles across London in less than twenty minutes.

Emergency vehicles were parked haphazardly everywhere in the street. An ambulance, two paramedic response cars. Marked and unmarked police vehicles. The white forensics van. A crowd of civilians was clustering in groups outside the tape, talking in hushed voices and watching the movements of the officers and paramedics. A woman in a peaked cap was tying flowers to a lamp post with yellow ribbon. Flowers and teddy bears had already been laid around the base.

Glancing at the scene, Sarah worked out the logistics. The walkway leading to the flat was very public. The press hadn't arrived yet, but it could only be a matter of time. It would be nice to get the body out before they arrived, but realistically that was probably not possible. It would be difficult to maintain privacy.

She walked towards the outer cordon. Lee was there, standing next to Joanne Robinson, the Crime Scene Examiner. Sarah knew Joanne from other jobs and was pleased to see her. The local detective inspector was there too with a couple of detective constables. He introduced himself with an extended hand – 'Chan Kapoor' – and nodded to his two officers. 'Louise Marsh, Andreas Lippi.'

Sarah took them in quickly – Andreas mid twenties, a bit dishy, floppy hair; Louise late thirties, hard-faced. Murder scenes were always like this. For a few hours she'd be dependent on these officers she'd never met to make sure that early opportunities were seized. Then she might never work with them again.

'Pleased to meet you,' she said, and smiled. 'Detective Inspector Sarah Collins.' She gestured to her two colleagues. 'Detective Constable Lee Coutts. Joanne Robinson, Forensics.'

There was a shaking of hands. Everyone knew it was a bad one, and it seemed, to Sarah at least, that there was a summoning of resolve in these extended courtesies. Kapoor had a day book in his hand, which he opened. 'OK, everyone?'

Sarah nodded. 'Yes thanks. Tell us what we've got.'

Chan gave a thorough briefing. He'd covered all the basics, controlled the scene, traced but not informed the next of kin, identified the suspect, seized the clothing of the first responders, begun a CCTV trawl. There were active arrest inquiries but the suspect had not been located.

Sarah said, 'Have you been inside?'

Kapoor grimaced. He had the maturity not to disguise the fact that it was a scene he would not relish. He gestured to a plump woman in a green uniform sitting on the step of one of the ambulances smoking while a uniformed officer took her shoe prints.

'That's the duty station officer for the paramedics. Very professional. She declared life extinct. There didn't seem any point contaminating the scene further while we were waiting for you guys to get here so no one's been in except the first officers on scene who had a good look for the child.'

'Good shout. Thank you for that. And it's the DSO who's told us what to expect inside?'

'Yep.'

Sarah scribbled some notes in her decision log, then said, 'Is there any update on the child?'

Kapoor shook his head. 'Nothing yet.'

'OK, we need to inform the next of kin urgently. Could you ask some local DCs to do it?' She handed Kapoor her card. 'That's my mobile number. The intelligence bureau need to do a risk assessment. Get the duty officer to give me a call and I'll brief him. Or her, of course.'

She looked towards the walkway. At the front door of the flat, a uniformed officer stood impassively holding a crime scene log. 'I'll just suit up, then I'll go in and take a quick look with Joanne.'

8

Lizzie put her overnight bag on the floor. She and Ash were the only officers working the late turn in the unit. She hoped they wouldn't be too busy. She was meeting Kieran after work.

'Good news and bad news,' Ash said, entering the office with the kettle. 'Good news: no prisoners in the bin. Bad news: I've given you a couple of non-crime domestics.'

She bent over her computer and scanned the first of the two crime reports. It was a third-party report: a neighbour had heard shouting. Both parties had been insistent they didn't need the police. Still, she had to call them.

The man who answered barely said hello. He called out: 'Justin, can you *believe* it? It's the police *again*.'

The phone was muffled. Then a different man spoke.

'I'm so sorry about Adam. The poor officer who came to the door – Adam was *so rude* to him. He tried to plough on – asked if we'd ever been cruel to animals. I pointed out our two Siamese and asked him whether he'd ever seen animals so downright spoilt . . .'

A uniformed inspector had entered the office – a small woman, about five foot three, blonde, quick-moving. Lizzie guessed she was the duty inspector, the officer calling the shots for all critical operational decisions on the borough until someone more senior arrived. Something big must be happening. She looked at Lizzie and made the wind-it-up gesture with her index finger.

The voice was still rattling on. 'How can I reassure you that we really don't need you?'

'You've done a pretty good job, actually. I'll close the report. Sorry to have troubled you.'

The inspector spoke with a low voice in an Edinburgh accent. 'Hello, CID folk. We've got a critical incident. Briefing in the canteen in ten minutes, everyone ready to go, please.'

9

Sarah and Joanne, the crime scene examiner, had put on their face masks, plastic overshoes and double gloves, then pulled up their hoods and pulled the drawstrings tight. It was stifling, hard to move freely, hard to see. Sarah's mouth and nose were already moist from the mask.

Joanne crouched down and pushed the door open from the bottom.

Inside, it was dark and cramped. Neither Joanne nor Sarah wanted to touch the light switch, so Sarah scanned the hallway with her torch while Joanne laid down footplates. Coats were hung on the wall, a pile of shoes below them. The laminate floor was trampled and smeared with numerous bloody prints. A door immediately to the left: Sarah pushed it open and glanced inside.

A small bathroom with a heated towel rail throwing too much heat into the small, airless space. Blood-soaked clothes lay in a heap on the floor. A bloody towel was in the bath. The sink and taps were smeared with blood, as was the hand towel.

Behind this remained traces of an unremarkable bathroom, tidy and feminine. Pumice stone on the side of the bath. A box of Tampax and bag of sanitary towels in a small wicker basket by the toilet. A dark soapstone oil burner on the side of the bath. Neat rows of nail varnish on the shelf under the mirror.

Sarah stepped back into the hallway. It ended in a frosted-glass door, a smear of blood on the opposite side. Joanne knelt down and pushed the door open.

There was a lot of blood: the sitting room smelled of it, a metallic tang. The woman was lying on her back in a pool that had seeped across the floor and created a shallow lake, its dark surface crinkling as the blood congealed and dried. By her side was an empty Johnny Walker bottle. There was blood splatter on the walls, blood on the glass coffee table, blood on the television screen. Two dining chairs had been overturned. There was a bloody handprint on the sofa, another on the wall near where the victim had fallen.

In the middle of this carnage the table was a strange oasis of calm: on its surface an empty whisky glass, a divided clear plastic tray of coloured rubber bands. There was also a half-eaten children's yoghurt, a spoon still inside it. By the sofa was a wheeled case with a pull-along handle. It was partially unzipped.

It was hard to know where to start. With so much blood and so much potential evidence, it would be difficult to work here. They could expect to need the scene for days.

Joanne laid down footplates along the shortest route to the side of the corpse.

The victim was clothed. Jeans. T-shirt with short sleeves, wet with blood. Bare feet, painted toenails, a tattoo of a lotus flower on the inside of her left ankle. Her mouth and eyes were open, her eyes staring towards the left corner of the room as though there was something there that had caught her unending attention. She had trauma to her right cheek. Probably just a punch, but an effective one. Her long hair was matted in a bloody clump to her left. Her right arm was across her chest and her hand, drenched in blood, had fallen palm down. It had probably slipped down from her neck where there was a bloody lesion, a slice of flesh that gaped. The whole of her neck and chest was soaked; Sarah guessed at an arterial wound that had squirted blood before the victim had quickly lost consciousness, fallen and died.

She squatted by the body to get a better view. Broken fingernails. Bruising to the inside of the forearm. This woman had put up a fight. On the victim's left wrist, two loom bands. Sarah would not touch her: it would be best to photograph first and get the pathologist down to make an initial examination at the scene.

'OK?' she said, her voice muffled in the mask.

Joanne nodded.

'Let's just check the child's room. Then we'll go out and have a chat about next steps.'

The curtains were drawn in the bedroom and a purple light seeped through them. The bed had a matching owl duvet and pillowcase. On the wall was a *Frozen* poster and a framed school certificate: *Student of the Month. AMAZING! Keep up the good work.* There was a picture of the girl herself, wearing pink sunglasses, a feathered headband and beads, her arm round the shoulders of a similarly dressed girl of the same age. They were both smiling. Underneath was printed in italics, *Happy Birthday! Best friends forever. Love you, Irit.*

One of the drawers was open. There was no sign of disturbance, just a neat pile of ironed and folded T-shirts. The top one carried the image of a dolphin jumping out of a calm turquoise sea.

The room was perfectly tidy. There was no clue as to where the child had gone.

10

The duty inspector had rounded up CID from all over the nick, and the drinks machine shuddered loudly as it dispensed Coke and Red Bull. Ash had celebrated the news by bringing the biscuit tin from the office to the canteen, and everyone was digging in, the tin rapidly emptying.

'I'm a rebel, me!' he said in a fake northern accent. 'Can't wait to see the DI's face in the morning when all the biscuits have gone. Do you think she'll put a crime report on?'

An officer in the act of stuffing two biscuits in his mouth at the same time said, 'You're fine, mate. No witnesses.'

The duty inspector walked briskly into the canteen and sat at one of the tables.

'When you're ready?'

They gathered round, mostly standing. She handed out the hastily printed briefing sheets.

'With the station grapevine fully operational, I expect most of you will already know what this is about . . .'

Lizzie was staring at the briefing. At the top was a custody image of a white male: round head, short cropped hair, QPR shirt. It was the most recent image, taken the last time he'd been nicked. She looked down the page and saw the name of the victim. She pulled out a chair and sat down. Ash was looking in her direction, but she avoided him, gazing steadfastly at the briefing sheet. Inspector Redwood was still talking.

'Chummy is believed to have murdered his partner. When I say "believed", I mean he is the suspect. There's no doubt she's dead, unfortunately.'

There was a brief silence, punctuated by a muttered 'Bastard.'

The inspector resumed. 'OK, troops, this is a live incident – the suspect is at large and there's a child missing. I've been briefed by Homicide, but if you've got any queries you can call them on their mobile – and I suggest you do. Everything done properly, please. This is a murder investigation. Those briefing sheets are numbered and they don't go out of this room – I want them all back at the end of our little chat.'

Ash said, 'Sorry to ask, ma'am, but it may be handy if we come across him . . .'

The inspector looked up. 'I hope this isn't one of your bloody jokes, Ash.'

'It isn't a joke, ma'am. Got to think of our safety. How did he kill her?'

'My apologies. Multiple stab wounds. We haven't recovered the knife. Nobody should try to arrest him without back-up.'

Ash and Lizzie were tasked with notifying the next of kin. Lizzie grabbed some car keys and they met up in the office to get their kit. That phrase that had come to Lizzie in the court kept returning. *Die then.* She tried to tune it out. She put on her covert harness that held her radio, baton, gas and handcuffs, and pulled her jacket over the top.

Ash said, 'Are you going to be all right?'

She looked at him. He was smiling at her. 'Yes, I'll be fine.'

'Why don't you stay in the office? I'm sure you can swap with someone.'

'No, it's all right. Really.'

She checked in her grab bag that she had blank statements and evidence bags and they went down to the yard. Lizzie flicked the lock to identify the car and a shabby old Ford flashed its lights.

'You don't want to drive?' she said.

Ash raised his eyebrows. 'Drive for the job? Me? Never. They don't pay you any more for it and there's all sorts of shit that can go wrong.'

She pulled back the seat, adjusted the mirrors. She'd delivered a few death messages in her short service, but this one held a special dread. Her heart was beating, her hands were cold. How was she going to get through telling Georgina's mother that her daughter had been murdered and that her granddaughter was missing? She turned the engine on. It was like everything the job threw at you: you just had to do it.

Ash said, 'You not checking the vehicle?'

'If there's something wrong with it, I don't want to bloody know. We'll never find another one.'

'There you are,' said Ash, belting up, 'offering yourself up to a world of pain. If something's wrong with it and there's an accident, it will be on you.'

Feeling numb, Lizzie turned the car and swung out through the gates. She accelerated towards the lights and Ash put his hand on the dashboard.

'Are you positive you're OK to deal with this? You seem in a bit of a state, to be honest.'

'Bloody hell. How many times are you going to ask me?'

'Well, OK then, but slow down at least. You did everything you could for Georgina. The death message isn't an emergency. That's been and gone.'

He produced a folded piece of paper from his jacket pocket and opened it out. 'Want to know the intel on the address?'

'Yes, go ahead.'

'*Go ahead* – listen to you. Such a *cop*. You bloody *love it*. How could you ever think you were going to resign?'

'Whatever. Fuck, Ash. What have we got?'

'Nothing too bad. Mum's boyfriend, Fergal, was a bit of a Billy Burglar but he's not been busy for a few years, at least not as far as we know. Works for the council now, on the bins.'

'And Mum?'

'Julie Teel. Lots of shoplifting, one fraud. No convictions for violence. Used to be on the juice big-time. Heroin. Seems to be off it now. Nothing recent.'

Built in the 1970s on a site created by German bombs, the Deakin Estate wouldn't have looked out of place as the set of a Kubrick movie: high-rise blocks, covered walkways, upturned orbs of white light. It was notorious among the local police as a place that could have done with another direct hit. The council had tried to demolish it in the 1980s and start again, but the residents had managed to get it Grade I listed. Now – spruced up with lottery money – it was here to stay, and, sure enough, could be found on property websites tempting the adventurous and cash-strapped as iconic, unusual, exciting. One of the entrances had a group of youths in hoodies hanging out. They clocked the two cops and drifted away.

The intercom to the block didn't seem to be working. Lizzie rummaged around in her grab bag and retrieved Hadley's fire-door master key. She'd found it dropped as if specially for her, just yards away from the roof of Portland Tower from which he had fallen. It haunted her – a talisman of his mastery of the lesser-known skills of policing that she felt she still did not possess. She stretched up on tiptoes but couldn't reach the lock. She turned to Ash and held out the key.

'You'll have to do it.'

Ash took the key. 'Bloody hell, what did I say? You've even got one of these. Only the really keen guys have these.'

'I inherited it.'

He glanced at her, then reached up and slipped the key down into the lock. The door clicked open and he handed back the key. They made their way along the white concrete walkways to number 14, at the end of a row. The lights were on.

A white man, clad improbably for the time and place in a high-vis jacket, answered the door. He was overweight, with round cheeks that looked as though they were under pressure and whose surface was mapped out by a thousand burst capillaries. His bitten nails were stained with dirt. Both Lizzie and Ash had offered their warrant cards, but it had only been a formality. He'd known they were cops the instant he opened the door. He put one hand on the door frame and looked at them coolly: without ever having met before, they all knew each other.

'What do you lot want?'

Ash said, 'Can we come in?'

'Tell me what it's about first.'

'No one's in any trouble.'

'You're not coming in without a warrant—'

Lizzie interrupted. 'Fergal, isn't it?'

He nodded. Something about her demeanour had changed him.

'I'm really sorry,' Lizzie said, 'but we do need to come in.'

Fergal hesitated, his face tense, as if he had already guessed what it was and wanted to think of a way to avoid what was to follow. Then he stepped back and let them walk past him into the living room. There was a strong smell of cannabis and on a large plasma screen a rerun of Master Chef was playing.

Julie was sitting on the sofa next to a fat pit bull dog which lay, its head resting on her lap, snoring quietly. Julie was thin and nervy, but with some style. She wore faded blue jeans and fingerless gloves, and was wrapped in a tartan blanket. The gloves suggested her circulation was bad after years of injecting, but they were beautiful nevertheless – Fair Isle patterns in the colours of autumn.

Ash offered the only single spare seat to Lizzie with an outstretched arm, but she refused and knelt on the floor opposite Julie. Ash took the seat beside her.

A low glass coffee table held the necessaries – cans of beer both opened and unopened, a large metal pub ashtray full of the dog-ends of roll-up cigarettes, a jumbo-size Rizla pack from which cardboard had been torn to make roaches.

On the wall was a framed photo of a baby with the legend *One Year Wonderful*. Next to it was a silver heart frame holding the image of Georgina in a 'World's Best Mum' T-shirt. On her lap was Skye, as a toddler, wearing wellies and a tutu.

Ash glanced over quickly to Lizzie, but she ignored him because Julie was searching her face for the news she had brought. Her eyes were surprisingly beautiful and lively in a face that was otherwise marked by long years of drug use: a sunken look to her cheeks and neck, deep lines around her mouth and eyes. After all those drugs, the passion and desperation, the fights, the arrests, she had finally settled for a saggy old dog and evenings of television, with a joint or two to keep things peaceful. But confusion was about to enter again.

She said, 'It's Georgie, isn't it?'

It was said fiercely, but it was clear that the real demand was for a refutation of her worst fears.

Neither Fergal nor Julie had offered to turn the television off so Lizzie had to give the death message to Georgina's mother while the bald chef commented on one of the contestant's meals.

Julie didn't move, but her lips went white as she pressed them together. Then her left hand went up to cover her eyes and she leaned forward with her mouth open. The fingernails belonged to an adolescent: polished pink with hearts and glitter. It made Lizzie immediately think of Skye. From the television screen she heard the words *What a fabulous thing to do with an aubergine.* Fergal put his arm round Julie and rubbed her back. 'I'm so sorry, love.' Julie shook her head but did not speak. She pulled her feet up onto the sofa and wrapped the blanket more tightly around her.

After about a minute she looked at the two officers. 'No,' she said. 'I can't believe it.'

Lizzie nodded: simply believing was usually too difficult. It could take days, months. The truth might never really sink in. She too was finding it hard. Before her eyes Julie was going through those shifts of understanding, as if grief were a staged chemical reaction, each transformation changing her forever. Her face now was etched with a deep frown, her mouth a tight circle. She focused on Lizzie as if she were a midwife helping her to deliver.

'Are you certain? Is she really dead?'

Lizzie experienced the usual temptation: to lie. After all, she didn't want to believe it herself. To tell the truth plainly was a simple enough discipline, but who would not flinch from it? Faced with Julie's denial, she felt her own confidence in the irreversible fact of Georgina's death wavering.

'Yes. I'm really sorry. It's true.'

Julie shuddered, but she didn't look down. Her mouth shaped into a twisted grimace. She spoke hoarsely. 'And little Skye?'

Lizzie forced her voice not to fail her. 'Skye's missing, Julie.'

Julie nodded, but without comprehension. 'Missing? What does that mean? Has he got her?'

'We don't know. The neighbour says she was with Georgina—'

She interrupted. 'How did he kill her?'

Lizzie remembered the inspector's description: *multiple stab wounds.* She searched for an alternative but found none. Ash, perhaps sensing her failure, stepped in.

'They haven't held the post-mortem yet. That's when they establish the exact cause of death.'

'But what do you know?'

'The information we have is that she was injured with a bladed weapon.'

A bladed weapon.

It took Julie a moment to figure it out, and Lizzie watched the understanding dawning in an expression of horror. 'Have you seen her?'

'No.'

Julie concentrated her gaze on Lizzie again.

'But you're absolutely sure?'

Lizzie recalled Georgina and her beautiful, elegant feet, and Skye standing with her outstretched hand in which she held a loom band. The band, she realized, was still around her own wrist. It seemed an impossible burden to have to insist on this news when she was finding it so hard to comprehend herself. And then she thought again of the court and her own impulse. *Die then.* How could she ever have thought that? How could her sympathy have so failed her?

She said, 'Yes, I'm sure.'

Julie inhaled sharply and then started to sob, holding her head in her hands and rocking back and forth. A cry came out of the desperate blanketed bundle.

'You have to find Skye! You have to.'

Lizzie leaned forward and put her hand on Julie's knee. 'They're looking.'

On the television, the one with the bald head was doing a piece to camera. Something about puddings.

Julie suddenly stopped crying completely. She looked slightly crazed, furious even. 'No, no. I can't believe it.'

The dog lifted its head. It jumped down from the sofa and ran towards the door, ears pricked, tail wagging low. A shadow passed across the window.

Ash said quietly, 'Are you expecting anyone?'

There was a knock at the door. A male voice, polite. 'Julie, are you in there, dear? We need to talk.'

It was unmistakably Brannon in full charm mode. Lizzie spoke very softly. 'Nobody reply. Julie, do you think he wants to hurt you?'

She nodded. 'Probably. He hates me.'

Another knock. 'Julie?'

Fergal spoke quietly but with complete conviction. 'Let's let him in. I'll kill the bastard.'

Lizzie shook her head. 'No. We need him alive to find Skye. If we let him in there'll be a fight. He wants to hurt Julie and he's got a knife. Worst thing would be to give him what he wants.'

A banging on the door had started and the dog began barking. Julie looked at Lizzie. There was a quiet urgency in her voice.

'You *can't* let him go. I'd rather die.'

Lizzie gestured towards the window at the far side of the room. 'Can I get out the back there and round to the front?'

Julie nodded.

Lizzie moved quickly over to the window and began unlocking the catch. Ash joined her. 'I'll go,' he said quietly.

'No. One of us needs to stay with Julie and Fergal. You're stronger than me if he forces entry. I'll go round and keep an eye on him. You call for support.'

Ash, frozen by indecision, didn't immediately reply. Then he said, 'He's killed, Lizzie.'

'I'll just keep an eye on him.'

'Don't bloody try to arrest him.'

'I won't.'

There was shouting from the walkway. 'I know you're awake. I can hear the telly and the fucking dog.'

Someone banged on the ceiling and a voice called out from upstairs. 'Keep it down, you lot.'

Fergal and Julie were looking at the two police officers. Lizzie beckoned for them to come to the window.

Brannon's voice again. 'Open the door, you fucking bitch.'

Fergal, now standing beside them, said, 'Let's let him in. I can hold on to the bastard.'

More hammering. Lizzie shook her head and put her finger to her lips. 'We'll get him, don't worry.'

She turned the volume on the radio as low it would go and passed it to Ash. 'Transmit from the bedroom . . .'

He took it from her. 'Duh!'

'I'll call you on my mobile.'

Ash grabbed her forearm tightly for a moment. 'Keep back from him.'

Climbing out of the window, Lizzie heard Brannon at the door again. 'I know you're awake. Open the fucking door.'

She dropped down from the window ledge and jarred her ankle. Briefly she was distracted by the sharp pain. She bent to rub it, then ran into the shelter of the wall, calling Ash on her mobile. He accepted the call but neither of them spoke. She kept the call open as she moved around the perimeter of the building. From here she could see the exit from the walkway. She could hear banging and shouting. Lights were flicking on in the other flats. Above her, someone opened a window. She took her asp out of her harness and racked it, holding it concealed by her left side. Her heart was thumping.

She leaned back against the wall and breathed deeply. After another burst of banging and shouting, she heard footsteps approaching, then passing and fading as a man walked rapidly away. She dipped forward out of the shadows, looked to her left and saw Brannon in dark jeans and a military-style khaki jacket. She waited for him to cross the green and turn left onto the pavement before she spoke into her phone.

'Left, left along Simmonds Street.'

'Got it.'

Only when he was out of sight did she run lightly across the green and into the shadow of the further building. She leaned out beyond the wall and watched him disappearing up the road. He was walking quickly. She closed her asp and slotted it back into the harness, then stepped out onto the pavement and began talking into her phone.

'Yes, I'm sorry I'm late. I'm on my way now . . . Don't be like that.'

'Very good,' Ash mocked. 'Very tradecraft, my dear. Just don't get stabbed.'

Brannon was ahead at the far end of the road. He seemed to be holding something in his right hand, down by his leg. He turned right at a T-junction and she lost sight of him.

'Right, right at the T-junction of Simmonds Street. Dark jeans, khaki jacket. Definitely Brannon. May be carrying a knife in his right hand.'

'For fuck's sake, keep back. He'd love to kill you.'

'It's OK. He can't even see me.'

She broke into a light run and then slowed at the end of the street, regulating her breathing and trying to calm her demeanour before she turned right.

He was ahead, walking quickly. His right arm was stiff and Lizzie was sure she had caught the silver glint of a blade by his thigh.

She spoke into the phone. 'I've told you not to worry, Mum.'

'Very funny. I'll mention that remark at your funeral. They're on their way. About six minutes, they reckon. You sure it's him?'

'Positive. You got the description?'

'Yes.'

'I can hear a siren. Tell them to switch the bloody thing off.'

'Get back. They don't need you any more.'

'He's started to run. Left, left at the next junction. There's a newsagent on the corner. I'm losing him.'

She was sprinting now, and as she rounded the corner, she could see he had gained a hundred yards on her. 'I can't keep up with him anyway.'

But then Brannon slowed and turned. He must have heard her running, known from her footfall that it was a solitary foot-chase.

'He's coming towards me.'

'Really, not funny.'

'No, he is.'

She dropped her phone and racked her asp. 'Get back.'

He was walking purposefully towards her, the knife in his right hand. She saw it clearly now under the street light. It had a smooth blade, about eight inches long.

She shouted out, 'Drop your weapon.'

Whatever he was shouting was incomprehensible. His face was wide, his eyes staring. She recognized this demeanour and guessed it was drugs making him look so crazy and invincible. He was holding the knife in a clenched fist with the blade facing up. In an absurd instant, all that officer safety training came back to her and she remembered how ineffective she had always felt when practising fighting against someone holding a knife. They'd laughed about it!

She had minutes, seconds perhaps, before he stabbed her. She stepped behind a lamp post, trying to use it as cover, striving for determination. *Keep thinking. Keep fighting.* A stabbing she had attended: blood all over the road. He was close, and in the urban half-darkness she could see a black stain on the blade of the knife. The training came back to her like a prompt for the multiple choice exam. *Keep out of his fighting arc.* He lunged and she stepped back and swung her asp, missing him completely. She had lost the cover of the lamp post. There was nothing between her and the knife now.

He lunged again, swiping the blade upwards in a brutal sweep that moved through the midline of her body. But he had underestimated her speed and was momentarily off balance. She stepped diagonally forward, swinging her asp hard. Her voice escaped her in a grunt like a tennis player's at Wimbledon.

The impact of the blow jarred her hand. Brannon didn't drop the knife, but he bent over, shaking his wrist. She swung again, at his head, but even now she lacked the conviction for this brutality and he swerved easily away from it. He stood straight and stepped towards her, speaking quietly.

'You little cunt.'

She wanted to run, but he was too close and she didn't dare turn her back. She was deaf and blind to everything except him. She drew the asp back to strike again, but he darted forward, moving the blade from left to right, criss-crossing it in front of his body.

'Want some of this, cunt face?'

The stain of blood on the blade was clear now. She needed to hit him again: one good blow. She moved backwards and said, 'Please, don't.'

'Turned her against me, didn't you? You cunt. You little cunt.'

He lunged forward again. Lizzie, retreating quickly, missed her footing on the kerb behind her. She fell, backwards and out of control. There was a splash of sharp pain in her sacrum.

The ground: the worst place to be. He was standing over her, his feet either side of her hips. In that instant, he was strangely familiar – his round head and pale eyes – and suddenly she was in the grip of terror. She could see every stabbing she'd ever been to. She twisted, tried to get on her side to kick. The asp still drawn back in her right hand; her left hand fumbling for her gas under her armpit.

He leaned down. She twisted and sprayed her gas. She couldn't see anything. She lashed out blindly and felt the impact of her asp hitting hard. Her eyes were stinging and beginning to stream. There was an impact in her shoulder, like a punch. Headlights were spilling down the road. She hit out again but made no contact. A glorious blurred flood of blue lights and a deafening siren. She felt another pain, a hard thump in her forearm. He had turned and was running, the blurred soles of his shoes disappearing down the streaming road. Blood was falling on her face.

A paramedic with a wide face and beaded braids was crouching down, offering her gas and air. She took deep gulps. She could see more clearly now, but her nose was streaming from the CS. Her head was spinning. People were working on her, cutting her clothing. Torn dressing packs were discarded on the tarmac and she saw blood too, like a spill of ink. The thump of her pulse in her ears. A police officer had his hand on her shoulder. She clocked the holster on his hip. He leaned in to her: short grey hair, thin face.

'Do you know where he's cut you, love?'

But she was thinking suddenly of where Brannon might be running to.

'Marley,' she said.

The paramedic passed her the mask again. 'Take a deep inhale. We're going to lift you in a second.'

'Marley,' she repeated before she inhaled and lay back. They were fitting the scoop around her and raising her up. Above her, the beating blades of the police helicopter searching for Brannon.

11

As soon as she heard of the attack on the officer, Sarah drove to the hospital. She was directed to a ward on the sixth floor, and the nurse on the desk pointed her to a bay in a room containing four beds, each with the screens pulled round them. There had been a mix-up on the report. It wasn't the male DC she had expected but a female in her twenties, who was lying in the bed pale-faced, eyes closed. In that instant of stepping past the curtain, Sarah knew the sleeping face but couldn't for a moment place it. Then, glancing to her left, she recognized immediately the man sitting by the bed: Inspector Kieran Shaw, not in uniform. She looked back to the sleeping woman. PC Lizzie Griffiths, of course it was.

Shaw looked up. Recognizing Sarah too, he got up quietly and signalled for her to join him outside. Standing in the hushed recovery ward, with the nurses passing them on their many rounds, he talked at her in a hushed but furious voice.

'What the bloody hell were you thinking?'

'What do you mean?'

'Did you even do a risk assessment?'

His eyes were hard with contempt and she remembered how, when she was investigating him and Lizzie Griffiths, he had mocked her. She had executed a warrant on his home address and he had brought her out a cup of coffee and asked her what on earth they had taught her at 'detective school'. The man was a bully, among other things.

'I tasked it out to the borough and the intelligence bureau . . .'

Even as she spoke, she realized she was a fool to respond to him.

'Were you aware that the victim's mother had an injunction against the suspect? Did you even stop for one moment to consider whether you were putting your fellow officers at risk?' He raised his voice. 'You're bloody incompetent!'

A nurse, walking past, slowed her steps and looked at them, obviously concerned.

Sarah smiled apologetically. 'I'm sorry for any disturbance.'

Kieran said nothing. He didn't need to: his face perfectly expressed the contempt he felt.

The nurse's eyes flicked between the two of them. Then she moved on towards the further rooms.

Sarah said quietly, 'I know you're upset, but this isn't the time or place.'

'She could have died! You aren't fit to lead the response to serious incidents. I'm going to do everything I can to get you a misconduct finding for this!' He stopped suddenly and looked to his left. Lizzie, in a hospital gown and with bare feet, was standing in the doorway. Her arm and shoulder were bandaged.

'Lizzie,' Kieran said, immediately softened.

Lizzie blinked, turned to Sarah. 'Detective Sergeant Collins, isn't it?'

In spite of herself, Sarah smiled. It was hard to see in this pale, shaky young woman the officer she had so recently wanted to charge with misconduct. 'Yes, it is. Are you all right?'

Kieran interrupted. 'Leave her alone.' He moved towards Lizzie. 'Come on, let me get you back to bed.'

Lizzie took a step backwards. 'Wait.' She turned to Sarah. 'Have you got him yet?'

'Sorry, no.'

'I need to lie down again. But come and talk to me. I told them in the ambulance about someone who might assist him in evading police. Did that get through?'

Thankfully there was no time to stay and argue with Kieran Shaw. Lizzie's information needed acting on at once. Sarah stood on the hospital stairs and called up Lee. She waited while he put together an intelligence search on Marley, the young woman who Lizzie said had persuaded Georgina not to give evidence against Brannon. Lee called back within fifteen minutes. Lizzie's suspicions had been corroborated by historic reports to social services that showed, after a bit of digging, that Marley and Brannon were in fact cousins who had lived together as children.

It was a familiar horror story: a big family under a too-small roof, a succession of boyfriends and births, a chain of incidents before the family was finally dispersed by child protection orders. Marley and Brannon had been placed together in the same local authority care before being moved into separate foster homes.

Lee had an address for Marley. The team was putting an emergency response together: Sarah should make her way over to the rendezvous point.

She left the hospital, running down the stairs and through the corridors of people moving slowly under the hospital's fluorescent light. The RVP was very close – just a short blue-lights run through the congested clearway towards the outskirts of the city.

Sarah was the nearest and arrived at the petrol station first. She waited, parked up by the darkened car wash, watching the traffic streaming past, the drivers pulling in and filling their cars in the illuminated forecourt, then moving towards the cashier, lit up behind his pay window. Soon the firearm BMWs pulled in. There was a dog van too, with an Alsatian moving around in the back.

Then the homicide car, with Lee and Fedden. The officers stood in a loose circle, Fedden at the head, his feet planted solidly and widely on the tarmac. Lee kicked off, briefing on the intelligence.

'Marley herself doesn't seem much of a risk. Her own convictions are all for dishonesty offences rather than violence – she seems to be a bit of an expert in catalogue fraud. But her criminal credentials are top-notch – links to the Young family and an ex-boyfriend in the Tottenham Bloods.'

Fedden wound up the decision-making. They couldn't access the CCTV around Marley's flat because the council offices were shut. Basic surveillance of the building had yielded nothing. The lights were off, the curtains drawn. What they had was only slightly more than a hunch. Still, intelligence suggested there was no one closer to Brannon than Marley. Fedden had weighed the options and gone for rapid entry. They couldn't risk talking at the door if Brannon was inside, desperate and violent, with Skye and a knife.

'Better to ask for forgiveness than permission, boss,' Lee agreed, and Sarah noticed two of the firearms officers glance at each other with the hint of a smile at the cliché.

Lee spoke up again. 'After the entry, do you want me to handle talking to Marley?'

Fedden smiled. 'Thanks, but I think a female officer would be best. You grab some sleep and be back in early. Sarah will handle Marley. That's if you don't mind, Sarah?'

'Of course not.'

'OK, boss. I'll take a job car home, if that's all right?'

'Yeah, sure. Back for six a.m. if you can manage it.'

'No probs.'

Lee pulled out of the garage and headed west. Sarah grabbed her stab vest out of the boot of her car and pulled it on. Fedden was her passenger now and they drove into the estate after the firearms cars, stopping a few hundred yards away from the property and out of view. They waited, leaning into the shadow of a wall, for the firearms team to do their job.

Sarah wished she was better at making small talk.

Fedden said, 'He's a good lad, Lee.'

'Yep, he is.'

He expanded on it. It was a subject he was comfortable with. 'He wanted to stay but I had to send him home. We'll need fresh legs tomorrow.'

'That's right.'

'Still, I like that about him. Doesn't look at his watch. Doesn't want to know what time he's getting home.'

Sarah thought of Fat Elaine, who had no choice but to look at her watch and who had been home hours ago. She thought too of her own camp bed, hidden away in one of the storerooms in Hendon, and of Daisy with the dog walker.

They heard the bangs and shouting of the rapid entry. The update came quickly: the flat was secure. Only one occupant: Marley Davies. She'd been allowed to call her solicitor.

Sarah entered the flat with Fedden. Marley, wearing purple silk pyjamas, was sitting cross-legged on the floor, hunched over her smartphone, leaving an angry voicemail. 'Call me as soon as you get this!' Her slim brown feet were bare, with bracelets round one ankle and toe rings on both feet. Two uniformed constables – a small Asian woman and a hefty white bloke with a big beard – who'd been deployed as back-up by the borough to assist with securing the scene were hanging back, waiting in the doorway to the kitchen. Fedden nodded at the two officers and stood with them. 'Thanks for helping us out.' He wanted Sarah to lead the conversation with Marley so he could observe.

Sarah stood adjacent to the table, letting Marley finish her call. Looking around the room, she could see the proceeds of the catalogue fraud – a huge TV, a dryer, a washing machine, a juicer.

On the coffee table in front of her was an open Apple laptop, cigarettes and an ashtray, a can of Diet Coke, a white porcelain hand with lots of rings and necklaces on the long fingers. Marley closed the call, put the white Samsung on the table.

'Right then. Mark's not here, so you can all FUCK OFF. You'll get the complaint first thing.'

Sarah tried for a smile.

'Hi, I'm Sarah Collins. I'm a detective inspector on the murder team.' She gestured towards Fedden. 'Jim Fedden . . .'

Marley looked at her with the blankness of someone who hates police from the depths of her heart.

'The neighbours have seen all this! What are they going to think?'

'I'm sorry about that. But can I just talk to you for a moment?'

Marley drew her finger across the laptop's tracker pad and started typing with two fingers. Without looking away from the screen she muttered, 'I s'pose so.'

'Thank you. Has Mark been here?'

'No.'

Marley hadn't looked away from the computer. Sarah moved cautiously round behind her. On the screen was a photograph of the improvised shrine of flowers, teddy bears and candles that she had seen being built earlier outside Georgina and Mark's flat. Marley was scrolling down, reading the newspaper account of the investigation. The tips of the four fingers of her left hand were pressed against her mouth. She went back to her search. Tapped in *Skye Brannon*. A collection of images came up and Marley clicked on one of them. It was a bunch of school kids horsing around outside Wagamama. Skye's head had been ringed by the newspaper. *Frantic search for missing girl.* Marley swore quietly.

Sarah moved away.

'We'll check the estate CCTV in the morning. If he was here, we'll find out. You can see from the news reports that you don't want to lie.'

Marley stared at Sarah for a moment. She was clearly thinking it through. Then she said, 'Yes, OK, *whatever*! OK. He was here. He turned up with Skye and the dog. But I didn't know about . . . all that.'

'What did he tell you?'

'That they'd fallen out. He was going to stay somewhere else, just needed to leave Skye with me while he sorted something out.' She looked back at her laptop screen. 'I can't believe it. I don't believe he killed her.' She looked back at Sarah with some sort of desperate accusation in her eyes, as if it were she, not Brannon, who was responsible for what had happened.

Sarah said, 'He left you with Skye? What happened next?'

But Marley had turned back to her laptop, was clicking and staring.

'What are you looking at?'

'Georgie's Facebook page. Everyone's posting on there, saying how much they miss her.'

'You're shocked.'

'Of course I'm fucking shocked!'

In an instant, Marley had taken the computer and thrown it across the room. In the process she knocked over the can of Coke that was on the coffee table. Coke was spilling everywhere, fizzing on the floor. Fedden turned to one of the constables. 'Get a cloth.'

But Marley was already on her feet. 'No! Leave it to me. It's my flat.' She moved to push past the officers and Sarah saw the hand of the male officer go swiftly to his cuffs. She didn't blame him. She was wondering too whether it was safe to let Marley go into the kitchen, where there was a fancy wooden knife block with a set of black-handled knives.

The female officer stepped in front of Marley. 'Just tell me exactly what you want and where it is and I'll get it for you.'

'This is fucking ridiculous!' Marley looked at Sarah and then back at the officer. 'For fuck's sake. Top drawer. Tea towel.'

The officer passed a towel. Marley was speaking as she mopped up the Coke angrily. 'He was out about an hour. Came back, took them both away. I had no idea.'

'OK,' Sarah said. 'And how was Skye?'

'Fine. Didn't say much, watched TV. She did seem quiet, but Skye's always quiet.'

'No injuries?'

'Injuries? What do you fucking think? Of course there weren't injuries. If there were injuries I'd have fucking said something, wouldn't I?' She left the wet towel on the floor, lit a cigarette, inhaled, the smoke going into her eyes.

'Any idea where he might be? Who's he close to?'

'He didn't tell me nothing. Said he'd ring me in the morning when he'd got himself straight.'

'Did he have a car?'

Marley took a long, deep drag of her cigarette. 'I don't know. Expect so. How else did he get them all here?'

'What sort of car?'

'I don't know! I don't know what he drives. He's always changing cars.'

Marley put her cigarette in the ashtray. She clutched the fingers of her right hand tightly in her left as though in some sort of spasm. The smoke was curling up slowly from the table.

'I know this is difficult. I want you to think—'

'I am thinking!' Marley stood up, picked up her phone. 'I don't know what's happened. But he's not a monster. I'll try calling him for you.'

Sarah stepped over, reached out and put her hand over the keypad. 'Please don't do that.'

Marley snatched the phone away. 'What do you mean, don't?

It's my phone! It's my flat!' She clutched the phone in a tight fist. 'I know you lot. You'll kill him if you get the chance. I can get him to hand himself in.'

She looked at her phone again, relaxed, began to touch the screen and Sarah took hold of it with one swift movement. The female constable had moved forward just in case, but the speed of Sarah's action had surprised Marley. There was no tussle. Sarah was already producing an evidence bag from the pocket of her stab vest and popping the Samsung inside. The temperature in the room was going up.

'What the fuck. That's illegal . . .'

'I'm sorry. We might ask you to call Mark. But not right now.'

'That's fucking illegal. Give me my phone NOW.'

'It's not illegal. I'm lawfully on the premises and it may contain evidence of a crime. Let's try to work together on finding Skye.'

'Well, you're not lawfully on the premises any more because I'm telling you to FUCK OFF.'

Sarah glanced at Fedden to see how he wanted to handle it. She'd tried to keep it friendly, but they'd been asked to leave. They were exceeding their powers now, it was true. Fedden took over, turned to the male officer. 'Can you arrest Miss Davies, please, for assisting an offender.'

Marley spat at Sarah. It hit her jacket.

'You fucking PIGS!'

The male officer was ready. He moved in swiftly with the cuffs. He was a big bloke and Marley knew better than to fight him. She was shouting as Sarah and Fedden moved out of the flat.

'I want my phone! I need to call my solicitor!'

They stood outside. Fedden produced a tissue and passed it to Sarah to wipe her jacket. 'Bad skills, letting her get you.'

'You're right there.'

'You want her nicking for it?'

'Course not.'

Most of the lights were out in the flats, but one woman was looking down at them from her open window. The police dog was sitting patiently next to his handler while the firearms officers gathered up their kit. The sergeant handed out Cadbury's chocolate éclairs. Sarah accepted one; the sergeant told her to take two. She popped another in her pocket.

Fedden said, 'No option but to nick her. She admits he left Skye with her while he went out to try and kill the grandmother. We need to spin the flat, seize any phones, computers.'

'Do you want me to try to talk to her again? Try to persuade her to help us voluntarily. We could de-arrest. We might get more out of her.'

'No point. She's as mad as a bag of snakes. I can't see her giving anything up, and I don't trust a damn word she says. That girl can't lie straight in bed.' He glanced at his watch. 'What time were you on duty this morning?'

Briefly Sarah recalled her visit to Hatchett's in the morning. It felt a world away now. 'Eight.'

'Organize the search team and go home. It's stupid o'clock already, and by the time we've completed the search, downloaded the phone and booked her in, it'll be morning. I'll get Steve and Lee to interview her first thing. Can you drop me at Hendon?'

12

It had been an anxious time but now he had entered that gap in the night, the one he could move through freely. Sleep was at its most profound. All the curtains were drawn on the little Victorian terrace. No lights were on in the windows. Brannon imagined the people lying open-mouthed on their backs or curled on their sides. The couples flung away from each other across their double beds. The babies in their cots with their bottoms in the air. The old people, solitary and smelling stale. He had stood and watched them countless times, savouring their insensibility to his presence.

He moved quickly onto the road that ran adjacent to the park. There was no moon, but the street lamps were bright so he had no cover of darkness. Still, the only seriously bad luck he could have would be a patrol car passing by chance – a lone man in a hoody at this time of night would be sure to arouse interest. But this wasn't central London. He was pretty sure he wouldn't be disturbed. There was still the question of Skye and Candy, whom he had left in the boot of the locked car down the side street a few yards away from the park. He'd had to do that once before, when he'd used the payphone at the railway station and even though he'd been quick Skye had hated it. The gates were Victorian, perhaps eighteen foot high, cast iron with gilded decorative spikes. To anyone who didn't know better, they would look intimidating, but the fact was that getting into the park was going to be a cinch. The great thing – the joke, in fact – was that the railings were less than two thirds the height of the gate and easily scalable. Fancy gate: shit railings. How many times had he seen that?

He worked the route out swiftly as he walked, head down, hands in pockets, a man on his way home, surely. The bottom rail with the decorative frieze at the bottom would be good for a foothold. Then, helpfully, a metal bracket supporting the notice giving the park's opening times. Another, matching decorative frieze at the top. The knack was to get over smoothly with the minimum of effort. He didn't look over his shoulder as he moved decisively in flowing movements: right foot on the bottom rail, right hand on the bracket, left foot swinging up to the bracket, right hand on the upper frieze, a precarious moment with both feet on the top bracket before he was able to swing a foot over. He dropped down into the park and began to run. He hadn't even winded himself.

It was darker in here, and there was the usual burst of euphoria. He was a hunter, better in the night. He'd always liked locked, deserted parks: the empty paths, the dark, silent ponds. The wooden fence was easy enough to scramble over, and he ran through the small back garden. The lights were out. He had the knife in the back of his waistband. He had taken Skye's nylon hairbrush with him and had a couple of bump keys in his inside pocket. The door to the garden had a single Yale-type lock. He slid a key in and gave it a light tap with the hairbrush. It didn't work the first time, but the second time he got the tap and the rotation just right. He felt the sweet movement of the pins inside the barrel, the synchronicity of his quick push against the door.

He stepped into the sitting room and breathed in the silence of the flat, trying to sense if there was someone here. Then he padded out of the darkened room into the hallway. There was just one bedroom, the door slightly ajar. He leaned round the threshold. The double bed was unmade but empty. White sheets. An unlikely detail: a teddy. Who'd have thought that of her? It was an old one, with hard grey fur and a missing bead of an eye. Anyway, he wasn't having that. He picked it up. Down the corridor on the left was the bathroom. He liked this: the intimacy of the home claimed by him. He'd never been one of those who trembled, who feared they'd shit themselves, who fucked up, cut themselves on glass or forgot to wear gloves. He'd always been in his element in the night in a house that wasn't his. He wanted to dominate the place, to explore, to rifle through the belongings, but that would be the work of an amateur. Besides, there would be time to look later on.

Still holding the teddy, he slipped the lock on the front door and glanced briefly out into the street. Lizzie's car was parked up, dark and lifeless. He closed the door, leaving it unlocked but holding it in place with a few of the shoes that had been lying in the hallway. He slipped through the flat, popped the teddy in the kitchen bin, shoving it down to the bottom. He washed his hands, dried them on her tea towel. Then he went back out into the garden. He could feel the time shifting. People would begin waking. Lights would go on. Doors would open. Within minutes he was back at his car and lifting Skye into the passenger seat. She had fallen asleep and was rubbing her eyes.

'I'm sorry to do that to you, darling, but I can't take any risks. You understand that, don't you, sweetheart? We'll be somewhere nice and comfy in a minute. I'll let you sleep with Candy if you want.'

13

Thursday 17 July 2014

Sarah let the hot water rain down on her head. It had been almost three when she got home. She could have slept in the office but had wanted to take the opportunity to sleep in her own bed. She wouldn't see Daisy for days. The dog probably thought Mrs Edwards was her owner. She did the necessaries – teeth, make-up, quick coffee – and was back on the road within twenty minutes, heading into Hendon by 7.30.

The office was buzzing, full of detectives. Everyone was busy, reviewing and coordinating the search for Skye. If people talked, it was quietly. Most were smartly dressed – murder detectives, the public face of the Met – but there was also a smaller number of back-room boys and covert types, mostly in jeans. Lee had obviously fancied himself as one of those today. Instead of a suit he was wearing a faded Los Pollos Hermanos T-shirt and jeans, a covert harness round his shoulders.

'You off out?' she asked.

'No, just got back actually.'

'You've been interviewing Marley with Steve?'

'Yes. He's fucking good!'

'He is.' Sarah looked at Lee and did a fake wince. 'Wear the wrong clothes into work, did you?'

He grinned. 'I did, yes. Thought it'd be warrants! Do you think the boss will mind?'

'He'll be fine, I expect.' She smiled. 'So. Marley give us anything?'

'Nothing. We got a prepared statement – Brannon was at her home but she had no idea he was wanted by police. Then she went no comment. Wouldn't give us a thing, not even off the record. Boss has bailed her and stuck some surveillance on her. He's given the phone back – he's hoping Brannon will call her.'

There was an awkward pause. For all their efforts at friendliness, they had reached the end of work talk. Lee said, 'You fancy breakfast?'

The offer made Sarah smile. He'd probably got a favourite greasy spoon lined up with the blokes. She was probably the last person he wanted along. It was good of him to invite her and she glimpsed something of what Fedden liked so much about him. He was one of the boys: cocky perhaps but not a bearer of grudges.

'Thanks, but I can't. Just got in. Got to catch up.'

She walked along the corridor. She wished she'd been better with Marley last night. Still, if Steve hadn't been able to get anything out of her either . . . The door to Fedden's office was shut, but through the glass pane she could see he was talking to Steve right now. She tapped and Fedden nodded.

As she opened the door he said, 'I'm busy right now, Sarah, but come and find me in about thirty minutes. I'll give you a dropped call when I'm ready for you. The identification of the body's scheduled for a couple of hours – can you supervise that?'

'Of course.'

She walked the few paces back to her office. Brannon was linked to the Young family. Steve handled informants, among other things, and he was probably trying to get people to talk to police. Conversations about that dark art would always be need-to-know only.

Her desk was piled with reports, her inbox full of updates. Some of the team had stayed on and worked the murder through the night. There was already an operation name: Woodhall. Thank God she'd bought that coffee machine.

An email from Elaine, which she scanned quickly, gave an update about the Egremont job. She'd got Stephenson's old address from the school and located the landlord through the land registry – not a bad bit of work. The landlord remembered Stephenson well, apparently, because he'd been an exceptionally pain-in-the-arse tenant. Always moaning, never happy, always wanting something – new windows, a better kitchen, a reserved space for his car on the road, for goodness' sake. One thing had just about summed him up: when he'd moved out, the landlord discovered that, without asking permission, he'd removed the carpet throughout the property and had the floorboards polished. It had been an expensive carpet, too – Axminster, pale green with flowers. The landlord had deducted the cost from the deposit. Stephenson hadn't been happy but he hadn't had a leg to stand on! Elaine made no further comment, but the suggestion that this might be a bit interesting was implicit, and Sarah agreed. Still, she thought, sending Elaine a quick thanks, by itself it was nothing.

Now wasn't the time to be thinking about Egremont. She slugged back her coffee and turned her attention to Brannon.

The team had produced an initial CCTV trawl and she glanced through it. Stills from Brannon's estate showed him leaving with Skye and the dog after the murder. Brannon was caught in profile: a short man with a round shaved head, dressed in dark Converse high-tops, dark jeans, a military-style khaki jacket. On his back a small duffel, at his hip a soft brown shoulder bag. Skye was on his left, her hand gripped tightly: blonde hair in two French plaits, ivory puffa jacket with a fur hood, lime-green pedal pushers, glitter pumps. The dog trotted along beside them, the lead in Brannon's right hand, a blue plaster cast on its front right leg.

The images were great – the clothing so distinctive, the combination of man, dog and child so specific. But they weren't fixed. Brannon might not be seen out with the child or the dog again. Remove Skye and the dog and he was much less recognizable. There would be changes of clothing in the bags too. Still, soon his face would be everywhere. Someone would spot him, surely.

She was studying the download of Georgina's phone when her own phone buzzed with a single ring. She walked back along the corridor to Fedden's office.

He was concentrating, head down, tie off, glasses on, scanning through papers. He had a pile of paper napkins on his desk and the carpet was littered with discarded balls of them.

'Yes, come in, shut the door.'

He took his glasses off and placed them on the desk. He wiped his forehead with one of the paper napkins, balled it up and threw it onto the floor. He looked at Sarah, a flicker of exasperation crossing his face.

'I got a call early this morning from Inspector Kieran Shaw. He wasn't happy about you sending officers to Georgina's mother's address without doing a proper risk assessment. He said you put them in danger.'

There was a pause.

Sarah said, 'May I sit?'

'Of course you can. Why do you ask? This isn't training school!'

Fedden moved his hand across his face and Sarah wondered how much sleep he'd had.

She sat. This wasn't the time for an explanation as to exactly why Shaw might be so keen to complain about her. Still, she remembered well enough waiting in her car outside his house in Sussex to execute the warrant on his home. His wife had been moving around inside; had stood briefly at the window and looked at her. The wife was willowy, with long dark hair. When Shaw had arrived home in his Land Rover, the daughter had run out to greet him in bare feet. He'd scooped her up in his arms and taken her inside. An idyllic little snapshot undermined only by the fact that Shaw was sleeping with Lizzie Griffiths. A few minutes later, Shaw had come out and taunted her about the pointlessness of searching his house. *If I had something, it would be gone by now.* He'd given her a cup of coffee and told her to leave the empty cup by the car. But behind the taunting had been real anger. Of course he'd objected to her searching his home, taking the investigation right into his family, risking perhaps his marriage if his relationship with Lizzie Griffiths were to be revealed. He'd be thrilled now at the possibility of turning the tables on her. She didn't underestimate either what a formidable enemy he could be. She remembered how he'd faced her down on everything she'd asked him.

'I want the basics,' Fedden said. 'Why did you task the borough to inform the next of kin, rather than us?'

'It was a judgement call. Because of the missing child and the public nature of the scene, I thought the investigation was likely to break very quickly onto social media and into the London press. I didn't want them getting to the next of kin before we did so I decided to request local CID to deliver the death message.'

Fedden nodded but he still looked irritated. 'OK, that sounds reasonable.'

'Thank you.' It wasn't over yet, she knew that. She went on, speaking precisely. 'I tasked the local borough and the intelligence bureau to conduct a risk assessment on the address and its occupants. That's in my decision log and there's a radio transmission that will confirm it. I'll email you the reference.'

He waved his hands as though she were making a fuss about nothing. 'Not necessary.' But she wasn't taken in. She was going to be really clear that there was no substance to Shaw's complaint.

'It's no trouble at all. The reference will be in my notes. I checked it out last night before I went off duty. It turns out the injunction against Brannon attending the property hadn't been entered onto

180

the Police National Computer. They missed the risk unfortunately, but it's not down to me.'

The DCI tapped the desk with his pen a couple of times. 'Good. That's us out of the shit then.' He smiled, but it didn't reach his eyes. 'There's no formal complaint anyway.' He still didn't look happy. He put his hands flat on the desk. 'One other thing and then we'll get down to business. I'm sorry to have to raise this, but there was no opportunity last night . . .'

Sarah felt an involuntary tension creeping into her face. 'OK.'

'Why weren't you back in the office yesterday for the start of your on-call?'

She thought for a moment before answering. Probably best not to back down.

'I had a lead on Operation Egremont and it took longer than I thought it would. But I drove to the scene direct. I wasn't any later than the others.'

Fedden tipped his chin upwards and his eyes searched the ceiling for a second. With his wide, sweaty body, his spread legs and his little hands resting flat on the desk, he looked very much like a clever frog. But it was also a bad-tempered frog she was looking at.

'Sarah . . .'

'It won't happen again.'

He smiled, obviously struggling to master his ill-humour.

'We may be getting somewhere with Egremont. I'm pleased you've taken it on. Word on the street is, if anyone can get anywhere with it, it's you.'

She was getting impatient too. She hadn't had much sleep either and she wasn't in primary school any more. It was time for the bollocking to end now, surely. 'Thank you.'

'You're like me. You want results.'

Like me. As a compliment, it was revealing. Anyway, she wasn't like him: that was surely clear to both of them.

'But I don't want you to forget what I said about me being the captain of the ship.'

She tried for a smile and for blokey reassurance, but she guessed that her body language was as unconvincing as his. 'It's OK, I'm hearing you. Bang out of order. It won't happen again.'

'Thank you. I didn't think I'd have to spell it out.' He nodded, but there was no warmth. She remembered last night – they had worked well together. But this morning it was as if once again he couldn't decide whether she was a good thing or not. 'Good. OK, so: Operation Woodhall. We'll have a scrum-down after the identification of Georgina's body – I want to get everyone together in the office, share information. Can you get straight back here?'

'Of course.' She moved to stand. 'Who's family liaison for Julie?'

'Oh blast, yes, I knew there was something else I needed to tell you.'

14

Eyes, lips, hands – the same act, and yet. An ache when she moved, a stiff neck. A pain in her forearm where she'd been stabbed, and in her shoulder. A grazing to the palm of her hand. They had to move carefully and in their caution she found something different. She felt his skin, the taste of him. It was almost embarrassing to be so alive to him: to the moment when he entered her. Then, as if he was overcome by the act, it was over in a sudden rush. He kissed her and smiled and said 'sorry'. She almost felt sorry too for his care for her, for his unexpected vulnerability, frightened by where this was going. He moved his hand down to touch her.

She awoke to hear the shower running. She leaned stiffly over to the bedside table and took two of the painkillers they had given her.

Kieran came into the bedroom and started dressing.

'I hope you're going to make a formal complaint about that Collins woman.' He rummaged through his drawers for clothing.

'I don't know.'

He was pulling on his jeans. 'What do you mean, you don't know? The boot's on the other foot now.'

She pulled the duvet up around her shoulders. 'Don't bother me with this stuff right now.'

He fastened the belt on his jeans. 'OK. We'll leave it for now.' He moved over and kissed her on the cheek. 'You can stay here today if you like.'

'No, I'm going in.'

'Are you mad?'

'Oh fuck off, Kieran.'

She rolled away from him and pulled the duvet over her head. She closed her eyes and drifted off. Then the sounds and smells of cooking. Toast, bacon, coffee. He put his head round the door.

'Breakfast if you want it. You've made the London papers, by the way. The Met's not released your name, but you should call your mum just in case.'

Lizzie lay back, thinking of Georgina, struggling to believe she was dead. She saw her leaving the court with her little family. Brannon scooping little Skye up into his arms, squeezing her tightly. Lizzie didn't understand, Georgina had said. She didn't know how loving Mark could be. *He's only like that when he's drunk.* There, in the court's foyer, Lizzie had witnessed that loving Brannon. He had placed little Skye on the floor and poked her in the stomach and Skye had protested, squirming with pleasure at her dad's teasing. '*Dad!*' But Georgina, in her memory at least, did not seem so happy. She had avoided Lizzie's gaze.

Kieran was shouting something to her. She caught it halfway through.

'. . . iron a shirt for you?'

Lizzie picked up her fractured iPhone, which was lying by the side of the bed. She'd broken the screen when she'd dropped it in the street. She pulled on a T-shirt and pants and walked barefoot through to the little corner that constituted a kitchen. A cup of coffee and toast waited for her on the table. Kieran had his back to her, putting the breakfast onto plates.

'Do you want me to iron a shirt – if you're going in, that is?'

Lizzie glanced at her overnight bag on the sofa. Kieran had picked it up from the nick on the way back from the hospital. There were a couple of shirts in there, some trousers, changes of underwear. Her make-up. She'd got into a routine, she realized.

'If you don't mind . . .'

'It's not the ironing I mind.'

Lizzie sat at the table and bit into a slice of toast. Kieran plonked a plate of scrambled eggs and big juicy field mushrooms in front of her. He sat opposite. His own plate was piled with bacon, mushrooms, tomatoes, eggs.

'You're crazy if you go in. You're not fit for duty.'

Lizzie forked a mushroom onto her toast. 'This is delicious. Thank you.'

'What on earth were you thinking last night? You're too experienced to take such risks.'

She slurped her coffee and rolled her eyes. 'Mmmm. Yummy.'

'Seriously. You're a bloody idiot, Lizzie.'

She shrugged. He persisted. 'I want to know what you were thinking. Running after a madman with a knife.'

Lizzie flicked through her phone. She had a text from Ash.

Good morning, crazy person. Are you fit for duty? I'm thinking that's a no? Just text me.

She texted back. *There in an hour or so.*

Kieran said, 'I'm way too old to have to wait for you to stop looking at your phone.'

Her phone buzzed again but Lizzie put it down.

Kieran said, 'Well?'

She looked at him, now a bit irritated. 'I didn't think it would be dangerous.'

Kieran laughed and smiled widely in disbelief. 'Really?

'The victim's mother was there. I couldn't just let him make off.'

'Why not? They always come again.'

She remembered Brannon banging on the door and the look in Julie's eyes.

Kieran spooned egg onto his toast and took a generous bite. He spoke with his mouth full. 'Was it the child?' He looked at her, and twisted his mouth to the left as if considering her state of mind. 'Because it wasn't worth taking that risk, not even for a child. Look at how it turned out. You didn't make any difference.'

She wouldn't be drawn, whatever he said. The painkillers had kicked in and she was feeling a bit better. She wouldn't get sucked into this.

She glanced at her phone. Ash again.

If you are coming in then a) you are mad and b) big enchilada wants to see you so wear something sexy.

Lizzie smiled and texted back: 😊.

'Lizzie, are you going to answer me?'

His voice was insistent. She snapped.

'Oh Kieran, can't you just leave me alone!'

She put her phone down, rested her forehead in her hands for a moment before she resumed eating her breakfast. The phone buzzed with a reply from Ash. She picked it up, glanced at it.

Love you too.

She sent an *x*, put the phone down, kept eating.

Kieran put his cutlery down.

'I'm sorry. That phone call last night saying you'd been hurt was awful.'

She pronged another mushroom, slipped it into her mouth. Kieran persisted.

'It was crazy what you did. I need to know you won't do anything like it again.' When she didn't reply he said, 'Was it to do with Hadley?'

She shook her head, swilled her coffee.

'Tell me you weren't trying to make up for past mistakes. That's what worries me.'

She didn't reply.

'Because you don't have to. You didn't make any mistakes. Those deaths were not your fault.'

She pushed her plate away. 'It was nothing to do with that.'

She started clearing the table, putting stuff in the dishwasher. He got up, stood behind her and put his arms around her chest. He kissed her neck. She shrugged him off and went back to clearing the table.

He said, 'Leave it. I'll do it.'

She turned to go to the bathroom, paused, then said lightly, 'I just like playing tag. There was no more to it than that. I've always liked playing tag.'

Lizzie had managed to fit the dressing on her arm under the shirt Kieran had ironed for her. Still, word had clearly spread about her fight with Brannon, and when she entered the office there was a ripple of applause and laughter. She went to sit opposite Ash, but he stopped her.

'Don't worry about logging on. Just go straight up and see King Kong on the third floor.'

She smiled. 'Thanks.'

'Don't thank me. I'm grumpy as fuck. Who the hell am I supposed to give today's crime reports to?'

She opened the bottom drawer of her pod and took out a pair of court shoes.

Ash smiled. 'Glad to see you're following my advice about looking sexy.'

Lizzie held them up sceptically. 'Sexy?' She slipped them on. 'I need to make a quick call. Do you think I can use the boss's office?'

'I wouldn't. She's about. You might end up having to talk to her.' He gestured towards a large walk-in storeroom at the end of the room. 'I find that's useful. If you go through the coats at the back, you might find Narnia.'

The storeroom was full of filing cabinets, plastic crates stuffed with assorted evidence bags and discarded Met vests. There was also a folding bicycle and, for some reason, a child's car seat.

Lizzie called her sister, Natalie.

'Hi, Natty, it's Lizzie. How are the kids?'

Natalie recounted the usual stuff. Seb had fallen off a swing. Her husband was working too hard. They'd got cheap flights to Barcelona and she'd found a fantastic villa on a hill, with its own pool. Not too expensive because it was last minute. Lizzie checked her watch, giving her sister five uninterrupted minutes.

'Yeah, uh, Natty. I called because I just wondered if you could ring Mum for me. Only there was this thing last night and I don't want her to get it from the papers. If you speak to her first, it might be the best thing. It's not a big deal.'

The borough commander, Detective Chief Superintendent Trask, had a large office on the top floor. It was hushed up there and the carpet was actually clean. His assistant's office was on one side, and there was a small waiting area with various frames on the wall: a hand-painted Hebrew inscription from a local synagogue, a picture of some officers in front of a bouncy castle, a shield from somewhere or other. The commander's door was propped open and he called her in immediately.

'Come in, Lizzie, come in.'

'Sir.'

As she entered, he stood up, and Lizzie could see why Ash had called him King Kong. He was indeed a silverback – probably six foot four, broad across the chest, with a big reach. Even now, approaching retirement, he would still be a daunting prospect in a fight. He wore a baggy suit with broad chalk pinstripes.

Behind him on the wall was a picture of his family: a tall son and a daughter both in academic gowns. A glass cabinet held mementoes from foreign police forces, framed commendations, news articles and photos of the various teams he had worked with. On the desk was a police radio and a Flying Squad mug.

'Take a seat.'

'Thank you.'

'Don't look so nervous. I don't bite.'

He sat too and spread his hands out on the desk. They were big hands. He looked at her, and in that look he conveyed effectively his working persona: lots of proper service, lots of difficult jobs, keeps himself tidy, won't take any shit. *You want to work for me*.

'Wondering why you're in here?'

She avoided the question. 'Sir?'

'Brannon.'

'Yes, sir.'

'Do you think you hurt him?'

'May have done. I hit him pretty hard.'

There was a pause. Then Trask smiled broadly, almost laughed. 'Bloody well done then.'

Lizzie found herself pulling a funny face – both frowning and smiling in spite of herself.

'Thank you, sir.'

Another pause. The borough commander tilted his head slightly to the left. It gave him an air that belied his tough-guy look. Evidently he was a clever gorilla too.

'When I say well done, do you understand what I mean?'

'I think so, sir.'

'I mean well done for trying to ensure Brannon was lawfully detained and well done for defending yourself effectively and proportionately.'

'Of course, sir. That is what I understood.'

He considered her response with the hint of a smile at the edges of his eyes. Then the smile broadened into a grin. He clearly couldn't stop himself. 'And if you broke his wrist too, then that's just a bonus.'

In spite of herself, Lizzie laughed. He laughed too.

'In the good old days,' he said, leaning back and spreading his arms wide, 'I would have offered you a drink. Not possible now, of course.'

He got up and held his hand out over the desk. It was warm and reassuring and he clamped a second hand over the first, fastening her small hand in his strong grip.

'Very brave, Lizzie.'

'Thank you, sir.'

'You OK? The stitches, all that? Fit for duty?'

'Yes, sir.'

He nodded. 'Good. Old school. I like that.'

She shrugged. 'Don't know about that.'

They both sat down again.

'OK,' he said, not entirely succeeding in calming his physical presence into a man-behind-the desk style. 'We need to cover the practical stuff. I've looked over the crime report for Brannon and it's clear you did everything you could. There's always a review for a domestic murder but I can't see any issues with your conduct. I'm old school too. You can expect me to back you all the way. As for last night – the self-defence is clear-cut. However, you never know nowadays. Some bastard in a wig might still choose to come after you. Any questions, I want you to come and see me personally. Don't be shy.' He scribbled something on a piece of paper. 'That's my mobile.'

'Thank you.'

'Day or night.'

'Yes, sir. Thank you.'

'The MIT team will need your evidence for court, but that's a long way off.'

'Of course.' She began to stand.

'Just one other thing.'

'Yes, sir.'

He waited. She sat again.

'Georgina Teel's mum, Julie? She's very grateful. Says she feels she can trust you after what you did. Wants you to help her through this – identifying the bodies, that kind of thing. The DCI over there is keen to have you on board but I'm not sure about it. I want you to be honest. Do you think you can handle it? It'll be a push. They're doing the identification in about an hour.'

15

S arah put the papers she was reading back down on her desk. It was drizzling onto the parade square outside her office window. She pulled on her jacket, slipped down the stairs. In the shelter of the building she lit a cigarette and watched the new recruits marching in the rain. They would be some of the last to tread this ground.

The covered walkways that meandered around the parade ground as if it were a college campus, the cold, echoey gym where Sarah had run the bleep test and revised handcuffing more times than she could remember, the glass-faced canteen where squads gathered on operations: in a year all this would be gone, demolished and replaced by a more compact vision of policing London's eight million inhabitants.

The rain petered out. She stubbed out her cigarette and started to walk the length of the site, the disused skid pan and then the playing fields on her right.

She needed to clear her head before the next-of-kin identification. She couldn't believe that Lizzie was going to act as family liaison.

Fedden had explained it to her in his office.

'Yes, the local officer who tried to arrest Brannon. The family was very impressed by her, as am I, by the way. Her commander's asking her this morning. I can't imagine she'll say no.' He'd looked down at his notes. 'PC Lizzie Griffiths. She's just a training detective with about five minutes' service in total.'

Sarah had involuntarily closed her eyes. Fedden was still speaking.

'Very brave, very brave indeed. The mum was very impressed—'

Sarah had interrupted. 'Jim.'

He'd frowned. 'Yes?'

'Lizzie Griffiths. She's the officer I investigated. The deaths at Portland Tower?'

'Shit.'

He'd paused, rubbing index finger and thumb together while he thought it through.

'Well, I can't see it's a problem really. She was cleared of misconduct. There are no issues. You both need to be professional.'

Be professional. Had she detected there the suggestion that maybe she wasn't? Or was that paranoia? Lately she hadn't been able to tell when it was and when it wasn't. Of course Fedden hadn't wanted to delve into the problem any deeper than that, didn't want to put two and two together about Kieran Shaw's complaint. He did, after all, have more pressing things on his plate. For her part she hadn't felt able to say that, apart from anything else, it was simply personally difficult for her to work with Lizzie Griffiths. It would look weak, she believed, to say she couldn't hack it. She hadn't even begun to prove herself to Detective Chief Inspector Fedden.

Ahead, the grey student tower blocks loomed into an overcast sky. She remembered the narrow bed, the thin mattress, the window overlooking the tube line. Soon the blocks would be gone too, demolished in a cloud of dust and brick. She could see the proposed future flats in her imagination – the architect's drawings of trees, of happy figures standing in atriums, a development that could be lifted and placed in any modern city. The Met was contracting, adapting, selling off the silverware, packaging up its relics like the standards of extinct regiments now hanging unloved in alien mess halls. She was surprised how it saddened her.

She turned her thoughts towards the evidence.

At 1100 hours Georgina had sent her mother a WhatsApp: *Mark in one of his moods.*

More WhatsApps had followed. Brannon was asking her about the statement she had given to police, niggling at her. *Did you want me banged up?* About an hour later there were a couple of missed calls to her mother, then another chain of WhatsApps.

Please call me Mum.

He's gone out. Probably drinking.

Can you call me?

I'm going to come over with Skye. Call me if you get this.

Julie hadn't picked up the messages because her Wi-Fi was down and she didn't have any data left on her monthly contract. If she had, maybe she would have gone over. Maybe things would have been different. Maybe not.

A CCTV trawl showed that during this time Brannon had visited the local off-licence. He bought two 70 cl bottles of Johnny Walker blended whisky. Cameras showed him drinking in the shopping precinct. An empty bottle of Johnny Walker had been recovered from one of the bins and been sent to the lab for DNA analysis and fingerprinting.

At 1257 hours he returned to the estate.

Another empty bottle of Johnny Walker had been found inside his and Georgina's flat. There was also a case by the sofa, full of Georgina's clothes.

Sarah thought through how it might have happened.

He returns home. He sees the packed case in the living room. Georgina perhaps is in Skye's room packing her bag.

Leaving: the most dangerous thing a victim of domestic violence could do. She could see how his solicitor might try for a lesser finding of manslaughter: Brannon had come home blind drunk, seen the packed cases and lashed out. He'd been so inebriated he hadn't even been capable of forming the specific intent to seriously harm necessary for a murder charge.

But it hadn't been like that. Sarah didn't believe the murder had happened immediately. There was that second bottle of whisky, on the floor by Georgina's body. On the table an empty glass.

Drunkenness wasn't such a simple indicator, either in law or in reality. There was the defence option, of course: my client was drunk, not in control of himself. It was manslaughter, not murder. But there was another possibility, the one she favoured.

She had read through Lizzie Griffith's account of the last failed charge against Brannon. It had been a detailed narrative and would support a prosecution suggestion that Brannon had known perfectly well what he was doing. Georgina had told Griffiths, 'He's only like that when he's drunk.' She'd said he had promised to stop drinking if she let him come back. And then there was the phrase recorded by Lizzie Griffiths after she'd sat next to him on the bench while they waited for the custody sergeant to become available: 'I'm a bit of a cunt when I've had a drink.'

Brannon hadn't murdered because he'd been drunk but rather the reverse: he had got himself knowingly, purposefully drunk. He had stood on that concourse drinking steadily, working himself up into an inebriated rage that he knew perfectly well would be satisfied only by violence. And then, after he'd drunk that entire bottle of Johnny Walker outside the shops, standing alone in a developing torment of jealousy and rage, he'd directed his steps back to the flat, able to do whatever he needed to do.

So here he was in the flat, sitting at the table, still drinking – that empty glass – asking Georgina about the bags, telling her what a bitch she was for giving a statement against him. Georgina knew the danger too. Why hadn't she left then? There was the tray of coloured rubber bands on the table too, and an opened child's yoghurt. Sarah had checked the protection reports on Skye written by officers over the years. Georgina was meticulously tidy, they all said that. The flat was spotless. If Skye had finished eating Georgina wouldn't have left a half-opened yoghurt on the table or a dirty spoon on the table. This was a meal that had never been finished, never tidied away. Had he pulled Skye to the table? Insisted she sit? *Fucking sit down, Skye. Get her something to eat!* Or was Skye crying by her unfinished yoghurt and Georgina fetched the coloured rubber bands to distract her?

It was at the very least believable that he'd made Skye sit with him while he continued to drink. And if Skye had been sitting there with him, a hostage to his sudden violence, Georgina wouldn't dare do anything, certainly not leave, make a call. Had he had the knife there already? On the table or in his jacket?

Sarah had arrived at the steps leading up to the old classroom block. In front of the white concrete entrance was a little platform on which was mounted a statue of Robert Peel. A nineteenth-century bronze, it was out of place beside the sixties building. There Peel stood, indifferent to the changes around him, patrician and debonair at the top of his plinth; buttoned waistcoat, scroll in one hand, the other hand lightly resting on his hip, verdigris spilling down the folds of his jacket. Apparently when they demolished the classrooms the plan was to package him in bubble wrap and move him elsewhere.

She turned her back on the statue and looked out over the playing fields, remembered her intake kicking a ball about out there, swearing at each other, falling over and laughing with no idea what awaited them out on the streets of London.

She pictured the scene again.

The violence had taken place in the sitting room. She hoped against all the evidence that Skye hadn't seen it, that she'd been shut in her room, but the yoghurt pot on the table suggested something else. The pathologist's early report from the scene showed Georgina with three punching stab wounds to the chest. The blood that soaked her T-shirt had been from these rather than the bleed to the carotid artery, which was subsequent to the chest wounds. It wouldn't have been quick. Before the arterial bleed there'd been a fight. Sarah knew about domestic murders, the unbelievable violence, the savage cruelty and rage.

She saw it. Skye sitting at the table. The dog cowering or barking. Georgina fighting – the punch to the face, the bruising to the arms. Then stabbed in the chest, one, two, three. Falling, perhaps. The slash to the neck that had punctured rather than severed the artery. Georgina on her back, bleeding out in minutes.

It was nearly three quarters of an hour after his return home that CCTV captured Brannon leaving with Skye. There had been a dark time inside that flat.

Brannon, drunk on whisky, soaked in blood, had washed. He'd changed his clothes, profited from the bag Georgina had packed for Skye and put his own clothes in another. Where had Skye been while he did this? How had he controlled her? Sarah saw only the CCTV of them walking away from the flat: Skye in her puffa jacket with her father and the dog. The image had been almost a parody of a family leaving for their holiday.

Sarah bent over her knees. She had had a vision of such cruelty, such a need to control. She'd watched those documentaries where men in suits explained ponderously as to the why. As though they knew! Sarah had seen the bodies on the slabs, the skulls with blunt trauma, the ligature marks. The act always drowned out any explanation. She knew why already and also would never know why.

She stood up and breathed in the moist air, looked across the empty playing fields.

The law, thankfully, was simpler, more binary than such contemplation. The moment they could show that Brannon had chosen this horror, he would be guilty of murder. Acting on your very worst impulse was no defence. She imagined the case files, the disclosure sheets, the numbered exhibits that would coldly detail Brannon's intention, unpicking any defence he might claim. Before the law there would be no excuse. A mandatory life sentence was all the police could offer Georgina's family and friends.

But first they had to find Skye. To do that she would be cleverer than her feelings. She would think herself into Brannon, see the world from his fragile, dissonant, furious point of view.

She began to walk the loop again, the playing fields now on her right, the blue Tardis police box, the tube line with its commuters running past parallel on the left.

Back in the office, she glanced quickly through the new statements that had arrived on her desk. There was one from Skye's friend Irit who had discovered Georgina's body. Irit had been playing hopscotch with Skye earlier that morning on the walkway and she'd wanted to play again. After lots of impatient knocks at the door, she'd climbed onto Skye's bicycle and looked through the window. She'd run straight home.

Mum, Mum, Mum. Georgie's lying on the floor.

Sarah scribbled her thinking in her notebook.

Operation Woodhall. Evidence of degree of premeditation and planning:
1. Drinking.
2. Timeline: 40 minutes at the flat. Protracted scene before Georgina is killed? Takes time to change, etc.
3. CCTV: Brannon leaves in different clothing to that he wore on entering. Carries bags. Takes Skye and dog. Intention to avoid arrest.
4. Discovery of body: earlier than Brannon planned? Did not know Skye had arranged to play with her friend Irit. Believed perhaps he had until the following day before the murder

was discovered. Irit's desperation to see her best friend meant things didn't go to plan.

She put her pen down and lifted the photocopy of Lizzie Griffiths' statement from the bundle. One of the homicide DCs had interviewed her at the hospital last night. She skim-read down to the part where Brannon arrived.

The first knock at the door was polite. Brannon spoke quietly. He said, 'Julie, are you in there? We need to talk.' It was only when no one replied to him that he began to bang on the door.

She marked the paragraph with a red asterisk and made another note.

5. Evidence of intention to surprise Julie Teel before she became aware of her daughter's death. (See MG11: PC Lizzie Griffiths.)

She walked quickly down the corridor. Fedden wasn't at his desk. Lee was alone in the incident room, working at a computer. She pulled up a chair. He didn't immediately look away from his screen, and when he did, his expression was perplexed, as if he couldn't understand why she was disturbing him.

'I'm sorry to ask, but I've no time to do it myself. I've got to do the identification . . .'

'Sorry, can't help. I'm doing a financial production order for Brannon. It's a priority.'

His tone was implacable. Even though she outranked him, she guessed she'd be a fool to challenge him. 'OK.'

Having won the point, he softened. 'What was it?'

'I need someone to set up emergency temporary accommodation for Julie Teel and her partner. A nice hotel so they're OK about staying there. And I want an alarm at their flat. I think Brannon had a plan and that killing Julie was part of it. If I'm right, then it's unfinished business and he may return. My assessment is that he still poses a threat to her.'

Lee didn't answer immediately, and Sarah felt a rush of irritation. Then he said, 'Elaine's about. I'll get her to do it.'

Lee didn't outrank Elaine. What was he doing tasking her with the shit he couldn't do? Still, there was no time for such quibbles. She was already running late.

'OK.'

'It's your name on the authorization?'

'Yes, don't wait for anything higher. I'll talk to the boss about it as soon as I can. I'll email him before I leave for the mortuary.'

Lee raised his eyebrows slightly but didn't say anything else. Sarah ignored the scepticism: she'd had to deal with worse.

She went into her office and sent Fedden an email explaining why she thought Julie needed safeguarding. Then she scanned her emails in case there was something live she needed to know about before she left the office. One from Elaine: she'd got a forensic hit on the camera she'd submitted in the cold case.

16

Lizzie had picked up Julie and Fergal from one of Julie's friends. Now she waited with them on metal chairs with blue fabric seats that seemed to belong in the waiting room of a GP's surgery. No small talk could cover the anticipation and dread they all felt. Julie smelled of alcohol. Who could blame her?

Sarah arrived. Acknowledging Lizzie with a brief nod and quickly introducing herself to Julie and Fergal, she began to talk through the viewing procedure. Julie listened intently, as though she was being talked through a high-wire walk for which she had insufficiently prepared.

'There will be a pane between you and Georgina. This is because we still haven't completed all the forensic work.'

Julie nodded quickly for Sarah to move on: the forensic exigencies were probably too much to contemplate. 'OK, OK.'

Fergal was holding Julie's hand and looking at her steadfastly. Lizzie's heart went out to him. Whatever greatness he had, he was summoning. For some reason, he was again wearing his high-vis jacket. Had he come from work? she wondered. Had he emptied bins this morning?

He must have read her mind because he said, 'Sorry for my clothing.'

She shook her head. 'No . . .'

'I don't get paid if I don't go in.'

Sarah looked between them and Lizzie immediately felt rebuked.

Sarah was resuming her explanation.

'We'll go through to the viewing room and she will be on the other side of the screen on a trolley. You can look for as long or as little as you want. We need just enough to be able to identify her.'

Julie had frozen. She had started looking beyond Sarah towards the door that led to the viewing room.

Lizzie said, 'Is that all right, Julie? Are you going to be able to do this?'

'Yes, yes. I want to do it.'

Sarah said, 'Do you want her face to be covered when we go in or would you prefer her to be uncovered?'

Julie turned to Lizzie as if she were some sort of expert. 'What do you think?'

Lizzie was at a loss. It felt like a perverse quiz and she was the 'phone a friend' who didn't know the answer. She said, 'Whatever you would find best.'

'I don't know.'

Somehow, they had got trapped by this matter. It was almost silly, except it wasn't. Lizzie thought that if it were any officer but Sarah, they might even laugh about it afterwards. *That dreadful moment when . . .* But any laughter in any case was in another dimension right now.

Sarah said, 'Would you like me to decide?'

Julie turned again to Lizzie, insistent. 'What do you think?'

The decision had magnified itself inordinately: it felt like a supernova. Then Lizzie realized suddenly it was of no import at all. There was no right answer. Covered, uncovered: it would make no difference. Any decision was bad because Georgina would always be dead. This hiatus around the simplest choice was nothing but the product of loss. The only way she could help Julie would be to move things on.

She said, 'I think I would rather she were uncovered.'

Julie sobbed. Then she gained control of herself and said, 'Uncovered then.'

Sarah picked up the initiative. 'OK, I'll go and make sure everything's ready. One last thing. Who do you want going in with you?'

'Just Lizzie.'

Here, emphatically, was the real thing, the veil torn away. The fact of the body on the other side of the screen usurped all other experience. There was nothing besides this. Julie froze and momentarily Lizzie saw the impassive wax-like face of Georgina Teel into which no life could ever be breathed. Then Julie threw herself at the screen, so hard it shook. She seemed to move downwards against a force of friction that had pinned her, smearing the glass with her mouth and hands.

'Georgie, Georgie, Georgie, Georgie.'

She was on her knees, clawing at her face and neck. A guttural voice came from her.

'No, no, no, no, no.'

Lizzie bent down beside her, clasped Julie's hands, held them tightly in her own. Then, when Julie's hands went limp, Lizzie wrapped her arms round her and cradled her as she wailed.

Afterwards, Julie was diminished, small, still. Like a bird resigned to its cage.

Sarah had already prepared the statement. She read it out in the anteroom.

'. . . I saw a woman lying on a trolley. She was my daughter, Georgina Teel.'

Sarah's phone started ringing. She checked the screen. 'I'm very sorry. It's to do with the investigation. I'll have to take it.'

She stepped out of the room. Julie sat looking straight ahead, entirely motionless and silent, as though she were suffering from some sort of severe sickness that was aggravated by movement.

Now Lizzie's phone started to ring too, the ringtone music loud and angry – 'Cleanin' Out My Closet'. Could it have happened at a worse moment? She fumbled quickly to kill the call before the lyrics got any worse.

'Sorry about that.'

Julie shook her head. 'No. It doesn't matter.' She looked dazed still, hardly taking anything in. 'Eminem, is it?'

Lizzie put her phone back in her bag, hoping Julie hadn't seen the caller ID. 'Yeah, it is.'

She'd known immediately who it was because she'd assigned the tune to her mother as a kind of joke. Clearly her sister had spoken with her and now she needed to do the full-blown panic-down-the-phone at Lizzie.

'Take the call if you need to.'

'No, it's fine. I should have switched it off.'

Sarah came back in. 'Lizzie, I've got to go. Can you finish here without me?'

Lizzie nodded. 'Yes, of course. Not a problem. Just the statement, yes?'

'Yes. One of my team's on her way over. Elaine Lucas. Can you wait for her?' Sarah took a step towards Julie. 'That was a colleague on the phone – we're arranging for you and Fergal to be moved into emergency accommodation.'

'I don't understand.'

'We think Brannon's still a threat to you. The officer's name is Elaine. She's on her way over to discuss it with you. I'm really sorry, I have to go.'

'It's fine. Please go. I want you to find Skye. That's all that matters now.'

The door shut behind Sarah. After a moment, Lizzie and Julie exchanged looks. Then a little smile broke out on Julie's face. 'You two don't get on very well?'

Lizzie blushed, embarrassed that Julie had noticed something. 'What makes you say that?'

'Dunno. You seem awkward together. She barely spoke to you.'

Lizzie's voicemail pinged – a message from her mother to call, no doubt. She said, 'Well, Detective Inspector Collins and I don't usually work together. But she is a very good detective, you can be sure of that.' And that was certainly true. Lizzie collected herself, put the statement on Julie's lap and gave her a pen. 'Could you sign here, please?' Julie signed. 'And here.' She signed again. 'Thank you.'

Julie spoke barely audibly. 'Thanks for doing this.'

'I wish I could do more.'

'You tried to arrest him.'

'That's just my job.'

There was a tap at the door and a fat woman in a floral-print dress, bare legs and flat boat shoes came in. She looked nothing like Lizzie's idea of a murder detective. Lizzie smiled but the woman seemed to barely notice her. She went straight over to Julie and offered her hand.

'Hi, I'm Elaine. I'm a detective but mainly I'm a mother. I am so sorry for your loss.'

Julie promptly burst into tears. Elaine hugged her, patting her back with her fat hands and stroking her hair as if she were a child. In spite of the gap in age and circumstances, the two women looked as though they had known each other for years.

Elaine took charge of moving Julie and Fergal to the hotel. It was a good thing: Lizzie was beginning to feel exhausted. A film of sweat had broken out across her top lip. Her arm was aching. She popped another painkiller. She was fine. She just needed to go off duty and lie down.

She sat in the mortuary car park in her police car and called her mum. She had to do it. Delaying the call wouldn't help. But as soon as her mum picked up, she felt even worse.

'Lizzie, I'm coming up.'

'No, Mum, thanks, really . . .'

'I can't bear to think of it. You've been stabbed, Lizzie! Stabbed! You've got to leave that bloody job.'

Lizzie held the phone away from her ear. If she'd waited until she got back to the office, she could have got someone to interrupt the call, pretend she was needed.

'Mum. It sounds much worse than it was.'

'Who's looking after you?'

'I don't need looking after.'

'Are you still seeing that man – the one who came to your dad's funeral?'

'I really can't talk now . . .'

'I can hear I'm annoying you. I *know* I annoy you. But I'm your mother. You have to understand. I love you. I really hate to think of you being in danger.'

'I'm not in any danger.'

'You don't seem to have any life . . .'

'Please. I'm fine. I wish I hadn't told you now. I'll come up and see you, I promise.'

She closed the call and rested her head on the steering wheel. She texted Kieran.

A bit under the weather. Any chance you could pick me up from the nick?

17

The traffic crawled all the way back to Hendon. The sky was heavy with smog. An electricity substation was surrounded by high green railings and warning signs. *Danger of Death.* A few colourful horses stood mournfully in a tiny patch of green, their rear legs bent. A builder's yard. *Pallets wanted.* Sarah thought of the call she had taken earlier at the mortuary from Elaine. She hadn't even said hello.

'I've booked the hotel for Julie and Fergal. I'm on my way to the mortuary now.'

'Thank you, I've got to get to that meeting . . .'

'Never mind that. I'm very happy to help that poor woman, but please, don't ever get that creep Lee to tell me to do anything again. He doesn't outrank me, he's got less service and he's a prick.'

'I'm sorry.'

'He's one of the Fat Elaine brigade.'

'Really. I'm sorry.'

'He knows what a good cop looks like because he sees one in the mirror every day. Mostly pisses standing up. Certainly can't look like me. No way. Definitely can't have kids that actually need looking after.'

'I'm sorry. You're doing a great job. I was in a rush—'

The phone had gone dead before Sarah had even finished her sentence. Now, clipped to the dashboard, it was ringing again. *Withheld number.* She answered, hands-free.

'Detective Inspector Collins.'

She heard the flat vowels of Walker's solicitor, Holt. He was shouting. Sarah put her hazards on and pulled over. She interrupted, 'Have you called 999?' Cars were beeping and pulling round her. She clipped the emergency beacon onto the roof and plugged it into the cigarette lighter. The siren began to wail. 'I'm driving there now. I'm going to have to close the call.' The road ahead cleared and she accelerated.

Minutes later, she had pulled off the North Circular and onto the richer residential streets near Tania's house. Big bay windows. Cherry trees and lilacs. There was a turning she recognized on the right and here, by an arcade of shops, the run-down house with plastic bins in the front garden. Outside the gate a marked response car was double-parked, lights flashing.

The front door was open. She grabbed her harness and ran through the small garden, taking the stairs two at a time, but when she arrived at the entrance to the flat, it was already over. Andrew Walker was lying on his side, clutching his ribs. His face was a bloody mess, one eye swollen and closed. A tall man was standing next to two uniformed officers, his hands cuffed behind his back. He looked completely out of place. He was dressed in a smart suit and what was clearly an expensive shirt. It was Ben Mills, Tania's father.

The security system in Ellersby police station was beginning to get on Sarah's nerves. It was always hard being an officer in a foreign nick, but Ellersby was on a different level. You had to swipe your warrant card to go anywhere in the building, and of course, as she wasn't a local, hers wasn't activated. It had taken her five minutes just to get into the station, another ten to find someone to swipe her into the lift so she could meet Fedden in the canteen. It was at the top of the tower: all glass with good views across the low-rise suburbs and out towards the green belt.

Fedden was waiting for her, Lee sitting beside him, in front of the remains of two portions of fish and chips. Lee had changed into a suit, Sarah noticed, and both men had taken their jackets off and rolled up their shirt sleeves. Fedden had a paper napkin tucked into his shirt top and one on his lap. He pushed an unopened bag of chips and a bottle of water across the table towards Sarah.

'On me. Hope it's still hot.'

'Thanks.'

'You're welcome.'

The chips were warm enough, and salty too. She was starving.

Fedden said, 'What a fucking shit storm.'

Sarah, eating, only nodded. It hadn't been her idea to release an appeal that suggested Walker as a suspect in the disappearance of Tania Mills. Walker's lawyer had already made a complaint about that.

Fedden said, 'Tania's father said anything about what made him do it?'

'Journo doorstepped him. He'd done his homework on the appeal. Told Mills all about the attempted abduction. Asked him what he thought of Walker being linked to Tania.'

'For fuck's sake.'

Sarah popped another chip in her mouth and made no comment.

Fedden said, 'And how did Mills find out where Walker was living?'

'He won't say. We can look at his computers and phone, but my guess is, it wasn't difficult. Walker's still in the area. People will know where he lives.'

'Lee's been with Walker at the hospital.'

Sarah turned to Lee and he said, 'Fractured jaw but it's only a hairline. Doesn't want a prosecution. Says it will only put him more at risk.'

Sarah, wondering how hard Lee had tried to persuade Walker to give evidence, said nothing. She concentrated on her chips.

Fedden said, 'Mills made any expression of remorse?'

Sarah shook her head.

Lee said, 'I wouldn't bloody feel sorry if it was my daughter.'

Fedden said, 'I've spoken with his lawyer. He's a barrister, works out of 3 Holden Court. Good set of chambers. He's a decent chap, actually. Not the kind of guy you normally meet in custody. Family friend, apparently. Anyway, he's going to talk to Mills, persuade him to accept a caution.'

Now that she was no longer hungry, Sarah realized with some disgust that the chips weren't really hot enough after all. She pushed them to the side. She said, 'We could try for a victimless prosecution. The officers' evidence might be enough.'

A muscle twitched in Lee's cheek. He said, 'I don't mean to be rude, Sarah, but I don't get it.'

Sarah turned to him. 'What's that? What is it exactly that you *don't get*?'

'I've told you. Walker wouldn't give me a statement.'

'Yes, and that's why I'm suggesting we prosecute without his evidence.'

'And that's what I don't get. Are you fighting for a charge against a man who was assaulting his daughter's murderer?'

Fedden intervened. 'Lee, hang on there.'

Lee clocked the boss's severe expression and checked himself. 'Sure thing. Sorry if I was out of turn there, Sarah.'

'That's all right.'

Fedden said, 'Could you give us a moment, Lee?'

Lee got up and left the canteen, but Sarah could still see him, standing by the lift, stranded by the fact that his warrant card too wasn't activated for the security systems. Finally he had to put his head back into the canteen and ask one of the local officers to help him out. Lee grinned and Fedden nodded at him, less enchanted than usual.

Fedden said quietly, 'Don't worry about Lee, I'll have a word. Can't have the troops disrespecting the rank.'

Respecting the rank: it was a phrase Sarah had never liked. She spoke quickly, hoping to cover her objection. 'Thanks for the support, but I think I'd do better to stand up for myself.'

Fedden frowned as if not conceding the point. 'Well, that's up to you.' After a pause he added, 'I hope you're not taking it personally.'

'Not at all.'

'OK: Mills. I want this shut down. That lawyer of his will squeeze a couple of words of remorse out of him, you'll give him a police caution and I'll sign it off. That poor man's daughter is probably dead. We really don't want to prosecute him, you know we don't.'

No wonder they called Fedden the Bulldozer. Sarah didn't know what to say, let alone think. She thought of Walker's bloody face. Everyone deserved the protection of the law. And yet she had to admit to herself that she also felt relief. It would have been hard to find the stomach to pursue Tania's father. Fedden was continuing.

'I want you to concentrate on getting a charge for Walker.'

'Jim—'

'I know what you're going to say but there's more than enough of us looking for Brannon. Walker has to be your focus now. Lee will arrange for him to be moved to a new address, but the only real way to protect him from further reprisals would be a conviction for murder and a decent stretch inside. No security like that provided by Her Majesty, don't you think? I saw you got a forensic hit on the camera you submitted. Well done for doing that.'

'That was Elaine . . .'

'She may have submitted it, but it was your idea. Rearrest Walker tomorrow by appointment, and interview him again.' He pushed his chair back. 'Now, if I can find a way to get out of Fort Knox, I'll head on back to Hendon. We've still got nothing useful on Brannon.'

18

Kieran had popped out to get a late-night curry. Lizzie lay in a hot bath drinking white wine. Combined with the painkillers, it was helping her to feel much better. She got out, dried herself, sat on the loo with a towel round her. Something occurred to her. She put her hand between her legs. When there was nothing she searched higher inside herself. She washed her hand under the tap, slipped on a T-shirt and pants, went to the bedroom.

The front door was opening.

'Stand by for the best aloo gobi in west London!' Kieran shouted.

'Great!' Lizzie shouted back. But her phone was in her hand and she was looking at her diary. Three days late. It was probably nothing to worry about. After the last twenty-four hours, it would have been surprising if her period hadn't been delayed.

The flat was filling with the scent of curry. She went to join Kieran. He was putting the aluminium containers on the table. It was a feast: biryani rice, cauliflower, prawns, spinach, poppadums, paratha.

'You've got so much!' she said with determined enthusiasm.

He was getting the wine out of the fridge and poured himself a glass. He took a gulp.

'We're celebrating.'

'What's to celebrate?'

He refilled her glass and handed it to her. 'It's about a year since we met.'

'*About* a year?'

'I'm rubbish at dates,' he said, and Lizzie thought of her calendar and the discreet little P that came up regular as clockwork once every twenty-eight days. Was he rubbish at those dates too? He was holding his glass out to her. 'Cheers then.'

'Cheers.'

They started eating. The food was good but Lizzie was distracted. She rested her hands on the table.

'Your daughter,' she said. 'You've taken her picture down.'

He smiled. 'Because I thought it might upset you.'

'But it doesn't upset me. It upsets me that you've taken it down.'

He got up slowly and took the frame out of a drawer. He hung it on the wall and sat back down. He smiled resolutely. 'Happy now?'

She glanced at the picture of the little girl dancing and then looked quickly away. She hated herself for making him put it up.

'Yes,' she said. 'Thank you. That's better.'

19

It was 10 p.m. and Sarah was driving east across London, dipping out of the busy traffic-laden roads into quiet, leafy Hampstead Garden Suburb. Her mind was on Skye: another night missing.

After Tania's father had accepted the police caution, Sarah had called Fedden from the police station to ask him again to delay re-interviewing Walker so she could assist in the hunt for Brannon. But Fedden had been adamant.

'We need a result for Egremont and I want you to concentrate on that. You said yourself: the moment we put Walker's door in this became a live investigation.'

And so Sarah had disciplined herself. She had put out of her mind her nasty suspicion that it was Walker's lawyer's complaint that was making Fedden so desperate to get a charge and made herself focus instead on Tania, walking out of the front door and disappearing. She thought too of Claire Mills, waiting since 1987 to know what had happened to her daughter.

Although it was late, she'd explained to Ben Mills the need to get some background questions answered urgently, and he'd agreed to talk to her back at his place.

The street of large detached brick houses was lined with young silver birches, the fronts of the houses wrapped in thick hedges. The cars in the drives were all high value or sweet little runners for the nanny or the grown-up children: two Porsches, a Daimler, a light blue Fiat 500, a classic Morris Minor Traveller.

Ben had changed into a soft grey sweater and indigo denim jeans. His handshake was quick and effective. He took Sarah through to a reception room at the front of the house. A large jug of fresh irises and tulips stood in a carved stone fireplace. There was a walnut baby grand in the corner, and Sarah, sitting, said, 'Do you play?'

'My daughters do. I couldn't stand it at first – the sound of practising in the house – but Olivia insisted. Her father's a pianist.'

It was hard to believe that Ben had ever been married to Claire Mills, or even that they were the same age. They seemed to belong not only to different worlds but to different eras.

There were no photos in the room, and she commented, 'Your ex-wife, Claire, she has a . . . well, a kind of shrine to Tania.'

'She does indeed. Every day I came home from work, there would be another photo up.' He reached into his back pocket and pulled out a dark leather wallet. 'This is the only picture of Tania I keep to hand.' He handed the wallet to Sarah. Behind a slightly cloudy plastic cover, she saw a photo of a toddler: a bit plump, fair curly hair, on a beach, sand on her knees and hands.

'How old was she then?'

'Must have been about three. I figure I'm allowed to remember her at any age since she's gone now. I accepted a few years ago that she must be dead.'

He took the wallet from her, slipped it quickly back into his pocket.

'You choose to remember her as a little child?' When he did not reply, she added, 'Why is that?'

His expression was unforgiving. 'I don't want to remember how she was when she disappeared. Claire may have made her into a little angel but she was up to all sorts of stuff behind our backs. I'd believed for some time she was putting herself at risk.'

'Up to stuff? What do you mean?'

'She was rude. She came back late and didn't tell us where she was. She'd stopped practising her violin . . .'

None of this sounded so bad.

'There was a shoplifting incident? Tell me about that.'

'I got a call from the police at work. She'd been in Selfridges. She'd stolen a belt.'

'Your ex-wife said she didn't steal it.'

He nodded. 'That's typical. Claire likes to go round with her eyes closed. Of course Tania had stolen it. When I turned up, a man had offered to pay for it. He was obviously a valued customer, because after that the shop dropped it.'

'This man – can you describe him?'

'He'd gone by the time I arrived. I thought nothing of it. Thought my daughter was just a pretty girl who had learned to cry her way out of trouble. Now you bring it up I have to wonder.'

Sarah wondered whether this could have been Walker. But he didn't strike her as the kind of person who, even then, could have smoothly intervened in such a way. Who had it been then? But there was no point speculating. Although she would try to trace the officers who had dealt with the matter she recognized it was probably impossible to identify the man in the shop now.

'So you took her home and that was an end of it?'

'I told her that I wasn't fooled by her story about forgetting she was wearing the belt.'

'You didn't trust her?'

'It wasn't just the shoplifting. There were other things. She had a tin in her room – undeveloped film, apparently. It was a hiding place, of course. It had cannabis and magic mushrooms inside it.'

'So, she was interested in photography?'

'So she said. There was an evening class at the local college of further education. I think she only went a couple of times. She'd stopped sticking to anything really.'

'Do you know the name of the college?'

'No, but Claire will.'

There was a brief silence. Then Ben said, 'What I've said doesn't mean I don't miss her every day.'

Sarah remembered her first sight of him in Walker's flat: blood on his hands, blood down his fine striped shirt. He'd punched until his knuckles were swollen. He was not a man at peace with himself – that much at least was clear.

She said quietly, 'Of course you do.'

He made no reply and she was mindful how late it was. She needed to review other evidence before interviewing Walker in the morning. She'd have to follow up on those evening photography classes with Claire, too.

'If there's anything else that would help me, anything . . . It might be something you don't even think is relevant.'

'I don't know whether it is relevant but . . .'

'Yes?'

'I was having an affair, you may be aware?'

Sarah nodded, waited.

'A couple of days before she went missing, I was in a café with the woman who became my second wife. It was bad luck – Tania spotted us. She marched right in. *Furious.* Swore at me. I was embarrassed. I took her by the arm, led her out of the café. I said, "This isn't what you think." She called me a liar and I slapped her. I told her it was none of her business: she needed to concentrate on her school work and do some violin practice and stop bunking off school.'

He curled over and held his head in his hands.

'I still can't believe I slapped her.'

Sarah wanted to lean forward and put a hand on his shoulder, but he didn't give the impression of a man who would welcome being touched. She said, 'I'm sorry for bringing all this up . . .'

He glanced up. His face looked as if it had been pulled tight by a string.

'If I'd reacted differently. That's what haunts me.'

Sarah couldn't help but think of Tania. Increasingly she did seem isolated, lost in teenage secrets.

She said, 'Please, Mr Mills. Don't blame yourself.'

'Yes, but it might have made a difference! Do you see that? If I'd been honest with her, she might have talked to me. Perhaps I'd have known more about what she was getting up to. Perhaps she'd still be here.'

20

Friday 18 July 2014

Finally, he thought. The last take was good. He'd nailed that one. Brannon had set up the video camera facing a white wall and draped a sheet over a chair. He'd been getting really irritated but he felt better now. He walked towards the camera, pressing the button to stop the recording. He'd been working on his statement on and off for more than a day. Those TV presenters seemed to have an easy life, but it was harder than you thought to get it right. Still, they had people helping them, whereas he'd had to do it by himself and all in one take. It was difficult to work on your own and under so much pressure. He had sat with the dog, Candy, by his side because he wanted to give the right impression. He wanted people to see that the dog hadn't abandoned him. That was important. The dog still loved him. He bit back tears. He needed to be strong. This was his chance to give his side of the story. He'd been a perfectly happy man before other people had started poking their noses in. He'd been forced into this. He'd tried to tell them how much he loved his family, how much his family meant to him, but they just hadn't listened.

He drew the curtains back and looked at the morning. The early light was golden through the window. It was a small room with a French window that gave onto a surprisingly long back garden. There was the dark-wood fence at the end with the little door into the park beyond. It was early, and he wondered whether he might risk taking Skye and Candy through for a few minutes. Skye's hair was short now, and dark. She hadn't liked him cutting it. She'd moaned and cried. He'd had to slap her. It had been a long day inside the tiny flat. Christ, it had been long! But changing her hair had been worth it. She looked very different. Still, taking her out was too much of a risk. Who knew what she would do? He couldn't trust her to know what was best. Only he could protect her. It would all be over soon, surely. That bitch couldn't stay away forever.

There was a quiet knock. He removed the video camera from the stand and put it under his left arm. Holding the dog by her collar, he took the knife from the table and tucked it into the back of his jeans, then walked swiftly to the front door. Skye had been asleep, but in spite of his efforts not to disturb her, she appeared in the bedroom doorway. Her arms were by her sides, her eyes watchful. He waved her away. 'It's a friend, Skye. Go back to bed.' He checked the spyhole, opened the door and handed over the video camera and a mobile phone from his back pocket. He shook hands briefly and said, 'Thanks,' then shut the door.

He was keeping a grip on things, but sometimes he felt like his mind was going to explode. He'd got some blow and some coke. The whisky he'd picked up that first night. That all helped. But Skye wasn't easy. All those bloody questions. He'd tried to explain, but she kept on and on. Was Mum all right? Was she really all right?

The handcuffs were on the table in the sitting room. He was ready at any point.

He went into the bedroom and pulled the privacy blind back to look briefly at Lizzie Griffiths' car, as resolutely stationary as it had been when they'd first arrived.

Skye was turning out the chest of drawers. Women's underwear, T-shirts and tracksuit bottoms were on the floor. He should have brought more things for her to do. On the table by the bed was a black-and-white photograph of a man in a soldier's uniform, and Skye picked it up.

'Who is this?'

'Never mind.'

Skye frowned and Brannon regretted his tone. She needed him to be the whole family now, father and mother. He should be reassuring, kind. He'd told her that a friend had lent him the flat for a couple of days until everything got sorted, so now he took a guess and said, 'It's my friend's dad.'

'Is he dead? Is that why there's a picture by the bed?'

The question made him cross again. It was bad, he knew, that she was obsessing about people being dead. That man probably was dead, but so what? Old people died.

'No. She just loves him a lot and that's why he's by the bed.'

'I'd like a picture of Mum.'

'Of course you would. And I'll get you one as soon as I can.'

'When will we know if Mum's OK?'

'Any day now. Hang on . . .'

'Was he a soldier?'

'Yes, he was. He was a hero. Now be quiet, Skye.'

He had heard a car pulling up outside. He tweaked the curtain. It was a black Land Rover Discovery and he could see Lizzie Griffiths in the front passenger seat. Quickly he got the handcuffs from the table in the living room.

'Come on, Skye. I've told you what we need to do.'

'I don't want to.'

He shut the dog in the bedroom and pulled Skye by the arm into the living room. The dog was whining and scrabbling to be let out. He hated that Skye looked so frightened and it made him angry. He was trying to find a way for them to be together.

'It's the only way I can keep you safe. Come on, like we practised.'

The flat had radiators and he cuffed her to the outflow. She was crying.

'Be a good girl and keep quiet. I'll be back in a moment. Then we'll be off.'

'Can I have Candy?'

'No, you can't have Candy!' He tried to cover his outburst with a smile. 'I've explained, sweetheart.'

He waited by the door, leaning back against the wall, knife in his hand. He was exultant. He would do this and then he would get away with Skye. He'd find a nice place for them to be together. Maybe in Yugoslavia somewhere. He'd heard they had lovely beaches.

The sound of a car pulling away. Good. That was probably the Land Rover. He waited for the footsteps, the key in the lock. He would act quickly. There would be no words, no attempt at negotiation. She had it coming. It was her who'd fucked it all up. He was trembling with excitement.

21

Sarah had worked until two the previous night preparing for the interview. She and Elaine had arrested Walker early doors at his new hostel, picking up his solicitor, Holt, on the way in to speed things up and taking them straight to Ellersby nick. Walker's face was swollen and bruised, the full palette of blues, purples, greens and yellows. He made no mention of it as he smoked in silence in the yard, Holt standing next to him to prevent any allegations of interference. Holt smoked too, with more energy than the activity really seemed to require.

Sarah tapped out a quick courtesy text to Mrs Edwards.

Won't be able to take Daisy for at least two days. Thanks for your help, Mrs E!

She patted her cigarette box. 'Fancy another?'

Walker shook his head. 'No, let's get on with it.'

They were none of them strangers to interview rooms. They found their places around the table quickly and Elaine completed the formalities.

Sarah opened her file. 'OK, Andrew. As Elaine explained when she arrested you, we are in possession of new information. I'm going to go through that with you. You can break for consultation afterwards if you need to.'

Andrew nodded.

Sarah put on her reading glasses. 'I've got a transcript of our first interview here.' She traced the highlighted words with her pen. 'Here it is. I asked you if you'd ever met Tania and you said, "Never." I asked if you'd spoken to her and you said, "No."' She removed her glasses. 'It's pretty categorical: you didn't know Tania. Do you agree?'

Holt intervened. He had a Mancunian accent and rapid delivery. 'Andrew, as discussed, I'm advising you to make no comment to the officer's questions until she has fully disclosed their new information and we've had an opportunity to further consult.'

Sarah nodded. 'OK.' She looked back at Andrew. 'We are re-interviewing you today because we have evidence that contradicts your account of never having met Tania. If you were in any way mistaken about that in your first interview, you can correct it now.'

Holt intervened again. 'For goodness' sake, Detective Inspector . . .'

'I'm only asking questions, Mr Holt. You can advise but it's up to Andrew to answer as he sees fit.'

She nodded to Elaine, who took a photo of Tania out of her file and pushed it across the table to Walker.

Sarah said, 'Just in case you're not sure who Tania Mills is, I'm showing you a photograph of her at the time of her disappearance. That's exhibit DJF/4. Looking at that image, do you wish to correct your earlier evidence that you never met Tania?'

Walker looked between her and Elaine. 'No comment.'

'A man called Robert McCarthy was arrested as a suspect in the initial stages of the investigation. He was subsequently eliminated from the investigation. Robert had a photograph of himself with Tania. When I asked him who had taken it, he said that Tania had taken the photograph herself, using a timer. Not in itself a big deal, you might say, but what was unusual was that the photograph was a Polaroid. Polaroids with timers were relatively rare. Elaine here met with Tania's mother and she confirmed that Tania to her knowledge only had one camera, a Pentax K1000 that used conventional 35mm film. The only other camera the family owned was a Kodak Instamatic. When we searched your flat, however, we found this.'

Sarah reached into the bag she had on the floor by her side and produced a sealed evidence bag. Inside was a big, clunky camera; grey plastic, shaped like a UFO and with the word 'Spectra' on the front. She placed it on the desk.

'Exhibit SBB/23 sealed in C3427680. It's a Spectra SE camera and it's relatively rare: a Polaroid camera designed for use by professionals. Unusually for a Polaroid camera it has a self-timer. The other thing that makes it distinctive is the size of the film, which is a specialist product: Polaroid 1200 film. The photograph Robert McCarthy has is printed on this film. Is this your camera?'

Holt raised his hand slightly. 'I'd just like to read something out to be entered on the record.'

Sarah nodded. 'OK.'

Holt read from his hastily scribbled notes. 'As Detective Inspector Collins has not so far fully explained to us the nature of the new evidence she wishes to put to Mr Walker, I am advising him to reply no comment to all her questions.'

Sarah made a note in her day book and then put her pen back on the table.

'Andrew, the choice whether or not to answer my questions remains with you. We seized this camera from your flat and I'm simply asking whether it's yours. It's a yes or a no.'

'No comment.'

Sarah said, 'Tania's mother told me last night that her daughter had attended photography evening classes at the Ellersby College of Further Education. Did you ever go there?'

'No comment.'

'You worked there, didn't you? As a technician?'

'No comment.'

'OK. Back to the camera. It's been swabbed for DNA and fingerprints. Any chance that Tania ever touched this camera?'

Again Walker looked at Holt, who shook his head.

Walker's voice was barely audible. 'No comment.'

Holt said, 'Is this some sort of roulette game? Do you actually have anything?'

'Indeed we do, yes. A swab of the feeding mechanism of the camera has produced a DNA hit for Tania. It's a low copy sample – not great – but there's also a partial fingerprint match.'

Holt said, 'Everything you have is circumstantial. Plus there may well be contamination issues . . .'

Sarah interrupted. 'I think I'd better stop you.' She turned to Walker. 'There are a couple of suggestions from your lawyer there, but the questions remain simple. Did you know Tania? Is this your camera? Might Tania have touched it?'

He shook his head. 'I've got nothing to say.'

'We've got a place where you and Tania could have met: Ellersby College. You had the right, unusual, camera. It's got a partial DNA hit and a fingerprint. Not much by itself, but taken together these things are compelling. You knew Tania didn't you.'

'No comment.'

'We've got a witness says you confessed to killing Tania.'

Walker pushed his chair backwards. 'I want to stop the interview.'

Holt pushed his chair back too. 'Stop the tapes then. Now.'

Elaine had persuaded one of the detention officers to lend her his swipe card. She and Sarah made their way to the canteen upstairs. Sarah grabbed them both coffee. Elaine pulled two chairs right up against one of the glass walls. She produced some cupcakes from her bag and offered them to Sarah.

'Don't even try to say you don't want one.'

'I wouldn't dare.'

She dunked it in her coffee.

Elaine said, 'So, did the boss say you couldn't have Lee for this interview? That he was needed for the search for Skye?'

Sarah wiped her mouth with a paper napkin. 'It was never an issue.'

'What do you mean?'

'I didn't want Lee. I wanted you.'

Elaine giggled. 'Why's that then?'

'It's not because I fancy you, if that's what you're laughing at.'

Elaine laughed. 'That's me told!'

Sarah laughed too. Then she thought she would try and tell Elaine why she had wanted her along. She would hide it as a joke but she wanted Elaine to know that she thought well of her.

'Lee's got no bloody idea what he really thinks,' she said. 'He cares too much for other people's opinion. He's always second-guessing what a good cop would say and that makes him stupid. You, on the other hand, don't appear to give a shit and I kind of like that.'

It was an hour before they reconvened in the interview room.

As soon as the tapes had been started and the caution given, Sarah said, 'Andrew, you're in the habit of lying to protect yourself.'

'No.'

'That wasn't a question actually. It was a statement.'

'Well, I don't. I don't lie to protect myself.'

Holt spoke up. 'Andrew, I remind you of my earlier advice.'

'You say you don't lie and you say you don't hurt people. Let's just test that. Last night I looked at the victim's statement from your last conviction. She gives a very different account to yours.' Sarah slipped her glasses on. 'Yes, here we are. I'll only read the relevant bits. "He came up behind me and said, 'Shut up or I'll punch you in the face.' He pulled me along the path towards the gate in the railings. I was pleading with him, saying, 'Please, please, please let me go,' but it was like I didn't exist . . ." She ran her finger along the text, skipping a bit. "He pulled me behind a fallen tree and forced me to lie down. When I tried to get up, he pushed me in the chest and slapped me across the face."'

Sarah looked at Andrew. 'None of this was in your account to me. You just wanted to touch her, you said. Nothing about telling her to shut up or you would punch her in the face. Nothing about slapping her.'

He shrugged.

'You say you're a reformed character who tells the truth, but from the evidence of your interview alone it's clear that's not true.'

'I am reformed.'

The solicitor said, 'Andrew—'

Walker said, 'I'll make my own mind up.'

Sarah turned to Elaine. 'Would you mind?'

Elaine opened the laptop that was sitting on the desk. There was a shuffling of chairs as they arranged their seats so they could all see. Sarah said, 'OK, Andrew. The statement of your victim was videoed. We're going to play some of it to you now.'

Holt said, 'I can't see what this has to do with the current matter. This will all be inadmissible.'

Sarah's tone was neutral. 'Maybe. We'll let the courts decide if they want to exclude it or not. For now, I'll continue, as I am entitled to do.'

The frame was frozen on a small teenage girl sitting in an armchair. She wore jeans and a hoody with the hood pulled up. In the right-hand corner of the frame was a female adult in a blue trouser suit who could only be seen in profile.

Sarah said, 'The victim found it hard to make the statement. She asked if she could wear the hoody with the hood up.'

Andrew nodded. 'OK. Uh huh.'

'The other female—'

'Yes, I know, she's the police officer.'

'OK, Elaine, when you're ready.'

The girl was speaking, but she was so quiet that to begin with she was inaudible. Elaine increased the volume.

'He told me to lie back and pull my skirt up. If I didn't do what he told me, he would punch me in the face. I told him my name and that I have a baby brother and two cats and that my mum was probably missing me. He told me to shut up.'

The young detective at the right of the frame leaned forward very slightly. 'What words did he use?'

The girl cleared her throat. 'He said, "Shut the fuck up."'

'OK. Go on.'

'He started to unbutton his trousers. He was sort of squatting over me and he made a grunting noise. He had my legs pinned beneath his knees and his left hand on my right shoulder. He said, "Say you like it." I couldn't help myself. I sort of squealed. He punched me in the face. He said it again and again, "Say you like it. Say you like it." He had started to masturbate . . .'

The girl stopped speaking.

The detective said quietly, 'I know this is difficult.'

After a long silence the girl began to speak again.

'I said, "If I do what you want, will you let me go?" But he slapped me across the face. My nose was bleeding "Shut the fuck up. Shut the fuck up. Say you like it."'

Sarah glanced across at Walker. He was frowning, completely absorbed in the recording.

The girl had pressed her hands hard against her face, covering her eyes. Then she wrapped her arms around herself. She was completely curled into herself, covered by her hoody. Only her voice escaped, very quiet.

'I was frightened he would punch me again. But he hadn't said he was going to let me go if I did what he asked and it was like something else took over inside me. I was so disgusted by him. I hated him. I couldn't say I liked it and then just be killed by him. He put his hand on my throat and started to tighten it. I could hear him saying, "Say you like it." I couldn't breathe. Then, thank God, there was a dog there.' She laughed in astonishment and shook her head. Sarah glimpsed the girl's little snub nose briefly. 'A beautiful black Labrador and it was barking. He was getting to his feet, pulling up his trousers, running off. It was the best moment of my life, ever, and later, when the police came and the helicopter was overhead, I hoped they would kill him.'

Sarah reached out and touched Elaine on the arm. Elaine paused the tape.

Sometimes it was hard to keep up with her own thoughts. Sarah struggled to identify the exact question she needed to ask. After a pause she said, 'You said – in the earlier interview, that is – you said that it's not part of your fantasy to hurt someone.'

'That's right.'

'Maybe that's true. You don't want to hurt people, but you do want very much to really do the thing that you fantasize about—'

He interrupted, putting his hands on the desk and leaning forward. 'Yes, right now, for example, I'm finding it hard to concentrate because I just want you to stop talking and talking and talking and open your legs and show me your pants.'

Elaine started forward.

Holt said, 'I think we need to break again.'

Sarah said, 'I see no reason to stop.' She turned back to Walker. 'I wondered when you might get to that. Why do you think you've said that now?'

For the first time in the interview he sounded angry. 'I don't know. It just came to me: you, with your legs open and your pants, a piece of fabric stretched over your hairy cunt. What sort of pants are you wearing?'

Holt said, 'Mr Walker is clearly upset. I'm warning you, any comments by my client could be excluded by a court.'

Sarah looked at the solicitor. 'I don't think so. Mr Walker's behaviour in this interview is relevant. The man we see now contradicts entirely the gentle, reformed character he feigned in the first interview.' She turned back to Walker. 'So, you've hit on a radical way to change the subject.'

He shook his head. 'No.'

'You're not the honest, non-violent person you made out in the first interview. You are not someone who *only wants to look*.'

'I am!'

'Hang on, I'll be precise. This looking thing, it's not just a – what did you call it – it's not just a fantasy. You desperately want to do it *for real*. And you are prepared to use violence when you think you can. You did that when you kidnapped your victim in the park. You threatened her. You punched her, you slapped her. You strangled her.'

'Just that once.'

'There are two kinds of sexual murderers. There are the people who murder because that's what they like – to hurt, to kill. You're the other kind: you're not interested in hurting people, but if it's necessary to get what you want or avoid being identified, then you'll do it.'

'No.'

'You're a dangerous man. You are a liar. You are manipulative. You are violent.' She paused, looked him hard in the face. 'You killed Tania. You met her and she trusted you. You did what you wanted to do and then you killed her.'

Andrew glanced between Sarah and his solicitor. Then he said, 'I didn't kill Tania.'

'You didn't want to, but you had to. It was the only way to get away with what you'd done.'

'No.'

'And you've been pretty successful. We've never found her. Where is she, Andrew?'

22

The hotel where Georgina Teel's mother Julie was staying, was just out of London. Lizzie planned to take her statement and then drive up to see her own mother, returning the following day and going straight into work. She had hoped to have time to pop in to her flat and grab some fresh clothes, but she had been running late and didn't want to keep Julie waiting. So when Kieran dropped her outside her flat, she threw her overnight bag straight into the back of her Golf. After all, her mother had a washing machine. She could wear the same work clothes for her night duty the following day.

The A41 had fields, trees, hedgerows but was too busy, too fast and too well engineered to be a real country road. Its leafy edges were interrupted by the outlying suburban things that suggested the too-close city. Hotels with conference facilities, car showrooms, a drive-in McDonald's, a Costco.

Lizzie swung into the ample hotel car park and made her way through the fake marble lobby to Julie's impersonal room with its patterned blue carpet and taupe-coloured pleated curtains.

Julie was sitting on the bed, a small, thin figure. The room was warm but she was still wrapped in a blanket, rolling up a cigarette in her fingerless gloves. 'I'm dying for a fag but I'm worried I'll set the fire alarms off.' She looked like a scrawny bird that had been taken from her nest, a bird you wouldn't bet on surviving.

Lizzie fumbled with the heavy, supposedly portable silver box of the double tape recorder.

Julie said, 'You seem a bit stressed with that.'

Lizzie looked up. Julie was smiling.

'Take your time,' she said. 'It's not like I'm going anywhere.'

The tape recorder's thin black microphone leads were tangled in a compartment in the back.

Julie said, 'This place has got a pool, a gym, a restaurant. I feel like I've gone to Mars.'

Lizzie slotted the tapes into place.

'Nearly there. Do you mind if I write out the statement while you speak?'

'Why would I?'

Lizzie knelt by the low glass coffee table and pressed play. Julie began.

'Being a mother: it's probably the most important thing anyone does. Anyway, whatever, I was no good. I know that's true. When I got pregnant with Georgie, I didn't even know what was happening I was so out of it.

'I was on the junk – heroin. We got so many names for it. Horse. Brown. Candy. Tiger. Smack . . . Anyway, all those names, it's like a love thing for H, making it sound glamorous, and it's got to be glamorous in a way, something that's so downright evil.

'When I started, right at the beginning, I was just eating it. Thought I could handle it. But then it hit me and I didn't know what was happening. It was like that song. "Can't Get No Satisfaction". I had to keep moving on just to deal with how much I wanted it. I started chasing – you know, inhaling the fumes – and then a mate of mine said he'd sort me out. Not his fault: I knew what he meant. He taught me how to mainline and that was that. I was a junkie proper. Had my works in a little pink embroidered Chinese pouch with press studs: a spoon, a lighter, my spike.

'The hit from shooting up, it's like nothing else. Blows your head right off. But when you wake up, you're so sick. No energy, just shivering. Sunny day, hat on, three T-shirts, jumper. And clucking, mind you. I was nothing but hunger. Junk, it eats you up from the inside, just craving it, like you've got ants under your skin. Only way to stop being sick is to score, and then you're sick all over again. It's the devil. You have your junkie friends, but really? Truth is you don't have no real relationship with no one, no one except the juice.

'I was all them things you hear about junkies. Couldn't have got any lower. Tarting myself out? I done that. At the time, I didn't even care that much. Just wanted to do it, get it over with, the punter give me the money, then I can go and shoot up. I stole from my own mum. Track marks down my arms and legs, looking for a vein in my inner thigh, in my big toe.

'Georgie was born addicted. They weaned her off it in the hospital. They give me a chance and I did really want her but they took her away from me. Spent all the money they gave me for food and heating on junk, hadn't I? Social worker come round and said it would be better for Georgie if I would sign her over. But I couldn't. Georgie was the only thing that was ever stronger than H. That's why I think she must have been some kind of angel, 'cos only an angel can fight the devil. I missed her so much that some better part of me got my shit together and got off the juice. Judge said I'd done really well and that the best place for Georgie would be with her mum.

'I did slide a couple of times, I admit it. My mum took Georgie, locked the door on me. Told me, "Don't come round here no more. Georgie don't need to see you right now."

'But we had good times too. I used to get myself together and then I would do everything with Georgie. Spend all my money on her. Park. Ice-skating. Took her once on a holiday to Spain. There was a pool and everything. Just her and me. We didn't need nobody else. I loved her.

'Georgie got real good at keeping secrets. Too good. She tidied the house, kept it looking nice for when the social visited. She did well at school. Never any trouble. Quiet, she was. Neat. My mum used to say, "Old head on young shoulders."

'Finally, I worked my way round the turn once and for all. Took that Chinese purse, filled it up with stones and dropped it in the canal. After that, it was just the two of us: Georgie and me. I didn't want no more trouble. Fergal only moved in after Georgie left even though he was always good to me.

'She left school at seventeen. Got herself a job in a phone shop. That's where she met Mark. Sold him a phone. God, I wish she hadn't been at work that day! She told me he treated her proper. Didn't come on too quick. Respectful. Always had money, of course, paid for everything. Right from the start he was the big I am. She moved out almost immediately. He gave her a home, all that. I think at the beginning she liked how he bossed her about, because when she was a kid I was never in control.

'She couldn't get enough of him. Mark this, it was, Mark that. Months before I was allowed to even meet him. She come round the day before he visited for the first time. Told me: dress nice, tidy up, clean out the ashtrays. No talking about the junk tattoos on my arms.

'She says, "Don't offer me a fag. I'm not smoking no more." I said, "Oh that's good." And she said, "Mark doesn't like it."

'I did what I was told. Wore a nice shirt with long sleeves and a long skirt. Then I was in the kitchen having a roll-up and he comes in and says, bit ridiculous really, pole stuck right up his wide-boy arse, "Don't be smoking around Georgie."

'If it wasn't for Georgie I'd have just told him to mind his own.

'But I didn't have a leg to stand on, did I? Did what he said then and there. Emptied out the ashtray in front of him, put the baccy in a drawer. Wanted to show him I could be a good mum, that he'd want me around when the kids come. Turns out I'd have been a better mum if I'd have told him where to stick it. You never know where you are in this life. I should have stood up to him. I've never done nothing right for Georgie.

'I'd started knitting – baby and children's knitwear to sell at one of those stalls for tourists in Covent Garden. Turned out I was good at it. Could do cable, Fair Isle, all that stuff. Real quick and neat. Think they said I was some kind of fisherwoman on a Scottish island. Only isle I've ever been on is the Isle of Dogs! Got my own little site on eBay now and I supplies some nice shops – Hampstead, Kensington, that kind of thing. Anyways, whenever Mark and Georgie come round, I used to knit for Britain. Kept my mind off the fags, didn't it?

'When Skye was born, I used to mind her. Mark would drop her off. Didn't speak hardly at all. Just says, "See you" and leaves. It's hard when you feel you can never make up for something. Makes you feel powerless. I was always on the back foot.

'She wouldn't tell me at first, but I noticed. Walked into a cupboard, hadn't she? Knocked herself on the table. Nobody never walks into a cupboard, do they? I wasn't born yesterday. Then there was little Skye. She says to me one day when she's round at my house, "Dad hits Mum." "Oh, does he?" And she says, "Yes."

'I would try to talk to Georgie. "If there's ever anything you want to talk about . . ." Or, "I know I wasn't the best mum, but you know I'm always here for you now. Whatever you need. I'd lay down my life for you." Georgie would say, "Everything's fine, Mum." Then he knocked her front tooth out and finally I sat down with her. "You ready to talk about it now? You know I love you all the world." She was a pretty girl and she couldn't hide that she minded. He'd left a great big gap in the front of her face. Told her if she went to the police he'd kill her.

'I couldn't sleep. Knew it was my fault because she had been looking for someone strong, with rules and all that.

'I said, "You've got to leave, you know you have. Think about Skye. She can't see him doing this to you. I know I made lots of mistakes. I'm not one to talk. But I'm going to be there for you now when I wasn't before. Me and Fergal, we'll do everything for you. Fergal loves you like you're his, you know that."

'But she couldn't see her way to leaving. There was Skye, the flat, everything. Plus he said he'd kill her if she ever left him. I was determined. I said, "One day you'll want to go, and when you do, we'll just do it sudden. Move you out one day when he isn't there."

'That's when he started coming round here, banging on the door, threatening me. "Mind your own business, you old slag!" That was a different side of him then, wasn't it? Got so bad in the end I had to stop him coming round. That's when I went to court, got an injunction.

'Georgie got a part-time job as a teacher's assistant. Just two days a week but it was a start. I helped her out with Skye. She'd drop her off. Skye would help me with the skeins of wool. I would put my hands out and she would ball it up. Knitted me a scarf, lovely colours. Must have taken her ages! Fergal would sleep on the sofa. Skye would be in the bed with me. Had her own little set of drawers with pyjamas, change of clothes, duvet, teddy, everything. She used to run to get that teddy, Roly Poly. We used to say he'd been waiting for her. Sally the dog, too. She'd sleep next to the bed when Skye was over.

'It brought me and Georgie closer. It was like I got the chance to say sorry over and over again just by being there for her. I never made no criticisms. Same time, it was like . . . like she maybe understood how we can all make mistakes and end up somewhere we didn't mean to be. Mine was different, of course, brought it all on myself. She'd just moved in with a bastard.

'Things were starting to look better. It's like she's turned a corner. Got her tooth fixed. Turned out she was still young and pretty after all. Says she's going to think about training as a proper teacher. She's clever and determined. I'm sure she can do it.

'I said to her, "The day you're ready to move out, you ring me and we'll do it together." Being a junkie taught me a few things, and leaving places quickly, that was one of them. Just a matter of time, that's what I was thinking. I think he sensed it too, that's what I think.'

It was only when Lizzie looked up from her scribbling that she realized Julie was crying silently, knees bent up like she was a little egg, arms wrapped tightly round.

'Should I stop the tapes?'

'That's why he did it. Knew she was going to leave him. Make herself a life.'

Lizzie moved over, put her hand on Julie's knee. 'I'll stop the tapes.'

'I saw them WhatsApps she sent, the day he killed her. I should never have encouraged her. It's like I killed her because I didn't have no data.'

'No . . .'

'He wasn't going to let her get away. Course he wasn't. I should have known that.' She had her head in her hands and was rocking, crying. 'He's broken me.'

'Julie . . .'

She looked up, her face now drawn tight and determined. 'Tell everyone at the police! I don't want him to die. I want him arrested. You be sure to tell them that.'

'Of course.'

'And I want my Skye back. I'm living for her . . .'

'They're doing everything they can.'

'I want him to live a long life because it'd be better for Skye. She could learn to hate him rather than feeling sorry for him. And for him, living is the worst punishment he can possibly have. I want him to have to stand up in court and listen to what he's done. The whole bloody lot. And then I want him to have to study it in prison day in, day out for at least thirty years. Because it's going to get to him in the end, what he did. And then he'll feel like me. He won't want to live no more.'

23

They had reconvened in the interview room and Walker's solicitor read out a prepared statement.

'I did know Tania Mills. A couple of times she came to an evening class at Ellersby College for photography that I assisted at. We got to know each other, but not well. She didn't seem like the kind of girl you could get to know well. There was something about her, always with her mind on something else. I must have seen her about five times in total.

'I had access to the darkroom at Ellersby College. A couple of times she bunked off school and I taught her how to develop photographs. I remember that well. She was wearing her school uniform. It was sexy in the darkroom with her, the claustrophobic feel, the red light. I fantasized about her. I lent her my Polaroid camera for a few days. It was to keep in contact with her.

'The day after the storm, the college was shut and I was at home. At about eleven, Tania called me from a phone box. She said she wanted to give me back the camera. About an hour later, she turned up at my house. She had her violin with her and a shoulder bag. I asked her in.

'She was in a strange mood. She had some cannabis with her and she rolled a joint. She looked through my cameras. I'm a bit of a camera nerd and I already had a collection – a Nikon, a little Leica, a Hasselblad 500C/M. Tania didn't know what else I was interested in, of course. But then she wasn't curious about me at all. She was just using me. She asked if she could borrow my phone directory and she lay on the floor on her stomach and looked through it, bending her knees and swinging her feet. She tore a page out of the directory. She said she was looking for someone, and now that she had the address, she was going round there. I could hardly hear what she was saying because I was taking photographs. I used the Hasselblad. You look through the top of the camera so if someone's not really paying attention it's not clear what you're focusing on. She was used to me taking pictures, moving around. She asked if she could see the pictures when they were developed so I took some conventional portraits to have something to show her when I saw her again.

'In the first interview you asked when I started fantasizing about Tania. It got really bad after I took those photographs. They were fantastic.

'Anyhow, she left and that was the last time I saw her. When I saw the reports about her being missing, I destroyed the photos because I understood how easily they could draw me into the investigation. But I never stopped thinking about them and that's why I told Erdem about that fantasy, over and over.

'In my first interview I lied about knowing Tania to protect myself but this account is the truth. I've put in everything I can remember.'

Elaine and Sarah had bailed Walker. They'd questioned him but everything he had to say was in his statement. They were both starving, but Elaine was keen to get home to her kids rather than spend time getting proper food.

'Secret weapon,' she said, producing an unopened pack of chocolate digestives from her bag.

'Good skills. We'll get coffee from the machine in the canteen and I'll call Fedden from there.'

They turned their chairs towards the view out west. Fedden picked up after a couple of rings.

'I got your text, Sarah. That's great news. It's time to start talking to the CPS.'

Elaine offered another chocolate digestive. Sarah waved her right hand to say no and continued talking.

'Jim, I'm not sure we're quite there yet.'

'There's still work to do, but what a lot we've got! Walker says he knew Tania, says he lied about knowing her and puts himself with her on the day she disappeared.'

'If I was a sex offender, I'd probably lie too about knowing a missing girl.'

'Yes, but you're not a sex offender.'

Elaine, munching steadily, watched Sarah with an increasingly amused expression. Fedden was on a roll and Sarah didn't interrupt his enthusiasm. When he had finally wound himself down, she said, 'I've been following another lead.'

He was no more than a disembodied voice barking into the headset of her mobile phone but she could almost see him, flushed red with a combination of rage and incredulity.

'Yes, I've seen that. A special-needs guy remembers a green car from more than twenty years ago and a teacher at Tania's school drove a Jag? Christ!'

'The investigator should pursue all reasonable lines of inquiry, whether these point towards or away from the suspect . . .'

'Tell me you're joking.'

'What I'm saying is that there is another line of inquiry, and if we do get a charge against Walker then we will have to disclose it to the defence.'

'Or, to put it another way, now that you've developed this nonsense, it's a problem for us. Do you not think that Walker did it?'

'I don't know yet.'

'*You don't know?* How much service have you got?'

'Less than you—'

He interrupted. 'Damn right, because you're obviously still naïve enough to think that a pervert who admitted seeing Tania on the day of her disappearance isn't responsible for her death.'

'It's my view that just because someone is repulsive and even dangerous that doesn't mean they are guilty of every crime we can link them to, however much we might want to.'

Elaine broke into a wide smile and shook her head from side to side. She wagged her index finger and tutted in warning.

Fedden said, 'Open a discussion with the prosecutor about Walker. Find out what more they need from us for a charge. Once Woodhall's under control, I'll give you some decent techs to develop it according to the lines of inquiry laid down by me and the prosecution service.'

There was a pause.

'And in the meantime, I can keep Elaine?'

'Yes, in the meantime you can keep Elaine and task her to do everything possible to eliminate this red herring. I want you to concentrate on getting a charge for Walker.'

The line went dead. Sarah put the phone in her pocket.

Elaine said, 'Sounds like that went well.'

'Uh huh.'

'He asked you how much service you've got?'

'He did.'

She laughed. 'That means he really doesn't like you. I bet he's never asked Lee how much service he's got.'

'No. I expect not.'

'The guy's an arsehole,' Elaine said cheerfully, putting the nearly finished tube of biscuits in her bag and standing up. 'Well, sorry, but I gotta go.'

Sarah stood up too. 'Look, I know you need to get off, but can I just talk the evidence through with you in the yard for five minutes so I can smoke.'

They stood in the covered area by the property store. Some local officers pulled up in an unmarked car and started unloading big plastic bags of evidence from the boot. There was a lot of stuff: three computers, a microwave, a food processor, a mini fridge.

'Guess the offence,' Elaine said.

'Handling, I'd say. Selling it all on eBay.'

'Yeah, you're probably right.'

Sarah lit her cigarette. She said, 'I want to think through what it would mean if Walker's telling the truth.'

Elaine nodded and Sarah continued.

'The day Tania disappeared she got a call from her best friend Katherine Herringham and organized to meet her. Claire Mills says Tania left home at about nine. She knows the time because Tania was leaving just as the baby she looked after was being dropped off. Tania went to Robert's hut and changed out of her jeans. And then that's it. After she leaves Robert's hut we have nothing definite.'

They were both silent for a moment, thinking through the evidence.

Sarah said, 'Walker says Tania telephoned and then came over. It was already late morning when she arrived, after eleven. So if he's telling the truth we've got a gap of about two hours between Tania leaving the hut and then turning up at Walker's in a bad mood.'

Elaine said, 'She was supposed to meet Katherine but went somewhere else?'

'Could be.' Sarah paused. 'Or Katherine's lying and Tania did visit her friend. After all Katherine never called Tania's home to find out why she hadn't turned up.'

'I asked her about that when I was trying to trace the Jag. Katherine said Tania was unreliable. She was pissed off with her and so didn't want to chase her. But Katherine could be lying, yes.

I suppose so. But then why would she lie? She'd want to help find her friend, surely.'

Sarah thought for a moment. 'Katherine and Tania played music together. Stephenson was probably Katherine's teacher too. Did she remember the Jag when you asked her?'

'No. She couldn't remember anyone with a green Jag.'

'Still, that doesn't mean much. I can't remember what cars my teachers drove.'

Elaine laughed. 'I remember my German teacher drove a Mini because we used to lie down in front of it and stop her leaving school.'

Sarah laughed. 'I can see you doing that!'

Elaine affected outrage. 'What on earth do you mean?'

Sarah went back to her thoughts. 'There's no particular reason to remember what your teacher drove, if indeed you ever knew.'

'I just got lucky with Stephenson?'

'Maybe. Or maybe . . .' She thought about it. 'Or maybe, like your German teacher, Stephenson was the kind of man who stuck in people's minds. The deputy head who remembered the car – what sort of an impression did he give you of Stephenson?'

'Didn't like him. Always had to have things his own way, apparently: rehearsal rooms, the organization of school trips for the orchestra. Stephenson was arrogant, but because he got results, the head always let him have his way.'

'And what about Katherine? How was she when you met her?'

'Unfriendly. Said she'd been through it all countless times, what more could she add? To be fair, she is a single mum, so maybe it was understandable that she was in a hurry to get rid of me.'

Sarah stubbed her cigarette on the ashtray attached to the wall. 'All I'm doing is finding lots of questions I can't answer. It's so hard to fill in the gaps.' She got her packet of cigarettes out of her pocket. 'And it could all be perfectly straightforward, like Fedden thinks. Walker killed Tania.'

She put another cigarette in her mouth and reached for her lighter.

Elaine said, 'You're going to make yourself ill.'

'Oh stop nagging. This is only my third today.'

'Well, hurry up anyway. I want to get home. Do you want me to interview Katherine again? I could go round there tomorrow.'

Sarah inhaled. 'No, not yet. Let's wait, see if we can get more to put to her. Have you actioned the request to other forces for intelligence on Stephenson?'

'Yes. They'll copy you in with any information.'

'Shame we haven't got that bloody telephone directory Walker mentioned. If it exists, that is. At least it might give us a first letter of the surname.'

'Did you believe him then?'

'I don't know. Fedden thinks I'm cracked to even consider believing Walker. It's just a question of finding enough evidence to convict him.'

Elaine said, 'If Tania went missing today then some older bloke she met from time to time and who dropped her in a park rather than taking her home would definitely be a line of inquiry for us.'

'Yes, but we don't even know Stephenson is that man. All we know is that he drove a Jag. Still, I keep thinking about his tree planting in Morville Park. It'd be a bloody good way to dispose of a body.'

Elaine laughed. 'I think you should keep looking into Stephenson but I don't think you've got enough to start digging up parks.' She picked her bag up and swung it over her shoulder. 'If we're done then I'm off. You staying on duty?'

But Sarah, stubbing out her cigarette, was still preoccupied with Egremont. Another detail had come back to her. She said, 'When did Stephenson divorce?'

'Six months after Tania's disappearance.'

'That's interesting. I'd like to talk to his ex-wife. What's her name?'

'Abigail Levy.'

'Can you get me an address for her?'

Elaine pulled a face. 'You're not suggesting I do that now, are you?'

Sarah shook her head. 'Of course not.' She smiled. 'It would take an age if you went back to Hendon to do it.'

'Bloody hell.'

Sarah opened her hands, a picture of innocence. 'What?'

'You're a pain in the arse.'

'You're not the first person to have noticed that.'

'OK. I'll do a quick intelligence search for an address from here, but if it's not immediate bingo, then I'm going to give up and go home.'

Sarah smiled and winked.

Elaine said, 'Don't you dare.'

'Trust me, I'm not saying a thing. I'd call you a star but I know that would really piss you off. I'm getting a bite to eat; do you want to come?'

'No way. I'll do this and then I'm gone.'

Road sweepers were clearing away the discarded coat hangers and trampled cabbage leaves from the day's street market. There was a McDonald's on the right, lit up as bright and strange as a shopping mall fish tank. Young men had stacked themselves around a table, police officers in uniform queued for takeaway, a solid-looking man with dirty hands and orange overalls sat alone eating his way steadily through two burgers. Sarah wouldn't have been surprised to see an alien in there: purple, with eight tentacles, looking through its laptop undisturbed and picking at a Big Mac and a side of fries.

The feeling of separation she had from the people behind the glass was familiar. How many times, she wondered, had she sat on crowded tubes and surveyed the faces of her fellow travellers wondering what lay concealed behind their bored expressions.

When she was only a trainee detective, she had prosecuted a Chinese DVD seller who, at the bottom of a bag containing rip-off copies of *Avengers* titles and *Batman* movies, had concealed some more specialist DVDs. As part of the case she'd had to produce an exhibit that dip-sampled and detailed their contents. Over an eight-hour shift she'd watched a succession of women performing all the various permutations of sex, mainly with dogs. One of the women had had a fairly convincing stab at enjoying it, others seemed professionally sexy. There were girls from all over the world. Asian girls. Americans in hot pants. Some blonde girls who seemed to be from Eastern Europe. There was one in particular who had stayed forever in her memory: a young girl with short black hair and tattoos across her stomach, whose extreme thinness suggested drug use. She acted in company with another woman, who moved with an air of experience. This woman had encouraged the girl, putting her hands where they needed to be, demonstrating how, bending, turning, doing the necessary acts with a practised air, while the girl who was making her debut smiled uneasily, blushed, avoided the gaze of the camera and covered her face, still no stranger to shame.

All kinds of moral cant and imperfectly hidden titillation covered people's reactions to any talk of sex offenders. Monsters-in-disguise was a much-favoured phrase that usefully marked out the territory of the decent. But Sarah found no comfort in it. The DVD seller had been selling the video of this girl out of a bag on the streets of London. Clearly there was a market. That was the problem, she thought as she crossed the road and entered the brightly lit mall: her job gave her too much access to the backstage areas of people's lives. Desire was tainted by its contingency to its many possible forms of harm.

She pushed open the heavy glass door to a sushi place. Whirring fridges held plastic trays of cubed raw salmon and clear plastic pots of perfect green beans. She ordered hot food at the counter and perched on one of the tall stools that faced out towards the mall. She prised the cardboard lid from the noodles and steam rose from the standard brown broth. There were the usual green leaves, the shavings of something that looked and tasted like wood. Healthy food, it promised. One of your five-a-day. God, she was tired.

There was a tap on her shoulder and she turned round. A wide, beaming smile greeted her. 'Hey, Sarah! Twice in as many weeks!' Caroline grinned. 'Can I join you?'

In her jeans and white cotton shirt Caroline seemed fresh and untainted. Sarah felt she needed a bath before she even tried to speak to someone so optimistic. 'Yeah, sure. But I've got to go in a minute.'

Caroline jumped up on the adjacent stool and popped a sushi box on the narrow shelf that overlooked the mall. 'You always this grumpy?'

Sarah smiled in spite of herself. 'Pretty much.'

'I'm catching a film in the centre with some friends. You can join us if you like.'

'No, honestly, I can't. I'm still on duty actually.'

Caroline broke the seal on the plastic top of her sushi box. She emptied the soy sauce into the little bowl, squeezed in a generous twist of green wasabi, dipped a sushi roll into it and popped it into her mouth with an enthusiastic slap of her lips. Sarah felt a teeming sense of her, the fullness of her lips, the pleasure she had in eating. Caroline had chosen another roll and was moving it around the bowl.

'So, what have you been up to?' she said.

'Ah, nothing much. Interviewing.'

'Interviewing, that sounds interesting.'

'Sorry, I don't want to talk about it.'

Caroline frowned briefly, a quickly dissipated hardness of bemusement between her eyebrows. 'OK.' She popped the second piece of sushi into her mouth and winced with enthusiasm at the heat of the wasabi.

Sarah rubbed her forehead with both hands. Maybe she should go now, say she was unwell. She looked back at Caroline, who was studying her with a curiosity that seemed both sympathetic and amused.

'Sorry about that,' Sarah said. 'Been a long day.'

'No, it's OK. You do look tired.'

There was a pause.

'Was it a bad one then?'

'Kind of.'

'You can't talk about your job?'

'Well . . .'

In went another piece of sushi. Another enthusiastic slap of the tongue. 'Is that because it upsets you or because it's confidential?'

Sarah tried to smile. 'I'm sorry, it's just . . . not the moment. Can we change the subject?'

Caroline's face gave a little flicker of discomfort that she quickly hid with another smile. 'Yes, sure. Why not.'

'Tell me about your day. You like teaching, right?'

Caroline talked about a girl who had done surprisingly well in a maths competition, but neither of them was interested. They were mired in courtesy. There were perhaps other things they wanted to talk about but they couldn't work themselves round to them.

Sarah said, 'I'm sorry. I've got to get back to work.'

Caroline looked at her sushi carton. 'But I've only got four more pieces to eat! Can't you sit with me until I've finished?'

Sarah looked at the box. There were indeed four rolls left. 'Of course I can.'

Caroline was searching out her expression. 'Don't you like me?' she said.

'I do, yes. Look, it's been a long day.'

'You said.'

Suddenly they both broke into a smile, a relieved acknowledgement of the awkwardness that both made them want to sit together and then made them uncomfortable when they did.

Caroline said, 'Don't feel you have to stay. Maybe we can do this again.'

'No. I want to stay.'

Caroline reached her hand across the table. 'Look, I admire you . . .'

'Don't be silly.'

'I don't know how you do your job.'

I don't know how you do your job.

It was the worst possible thing she could have said. It must have shown on Sarah's face because Caroline shook her head in confusion.

'What?'

'Nothing.'

'What did I say?'

'It's nothing.'

There was a long pause. Caroline had stopped eating. She was waiting with a questioning smile for an answer.

Sarah said, 'It's silly really.' When Caroline still didn't say anything, she added, 'It's just that phrase.'

'What phrase?'

'*I don't know how you do your job.*'

'What's the matter with it?'

'Everyone says it.'

'So what? I mean it. I do admire you. You do a difficult job.'

Sarah nodded. 'OK.'

'OK?'

'Yes, but what exactly do you mean when you say you don't know how I do it?'

Caroline frowned. 'I mean what I say – that I couldn't do it. Couldn't *bear* it. All that suffering. What's the matter with that?'

'Do you really want to know?'

'Come again?'

'Just think for a moment. Do you really want to hear this?'

Caroline looked cross now. 'Yes, I do. Finish what you're saying.'

'OK. When people say they can't do my job, they don't mean they're not clever enough, or cunning enough, or that they simply couldn't work hard enough. They don't mean they can't get up after just four hours' sleep after sixteen hours on duty the shift before and start again, or that they can't be professional and stop themselves vomiting when someone's been lying dead in a bath for a week. They never mean they haven't got the patience or the resilience or the sheer determination. No, it's self-flattery. If they can't do my job it's because they're *too sensitive*—'

'Sarah . . .'

'I'm going to finish.'

'OK. Go ahead. Finish.'

'They can't bear to witness bad things. Or they're too moral, poor souls. They couldn't bring themselves to be patient with bad people. They couldn't sit and listen and be fair and befriend them because that's all part of the job, however repellent the person is.'

She stopped. Caroline had stood up and Sarah was hit by sudden regret.

'You've always seemed so lonely.'

Sarah was shocked by her own outburst. She said, 'Look, I'm so sorry I said all that. I haven't been well.'

'I've only ever tried to be friendly to you.'

'Yes, you have. I'm sorry. I don't know why I said all that stuff.'

'I don't know you well enough for you to speak to me like that. You know nothing about me.'

Sarah's phone was ringing. Out of long habit she immediately took it from her outside pocket and checked the screen. It was Elaine, but she rejected the call. Caroline had begun to walk away. Sarah stood up, called after her, suddenly not even embarrassed that people were looking at her.

'I'm sorry . . .'

But it was too late. The glass door had opened and then shut. Caroline was walking quickly away through the mall and Sarah was left standing. Her phone was ringing again. She sat down and answered. Elaine had an address for Abigail Levy.

Stephenson's ex-wife lived in a converted mews in Primrose Hill. It was one of those romantic pockets, hidden away in the mega-city, that the wealthy had long since spotted and nabbed. The horses and the stable workers were long gone: if ghosts haunted the cobbled pathway then it was surely only in a friendly way. Terracotta pots outside Abigail Levy's door burst with flowers: savagely yellow rudbeckia, jagged green and purple acanthus.

Abigail was small and thin: five foot two and probably less than eight stone. She was in her well-kept fifties, had dark brown eyes and a slightly bouffant blonde bob and was wearing a smart pink suit with dark piping on the pockets that might be Chanel or, if it wasn't, was at least hinting that it might be. She wouldn't have looked out of place filming a lunchtime chat show for women of a certain age. She smiled with slightly hostile confusion when Sarah showed her warrant card, but asked her into her little house. The sitting room was perfectly done: a Persian silk rug lying like a sky-blue meadow, side lamps that cast a soft light, a matching pair of antique open-sided armchairs. Abigail offered tea and brought it in on a round silver tray. She sat in one of the armchairs and stretched her legs out in front of her, her feet crossed at the ankles. She tilted her head to one side.

'How can I help?'

'Thank you for talking to me, Mrs Levy.'

'Not Mrs, Miss.'

'I'm sorry, Miss Levy. I'm making inquiries about a girl your ex-husband taught, Tania Mills.'

Abigail gave a tight little smile that crinkled the lines at the sides of her eyes but didn't seem to contain any happiness. 'The name doesn't mean anything to me.'

'Your ex-husband never spoke about her?'

'Not that I remember.'

'Because she went missing. She was never found. It must have been quite a talking point.'

Abigail drew her feet towards the chair, her knees bent at an angle to the side, her heels off the floor. 'I remember that, yes. I just didn't remember the name. But he didn't really talk about her. My husband was never interested in anyone except himself.'

'You divorced the following year.'

'Not a day too soon.'

'Can I ask you about that?'

Abigail placed her hands together and brought them to her chin. She stayed like this for a moment, then said, 'I'd rather not talk about it, if you don't mind. I can't see what relevance it has to any police inquiry.'

Sarah considered whether to press, decided against. 'Your husband, was he involved in charitable activities?'

'Not when we were together. I don't think so.'

'He didn't get involved in the community? That sort of thing?'

Abigail exhaled a mirthless laugh. 'God, no! Why would he do that? You clearly don't know him. He's not interested in other people.'

'But he's involved in charities now.'

'I wouldn't know.'

'There was a storm . . .'

'Yes, the storm. I remember.'

'He volunteered to help replant Morville Park.'

She seemed surprised, interested even. 'Did he?'

'You didn't know about it?'

She sat back in her chair. The animation she had briefly revealed was once more contained. 'No, I didn't know. We were already not close.'

Sarah's phone buzzed. She glanced at the screen. It was a group text to her team. *OPERATION WOODHALL: URGENT*. She put the phone back in her pocket, paused for a moment before speaking, allowing the interruption to dissipate in the elegant little room.

'I'm sorry about that.'

'That's all right.'

Abigail smiled again, stretched her legs out and recrossed her ankles.

Sarah said, 'Can I just ask you . . .'

'Yes?'

'Your ex-husband and you, how did you meet?'

'He was my violin teacher. He was a very good teacher.'

'Do you still play?'

Abigail shook her head. 'God, no. I haven't played for years.' She smiled and tilted her head to one side. 'Is there anything else you need to ask? Because if not . . .'

Sarah smiled too and stood up. 'No, thank you for your time.' She offered her card. 'If you think of anything that might help me with my investigation.'

Abigail said thank you and placed it neatly on the table.

24

Brannon had been drinking for a while. Skye was still in the sitting room. He couldn't look at his daughter because that just wasn't possible. Not yet. He needed to keep drinking for a bit longer.

That moment when Lizzie had driven off and he'd been left standing with the knife in his hand: he couldn't stand it. He could actually *hear* the people laughing at him. Then it was as if he'd been struck on the side of the head by a bar. It had overwhelmed him. He had had to sit down.

He'd got up like someone seeking first aid and gone to the sitting room. He thought Skye, still cuffed to the radiator, had said something to him but he couldn't be sure. He couldn't look at her or respond. He'd gone and got the bottle of Jack Daniels and returned to the hall.

He was familiar with the dark crevasse where he had now settled. He'd known a version of it since he was a child, but it had been smaller then, a narrow, cramped space, like being inside a closed cupboard. The first time had been one of his mother's boyfriends. The memory was so distant that he had no sense of how old he had been. He had been standing, his back against the wall, watching. The man had hit his mother, more than once, and a terrible panic had coursed through him. He hadn't known what to do. He'd seen a film – *Jason and the Argonauts* – and he wanted so much to be Talos, the moving bronze statue with the huge legs, towering expressionless above the weak and feeble warriors, no more than fearful ants beneath his pitiless sword. Instead, he was one of the ants. Why was no one in charge? Why was no one helping?

Another memory rolled over him like a bank of cloud. His mother had called him into her bedroom. The curtains were drawn and the room was dark. He couldn't remember the man's face at all, almost as if he had actually had no face; just the shape of his body raised over his mother like a beast. Like the Cyclops in *Sinbad* with his heavy brow and his furry thighs. She'd raised herself up on her elbows and told him to get her some cigarettes. The money was on the bedside table, right by them. When he hesitated she told him to GET A FUCKING MOVE ON.

He'd had to ask an old drunk outside the shop to buy the cigarettes because he was too young. The drunk took the cellophane off the packet and removed two cigarettes. 'Tax,' he said, tapping the side of his nose. The box was ruined without its cellophane. He remembered it now, the gold packet of Benson & Hedges resting in his hand.

That must have been shortly before the police came. That day a woman sat next to him on the sofa and read him a book, while the others held conversations just out of earshot. The police moved through the flat with their radios chattering and the family in the book went tumbling down through fields full of flowers looking for a bear.

In the foster home, he'd had Marley to begin with, but then decisions had been made. He'd tried to listen to what they were saying but he couldn't follow it. All he'd understood was that Marley had gone. He'd wet the bed. The other kids had laughed at him. That was when the darkness had begun to change. It had begun to be capable of movement, had developed range and power. He could feel it building, like those maps of storms, the isotherms moving across, gathering force and intensity. There was something wonderful about it really.

He'd done shit at school, been sent to a unit. But why should he care? He'd made plenty of money without all that crap. Soon he was working for the Youngs. They could rely on him. He wanted them to know that. It wasn't just a professional thing; it was more than that. And it seemed they did know, because they trusted him, treated him with respect. He was part of the family. Not one of the main guys, sure, but still, they looked after him. He was beginning to be someone. And on the back of that, he'd made his own little family. They respected that too. He could see it in how they talked to him.

He'd loved Georgina the moment he set eyes on her. Besotted he was. She was his ideal woman. What a beautiful home they'd built. His beautiful family! It was other people who had come between them, people who should have helped them. Georgina's mother, and that bitch Lizzie Griffiths . . . No one ever wanted to help him! No one had ever looked after him. He couldn't trust anyone. Not a soul. He had to be a man for everyone. No one else made clear rules. No one else kept their promises.

He thought of Skye in the sitting room. At first she'd been crying, but now she was silent. He felt so very, very sorry for her. She was so small and so precious. So innocent. No one could ever protect her from this world. He had thought he could, but he couldn't. And when they caught him and killed him, she would be sent to just the same sort of home that he had been in. Never! He would never let them do that to her. It would kill him to do what he had to do, but he was strong enough. He would look after Skye. He needed to keep drinking and then he could do it.

He turned the Samsung in his hand. It was like a glimmer of light here in the darkness. In spite of everything, he could still take pride in his skills. Tradecraft: that was what they called it. He knew better than to make phone calls. This high-quality burner was pristine.

There was an app. He clicked on it. He'd just check up and see where the bitch was. Studying the log, he could feel a chink of light opening inside him. *He could track her.* Even at this distance he had some control over her. She'd stopped at a hotel just outside London for a few hours. He wondered briefly about that. The cheap bitch had probably met some married man for a fuck. Now she was moving up the M6. He felt his power: at some point she would have to come home. Perhaps he could wait after all.

He logged on to the internet browser. His video had been uploaded to YouTube. It had thousands of hits! The comments were coming in.

Truk407: Mark Brannon, U R my hero.

Fedora-Man: Die you murdering piece of shit.

He didn't give a shit about that loser Fedora-Man, whoever he was. He was bigger than that!

Brannon went into the sitting room. Skye was lying asleep by the radiator. He went into the kitchen and checked the cupboards. Luckily Lizzie had flour and eggs. He whisked up some batter. He knelt by Skye and gently unlocked the cuffs. He picked her up, cradling her in his arms, stroking her hair.

'Come on, beautiful, wake up. I'm making pancakes.'

25

The homicide team's offices felt like a late opening library where only the studious remained. There was so little movement that the lights were out in the corridors and flickered on only as Sarah passed along. Nearly everyone was out, tasked with urgent inquiries relating to the video that had been uploaded to YouTube. Those who remained worked silently at their desks. Lee was alone in the major incident room. He pointed her in the direction of a stand-alone computer, and when she clicked on the link, he got up and stood beside her while she watched.

The video already had nearly eight thousand hits. Mark Brannon was sitting in front of a white wall in an armchair over which he had draped a white sheet. His demeanour crazily suggested the pre-interview anxiety of a candidate who had insufficiently prepared but was hoping against the odds to get a job he wanted too badly. He wore an ironed buttoned shirt but was unshaven, and his hands rested on the arms of the chair as if they had been strapped there. The dog, Candy, was lying by his side.

Georgie was my perfect woman. All I ever wanted was for us to be together . . .

Lee said, 'Twitter's going crazy.'

'Are we getting YouTube to take this down?' Sarah asked without taking her eyes off the screen.

'The boss is working on it.'

Tears were pouring down Brannon's face. The dog shifted position.

I had a family. I had love. I had everything. If it wasn't for the police, Georgie would still be alive.

'Self-pitying bastard,' Lee said.

'Any ISP address for where it was uploaded?'

I never wanted to hurt Georgie, but what could I do? She was leaving, taking Skye with her. I couldn't let her do that.

Lee said, 'It's an internet café. We've got officers down there doing a CCTV trawl.'

Brannon had broken down completely. He was sobbing, holding the shaved dome of his head. Then he seemed to tire of that. He looked up, wiped his hand across his nose and sniffed, used the heel of his hands to wipe the tears from his face. He gathered himself. His piercing blue eyes looked directly at the camera.

I'm being really clear now. I'm warning you. Skye is all I've got left. I'll never let you take her from me. Don't come near us.

'The shrinks are warning about murder-suicide apparently,' Lee said. 'The boss is very worried for Skye.' His phone pinged and he checked it and swore. 'Fucking useless.'

He showed Sarah the screen of his phone. It was a WhatsApp with a CCTV grab from the internet café where the video had been uploaded: a man with his hood pulled down. No facial image at all, but the man was too tall and thin for Brannon.

Sarah said, 'So he's getting help but we don't know from whom.'

She glanced back at the screen. There was a hint now of a terrorist video: Brannon's tear-stained face looked so certain, so determined.

This isn't the end of it. This isn't going to end here.

The title of the automatically loading next video played – a true-crime clip called 'Crocodile Tears' – and a banner advert ran underneath for a West End musical. Sarah closed the internet window, her mind tracking the video for evidence. Although she'd been told to concentrate on Tania, every instinct she had cried out to find Skye.

26

Fedden was in his office, head down, tie off, glasses on, reading through papers. He looked up and his expression changed from absorption to annoyance. He pushed his glasses to the top of his head.

'Yes, shut the door. Sit down. You see the video?'

Sarah nodded. Fedden shoved his chair back from the desk. His shirt was unbuttoned at the neck and damp under the arms. He was drafting an appeal to Brannon, he said, waving a sheaf of paper in his right hand.

'I've got this advice from a forensic psychiatrist. It's all disclosable, and if we catch the bastard before he tops himself, it'll go towards an unfit-to-plead application. Can't make head or tail of it. I've got to offer to help him, apparently. I'd murder the bastard with my bare hands if I could.' He put the psychiatric report on the desk, leaned forward and passed Sarah a printout of an email. 'Right now, this is the last bloody thing I need landing in my inbox.'

Sarah got the gist of it pretty quickly. It was a formal complaint from Mr Richard Stephenson's lawyers. He'd consulted, she noted, one of the more prestigious firms, based in Westminster. The guy both had money and also knew who to go to. The threat of civil action was palpable. The lawyers ticked off the main points – the damage being done (*staining Mr Stephenson's name*), the value of the thing being damaged (*a respected member of the community, an MBE who has enjoyed a long and eminent career*) – and of course hinted at the possible cost to the police when the dust settled: *It is hard to estimate the distress and financial loss . . .* What actual evidence, they requested to know, were the police acting on?

Wondering who had told Stephenson about the inquiries, Sarah put the email down on the table. The boss tapped the desk lightly with his fat little fingers. 'Any thoughts before you write the apology?'

'Just that I don't like being told to back off. I'm sure you're the same.'

Fedden shook his head in disbelief. 'You've got *nothing*! He drove a green Jaguar!' He slammed the desk with the flat of his hand. 'I've no time for this.'

She pressed her lips together, waited.

'Just give me the facts. What have you had Elaine doing?'

'I asked her to talk to schools where he worked, orchestras he directed—'

'For Christ's sake!'

'If I may say, you rather forced my hand with speeding up the inquiries.'

Fedden blinked quickly at this. 'I certainly didn't give you carte blanche to ruin a man's reputation. If you had had more evidence to go on—'

Sarah tilted her hand up to stop him. 'If you'd let me get a word in, I'm sure you'd feel better quite quickly.'

Fedden stared hard at her. He really did look as though the pressure was building sufficient for an explosion. His expression was almost funny, but she suppressed a smile and tempered her language before they were so rude to each other that there was no way back.

'I don't think you need to worry. We're pretty much covered for our inquiries into Mr Stephenson. I just checked my emails. Elaine put out a request to other forces for any intelligence relating to him. There are three open investigations into historic complaints of serious sexual assault including rape against Mr Stephenson by girls who were taught by him. One of them was thirteen at the time. They are from different schools in different force areas and the women don't know each other. The method appears to corroborate their accounts. Given time, there may be more.'

Fedden put his elbow on the table and rested his chin in his hand. His eyes widened as he considered this new information. Then he grinned. 'Thank fuck for that!' The good news dawned more fully and the creases lit up at the edges of his eyes. This was the cheerful Fedden who liked nothing more than to stick it to the bad guys. Seeing him now, Sarah could well believe that his rendition of 'It's Not Unusual' might actually be rather good. 'He can stick his complaint up his arse then,' he said with tremendous emphasis. He shifted in his seat and studied Sarah for a moment. 'I'm not going to have to apologize to you, am I?'

Sarah shook her head. 'No.'

'Good, because I think I'm going to explode if anything else happens.' He paused again, but then leaned across the desk and offered his hand. It was warm and sweaty. 'To hell with it, I'm sorry anyway. This Skye thing . . .'

'It's all right. You're under a lot of pressure.'

He sat back down.

'Damn right I am. Run it all past me, quick as you can. How much have we got on Stephenson apart from the Jag?'

There was a tap on the door. It was Steve Bradshaw. Fedden rubbed his forehead and beckoned him in. 'Sorry, I'll have to deal with this. It's Brannon.' Sarah got up to leave, but Fedden said, 'No, stay.' He glanced at Steve. 'If that's all right by you?'

Steve pulled up one of the spare chairs that was against the wall. 'Of course.'

Sarah looked between the two of them and sat back in her own chair. This was a turn-up. Steve had already begun the briefing.

'Bit of background, Sarah. Earlier today Marley – she's a relative—'

Sarah interrupted. 'Yes thanks. I know who she is.'

'Good. So she got a call from a prepaid unregistered mobile. Bit of a long shot but obviously we're desperate, so the boss sent some officers down to check the shop where the mobile was bought six days ago.'

Fedden interrupted. 'Hurry up, Steve. Let's not wait before we unwrap our presents. I'm guessing you got a hit on the CCTV?'

'Yes, boss. It was Brannon bought the phone.'

27

There was no peace like concentration.

Sarah had briefed Fedden. She'd told him about Stephenson's sudden interest in community work following the night of the great storm and about his landlord's complaint about the removal of the carpet from his home. Under the circumstances Fedden had agreed it might be worth getting a proper look at Morville Park.

Sarah made the arrangements and texted Elaine to meet her at the park the following morning.

An hour later, Fedden put his head round her office door. The warrant on Marley's flat had been executed and Marley had been rearrested.

Sarah drove steadily across London, tracking east through side roads. The neighbourhoods changed as if London were not a city but rather a coalescence of villages, transforming within yards as she crossed invisible boundaries. Here were religious Jews walking with their children on their Friday-night excursions; then wide leafy streets, eighteenth-century houses, people relaxing outside a pub with a collection of glossy dogs. The neighbourhoods got poorer. On the left, a girl in high heels and bare legs standing in the early-evening light hoping for a punter. On the right, Astro pitches and groups of lads playing football under eerie white light.

Fedden had asked that Sarah lead Marley's interview with Steve but she wasn't sure who the idea had come from. She hadn't worked with Steve since they'd interviewed Lizzie Griffiths. Was it

Steve himself who'd suggested they should suddenly do so again? Or had the news about Stephenson been so decisive as to finally swing Fedden's vote in her favour? In any case, she wasn't unhappy. She remembered how well she and Steve had understood each other in interview. He had always known the moment to speak, the correct emphasis, the right tone. And she relished the task ahead, which was, if difficult, straightforward: they needed to squeeze Marley into giving up everything she knew about Brannon's plans. As she started to drive over the speed bumps that broke up the approach to Caenwood police station, she experienced a rush of adrenaline tinged with something like the nervousness that she imagined athletes felt before they ran a race worth winning.

The custody suite was busy: prisoners and police waiting on the bench, a detention officer taking fingerprints in the side room, officers moving back and forth with bags of evidence. Marley was all front: leaning on the custody desk, sticking her commendable arse out. She was wearing a wide-brimmed black hat from which her golden frizz escaped stylishly, and was chewing gum as loudly as if it were a performance art. She also wore black-and-white ankle-strap heels, a very short skirt and a cropped top that showed her flat stomach. Lee and the custody sergeant – a short, feminine-looking white bloke with a square head, a dimpled chin and the hint of soft breasts beneath his shirt – seemed to be working according to unofficial police standing orders by responding to Marley's behaviour with impenetrable boredom. A young man was led past Marley towards the male cells and she high-fived him.

'Safe!'

'That gum?' Sarah heard the custody sergeant say.

Marley spat it into her hand and stretched her arm out to offer it to Lee. He held out a small evidence bag with disdain and she placed it slowly inside and pouted at him.

Steve walked up beside Sarah. 'Come on,' he said quietly, tapping his shirt pocket.

They smoked outside in the yard. It was almost like old times.

Steve took Sarah through the arrest.

'We got a couple of wraps of cocaine in her bedside drawer. So we nicked her for the Class A and assisting an offender.'

'Have we got the phone work?'

Steve nodded, inhaled his cigarette and threw the stub on the floor. 'Yes. The phone linked to Brannon called Marley from a park in Haringey. We haven't had time to check CCTV at the location yet. Now the phone's left London, as you know.'

Sarah remembered briefly how often they had stood on that low roof outside their old office talking about their various investigations and smoking too much. She remembered how the crow had jumped about hoping for food. They'd been good times.

Steve said, 'She's put herself on offer for him.'

'Have you read the intelligence on her, what the two of them went through together when they were children?'

Steve nodded. 'I know why she's doing it, but I don't feel sorry for her.'

There was a pause.

Sarah said, 'I believed her when she said she didn't know he'd killed Georgina when he went to her straight after the murder.'

'Perhaps we can work on that, on how he's let her down.'

'You dropped any hints about how much time she might be serving?'

'Yes, she's giving the couldn't-give-a-fuck routine, but I think she's bricking it.'

Sarah stubbed her cigarette out on the wall. 'Good.'

———

As soon as the interview preliminaries were over, the solicitor intervened.

'Marley has made it clear to me that she's very keen to assist the police in finding Mark Brannon. She is motivated by her concerns for the welfare of Mark's daughter, Skye.'

Sarah took off her reading glasses and considered the solicitor. He was thin, wore jeans and trainers and looked as though he might still be in his twenties. An idealist, she guessed. Anyone his age with a decent law qualification had to be to choose to work in criminal defence. Advising Marley was probably his biggest professional shout to date, and the responsibility of it seemed to be leaking into his pale eyes. She wondered if he believed his client.

'Thanks for that.'

She looked across at Marley, who was drawing her bottom teeth slowly down her top lip. First things first. They'd get back to the lawyer's offer of help, but not yet. This was the time to squeeze.

'Marley, I first met you two days ago when I came to your flat looking for Mark and Skye. You said to me then that you didn't know that Mark had killed Georgina. You hadn't been helping him to avoid arrest.'

When Marley didn't answer, Steve placed the mobile phone in its evidence bag on the table. He did it without drama, and Sarah remembered how he had always known when she wanted him to do something and how to do it.

She said, 'Exhibit LMC/4, your mobile phone that was returned to you after your arrest in the early hours of 17th July. A download has shown one call made to you by a prepaid unregistered mobile phone linked to Mark Brannon.'

Marley kissed her teeth, but there was anxiety behind her disdain.

Sarah said, 'You knew Mark was wanted. You knew he'd killed. Did you speak to him? Assist him?'

'I tried to persuade him to hand himself in!'

'If you'd told us about the phone, we could have cell-sited it.'

'You still can. He doesn't know you know about it.'

'What did he say to you?'

'He just talked about how he was feeling, about how hard it is. He said it was all the police's fault and that I shouldn't worry. He'd never hurt Skye.'

Sarah leaned back in her chair. 'The phone he called from has been cell-sited going up the M6.'

'He's got mates up there. People he's worked with. I can give you names.'

Sarah rubbed the back of her neck, as if something pained her there. 'I know you and Mark went through a lot together. I know you want to stick by him.'

'I was just talking to him. I didn't help him. It's not assisting.'

'I notice you've got your story very straight.'

Marley looked between Sarah and Steve. Steve put his biro in his mouth, cigar-style, and affected an American accent. 'I love it when a plan comes together.'

The solicitor began to protest, but Steve dismissed him with a wave of his hand. 'It's *The A-Team*. Bit before your time.'

Marley had jumped in. 'I know what it is.'

Steve said, 'I think your cousin fancies himself as Hannibal Smith.'

Sarah said, 'What Steve's saying, Marley, is that Mark's been using you.'

'What do you mean? I'm helping you. I'm willing to give you names, addresses, everything.'

'Skye's life is in danger and you're playing games.'

'I'm trying to help!'

'No, you're not.'

The solicitor tried to intervene. 'Why don't you just take the information my client is offering and act on it?'

Sarah ignored him. 'It's too neat. That burner he's using. It's only dialled one number, your number, the number the police know—'

'He made a mistake! He was lonely, wanted to talk to someone.'

'And having made that mistake, he's not noticed he's done it, and that phone – which has been switched off apart from the call to you – is now switched on and helpfully making its way up north. We can get a cell site on it. After two days successfully hiding from us, suddenly Mark's become an idiot.'

Marley looked caged, backed up, as if they had captured one of those fierce, untrusting cats that scrape their survival on scrubland. Sarah had an intimation of her, of the kernel of something desperate inside.

'You've stood by Mark, you always have. You two have been through a lot together.'

Marley's eyes were darting about as if the answers were sprayed over the walls in indecipherable script.

Steve spoke reflectively. 'Maybe it's not *The A-Team*. Maybe Mark's watched *The Bourne Conspiracy* once too often. You know, that bit where he drops his mobile phone in someone's pocket and they follow the phone instead of Matt Damon?'

Sarah said, 'By the time we can't find him in Manchester it'll be too late. The evidence against you by then will be overwhelming. You've been nicked and asked to tell the truth, but you're still lying.'

Steve said, 'Are you really going to stick by him to the bitter end?'

Sarah said, 'I don't think you're a heartless person. Have you really considered the possibility that he might kill Skye? Have you thought of her stabbed to death like her mother?'

Marley's mouth was clamped tightly shut. She shrugged as if none of this really concerned her, but she also drew her nails across the surface of the table, seemingly unaware of what she was doing. Sarah reached her hand across into Marley's eyeline, drew her gaze up.

'Do you honestly trust Mark not to hurt Skye?'

Horror flickered across Marley's eyes. She shook her head.

Steve said, 'We'll stop the tapes for a minute.'

Sarah had a sensation inside her chest like galloping horses. Somewhere, dead or alive, Skye was with her father. Steve went to put Marley briefly back in her cell. Sarah remained in the interview room with the solicitor.

With no impression of hurry, he opened his notepad. He popped the nib on his biro. Sarah tried to calm herself. Her urgency might be the very thing that stopped her communicating. She wondered if the brief was realistic enough to know that his client's best interests lay in playing ball.

'Do you need a coffee?'

He shook his head.

She understood: her friendliness might be treachery. She was the enemy, the person who would harm his client. This was the singular honour of the defence lawyer: to protect his client to the utmost no matter what the circumstances. His heart might be crying out to find Skye, but his duty was to stand by Marley.

Sarah ran her fingers through her hair.

'I'm not sure Marley really understands what she's done.'

He looked at her warily. 'I can't comment.'

There was a pause. Sarah said, 'I'll lay out the police position, OK?'

'OK.'

She pinched her bottom lip for a second while she thought it through.

'Marley and Mark Brannon were raised in an abusive household together. It's not surprising that she's loyal to him, whatever happens. That's mitigation, of course, but it's nowhere near enough to stop her going to prison. What I'm saying is that Marley's loyalty to Mark Brannon mustn't be yours. Mark's not your client: Marley is. Mark's getting her into a lot of trouble and it's your job to help her.'

'I won't help her by making her look guilty.'

'I get that. But look at the evidence: that phone's called no one but Marley. It's a set up, an attempt to misdirect the police and Marley's assisting that attempt. She needs to hurry up and tell us the truth about what was said during that phone call and who she spoke to.'

'Don't try to pressure me. I wasn't born yesterday.'

'Yes, you can hope she squeezes in under the wire of "too difficult to prove". But do you honestly think a jury will look kindly on her if she could have saved Skye's life and didn't—'

He raised his voice. 'I won't comment on my client's instructions.'

He was feeling it: that much was clear. She needed to give him space to come to the right decision.

'I'll finish telling you how we're seeing it, then you can have a talk to Marley.'

He popped his pen again, looked down at his pad, clearly keen to have something to write.

'Our priority is to find Skye alive. Right now, Marley's only a small part of a much bigger picture and she's got leverage because she can help us. The moment Skye is found, all that changes. The leverage is gone, and if Skye's dead and Marley didn't help, then trust me, our perspective will change. We'll have a lot more energy to focus on her. You can count on that.'

———

All Marley's bravado had gone. She sat hunched up in her chair. Perhaps she'd looked like that when she was taken into care aged nine – fearful and small.

'I didn't speak to him,' she said, chewing her nails down to the quick. 'It was someone else, someone I don't know. He said I was doing Mark a favour by answering the phone. I didn't need to know anything else about it. I asked him if the police were going to nick me and he said, "If they do just say Mark talked to you about how he's feeling, then you're not assisting." An anxious frown was etched between her eyebrows. 'I did ask the man about Skye and he said she was fine. Mark had promised he wasn't going to hurt her.'

Sarah left Steve charging Marley. They'd agreed with the solicitor that after she'd been bailed to court, Marley would sit with Steve and talk through everything she knew about Brannon. It would take a while, because any detail might be helpful. Sarah would update Fedden and then go home for her early start in Morville Park.

There was a mug on the table in the canteen, and Fedden pushed it towards Sarah when he saw her entering.

'I ponced some coffee from main office,' he said. 'Good enough for you?'

'Yes. Thanks.'

'I won't keep you. What's your instinct on Marley? Is she telling the truth?'

'Unfortunately, I think so, yes. She doesn't know anything. She's never even spoken to Brannon. Someone else called her from the phone. The information she gives Steve about his associates may be useful, but I doubt it. Brannon's been very careful.'

'I've sent officers to follow the phone up to Manchester. We might be able to nick the people who are helping him. My guess is they're attached to the Youngs. Brannon probably knows stuff they don't want sharing and so they have to show willing.' Fedden glanced at his watch. 'You need to get some sleep.'

'I'll rejoin the search as soon as I can.'

'Don't worry about that. Just keep Egremont tidy.'

Every traffic light seemed to be turning red at her approach. She waited for them to change with the patience of concrete. This was the secret weariness of police work, the running on empty that you had to simply endure.

London was proceeding around her. That was what she observed as she sat in her car, not even noticing the lights had changed until someone behind her honked his horn. She pulled into the two lanes of traffic stop-starting along the Euston Road. Something was bothering her. Finally her brain fished it out of her exhaustion and presented it to her: that chance meeting in the sushi place. Caroline's smile and her laughing eyes. The traffic stopped and she rested her forehead on the steering column in sheer frustration at her own rudeness.

She turned off through back streets that ran between the railway lines, conjuring the algorithm that would avoid the traffic and take her home.

She'd found her way to the Turkish mini market. The owner was outside winding in the awning. A flicker of recognition crossed his face.

'All right,' he said, 'but be quick. We're closing.'

But she wasn't quick. She lingered in front of the fridges, dawdled by the breads and cakes. She wasn't hungry. She didn't need anything. Daisy wasn't at home waiting for a treat. The house would be empty and silent. She threw a clear plastic pack of leathery fresh pasta into her basket and made her way towards the till. The man was waiting for her, impatient to close. She put her basket on the counter. He said, 'No point coming in here on the off chance. You'll have to ring her.'

'What are you talking about?'

'Yeah, all right.'

He rang the pasta into the till. Sarah handed over a twenty-pound note.

'Look,' he said, fishing out the change. 'You can't count on bumping into her. Particularly at this time of night. If you want to see her, you'll have to call her. Have you still got her number?'

28

The trees stood like a silent congregation. The early-morning sun threw shafts of light between the aisles of their trunks and ploughed bright furrows across the woodland's floor of decomposing leaves. These were city trees, in the less populated reaches of a London park. Still they seemed inviolate, primordial. Sarah remembered vaguely some myth of trees walking, talking, watching. In reality, though, although the woodland itself was ancient most of these trees were not old. Their height and girth measured only the years that had passed since that night in October 1987 when, unforeseen and unchecked, an armada of wind had swept across southern Britain unroofing houses and crushing cars like tin cans.

Some said then that the storm was a punishment for the south's re-election of Margaret Thatcher but the local councillors had resisted firmly any suggestion of the supernatural. It was a practical matter. Swiftly they completed their necessary meetings and discussions. They bent over papers and signed whatever orders were needed. Funds were released. Earth-movers with caterpillar tracks, and tender saplings – their delicate parts preserved in sacks – were dispatched to the battlefield of stooped trunks and upturned roots.

And perhaps, Sarah thought as she walked steadily along the wooded path; perhaps someone both seen and unseen had come too. Someone quick and furtive in the night. Someone with a body to cradle in a growing hand of roots.

There was no intimation of the devastation now. The trees were not telling. There was only the sound of birdsong.

The site was busy. A couple of uniformed constables were standing at the cordon. Two people in jeans and T-shirts were marking out the ground with white tape. Elaine was standing next to a huge spreading oak with a man in shorts and sandals. Another figure – the geophysicist probably – sat alone on a sandy bank with a laptop. Sarah walked over.

'Dr Stichill?'

He looked up. 'You're Sarah?'

'That's right. You've started already?'

He glanced over at Elaine and the man she was standing with.

'Yes, well, your colleague has been very helpful. And Mr Medcalfe, of course. Thanks to him, we know exactly where the school helped with the planting. Luckily it's a relatively small area.'

'Great. If you don't need me immediately, I'll go and say hello. I'll be right back.'

'No trouble. I've got plenty to be getting on with.'

Sarah walked over to Elaine and the man she was standing with. She stretched out her hand to him. 'Mr Medcalfe?'

Medcalfe was tall, late seventies probably, his tightly corkscrewed hair cut close to his head, perfectly grey, like soft lambswool. A simple checked cotton shirt, a lanyard with a key on it round his neck, blue shorts that finished below the knee, the slight knots of varicose veins beneath the dusky black skin of his calves. His handshake was quick and strong. The stressed 'r's of the Caribbean had not left him, nor the rhythm that made it sound as though the simplest sentence carried a hidden pleasure.

'Detective Sarah Collins?'

'That's right. Sarah, please. Thanks for making it over so early.'

'It's all right. I'm an early riser.'

Sarah glanced at Elaine. 'You've taken a statement already?'

She nodded. 'Yes.'

Sarah looked back at Medcalfe. 'You worked for the council, sir?'

He laughed. 'Nah, Harry.' He looked around him. 'Yes. Parks, allotments. Loved it.'

'And you're retired now?'

'Yes, long time now. I'm busy enough.'

'I'm sure you are. And you remember Mr Stephenson?'

He smiled sceptically. 'Yes. Him *very* keen to be part of the planting.'

'And the volunteers from the school, they only worked here? Nowhere else?'

'Yes, me sure about that. A hundred and ten per cent.'

Sarah glanced across at Elaine, who nodded. 'It's OK, I got it all down in the statement. Harry kept a timetable and a map of who worked where and when. Very organized. We couldn't be luckier on that score. He's let me have his notebooks.'

Sarah said, 'That's fantastic.' She turned back to Harry. 'But you're not sure about which trees exactly he might have planted.'

Medcalfe laughed. 'Lord no! But he not plant many, that's for sure. I think he was here to make an impression. Not to plant trees, no.' He looked around at the spreading canopy. He was breathing in the woodland. 'Can you tell which is the youngest?'

'We've got a botanist doing a survey.'

He laughed. 'You don't need no botanist!'

Sarah laughed too. 'Well, we've got one.'

He smiled. 'Me know.' He stretched out the word sceptically. 'Pro-cee-dure.'

Sarah smiled. 'Harry, I can't thank you enough. Do you need a lift home?'

'No thanks. I'll go bore the young people.' He offered his hand and Sarah shook it again. He looked up along the fissured bark of the oak towards the canopy above. 'You can't have this one. This one's old.'

Sarah looked up too through the map of leaves, almost translucent in the sunlight, and glimpsed the sky beyond, blue and distant. 'We'll leave that one alone.'

Harry put his hand flat on the broad trunk of the tree as if it were an old friend that needed comforting.

'You think you'll find her?'

'I don't know.'

He exhaled sadly. 'What a thing.'

'Yes, it is.'

Dr Stichill was younger and shorter than Harry, but he was, somehow, of the same ilk: a lean, practical man. He wore cargo trousers and a Helly Hansen fleece with more pockets than a person could ever need. He patted the ground beside him. 'Pull up a chair.'

She spread out her mac. 'So, you'll have found her by lunchtime?'

He laughed. 'That's right. Sooner maybe.'

Sarah rested back on her forearms. 'Tell me what's happening now.'

'We're looking for anomalies – depressions, that sort of thing. If there's a body, there will have been decompositional fluid but it might not show up. Depends on all sorts of thing – how long after death she was buried, whether she was clothed, wrapped in any way.' He nodded in the direction of the young man and woman in jeans who were stretching out tape. 'My underlings are mapping the site so we can make topographical corrections . . .'

Sarah didn't need to follow the technical stuff and her attention wandered. She could easily fall asleep on this nice warm hill.

Dr Stichill was wrapping up. 'I'll call you if we come up with anything interesting.'

'Thank you. We'll have Uniform always on site. My colleague has briefed them, but if anyone seems particularly interested in what you're doing, be sure to let me know.'

The path back towards the car was marked with objects left prominently for their losers to find. On a fallen tree a pair of sunglasses. Hanging from a branch a beaded necklace, made by some child's hand. By a drinking fountain a toddler's drink cup. Sarah found a bench opposite a view of grass that fell away towards trees.

A girl, eight or nine years old, her skin the colour and shine of polished ebony, was cycling slowly through the long grass in a red dress. Her father walked a few feet behind her. At first Sarah thought he was talking with his phone on speaker. Then she realized he was filming his daughter, trying to capture that moment of beauty.

Today was Susie's memorial service.

Sarah remembered the darkness of the classroom, the ink-stained wooden surface of the desk. They had been revising the *Aeneid*, reading it aloud, each girl assigned a phrase or a line. A blind professor had come in from the local university and he hadn't noticed the need to turn on the lights. Her own line had stayed with her forever, as she sat in the deepening gloom, her finger on the page, the words coming up but never reached. *Et vastos volvunt ad litora fluctus* – 'and they roll their huge waves towards the shore'. There had been a knock at the door. The school secretary entered, switching on the lights in a blink of fluorescence and asking for Sarah to be excused please. She led Sarah to the headmistress's office – *no, I'm sorry, the headmistress will explain* – taking short, hasty steps slightly ahead all the way and remaining behind Sarah in the hallway as she awkwardly reached over and pushed the door and ushered her into the office. The headmistress – red-haired, flamboyant, an Oxford scholar, much admired by both girls and parents – stood up when she entered and said her name with kindness.

Sarah.

Usually the 1970s rectory had been a hub of activity, a place where the door was never shut. Suddenly it had become quiet. The shared areas – the living room, the kitchen, the dining room – were deserted, and she moved through them like an interloper. Her father was praying earnestly, steadfastly in his study, and the door to her parents' bedroom upstairs was firmly shut. Her mother was not to be disturbed.

Sarah, off school until after the funeral, sat on the sofa and flicked through TV channels with the sound off. The doorbell rang constantly, and even though her attention was focused nowhere in particular, it was only reluctantly that she got up to answer the sympathetic parishioners who stood with arms outstretched holding casseroles and cakes. Her father was loved by his congregation and they wanted to help. This was all they could think of. They came in, offered to make tea. They cleared up the kitchen and asked how her parents were doing. When her eyes filled, they quickly changed the subject, found something useful to do like cleaning the floor.

After they had left, the cakes remained: confectionery oxymorons, bitter sweetnesses, exuberant expressions of a compassion that no one could bear. Coffee and walnut. Victoria sponge that tasted of sand. The tins, too – pictures of hens, of hot air balloons – splendidly inappropriate, bunting at a bomb site. A vast loneliness was the overwhelming sensation. Susie had gone. Dear Susie: practical, straightforward, warm, funny. Sarah had taken her for granted. Susie was just *there*. She wasn't the stuff of tragedy. She was stupid jokes and having a good time. She'd been as assumed and as necessary as water and daylight. What kind of a God could click his fingers and snuff her out?

Then there was the funeral. Her mother had come downstairs, her face forever altered, and life had resumed. But without Susie, the house was silenced. How could Sarah not have thought that God, in his perversity, had taken the wrong child?

She stirred. She should get back to work.

A family walked by – children of different ages, two dogs, a baby on a man's shoulders, her hand curled round her father's neck – and it seemed suddenly to Sarah that if a distant satellite had a camera with a lens designed to seek out human happiness, then this park would glow through the darkness of space. Perhaps there was some kindness after all if this was the place where Tania had been resting.

She reached in her bag and dug out her purse. Caroline's number was in there and she dialled it and left a voicemail.

'It's Sarah here. You know, the police officer? I'm really sorry about the other day. I was awful. I'm a bit busy for the next few days, but if you could face seeing me, perhaps we could meet up and have that drink when things have calmed down.'

29

It was late morning already, and Lizzie stirred in the single bed of her childhood. On a shelf opposite the bed were her running trophies and medals. She reached to the floor, picked up her phone and googled Mark Brannon. The search window filled within seconds. There was a video appeal and she tilted the phone to landscape and pressed the play triangle. A fat man in a grey striped suit, white shirt and shiny grey tie was addressing the camera. The strip beneath read: *Detective Chief Inspector James Fedden.*

'Mark, I am reaching out to you. You must feel terrified about what is going on and you must be looking for a way to stop it. We know . . .' The video buffered on Lizzie's mother's slow Wi-Fi and then resumed. '. . . how much you love your daughter, Skye, and we're appealing to you to help us to help you . . .'

The DCI's effort was palpable, and Lizzie understood from the words how hard they had tried to get this appeal right. They must be desperate. Three days after the murder of Georgina, Brannon was still on the lam and Skye was still missing.

The doorbell rang. Lizzie rolled over and ignored it. It rang again. She shouted out.

'Mum, someone at the door.'

Another insistent ring. She got up, stood at her bedroom window in her pants and T-shirt. There was a white Mercedes A-Class on the drive and three people were standing beside it. One of them, a man in a grey suit, looked up and waved cheerily. Lizzie pulled on

the pink-and-white-striped towelling dressing gown her mother
had left out for her and padded down the stairs in her bare feet.
She opened the door. The man smiled at her.

'Denning and Reeves? We've got a viewing booked.'

'Uh, yes, come in.'

They crowded into the entrance hall. The man in the suit had
pimples. His shirt was white but the collar was light blue and
matched his tie. He had a couple with him, both with gold bands
on their ring fingers. The woman was pregnant.

Lizzie ran her hand through her hair. 'Sorry, just got up.'

'That's OK,' the estate agent said. 'I can do the tour.'

'Yeah, thanks.'

She wandered off to the kitchen, put the kettle on to boil and
shovelled coffee into the cafetière. A note from her mother on the
table. *Shopping. Back soon.* Her shirts and pants had been taken out
of the washing machine and hung neatly on the rack. As the kettle
hissed, she stood in the kitchen doorway, watching the estate agent
in the sitting room commenting on the view beyond the window.
She remembered how her father had loved it, how hawks used to
hover there over the bulrushes and coarse grass before the wild
land was drained for playing fields and a children's playground.

'It's a good place to raise a family,' the estate agent was saying.
'It's a bit tired, needs freshening up, but that's reflected in the
asking price.'

Lizzie cast her eyes over the sitting room. The adjustable reclining
chair that her father had sat in like a rigid totem as he faced down
death, the glass coffee table, the sash curtains, the contrasting green
flowery wallpaper borders.

The estate agent turned back, saw Lizzie with her bare legs in
her mother's stripy dressing gown. The pregnant woman smiled
with embarrassment. 'It's a lovely place,' she said, unconsciously
resting her hand on her bump. 'Was it your childhood home?'

'Yes. My father died here last year. That's why my mother's selling.'

'Oh, I'm sorry.'

'That's OK. I'll leave you to it.'

Lizzie walked past them back into the hall and up the stairs to her mother's room. In the wardrobe was a box of photographs that had not made it into the heavy albums that lived downstairs in a pine chest of drawers. She lifted the box onto the bed. The tour was already climbing the stairs, talking in low voices. If she wasn't there, Lizzie thought, they could speak more freely rather than treating the place like a National Trust property that gave you a unique opportunity to encounter the full semi-detached suburban experience. She sat on the bed and began to look through photos. Her passing-out parade. Lizzie smiling and smart in white gloves, tunic and dress trousers. Her father in a wheelchair beside her, holding her hand and wearing his guarded but bursting-with-pride look. She leafed through the other pictures. Her sister, Natty, no more than a toddler, sitting on the newly made drive of the house on her tricycle. Herself burying her father on the beach, the light flaring orange across the print. A few photos from athletics competitions: Lizzie hurdling, another with her standing on a podium.

At the very bottom of the box was a single photograph: a man she didn't know standing on an ornamental bridge over a river. The sun was diffusing across, but she saw a sensitive mouth, a slight kink in his blonde hair. He wore nicely faded jeans and a light cotton shirt and he looked calmly at the camera. Beneath the photo were a couple of heavy envelopes. Lizzie lifted a flap and saw cream paper, blue ink handwriting.

There was a tap at the door. She closed the box, put it back in the wardrobe, opened the bedroom door. The estate agent was waiting on the landing with the two prospective buyers. They looked nervous but keen, like missionaries from the Church of the Latter-day Saints. The estate agent said, 'Is it OK for them to view the master bedroom?'

Lizzie tried to smile but feared that she was radiating hostility. 'Of course. You finished with the bathroom?'

They nodded and smiled back at her warily, an unpredictable stranger in her own house.

Lizzie standing in the dim light that filtered through the blind in the bathroom put her hand between her legs. She withdrew her hand and looked at her fingers. Still nothing. She ran the bath, stripped to nakedness, picked up a square glass jar of bath crystals, opened the stopper and inhaled the perfumes of a different generation. She stepped into the hot water, keeping her injured arm resting on the side of the bath, and lay back. Worry spread over her skin like heat. She should get a pregnancy test, just in case. Her thoughts turned to the man in that photo in the box. The fragmented memory of her mother dancing too close to him at a grown-ups' party when Lizzie was at primary school. Her mother's head nestled into the crook of his neck, his arm curved round her waist. After that party her mother had been gone for five months. She'd seen him – Alan, his name was – the day her mother had returned home. Looking down from the bedroom window of this same house, she'd watched the car pull into the drive. It had been red and had a horse galloping across the radiator grille. Only much later, when she saw another similar car in the street, had she realized fully that it was in fact a cool car, a fun car: a small vintage American Mustang. How her father must have hated that. But there'd been no sign of any displeasure when he had stepped out onto the drive and helped Alan to get her mother's cases out of the boot of the car.

She ran her hand over her stomach and a shimmer of feeling passed across her skin. She held her nose, lifted her injured arm into the air and plunged backwards so that the water covered her face. She thought of Kieran and his wife and daughter somewhere out towards the south coast. God, she hoped she wasn't pregnant.

The sound of the estate agent leaving. Then another car pulling in and drawing up the drive. The front door opening. Lizzie dressed herself in a pair of her old tracksuit bottoms and a T-shirt. She went downstairs. Her mother was in the kitchen unpacking bags of shopping. Lizzie reboiled the kettle. She took out the porcelain cups with the blackberries painted on the inside.

Her mother glanced over her shoulder. 'Using the china, Lizzie? Special occasion, is it?'

There was that familiar twist of irritation. 'Does it *need* to be a special occasion?'

'I s'pose not.' Her mother gave one of her tense smiles. 'You're absolutely right. They just sit in the cupboard. Better to use them.'

She abandoned her shopping, came and stood by Lizzie's side while she poured the now boiling water over the coffee in the cafetière and into the cups to warm them. Here was the familiar search for intimacy.

Her mother said, 'So, how are things?'

'Fine.'

Lizzie moved away towards the washing on the rack. It was still wet and she began to put it in the dryer. Her mother said, 'Will they be all right in there?'

'I need a dry shirt for work tonight.'

'But they're good shirts. You could leave it another hour or so.'

Lizzie twisted the dial and pressed on. 'They'll be fine.'

She poured some milk into a jug and popped it in the microwave. Her mother's eyes were on her as if her banal actions were in fact interesting.

'Your arm not hurting you too much?'

'No, it's nothing.'

Her mother tried to catch her eye. 'Anything to tell me about?'

'What do you mean?'

A nervous laugh. 'Well, that man who came to your father's funeral, for example. Am I likely to see him again?'

She thought hopelessly of the missed period and of Kieran's little girl and made a sort of grunt in reply. Her mother picked up on that and an anxious little frown creased between her eyes. 'Is everything all right?'

'Yeah, yeah, everything's fine.'

Her mother went back to unpacking the shopping. Even as she rejected her attempts at closeness, Lizzie regretted her own hard heart. She watched her mother: brave somehow in her tidy widowhood, still neat and slim in her blue cardigan and well-fitted trousers. She thought of the man in the photograph with his faded jeans and his red mustang. It was a possibility for her mother that she could never imagine.

She said, 'Have you ever thought of trying to find Alan?'

Her mother turned to her. 'Why have you brought that up? After all these years!' She shook her head, turned back to the bags on the floor. 'Really.'

'Well, now that Dad's dead. Where would the harm be?'

There was no immediate reply. Here were the tins for the high shelves. Her mother piled them steadily onto the work surface.

'That's a long time ago, Lizzie. Please don't resurrect it now.'

The microwave pinged. Lizzie turned towards the sink and emptied the hot water from the cups down the plughole. 'Our coffee's hot,' she said. 'Why don't we sit and drink it together?'

Her mother stopped, smoothed down her trousers, ran her hands under the sink, spoke brightly. 'Yes, why don't we?'

They sat at the table in the conservatory together. Lizzie tried to keep her tone nonchalant.

'It's actually quite easy to find people nowadays. Social media, Facebook, that kind of thing. I could help you.'

Lizzie's mum pursed her lips, and Lizzie remembered the tidiness, the scrupulous organization, the stern tellings-off that had characterized her later years with her mother.

'I asked you not to bring that up. He's dead. He died a couple of years after I came back to your father. Can we change the subject now?'

30

Sarah parked in a suburban cul-de-sac populated by 1930s semis. Children were playing on bikes in the turning circle at the end of the street.

When Katherine answered the door, Sarah realized that, in spite of her bad-tempered attitude on the phone earlier – *I've only just talked to that other woman from the murder squad!* – she had still somehow persisted in imagining Tania's friend as she had been in 1987. Claire Mills had shown her a photo of the two girls, side by side in school uniform. They were both smiling as if sharing the same joke, unconsciously sexy in their schoolgirl knowing-unknowing way – long hair, ties loose at the neck, arms flung round each other's shoulders, hips out to the side. But here was a middle-aged woman, older than Sarah herself. She wore jogging pants and a sleeveless T-shirt and had the hard-muscled calves of someone who had remained fit way beyond her youth. Her highlighted blonde hair revealed strands of grey. There were deep lines at her mouth and eyes.

She didn't say even hello; instead just 'You're later than you said you'd be.'

Sarah slipped her warrant card back into her pocket. 'I'm really sorry. Do you want to reschedule?'

Katherine threw up her hands in exasperation. '*Reschedule?*' She turned away with a heavy sigh and led Sarah into the house.

Sarah followed her into the sitting room and watched her moving rapidly around, scooping up objects that littered the floor and the furniture – swimming goggles, sweet wrappers, a football.

'I tell them to put this stuff away, but do they *listen*?'

She hadn't offered to make tea, hadn't offered a seat. She paused from sorting a pile of things under the television, talking quickly as she did so.

'This is the weekend my ex has the kids. It's the only time I get to myself. Did you come to ask me anything specific?'

Sarah had hoped to get something perhaps that others hadn't been able to, but everything Katherine did seemed designed to prevent her making any connection. The only thing was to plunge straight in. 'You and Tania had agreed to meet up—'

Katherine interrupted. 'I've explained this, feels like a hundred times.'

'I'm sorry.'

'Tania was unreliable.'

'Unreliable?'

'You know teenage girls – say they're going to do one thing and then don't turn up. We didn't have mobile phones in those days.'

'And you didn't think to call her home, find out what was going on?'

'Call her mum? Who does that?'

Sarah didn't sail on, as Katherine's tone suggested she should, but rather paused to weigh those words. Would no teenager have even considered picking up the phone to find out where her friend was?

'I think at that age if one of my friends hadn't turned up, I would probably have called her family.'

Katherine looked at her and scratched the back of her head. 'Goody two-shoes, were you?'

'Why do you say that?'

'Look, I'm sorry. I just didn't want to get her into trouble.'

'Why would she be in trouble?'

'If Tania hadn't come to me, that meant she was probably up to stuff.'

'Stuff? What stuff?'

'Oh come on! All teenagers get up to stuff.'

Here was the information that had to be unpicked, insisted on.

'But Tania wasn't *all teenagers*. She was one of the rare ones who seems to have come to harm. That's why I'm trying to find out any detail, any piece of information you might have – even if you don't know you have it – that might help us to find out what happened to her. If she was up to stuff, then I need to know what that stuff was. That's why I'm asking you these questions.'

'And I'm answering. I don't mean to be rude. It's just I've already been asked all this. I really don't think I can help you.'

Sarah attempted a smile. 'So, what kind of stuff *was* she up to?'

Katherine shrugged. 'I don't know. We weren't as close as we had been. She'd stopped telling me what was going on.'

'Had you fallen out?'

'Not really. You know how teenage girls are. I've got one myself: always in and out with her friends. I lose track. You not got kids?'

There was a look that went with the question, a suggestion that Katherine had guessed that Sarah certainly didn't have kids.

Sarah said, 'So you were still friends, yes? Best friends. Confided in each other?'

Katherine shrugged. 'I s'pose so.'

'You knew, for example, her dad was having an affair?'

'Oh yes, she told me about that.'

So, still close enough to talk about personal things. 'Were you aware of Tania being in any sort of relationship?'

'Everything you're asking me, I've already been asked. Have you not read the files?'

Of course she'd read the files, but she'd wanted to hear the answers first hand. She nodded, waiting for Katherine to reply.

'There was no boyfriend I knew of,' Katherine said thinly.

'And what about you?'

'What about me?'

The persistent difficulty of asking the questions was interesting in itself.

'Did you have a boyfriend?'

Katherine made eye contact, hesitated momentarily, then said, 'No, I didn't. I was fifteen. Anything else?'

'Just one other thing? Your music teacher, Mr Stephenson . . .' She felt Katherine's eyes on her and searched for the words. 'Was he around a lot? I mean more than you'd expect in a teacher?'

'That's an odd question.'

'Still, was he?'

Katherine studied her. 'Of course we saw a lot of him. We were both in the orchestra, Tania and me. Why do you want to know about Mr Stephenson?'

'It's just a line of inquiry. Did you ever go in his car?'

'I can't really remember. Look, Mr Stephenson wasn't a nice man—'

'Oh, he wasn't? Could you tell me about that?'

'He was nasty. A bully . . . But I'm sure he didn't kill Tania, if that's what you're thinking.'

'That's interesting. How can you be sure?'

Sarah noticed something, a stiffening perhaps that was almost instantly interrupted by Katherine relaxing and frowning. She sat on the sofa. 'Of course I can't be sure. But I can't see him killing. That's too much.'

'Too much?'

Katherine shrugged.

Sarah said, 'This bullying?'

Katherine shook her head. 'He was just a horrid man.' She stood with an air almost of surprise at having found herself sitting at all. 'Have you got any more questions? I'm hoping to go for a swim.'

Standing in the hallway by the open front door, Katherine apologized.

'I'm sorry. If I was rude, I mean.'

Sarah waved her hand. 'Please, don't worry.' But she slowed her exit, hoping for a breach in Katherine's guardedness. What she heard was not really information, but rather a little nervous outburst.

'I seem to live my life in a hurry!'

Sarah waited.

'I've got into the habit of doing things at top speed since my useless husband left me . . . OK, it's not only that. Tania was a long time ago and I prefer not to think about it.' Her face gave a little twitch. 'So, that's probably what made me rude.' She looked at Sarah directly. 'But I do pray this new lead, whatever it is, will go somewhere; that you'll be able to tell me what happened. Even if Tania's dead. I'd like to have a grave I could visit. Even that would mean a lot to me.'

Sarah hesitated. She was so tempted to ask her outright. *This bullying* . . . But she was getting ahead of herself. She'd tried, given lots of opportunities. Any suggestion of what she was beginning to allow herself to suspect, would contaminate the evidence. If it was going to come, then it needed to come from Katherine, unprompted. But the moment was already gone. The breach had closed. Katherine gave another one of those smiles that never touched her eyes.

'So,' she said. 'Is there anything else?'

'Not that I can think of right now. Thank you.' Sarah made herself stay a second more, even though she could feel the sheer force of Katherine's will pushing her out of the door. 'But look, I made a mistake. Coming here at such short notice. I'm sorry about that.' She offered her card. 'I'd like you to think you could talk to me. About anything. If you think of something, would you give me a call?'

31

Brannon woke stiff and aching on the floor beside the bed. Skye was stirring, rubbing her eyes. Anxiety had him firmly in its grip: he'd slept too long. He was losing it. Someone needed to be in control and that someone was him. He sat up, rubbed his head, tried to think positively.

The pancakes had been a success. That had been good. He had wanted everything to be perfect for Skye, and he'd managed to stick to that. No rules, no tellings-off. He'd let her toss the pancakes herself, and he'd cheered when she succeeded, laughed and cuddled her when she'd failed. The dog hovered around their legs hoping for dropped catches. When one fell, she scuffled after it and gulped it down. Mrs Greedy, Skye said, and he'd suddenly remembered all the names Georgie had used to steer their daughter in the right direction. Mrs Lazy, Mrs Sleepy-head, Mrs Once-You've-Done-Your-Shoes-Up-You-Can-Have-a-Treat. The memory was like an oncoming truck that seemed to leave no room to swerve sideways. He'd opened Lizzie Griffiths' kitchen cupboards and tried to veer away from it, staring at her jars of Marmite and peanut butter for inspiration. It wasn't his fault! Gradually the cupboard came into focus. Maple syrup; there was an unopened bottle of maple syrup. He reached out, held it up like manna. 'Look what I've found!' Skye poured with her child's hand. The pancakes were swimming in lakes of sweetness.

Then they'd cuddled up with the dog on the sofa, watching *Ice Age* for the thousandth time. Georgina had put it in the bag she'd packed for Skye when she was going to leave. He was indulging her. He'd never liked the film – the soft-hearted, boring mammoth, the dumb sloth, Sid. His mind drifted. Skye was protecting him from the monsters, holding his hand. When he woke to the credits, she was asleep in his arms. He'd snuggled up to her, smelling her child's head. At two in the morning, he'd woken her and taken her out through the back garden into the darkness of the park. It's a magical holiday, he'd told her. Remember you must be a good girl, though, and he'd caught her eye and checked she knew what he meant – that behind the perfect day together was also the warrior who had to keep the family safe, the knife in his jeans, the dog by his side.

'Do you like the park at night?' he'd asked. 'All to ourselves.' And she'd said yes.

He'd pushed her on the roundabout, held her in his arms as they slid together down the slide. He'd pushed her on the swing for as long as she wanted. Her little hands clutched the metal chains and she closed her eyes as he swung her high into the starless orange sky. She'd sung, 'Lavender's blue, dilly, dilly, lavender's green, when I am king, dilly, dilly, you shall be queen.' But when she'd run to the edge of the playground, he'd had to call her name. She'd stopped dead as if it was Grandmother's Footsteps and turned and seen he'd got the dog by the collar, the knife to its neck.

When they got back to the flat, the birds were beginning to sing and she was dropping in his arms. He tucked her up and kissed her cheek until she told him to stop. He stroked her forehead as she fell asleep. It was only then that the beetles had really come crawling. Scuttling under his skin and behind his eyes. The recriminations. The injustice of it all. He'd created that beautiful family and others had destroyed it. He thought of the film he'd watched with Skye: that stupid woolly mammoth in the cave seeing the picture of his wife and child, murdered by the humans. The sloth narrating, 'Oh, and he's got a family. He's happy. Look, he's playing with his kid.' It made him furious: the lies, the false sentimentality of it all. He wouldn't have *forgiven*. He'd have killed, destroyed. He didn't want to be that soft mammoth with the vacant expression and the slow speech. He wanted to be the wordless, pitiless bronze statue, lifting Jason's boat and tipping the Argonauts into the sea.

At six in the morning, he'd checked the app and seen that Lizzie Griffiths' car was still stationary, 150 miles away up the M6. What if she was on holiday, gone for days? Weeks even. His options were narrowing, the dark clouds rolling in, the deadline approaching. He needed to think straight while he still could, before it overwhelmed him. That trip to the park. Weakness! And he couldn't trust Skye, not really. He saw how she looked at him sometimes. No, he couldn't risk that kind of thing again! If he was caught, it would be catastrophic. They would grab Skye, and him. He wouldn't be able to save her – she might even run to them. And once they'd got him, he could see it all: the cramped seat in the cage in the Serco van, and him shut in there like a neat little pony in a horsebox. He could see the dock, the court security numpty sitting beside him wearing a blue jumper and a bored expression. He wouldn't even be able to kill himself in his cell. They'd have people watching to stop him doing that.

He'd seen that stupid appeal by the fat man with the little teeth. *You must feel terrified about what is going on and you must be looking for a way to stop it.* Those words: it was like Jason in the film creeping up and taking the valve out of bronze Talos' huge foot. The lifeblood gushed out of the statue's ankle. It grasped its own neck, fracturing, falling. A terrible sound like grinding gears. *We know how much you love your daughter.* Those words had to be resisted. They were meant to sap his strength. They were tricks to break up his family. And Skye, Skye, Skye . . . What she didn't understand was that that would be the worst thing! Without him, she would be on her own. No one to look after her. He couldn't let that happen, wouldn't let that happen. He should have left the country with her straight away instead of waiting.

He tried to work out his options. The Volvo had got ringed plates. Perhaps they didn't even know about it. He'd checked the news reports and there was no word of it. But he knew better than to trust the police. They probably knew about the car. There'd be a description of it for police and customs officers. He hadn't visited it in days, parked up where he'd left it on a side street. Perhaps they'd already picked it up, or, worse, had left it where it was and were waiting for him to return to it. If they surprised him without Skye, he'd be no more than a cornered animal.

Maybe he could break into someone's house and take the keys to a different car. But the theft would be reported straight away. There was no way he could change the plates now, not in a way that wouldn't be almost immediately detected.

He watched the rise and fall of Skye's breath, the softness of her sleeping face. Time and options were running out. How hard he'd tried for her, harder than he'd ever tried in his life. Those bastards, those bastards. Nobody had ever cared for him.

He wouldn't abandon Skye and he wouldn't let her down. She wouldn't be on her own like he had been. It would be easiest to do it while she was asleep. Would a pillow be the gentlest way? He imagined pressing it down over her soft little face, her struggle, his overwhelming strength. He was crying. He wiped the corners of his eyes. His hands were wet. Georgie had always been the only one for him. The only one. Now here he was, on his own, having to make all the decisions.

Lizzie was his one hope. If only he could get her in the house, he could take her car. She was a cop. Her car wouldn't be flagged. It might be days before anyone even noticed she was missing. He stared at the app. The car was stationary. The fact of it pounded in his head like a piston engine. She wasn't coming! He tried to breathe, to think. Perhaps now was the time to take the action he needed to take. No more false starts, no more failed resolutions. He would do what he had to do.

But Skye was waking. She rubbed her eyes and her soft face puckered charmingly. 'Can we have more pancakes?'

That gave him a lump in his throat. Some pancakes and then what?

'In a minute, Skye. I just need to look at something.'

He checked the app. At last! The car was moving. The dog had jumped onto the bed and was licking Skye's face. Skye smiled at him, something desperate in the creases at the edges of her eyes. 'Please, Dad, can we have more pancakes?'

He checked the phone again. The car was still moving, turning left in the direction of the motorway. He smiled at Skye. 'Of course we can, Mrs Greedy. There's still some maple syrup left.'

32

Sarah had decided to return to Morville Park before heading back to Hendon and assisting in the search for Brannon. It was late afternoon and the fine weather had held. The park was packed with picnickers lying out on blankets. Some had hampers, others the more basic version: plastic cups, packets of crisps, supermarket taramasalata. Children roamed, set free by their dozing parents. A group of young men, their shirts off, were throwing a Frisbee while a collie ran around frantically barking between them. A couple were making out under the shade of a tree, she on top of him, her skirts lifted, her shoulder strap pulled down.

The site was down wooded paths in a more secluded area of the park. The scientists were packing up their kit for the day. Dr Stichill was sitting on the bank as if he had never left it. He moved the laptop so that the screen was in shadow. Sarah saw blobs and splashes of green and blue.

Stichill said, 'Let me explain.'

She laughed. 'I think you'd better.'

His finger moved over the screen.

'Basically we're looking for a resistivity anomaly – something produced by decaying organic matter. The light-blue areas are all anomalous.' He tapped the screen. 'I think this one looked the most promising. We've done another survey here. It's an ERT profile . . .'

'I don't need to know the technical stuff.'

'OK, so basically . . .' He clicked on another icon. There was a black-and-white image in which the depth was laid out against an axis in metres. 'This,' he said, tracing his finger across the image, 'looks down vertically and reveals . . .' He moved his pen to the middle of the image, where there was a bright depression.

Sarah said, 'A grave?'

Dr Stichill tilted his head from side to side. 'Maybe. Maybe not. All I'm telling you is that this depression is anomalous, not that it's a grave. Don't get your hopes up.'

Sarah shook her head. 'I won't. But are we ready to start digging?'

33

Lizzie left her car in the yard. She wasn't really supposed to do that, but on nights, no one was likely to check. She walked to the shopping centre and bought a pregnancy test. Back in the nick, in the ladies' toilets, she unwrapped the packaging. Sitting on the loo with her pants down, she read the instructions. It was more awkward than she'd imagined, holding the stick under the stream of her wee. She should have waited until she got home. But there was this impatience to be let off the hook. It would be good news and she could stop worrying. And if it wasn't good news, well then, she could deal with it. The sooner the better.

She'd imagined it would take ages, but no, bang, there they were: two lines. Undramatic but clear.

She stared at the lines as though that would make them go away. Perhaps they didn't mean what she thought they did. Or perhaps she had done the test incorrectly. She read the instructions again, checked and double-checked, looked at the stick and the two lines.

She stared for a while at the toilet door.

Someone used the cubicle beside her. She heard the tinkle of wee. Whoever it was washed her hands and left.

Lizzie hadn't even realized she was still sitting there with her pants down. She bagged up the kit in the paper bag the chemist had given her. She threw it in the waste bin, washed her hands. She told herself to be practical.

She couldn't tell anyone, certainly couldn't tell Ash – she'd be immediately signed off front-line duties. She went upstairs, ate the cheddar and Branston pickle sandwich her mother had made for her.

The night duty began.

First off, Lizzie administered a caution for a common assault as a favour to another officer who wanted to go off duty. Only an hour in, they got their first call-out. An old boy – shirtsleeves, black trousers, brown checked slippers – lying on his back in his sitting room, stiff as a board. His arms were bent at the elbow and raised above his head, and the look on his face seemed to suggest the arrival of death had completely astonished him. The two uniformed officers stood back from the corpse as if denying it had anything to do with them. On the sideboard was an analogue transistor radio. Dishes dried on a rack on the sink's stainless-steel drainer. On the arm of the sofa an open Len Deighton.

Ash said, 'Doesn't look like that bad a way to go.'

Lizzie turned to the uniformed officers. 'Those windows?'

The younger officer, whose dark hair was gelled up into a ridge above his head, looked shamefaced. 'Sorry, yes, we opened them. The smell, you know.'

So it continued. They moved from call to call. At midnight there was a rapid chain of burglaries. They listened over the radio as the suspect – as manic as a gerbil on a wheel – was detained after a chase across the roofs of a terrace. Relatively speaking, it was an easy job: it was too late to take statements and the suspect had been admitted to hospital, off his face on crack cocaine.

They entered the dead part of the night. The street outside the station was deserted and transmissions on the radio became infrequent. Lizzie thought of that plastic stick with its two lines in the bin in the ladies' toilet. No one needed to know, not even Kieran.

One of the station mice, emboldened by the stillness of the office, came out onto the carpet and crouched in plain sight, twitching its nose. Ash shook his head in wonderment. 'Look at the bloody nerve on him.'

They wrote up the Overnight Occurrence Book, put their takeaways in the microwave and crossed their fingers hard that there'd be no more calls.

At 0530 hours, the CID mobile rang again. It was the duty inspector informing them of an allegation of rape in a nightclub.

Ash rubbed his face wearily. 'The timing couldn't be worse.'

They drove to the scene: a busy nightclub open into the early hours. Three empty marked cars were parked up. Lizzie and Ash – the same age as the young people who filled the streets around the club, staggering about, smoking and talking – walked through the crowds and made themselves known at the door. They were ushered through.

The girl had reported that she'd been assaulted in the toilets. Security – blokes with arms like hams and wearing lanyards and earpieces – were waiting for Ash and Lizzie in a cramped exterior space beneath a metal staircase. They looked embarrassed and out of their depth. The girl was in the security room, up the staircase, sitting on a shabby sofa that was crammed in against the back wall. She looked about sixteen, wore leather shorts and blue cotton braces over a T-shirt that bore big red embroidered lips. On her legs were laddered tights, on her feet unlaced purple Doc Martens. She was drunk and crying. She begged to be allowed to smoke, and Lizzie knelt in front of her and explained she couldn't smoke, not just yet.

Lizzie switched off her mobile – she didn't want to be interrupted by a personal call right now – and guided the girl through the Early Evidence Kit. Here it was: sex reduced to bodily fluids and chemicals. A swab around the mouth and teeth. The girl sitting on the dirty loo and weeing. Lizzie carefully putting the toilet paper, the urine sample into bags. All the way through the girl cried and Lizzie tried to reassure her. No, being drunk didn't mean she wouldn't be believed. Was there anyone she'd like to call? She bagged up the girl's pants and tights, her leather shorts, her T-shirt with the embroidered kiss. A female uniformed constable put her head round the door and held out the standard-issue white T-shirt and cotton bottoms wrapped in cellophane, the flat black pumps that always made Lizzie think of jumping over a wooden box in the school sports hall. The girl said she'd taken some E and wept some more. The specialist sexual offences officer arrived about an hour later, a tall guy in jeans and checked shirt with a shaved head. Professional and friendly, he took the girl off for the full medical examination and statement, hugging the evidence bags to him.

It was already past their rostered duty by the time they got back to the nick. They worked silently and with concentration. Lizzie glanced at her watch. If she was lucky, she could still miss the morning traffic and be in bed not long after eight.

34

Sunday 20 August 2014

Six in the morning and Sarah's alarm was going with the irritating chirp of electronic crickets. She stirred carefully on the camp bed she had set up in the office. Her bones ached. She packed the bed away and took her towel and wash bag along the corridor to the bathroom. There was no sign of life in any of the offices she passed, but she guessed that other people were probably also sleeping in hidden places in the building.

After visiting the park, she'd worked late into the night with the rest of the team, trying to find and develop leads for Brannon. There was a feeling of desperation in the office: Brannon had been missing since Wednesday afternoon.

CCTV from the M6 service station where the phone linked to Brannon had been sited provided no helpful images. Nor had Brannon or anyone else appeared at his friend's flat in Manchester, where surveillance officers had established an observation point. There'd been no further activity on the phone.

At 0100 hours the phone had started pinging at an address in Manchester. There was no intelligence linking Brannon to the address. No intelligence at all in fact regarding the address. Still, the phone was pinging and a local firearms team made a rapid entry to find a middle-aged couple asleep in bed and a teenage boy alone in his bedroom, calling premium numbers. He'd spotted the phone in a litter bin and thought he'd got lucky. He didn't even seem to realize he'd committed an offence by taking the phone without reporting it.

The mood in the office sank lower. Brannon was proving to be cunning and clever. The shrinks had warned of murder-suicide. Brannon's own words on the video had confirmed the threat.

This isn't the end of it.

It was a question of digging in. Whatever criticisms they were facing – and the clamour was increasing – they didn't have the option to give up. Fedden prepared another appeal with another CCTV image advising members of the public not to approach Brannon. They also sent out a warning to officers that the content of the video suggested he might target police.

Sarah had sat in her office, lost in the intelligence, looking for any unexplored link that offered a possible lead. At 2 a.m., she could think no more. She retrieved her camp bed and sleeping bag from its hiding place in the storeroom. She had been so tired that sleep came instantly.

Now, as she stood wearily in the shower, her mind travelled again over all the information. Brannon had made a threat. The question had to be was that specific or general? Sarah had taken Georgina's mother out of the equation. She was still safe in the hotel. Who else might he target? She brushed her teeth at the sink and played over the content of the video again in her mind.

If it wasn't for the police, Georgie would still be alive.

Who would he blame? One officer stood out head and shoulders above the others. In spite of years of violence, Lizzie Griffiths had been the first to secure a charge for a domestic matter against him. Sarah had read Lizzie's write-up of the case dismissal – how Brannon's lawyers had been briefed to go after her. That there was a personal grudge seemed certain.

Still, she wondered, how could he possibly target Lizzie? Unless he knew her hours of duty and could place her at the police station

– a risky location for an attack – he wouldn't be able to find her.

It bothered her. She'd tell Fedden her concerns before going back to the park.

She dressed and stood at the sink, considering her make-up bag. She'd do it later, before she left the office. She popped by Fedden's office, but he wasn't in. Probably snatching a few hours' sleep himself. Then, standing outside his closed door, she remembered a piece of intelligence.

She unlocked her sleeping computer and scanned through the briefing document. That was it: one of the Young family's criminal activities was alleged by a snout to be the theft of high-value vehicles. The intelligence was that this was linked to the attachment of transponders to the undersides of cars. The vehicles could be identified parked up in central London and then scanned until an opportunity offered itself for a robbery somewhere safe and remote. They were nasty robberies and the cars always disappeared quickly without a trace. Sarah tried to follow the thread of the thought. It was a remote chance. There was nothing specifically linking Brannon to this activity. Yet he was a minor player in the Youngs' criminal network. It wasn't such a far reach to suggest he might have personal knowledge of this method. Still, how could he possibly know which was Lizzie's car?

Sarah checked her watch: 7.10. She'd said she'd be at Morville Park by eight.

Lizzie's mobile number was on the major incident database. Sarah decided to warn her just in case, but the phone went to voicemail and she had to leave a message. She called Lizzie's station. The sergeant who answered wasn't in any particular hurry to help. After the customary exchange of emails to verify her identity, he told her Lizzie was on night duty and had been due to go off at seven.

'Knowing CID,' he opined, 'she's probably been in bed for an hour.'

Sarah dismissed the brief burn of irritation. 'Can you tell me something else?'

He laughed at the imposition. 'Sure, why not?'

'Can officers leave their cars at the station?'

'Some of you CID lot leave them in the yard over a night duty because you think you can get away with it, but you're not supposed to.'

'What about when an officer transfers in?'

'There are some reserved bays outside the station. She might be allowed to park her car there for a day or so.'

'And where's that recorded?'

'There's a book.'

'Of course there is. I want you to check that for entries for PC Lizzie Griffiths. She'll have joined borough within the last two weeks.'

'You're joking. That's a CID job. I'm busy.'

'I'm not joking. This is an emergency. I haven't got time to ring around your station and get someone else to do it. I'm a detective inspector on Homicide Command and I'm telling you, not asking you. I've made a note of that and the time I've told you to do it. Call me back with any updates. Thank you.'

She put the phone down before he could start arguing about the chain of command. Neither Fedden nor Lee were answering their mobiles. She made herself a quick coffee using the unwashed cup that was on her desk. The sergeant called her back on the office phone with the dates that Lizzie had been authorized to leave her car in the police bay.

'Have you got CCTV covering that area?'

'Don't even try to ask me to check that . . .'

'Pull the working copies and get someone to view them. Urgently. I'm looking for Mark Brannon hanging around the parking bays.'

Was she panicking? After all, Lizzie had surely been back to her flat since Georgina Teel was murdered. There'd been no attack. On the other hand, what if she was right and Lizzie was on her way home right now? She tried the mobile again; again it cut straight to voicemail.

She was going to be late. She called Steve and told him her concerns.

'I'm supposed to be at Morville Park by eight. We've got a scene out there for another job.'

'Don't worry. I'll take over.'

Sarah decided she could pick up some breakfast in the café in the park after she'd seen Dr Stichill. She headed west across Sunday-morning London, risking the main roads. Her phone rang and she pulled over. It was Steve, speaking quickly.

'I've just had a call from Caenwood nick. On the tenth of July, Lizzie's first day of duty, she leaves her car outside on the street in one of the police bays. You can't actually see the whole bay, but you see the car enter. It remains there for two days except for three hours in the afternoon of the tenth, when it leaves and returns. I've checked the custody programme and this is when Brannon's in custody for a common assault on Georgina. Lizzie took a withdrawal statement at Georgina's house. The DC who checked the CCTV says they never have enough cars – the worry is that when the car is out of the bay it's because she's using it to drive to Georgina's.'

'So Brannon could have got information on the car: someone saw her arrive and told him about the vehicle?'

'She leaves the car beyond the time she's allowed on the permit. CCTV shows her on the evening of the tenth being picked up by a black Land Rover. Then, on the eleventh, at 15.57, after the case against Brannon has been dismissed, CCTV shows him on the street outside the nick. He wanders off camera in the direction of the bay where Lizzie's car is, then back into view. The two of them actually bump into each other before she drives off – home, I presume. I've tried to ring Lizzie, but there's no reply. I've got a firearms team making their way over there just in case, but you know how long it takes to get these operations up and running. I can't trust that I will fall on good officers if I task the locals to keep an eye until the entry team get there. I think Lizzie's in the right direction for you?'

'I'm making my way over there now on blues and twos.'

35

Lizzie pulled up outside her house with the haste of someone who was going off duty late with six more night duties still to do. The light was already full in the sky. She had to get to sleep as quickly as possible. Reaching for her bag on the passenger seat, she realized she hadn't switched her phone back on since dealing with the rape victim. Better check it in case there was something from the night-duty jobs. Then she could deal with it and sleep undisturbed. She stood on the pavement, the bag on the driver's seat, and fumbled around for the phone. When she switched it on, it pinged straight away with voicemails and missed calls. Whatever it was, she'd deal with it when she got inside. She pulled the bag onto her shoulder, locked the car. But the phone started ringing and she fished it out again. Sarah Collins! For God's sake. She was the last person she wanted to speak to. She swiped to answer.

The voice started immediately.

'Lizzie?'

'Yes.'

'Don't go inside your house.'

'What?'

'Are you there?'

'Yes, just outside.'

'Get back in your car, drive around the corner. Call me from there. I'm on my way over. Please, do it now.'

'Hang on a moment . . .'

The voice was talking away urgently inside the phone, but Lizzie could hear nothing of what was being said. She was transfixed instead by something else: the sight of a little girl at her bedroom window. The girl was lifting the blind away from the window and beckoning to her. Lizzie talked over Sarah's voice.

'Skye Brannon is inside my flat. I can see her at the window.'

'Get away from there now. We've got a rapid-entry team on the way. Brannon's inside. If he thinks his cover's blown, the shrinks have told us he'll probably kill Skye.'

'She's beckoning me over. What if she tells him she's seen me?'

'Wait . . .'

'She's tapping on the window. He'll hear it. I'm going to try to get her out of there.'

Lizzie put her phone in her pocket with the call still open and ran quietly down the path to her bedroom window. She put her finger to her lips. Skye was close up to the glass, an urgent frown on her soft white face. The window was double-glazed with toughened glass. Lizzie had had it improved against burglary and knew she wouldn't be able to break it. But the catches were new and easy to move, if maybe not for a child. She considered entering through the front door, but didn't dare lose sight of Skye for a second. She put her finger to her lips again, pointed to the catches and made a careful rotating movement with her fingers. Skye shook her head. Her face was stricken with worry. She cupped her hands close to the window and spoke. 'Dad says he'll hurt Candy.'

Lizzie answered in an insistent hush. 'Open the window, Skye. I'll get the dog.' Skye hesitated. 'I'll get the dog. I promise.'

Skye stood up on the bed and reached towards the catches. She struggled, her little mouth twisted to the side with effort and concentration. But then the catches were free. Lizzie climbed onto the ledge and put her hands on the bottom of the window frame. She pushed it up about a third of the way before it jammed. She got her hands underneath and tried again with all her force. It wouldn't budge. She'd never opened this window from the bottom. Still, Skye could probably squeeze through. 'Come on, Skye, wriggle through.'

Skye's face was anxious through the glass. 'How are you going to get Candy?'

'I'll get her.'

But suddenly, it was too late. Brannon was standing behind Skye and he'd got the dog by its collar. His left hand was held behind his back.

'Come away from the window.'

Skye turned, hesitated for a terrible moment.

'I've told you, Skye. This isn't a game.'

Lizzie began grappling with the window, desperately trying to force it upwards. There was a yelp of pain and Skye screamed. Lizzie looked up. Brannon had put the knife into the animal's side and Skye was bending down towards the dog. Brannon grabbed her by the upper arm. 'I told you to do what I said!' The dog was whimpering and lifting one paw into the air. Skye held its head in her hands and started crying. 'Candy, Candy, Candy.'

Lizzie had a moment of utter shock: her jaw was clamped, her arms by her sides.

Brannon was looking at her. 'Look what you've done.'

It was ridiculous. She almost laughed.

Skye had the dog's blood on her T-shirt and smeared on her face where she'd tried to wipe her tears away. 'Daddy, Daddy, please. Help me look after Candy.'

'I told you to do what you were told. I warned you.'

He seemed to Lizzie some strange parody of a disappointed, angry dad. This was a world of craziness. She said, 'Mark,' and put her hands up to the window in a gesture of surrender. In that instant she'd worked it all out. Even though it terrified her, she had to get in, offer herself up to him, had to let him take Skye away.

That was the only way to stop him killing his daughter there and then. There was no point negotiating, no point in those offers the police had tried to make in their appeal. She spoke loudly, hoping Sarah could hear the open call in her pocket.

'I'm coming in, Mark. Through the front door. I've got my key. Nobody knows you're here. I saw Skye at the window. That's how I know. You can take my car and get away with her. It'll be ten o'clock tonight before I'm missed; even then they won't send anyone round, not for an hour at least. You could be in Europe with Skye before they work it out.'

Brannon hesitated.

The dog was whining and trying to lick its side. Skye was kissing its face and weeping. It occurred to Lizzie that with treatment, the animal might survive the wound. It would certainly take a while to die. It might perhaps have been easier for her if it *had* died. Skye might have been less likely to do what Mark told her. But she understood fully: that dog, it was all Skye had left.

Lizzie said, 'It's me you want, isn't it? That's why you've been hiding here. I'm on my own. Let me come in before someone sees me and gets curious.'

Brannon put his arm around Skye's neck and pulled her to her feet.

'Get down from the fucking window then. Move to the front door. Be quick. Don't call anyone. Do exactly what I tell you, or I'll kill her.'

Skye whimpered and Brannon wiped his hand across her face in a consoling gesture. 'I'm sorry, sweetheart. I've got to take charge for both of us. We'll look after Candy afterwards.'

There was a craziness in his words, but something still remained of the Mark Brannon Lizzie had known. He was a dark exaggeration of the man she had first met, the man who had said he loved his family.

'I'm going to the front door. Just don't hurt Skye.'

Lizzie delayed, fumbling the key into the lock, but she dared wait no longer. The hallway was empty except for the dog, which was lying panting on the floor. There was the stale smell of cooking, of the confined dog, of a flat that had not been aired.

A low shout from the living room. 'Shut the door. I want to hear the lock click.'

She could hear Skye sobbing.

'Skye, are you OK?'

'She's OK. Shut the door or she won't be.'

For the first time, Lizzie feared for herself. With a reluctant look at the pathway beyond, she pulled the door shut so that the lock clicked. Then she held the lock firmly in her left hand while she slowly twisted the catch back and bolted it open. It would probably make no difference to a rapid-entry team, but every second might count.

The hallway was empty. She scanned around for anything that might work as a weapon and stepped into the bathroom. There were nail scissors in the cabinet. They wouldn't do much harm, but she could hurt him with them if she jabbed them in his face.

She caught sight of herself in the mirror, had a sudden intimation of the other life tucked secretly inside herself.

Brannon spoke. 'Come into the living room.'

She put the scissors into her right front pocket and stepped into the hall. 'The dog, can I just help the dog. I've got a first-aid kit in the bathroom.'

Skye cried out. 'Daddy, Daddy, please let her help Candy, let her help Candy.'

The sound of a slap. More sobbing. 'Get yourself in here.'

She felt inside her pocket. She'd be able to show empty hands but could grab the scissors easily, just slide her hand down and take them out.

'I'm coming.'

She was afraid he would be waiting to cut her throat as she stepped into the sitting room, but he was opposite her, in the kitchen area, holding the knife casually by his side. He was shaven, wearing a clean shirt. Skye was lying down, handcuffed to the radiator. The curtains were drawn against prying eyes. The stove top was filthy. The cupboard doors open. The sofa covered in dog hair. One of her armchairs was draped in a sheet. It was here, she realized, that he had shot the video.

'Throw me your car keys.'

She tossed them across the space. He caught them easily and put them on the kitchen worktop.

A strange sort of calm had descended. Lizzie understood what, in his mind, had to happen. He had to kill her so he could get away in her car. She glimpsed also how he had persuaded himself of the sanity of his plan. There was no alternative that included surrender.

She knelt down next to Skye, intentionally turning her back to Brannon, and showed her the loom band threaded round her wrist. 'Look, I've still got it. I told you I'd treasure it. I don't want you to worry about anything.'

Skye's eyes were looking past her towards her father, full of fear. Lizzie wished so hard she had some way of undoing the cuffs, of getting the little girl out of the flat. She was thinking, thinking. Perhaps if she said she was pregnant, he might show mercy. But her police brain warned her not to. It would be like throwing a hand grenade into the room. Why should she have a family and he not? She squeezed Skye's hand. 'I've let your dad have the car so he can drive you to safety.'

She felt Brannon's arm on her shoulder, the knife a sharp point against the back of her ribcage. A shudder of fear passed through her.

Skye sobbed. 'Don't hurt her!'

'Don't tell me what to do, Skye. You don't understand any of this.'

He pulled Lizzie against his body and she yelped as she felt the point of the knife press harder.

Skye whimpered. 'Daddy, please.'

Brannon hissed into Lizzie's neck.

'You wouldn't leave us alone. You were trying to send me to jail, trying to break up my family.' He jabbed, and she felt a wetness spreading down her back. He was still talking. 'I've had nothing but grief from you lot. I had a good relationship with Georgie . . .'

Skye sobbed. 'Daddy.'

'I did everything for her, provided for her, bought them a dog.'

Lizzie could feel tears of fear running down her face, but she tried to keep thinking, tried to hold on to the most important thing she had learned in officer training. Never give up. 'All right, Mark. All right.'

'I didn't want to hurt her. I didn't want to.'

He jabbed again and she sobbed in spite of herself. The wetness was spreading. She felt her right hand down to her pocket, to the hard little handle of the scissors.

'All right. You've got the car.'

'I told you I was coming to get you. I warned you. You've done this to me. You've made me like this . . .'

He had started to drag her out into the hallway. Skye was pleading. 'Daddy, Daddy, please, please, please.'

He said, 'Pull the door shut.'

Lizzie reached out with her hand and pulled the door to.

He was dragging her backwards. She slipped her hand into her pocket, to the nail scissors. The dog was lying with its head on its front paws, still panting. She hesitated for an idiotic, terrified moment. Then she jabbed backwards with all her force.

With a gasp of pain Brannon lost his grip and reeled back. But almost immediately he was standing upright. There was a wound below his eye, but he still had the knife firmly in his hand.

36

Sarah was parked up out of view of Lizzie's flat. She listened with the phone to her ear. Everything relied on Brannon not realizing the police were coming. She remembered the street well from the warrant they'd executed there in the early days of the investigation into Farah and Hadley's deaths. She remembered the cupboards and drawers, the intimacies of PC Lizzie Griffiths' life exposed to the cold investigating gaze. She remembered smoking and chatting outside with Steve Bradshaw.

The sound of the fabric in Lizzie's pocket rustled and crackled painfully in her ear. The firearms team were approaching. She relayed to them over the radio what she understood from the open call. They were putting together tactics even as they screamed across London on blues and twos. They considered negotiating but decided against. Brannon was too volatile, his proximity to Lizzie and Skye too close. He should be given no opportunity to kill again. They'd do a rapid entry with weapons drawn. But it was all taking too long! She cut into their transmissions, requesting an estimated time of arrival.

Seven minutes.

On the phone, the little girl's voice cried out. 'Don't hurt her!'

Sarah got out of the car and put her stab vest on, slipped her harness over her shoulder. Then an unmistakable sound: a female yelp of pain came from the phone.

A shimmer like electricity passed over Sarah.

The street was unnaturally calm, the leaves on the young trees fluttering in the summer breeze. She felt very alone.

She transmitted. 'Threat to life. Officer believed injured. I can't wait for the entry team. I'm going in.'

She could hear them telling her how close they were, but she couldn't risk the sound of the radio either. She turned the speaker to mute and transmitted using her emergency button that would override other officers.

'Threat to life, repeat, threat to life. PC Griffiths believed injured. I am attempting entry through the front of the property.'

Brannon was rattling manically down the phone, like a tinpot dictator captured in a metal box.

. . . trying to send me to jail, trying to break up my family . . .

Sarah ran silently past the bend of the street and had a clear view of the flat. The front door, she saw, was slightly ajar. Her heart was thumping. She pulled out her baton and grasped it tightly in her clenched fist. There would be no room to swing it inside the house.

She heard the voice from the phone, the angry staccato of a man who would not be gainsaid.

I warned you.

She slipped the phone into her pocket, ran quietly up the pathway. Her hands were sweating with fear. She pushed the door quietly forward and stepped into the flat. She could hear what she thought was the sound of a door handle and movement just beyond her in the hallway. Brannon's voice was unnaturally close.

Pull the door shut.

She bit the tip of her tongue hard to steady herself, raised her closed baton to shoulder height. Almost immediately there was an angry cry of pain. An explosion of rage.

'You fucking bitch.'

Sarah stepped left into the hallway. Brannon had his back to her, the knife raised in his right hand. She punched her asp hard into the back of his skull and he fell forward with a sudden heavy exhalation. Almost immediately he was struggling to all fours, still clutching the knife. She hit him again, against the curve of the back of his head. He fell forward, but the knife remained in his outstretched hand. Lizzie was sliding down the wall. Sarah stamped on Brannon's knife hand. A stifled grunt of pain that sounded almost like exhaustion came from him. The hand relaxed. She stood over him with the asp.

'Lizzie, can you help me, handcuff him.'

But Lizzie's face was ashen, her lips blue. Her shirt was wet with blood. She shook her head.

From the living room beyond the hallway, the sound of a child crying. 'Mummy, Mummy, Mummy.'

Then, crashes of entry, shouts of 'Armed police!' Sarah dropped her asp and put her hands in plain view. An officer was standing in front of her, firearm drawn.

She said, 'Detective Inspector Sarah Collins.'

A tall, lean man who had entered behind her pushed her away from Brannon into the bedroom. He verified her ID without apparent emotion. 'You OK?'

'Yes. The adult female, she's Detective Constable Lizzie Griffiths. She's been stabbed.'

The officer turned away from her and went back into the hall. He was transmitting, updating.

'Officer injured. Stab wounds. Conscious, breathing. Urgent medical aid required.'

She followed him into the hallway. Brannon was in the recovery position. A firearms officer was standing over him. Behind them, leaning her side against the wall, was a white-faced Lizzie Griffiths, barely conscious. Her shirt had been ripped off her and an officer was taping a plastic cover over a wound in her back. Sarah could see it sucking in and fluttering open. She stepped towards her. 'Lizzie.'

Lizzie opened her eyes. 'The dog, Sarah. For Skye. Save the dog.'

Sarah looked at the dog. It was completely collapsed but still breathing in short pants. She took her radio out of its harness. 'Any uniformed officers outside, come in and get an injured dog out of here immediately. Take it to a vet.'

Two paramedics arrived and began working on Lizzie. She had an oxygen mask over her face. Sarah moved into the living room seeing the world as if through a filter. Somewhere above was the beating roar of a helicopter. The door to the garden had been smashed open. Skye, her face streaming with tears, was in the arms of one of the firearms officers, crying out, 'I want to see my daddy.' Sarah turned to the window and saw the medical helicopter descending into the park like a big red dragonfly. Doctors and more paramedics ran in through the garden. She followed them back into the hall. Lizzie was unconscious and the doctors immediately turned their attention to her. Brannon was on the floor in the bedroom. Grey, pasty-faced. The paramedics, a busy team of green bees shut into their own world, were getting ready to move him out. Sarah moved towards one of them, a tough-looking woman with cornrows and the pip on her shoulder of a duty station officer.

'Is he conscious?'

'Partially. He's got a possible skull fracture.'

'OK for me to arrest him?'

The DSO glanced at her with clear impatience. 'It's hardly my priority.'

'He's killed his wife and tried to kill a police officer.'

The DSO nodded, more sympathetic now. 'Be quick then.'

Sarah sat down next to him. 'Mark, it's Detective Inspector Sarah Collins.'

He groaned, looked at her. Mumbled something.

'I'm arresting you for the murder of Georgina Teel, the kidnapping of Skye Brannon and the attempted murder of Police Constable Lizzie Griffiths.'

She was distracted from the arrest by a raised voice in the hallway.

She stepped back into the hall. Lizzie was now horizontal and still unconscious, her upper body completely naked, her light blue cotton bra – snipped in half at the middle – discarded on the floor beside her. Sarah looked at that for a moment, the delicate, vulnerable femininity of it brutalized, irrelevant. Unconsciously Sarah's hand was covering her mouth with anxiety. She stared. There was something bewildering about the nakedness of Lizzie, her floppy indifference to the urgency of the medics moving around her. She had the passive, grey look of the dying. Blood was smeared on her skin and on the blue plastic gloves of the medics. A cannula was in the left-hand side of her ribs and the doctor was applying the defibrillator pads to her chest and back. Sarah's own lips felt cold and numb. She heard the words: *Shocking! Stand clear!* But she couldn't really take them in. A shudder of electricity passed through the inert young body in front of her, and what was happening came to her in a sentence.

Lizzie's heart has stopped. I should have gone in sooner.

PART THREE

37

Thursday 24 July 2014

Ever since Brannon's arrest, Sarah's team had been flat out, picking up the pieces.

Sarah had been interviewed about her entry into Lizzie's flat and her assault on Brannon, which had given him concussion severe enough to see him hospitalized. She'd had a representative from the Police Federation to support her, and a lawyer – after all she'd hit Brannon hard in the back of the head twice with her asp without giving a warning. When she'd got back to the office, there had been flowers on her desk from the team and a signed card with that quote about the sheepdog: *The sheep do not want the dog around . . .* She suspected she knew where the idea for that had come from. Still, it touched her to see the flowers. Elaine had left a gift pack of speciality Nespresso capsules. *Only thing I could be sure you wanted. No way was I buying you fags.*

In between all the work on the Brannon case, Sarah had found time to visit Morville Park.

The ground had been churned up in several places. Three trees had been felled: a broad beech and two oaks. Sarah had watched as they came down, heard the whine of the chainsaws, seen the young tree surgeons swinging over on their ropes, amputating the broad branches until the trees stood only as denuded trunks. She'd smelled the petrol fumes of the chipping machine as the trees were fed into its teeth.

Feeling fragile, she hadn't wanted to inform Tania's mother that they were digging. She knew the turned earth would be a territory of strange hopes and fears, of wishing and not wishing. And that at the end, it might all be for nothing. They might well not find Tania. But Elaine had insisted it was her duty to keep Claire informed, and of course Elaine was right and Sarah had let her do it. Claire, who seemed to see putting herself through every painful failed line of inquiry as an act of continuing devotion, had wanted to see the site where her daughter might have been lying. Early morning, Sarah had waited for her in the Morville Park car park. She arrived in her new Hyundai, smart and practical in trousers and a windcheater and sensible flat brown shoes, holding a bunch of cream roses. Sarah sat next to her while the park keeper, Tom, drove them both to the site in his electric vehicle, bouncing over the ground and quickly giving up on small talk about the weather. Claire laid the flowers on the ground by an oak tree and then stood at the edge of the dig and watched as the leafy beech came down. She mentioned quietly how it reminded her of the lilac that had fallen opposite her house on the night of the storm.

But today Sarah had had to accept that they would find nothing except the frame of a bike and the skeleton of a dog. Again Elaine had taken responsibility for telling Claire, quietly understanding that Sarah didn't feel up to that either.

Dr Stichill, his boots caked in mud, had packed up his equipment. Seeing Sarah standing smoking on her own, he had turned and taken a few steps to talk to her in private.

'I'm really sorry,' he said. 'If she's not there, I can't find her.'

'And you are sure now, sure that she's not there?'

'Yes, as positive as I can be. It's not an exact science.'

Sarah had looked out over the muddy ground. It brought to mind those photos of the dismembered trunks on the battlefields of France. But it was neither a battlefield nor a grave, just a suburban wood that she had wilfully shattered on a hunch.

Before she got back into her car, she called the hospital for the regular update on Lizzie: still critical. Still stable.

The envelope had been waiting in the hallway when she got home, conspicuous among its less remarkable companions, which included an electricity bill, an offer of a credit card, and a mail-out from a local estate agent. The heavy textured paper and the black ink handwriting immediately identified the sender. There persistently, in spite of his years running an inner-city parish, was her father: the grammar-school boy with his gradually emptying bottle of ink. She had not wanted to read it straight away. Instead she'd let the dog out, run a bath, placed her glasses, a towel and the envelope by the side of the tub.

She pretty much knew the letter's contents. It would be an account of the memorial service for her sister that she had missed. She knew how hurt her father would be that she hadn't been there. She knew how much it meant to him. Every year he laboured over the service, poring over his books, looking things up, sticking post-it notes in pages. Always the same village chapel, light filtering blue and red through the simple triple lancet window. Susie's old school friends arriving, parking their cars higgledy-piggledy on the lane, bouncing up the bank and into the hedgerows. At first they brought boyfriends then husbands, then children who broke free to run around unchecked in the aisle and pews, finally running away forever as they disappeared into their lives. Her father climbed the wooden stairs of the pulpit more slowly now than in the beginning.

She couldn't deny that some part of her had done it on purpose. He'd asked her for dates and she hadn't told him to rule out the upcoming on-call period – always the busiest time when it was impossible to get leave.

She lay in the bath and read. There were no crossings-out, no blotches. That spoke to her of how careful was the chatty tone. He'd edited until he was entirely satisfied and then taken a fresh sheet to copy it. She imagined him sitting at his desk in his slippers, drafting, just as he had once written his sermons.

She knew what she hoped for from the letter. She could have written it herself, supplied the scripture she would have liked to read.

Everyone that loveth is born of God.

That would do well enough. Why the hell not? But the letter was carefully scant on scripture, and her father's tone was determinedly cheerful. There was a joke about Job and his boils before her father moved on to understanding completely that her professional commitments had prevented her being there. Still, what a shame that she couldn't make it! Everyone had missed her, and so many of her old school friends had been there. He hoped the investigation was going well. How much people need and long for justice! He was proud of her and her work.

Mum and I love you dearly.

That was true enough. Dearly certainly. She remembered falling from a wall in the back garden when she'd still been at primary school. She'd looked at the deep cut, sickeningly white and blue the moment before the blood gushed. Her father lifted her up and carried her through to the sitting room where he'd dressed the cut and then, smiling, pinched the tip of her nose gently between thumb and index finger'. He'd been more free with his use of bible quotation in those days. "'A merciful and gracious God,'" he had said with a huge smile, "'abundant in loving kindness.'" Then he had kissed her on the forehead and given her a big slice of chocolate cake.

Things had been simpler then.

Now, more circumspect, he signed off his letter with the only bit of scripture he had permitted himself.

And so, my dear daughter, may the God of hope fill you with all joy and peace, always your loving father.

It was there, she thought, hiding in that quotation – the faintest suggestion that he might know she was not in truth filled with joy and peace and that there was some stumbling block that could not be alluded to.

The letter was swollen and warped where she had been holding it. She dropped it on the floor beside the bath. She should be filled with joy and peace but not be herself. That was a hard trick to pull off.

No point going round all those thoughts again.

It wasn't her father's fault. He was a man of principle. He couldn't let himself off the hook just because it was personally painful to him. She had some sort of intimation what that was like. Wasn't it after all the sin Steve had accused her of when she'd gone after Lizzie over the Portland Tower deaths: dogmatism, not seeing the bigger picture, not having a heart.

Perhaps that was why he had mentioned the agony of Job in his letter. Perhaps he wanted to say it pained him too – to be always loving her but never permitted to accept her. Job was all about the unfathomability of God. To not only take Job's children, but to send boils too! And when Job complained what did God answer?

'Where were you when I laid the foundations of the earth?'

When her sister had died, Sarah had dreamt that a hole had been beautifully carved in her, as if she were a sculpture that the wind was blowing through.

The water was getting colder and colder, but she continued to lie in the bath, the spaniel stretched out on the stone floor beside her. She looked down on the fish-eye view of her own body. The small floating breasts, the vulnerable flat curve of her stomach submerged beneath the line of water, the crest of her hips . . . She, who spent so much of her working life examining the intimacies of strangers, felt as though she was a stranger to herself.

She remembered the body of the teenager Farah Mehenni, too young to be so cold and dead. Sarah had been certain then too – not only that she would get a result, but also that it was the right thing to do. But in the end, even that conviction had wavered. She'd been left with nothing, a feeling of empty hands.

Then she thought of Lizzie in intensive care, still critical. She'd seen her just once: unconscious, attached to monitors, a tube feeding from her chest into a bottle of liquid by the side of the bed.

She should have gone into the flat sooner.

She stood up and stepped out of the bath. She began to dry herself quickly with some determination.

After the conclusion of the investigation into Farah and Hadley's deaths, the counsellor had explained that this habit of turning her thoughts over and over wasn't part of the problem. It *was* the problem. It had a name all to itself. *Rumination.* Sarah had come to think of this Rumination as a cowled sci-fi character, a Darth Vader that moved around secretly with her, sucking the flavour out of her food and the colours out of her day.

Every day, on waking, she'd reached out and religiously squeezed those little pills the doctor had prescribed out of the blisters of their packaging. She had done what she'd been told. Kept moving. Not let Rumination sit down next to her and take her by the hand. She'd exercised. Changed her routines. Gardened. Taken the tablets. It had been like hoping a rope would hold in a very strong current.

Recently she had been able to tell herself that her self-discipline had been effective. She had been getting better.

When she'd found that Stephenson was being investigated for child sexual exploitation, she'd felt vindicated. Even driving over to Lizzie's and parking up and waiting for the rapid-entry team, she'd felt clever, cleverer than the other cops. On top of her game. It made her shudder now, the silly vanity of the excitement she had felt. She could see Lizzie, unconscious, the shudder of the electricity passing through her unresponsive body when they administered the defibrillator.

It was time to tell someone now, get signed off sick before things got worse. She needed help, she recognized that, much more help than those tablets could offer. She needed to make a big change. She'd resisted it, feared the damage it would do to her career and what in turn that would do to her life. There was nothing she could think of that she could do except policing; nothing else that gave her such a deep satisfaction. But she had to face that too. She couldn't survive on prosecutions and guilty findings. It wasn't dedication after all. It was a personality disorder.

Daisy had got up from the floor and was wagging her tail.

'Yes, darling, just enough time for a late-night walk.'

But as she climbed the hill, Rumination walked steadily beside her.

She'd set too much store by finding Tania Mills. How pathetic it was to pin so much on an investigation over which you had so little control.

She turned. The great city of London cast an orange glow on the curve of the distant horizon. The dog was fussing around her legs. Sarah felt her hard claws through her trousers. She knelt down and stroked her. Thoughts came to her now that caused her shame and slid away from her as she tried to look at them. She remembered once standing on the edge of a tube station platform, the rush of the train . . .

Her phone pinged. She withdrew it from her pocket. A message from Caroline.

So what about that meet-up you promised?

She texted back, aiming for an upbeat tone. How very like her father she was.

Yes, sorry. Still busy, I'm afraid. I'll be in touch in a week or so.

The phone started ringing. She looked at it for a moment, then answered.

'Don't give me that bullshit. If you want to see me, make a date.'

'I'm busy . . .'

'You're *always* busy, aren't you? Did you get cold feet?'

Sarah looked out over London. She thought of her father's letter – *may the God of hope fill you with all joy and peace* – and she thought of the cold wind blowing through her. Despair, after all, was a sin too.

She made herself choose a date. Just over a week away. It would be a Friday going into a rest day. 'The first OK for you?'

'You'd better not cancel.'

Caroline hung up.

The dog was nosing Sarah's face. She stroked her little shoulders and head while her tail wagged from side to side.

'Yes, good dog. Good dog. Don't you worry, don't you worry.'

She started walking back towards her house.

And then it came to her with the force of utter conviction. Richard Stephenson, the fastidious violin teacher, volunteering to dig in a park? Of course they'd missed Tania. She *must* be there.

Her footsteps stopped and the dog stopped too and looked back at her. As soon as she had had the thought, Sarah was questioning it. It was an unpleasant sensation to no longer trust her own judgement. Was this latest impulse the informed perception of a trained investigator, or was it rather the irrational compulsion of someone on the edge? Was she suffering from a detective's fixation on a suspect? That trait was notorious – even the best could chase a subject blindly, leaving other serious lines of inquiry unexplored. There was a nervousness to her thinking, a hesitation that she didn't like. She'd already made a fool of herself with all that digging. But once she'd had the thought, she couldn't not follow it . . . It was an untrustworthy phenomenon: police instinct. The just-doesn't-feel-right that could be either genius or prejudice.

Daisy wagged her tail anxiously. Sarah had the retired park warden's number on her phone and she got it out of her pocket and contemplated the keyboard before beginning to text. She might as well go the whole hog and completely blow her reputation before she admitted she was having a breakdown.

Harry, sorry for texting late. Any chance you could meet me early tomorrow morning?

38

Friday 25 July 2014

Sarah stepped out of the car and threw the police logbook onto the dashboard. She pulled her jacket around her, zipped it up and threaded her way past the gate and into the park. The tree canopy moved darkly in the wind. A cold front had swiftly dispelled the clear skies and the path to the park wardens' rest area was gloomy compared to the dappled sunlight of the previous days.

Harry was waiting for her in the hut, sitting with Tom and two other wardens – a young man and woman – all having early-morning coffee and toast.

'Hide your weed,' Harry said loudly. 'Police officer.'

Sarah shrugged and opened her hands in mock despair at Harry's remark. 'What can you do?'

Tom smiled. 'I could have picked you up, Sarah. Do you want a bevvy?'

'No, it's fine. And thank you, but I wanted to walk anyway.' She turned to Harry, who was already pushing back his chair to stand. 'So are you going to give me the tour?'

'Yes, ma'am, but it won't take long.'

They moved through the single door and Sarah saw a small changing area. Harry was already talking.

'Yes, he always got here early, give him that. Arrived before me.'

Sarah looked around her. The floor was scuffed with mud. There was a bench, pegs. A shower and toilets.

'And did he or the children use this area?'

'Not really. Sometimes if we were feeling soft-hearted we woulda let the children use the toilet. But not usually. There's one in the park.'

'OK, so how would the school volunteers have got here? Did you pick them up? Did they make their own way?'

'Woulda used the bus, been brought here by their teachers. 'Cept for Mr Stephenson, of course. Him too grand for that.'

'Oh?'

'Yes, Mr Stephenson should be treated like royalty man. Had to have him a parking space.'

She followed Harry outside to the small tarmacked area. It was jammed. There was an electric truck parked up, a small tractor and three private cars, all old.

'We was digging the place up at the time, re-tarmacking. Still, him got to bring his car in, no question 'bout that.'

'And he was here before you? He had a key to the gate?'

'Yes, Sarah, always. Had him a key, insisted on that.'

39

The insides of her nostrils were sore. It was painful to swallow, an effort to breathe. Lizzie reached up through the darkness to remove whatever it was that was rubbing, but her hand was stopped and placed back by her side by another, bigger hand.

'Best to leave that in for now.'

She opened her eyes. Kieran was there, sitting by her side.

He smiled. 'Welcome back.'

She said, 'Skye, is she all right?'

'She's fine.'

'Brannon?'

'On remand. Murder and attempted murder, false imprisonment.'

'Collins didn't kill him then?'

He shook his head. 'Unfortunately not. Gave him a decent headache, though.'

She leaned back against the pillow. 'Good. Julie wanted him alive.' She was drifting off. Then she remembered something else: the dog panting next to her with the blue plaster on its leg. She opened her eyes.

'What about Candy?'

'Candy?'

'The dog.'

He put his hand on hers. 'Don't worry about the dog.'

She tried to sit up. 'No. How's the dog, Kieran?'

He squeezed her hand. 'The dog's dead. But it doesn't matter. You saved Skye.'

She closed her eyes. She wanted to cry. It did matter! She could see that poor dog panting slowly. 'It mattered to Skye,' she said quietly. Tears were running down her cheeks. 'Skye loved that dog.'

Kieran leaned into her. 'What was that?'

But she shook her head. She was sinking beneath the morphine again.

40

Saturday 26 July 2014

Sarah was lucky. Dr Stichill had been able to return the previous day. The site of the car park was small and level. By late afternoon the team had identified a clear anomaly in the ground. They began excavations the following morning and Tania was quickly found. She was wrapped in a carpet, lying on her back, her clothing still not completely decomposed. It had not been the roots of trees that had held her but the hardcore of the car park. She was remarkably well preserved. Her jacket and short woollen skirt were still there to hint at the young person she had once been.

Hidden inside the scene tent, Joanne Robinson, the crime scene examiner, carefully cut the jacket pockets down the seams and peeled them away. In the top inside pocket was a torn fragment of thin paper, the print decayed. She removed it with tweezers and examined it. 'It's a piece of paper, certainly, and the light weight of it suggests it could have been taken from a phone directory. I won't be able to give you more than that.'

Sarah said, 'What about the carpet? Can you clean that up? Get me anything on it?'

'We can try. We can probably identify the fabric. We might recover some pattern.'

'Can you make that a priority, please?'

Sarah rang Fedden and arranged to arrest Stephenson. Just as she was about to hang up, Fedden detained her.

'Look, you're not to worry about this, but I've just spoken with the surgeon. Lizzie's not out of the woods yet. They're going to have to operate, first thing tomorrow.'

'On a Sunday?'

'I wrote it down, hang on . . . yes, a haemopneumothorax. Ever heard of that? No, me neither. Anyway, there's been a lot of blood going into the drain from her chest and they've decided they can't leave it. She's running a temperature and they reckon there's a bleed that's not healing. But he says they're not too worried.'

41

Sunday 27 July 2014

The diurnal passage of light and darkness was masked by other rhythms. Always the soft footfall of shoes. The opening and closing of curtains. People touching her skin, lifting her, moving her. Pain in her side and back. A dry mouth. A difficulty swallowing and a soreness in her nose where the oxygen feed rested. It was always a penumbra here.

Breathing was effortful. She put her hand to her chest and the skin crackled beneath her fingers like tissue paper. She tried to raise herself, looked to her left and saw her vital signs spelt out on the monitor. Her heart was beating, slow and steady. On her index finger was the light of the pulse monitor. She tried again to sit but a woman in a royal blue dress stayed her with a hand on her arm.

'I'm taking you down to theatre. Do you want to say a quick hello to your mum?'

Theatre? She wanted to say, 'What are we going to see?' but she knew that was silly, although in her confusion she wasn't quite clear why. She opened her eyes, saw her mother.

'Mum.'

Her mother smiled. 'Lizzie.'

She closed her eyes. The woman in the blue dress was talking about stuff but it was too hard to follow the words. The bed pulled away. Suddenly she was really confused. Frightened. Where was she going? What was she doing, moving like this? What was happening? Or was it just her sister, Natty, pushing her around the garden blindfolded in a wheelbarrow, like she used to do?

She had come to a stop. People were talking. She heard them discussing her – confirming her name, date of birth.

'You're aware of the positive pregnancy test?'

She opened her eyes. In front of the super-bright theatre lights a man was standing looking down at her. He had a hairnet on over his grey curly hair.

She said, 'I'm still pregnant?'

He said, 'You are, but don't worry about that now. Plenty of time to talk about that as soon as we've sorted out that nasty wound you've got in your lung.'

She looked at the people around her in their blue scrubs. Her heart filled. They looked so kind. 'Thank you.'

The man with the grey hair smiled. He said, 'Our pleasure, PC Griffiths. You're a hero. Now, count to ten.'

42

The early morning was golden on the wide streets of Hampstead. Curtains were drawn. The immense trees with their grey patterned trunks and broad leaves had the neighbourhood largely to themselves. A few men and women in smart suits and expensive shoes hurried with an air of brisk satisfaction towards the tube. Elaine was driving and Sarah, in the passenger seat, was free to look at the blue plaques that remembered the former occupants of the million-pound houses. Poets, writers, dancers, photographers, painters had all lived here.

Lee, sitting in the back seat, said, 'More plaques on these streets than you can shake a stick at.'

Elaine said, 'I wonder when they'll start doing them for hedge-fund managers.'

They parked a few doors down from the address and the search team drew up behind them. Opposite was an eighteenth-century house with wrought-iron gates and a large cobbled courtyard. On the other side, a row of imposing brick Victorian semi-detacheds with stone steps up to the front doors.

Sarah said, 'OK, we'll go in and explain what's happening. Then, Elaine, you make the arrest and we'll get the search team in.'

They climbed the steps together, warrant cards ready in their hands. Sarah gave the brass knocker two taps and waited. Lee smoothed down his hair.

Richard Stephenson looked all of his sixty-two years but was still an imposing figure: tall and angular, with a large mouth, a craggy look about his face – tan lines and a hint of stubble. His hair was grey, short on the sides and long on top, with just the suggestion of a quiff. He wore indigo jeans and black brogues. Over a white cotton shirt with an open mandarin collar was a dark-blue velvet waistcoat. The look was theatrical – Confederate colonel perhaps – and he bore himself like an actor who had perhaps come to believe he really was one of those men he'd spent a lifetime playing.

Sarah showed her warrant card and Stephenson greeted her with an impatient smile. His eyes travelled to Elaine and Lee, standing on the step behind, and then back to Sarah. He spoke as if he was distracted, as if he belonged to a category that didn't usually have to concern itself with police officers. 'Yes. What can I do for you?' He glanced up the street. 'Has there been a burglary?'

'Detective Inspector Sarah Collins. Can we talk to you inside?'

'Certainly.'

He led them down the hall.

A black baby grand stood in the sitting room. On its shiny top was an open violin case. Above the mantelpiece was a dark oil painting of two young women in hats sitting in a café. The surface of a glazed walnut cabinet was covered with silver-framed photos. Elaine had moved over to the big bay window that looked out over the Hampstead street.

'Lovely place you've got.'

Stephenson appeared briefly gratified and bestowed a gracious smile. 'Thank you.' He opened his hands despairingly. 'Unfortunately commuters use the road as a rat run.'

Elaine turned to him with a deadpan expression. 'That must be irritating for you.'

There was enough rudeness there for Stephenson to have

noticed it. He addressed Sarah with raised eyebrows, as if puzzled by the lack of manners displayed by her officer.

'So, Miss, um, Collins, I believe you're the senior officer here. Why don't you tell me what this is about?'

'We've found the body of Tania Mills.'

He frowned as if he was struggling to place the name.

Sarah said, 'Come on, you must remember Tania Mills? She was a student of yours.'

He nodded gravely. 'Ah yes, you're right. The poor girl who disappeared after the great storm.'

'We found her body yesterday beneath the car park of Morville Park, where you helped with the replanting of trees. The warden there has given a statement that you had access to the car park not long after the storm – in fact, you insisted on leaving your car there even though they were re-tarmacking. There's been no work done on the area since, so Tania must have been buried in just that interval. Have you anything to say about that?'

A shimmer of tension flickered across his face. 'No, nothing.'

Sarah turned to Elaine. 'I think you should go ahead.'

She stepped forward. 'Richard Stephenson, I'm arresting you for the murder of Tania Mills on the sixteenth of October 1987 . . .'

He appeared to be listening with intense concentration. While Elaine completed the arrest and explained that they had a warrant to search his house, Sarah moved over to the cabinet and studied the photos in their silver frames. All recorded professional triumphs. Stephenson looking chummy next to celebrity musicians, both popular and classical. A photo of him outside the EMI recording studios on Abbey Road. Another with a man Sarah couldn't place but whom she thought was a film director. Stephenson in white tie outside Buckingham Palace, holding up the red ribbon and silver cross of his MBE. A woman maybe twenty years his junior in a blue silk suit with a matching veiled pillbox hat was by his side, smiling.

'Miss Collins'

She turned back. Elaine had handcuffs ready. Stephenson, his hand up to delay her, said, 'My lawyer's card is in my wallet. May I call him?'

Sarah nodded. 'Lee, can you help Mr Stephenson with that?'

Lee took the card, dialled the lawyer's number, then passed the phone to him.

'May I have some privacy?'

'I'm sorry. We've got nowhere here where we can give you privacy that's secure. You can talk to your lawyer in private once you're in custody.'

Stephenson muttered under his breath but loudly enough for everyone to hear.

Fucking little Hitler.

Elaine grinned.

He spoke into the phone, giving brief details of the arrest and listening to the voice at the other end. After a few moments, he passed the phone back to Lee.

'They're sending someone over here to be present during the search. If you would be so kind as to wait till then before starting?'

'Of course, the search team will wait outside. We'll put a seal over the door while we drive you to the station.'

Elaine stepped forward with the cuffs in her right hand. 'Sir, if you'd just crook your right hand in your elbow, please?'

His lips gave a little twitch. 'Is that really necessary?'

'You're an unknown risk, sir. It's just to protect you and us until we get you to the station.'

He flicked the fingers of his right hand out as though he was dismissing a fly.

'Well, I suppose I won't wait for the lawyer then. Save you the trouble of taking me away.' He flicked his hand again. 'I have an alibi for the sixteenth of October.'

Sarah intervened. 'Mr Stephenson, you are under caution. You might want to wait—'.

'No. I don't want to wait!' he snapped. His lips shaped themselves into a tight little moue. Then the words rushed out of him. 'Why should I waste my day when it's simply *not necessary*? I remember the sixteenth of October very well because of the storm. I was with Tania's friend Katherine Herringham all day.'

There was a pause.

Stephenson cleared his throat in two little quick twitches of his Adam's apple. 'So.' He seemed all expectancy, as though he had just cleverly played an unexpectedly high card. But there was fear there too, lingering behind the brittle smile.

Elaine had put her cuffs away and was scribbling in her arrest book. Sarah glanced across at Lee, just to make sure he was paying attention. Then she spoke in slow, measured tones. 'You remain linked to the discovery of Tania's body in the car park. You are still under arrest. We need to investigate your alibi and to interview you under caution.'

'That's bloody ridiculous!'

Sarah saw, out of the corner of her eye, Lee's hand go to his asp. She said quietly, 'Lee, why don't you put the handcuffs on?'

For just a second there was something wild in Stephenson, as though, against all odds, he might actually fight, but as Lee stepped forward, he nodded tightly and complied.

Elaine, who had been leaning her arrest book on her knee, looked up and said, 'I've written down your comments. I think I've got this right. Let's see: "I remember the day very well because of the storm. I was with Tania's friend Katherine Herringham all day." Would you like to sign that as a true record of what you've said?'

'No, I wouldn't! I am going to sue the arse off the Met when this is over.'

Sarah said slowly, 'I did warn you, Mr Stephenson, that you were under caution. It's correct procedure to record everything significant you say from now on.'

Elaine had started writing in her notebook again and Stephenson turned back to her, furious.

'What the FUCK are you doing now?'

'Just writing that you're refusing to sign. It's standard procedure. The other officers present will sign to corroborate that.'

'But I'm not refusing to sign!'

She offered the notebook again. 'So would you like to sign my notes then?'

'Oh for Christ's sake. It's like speaking to *idiots*! Look, if you're taking me to the station, you might as well forget I ever said that!'

Sarah spoke as if she was genuinely baffled. '*Forget* what you've said, Mr Stephenson? You've been arrested for murder.'

'And I am innocent! Why don't you write that down?'

'Sir, you are under caution. Did you listen to the wording of that – anything you say may be given in evidence? Elaine will be writing down anything significant you say – including, please, Elaine, Mr Stephenson's suggestion that you forget about his alibi.'

'Yes, I've got that, Sarah.'

Stephenson pressed his lips together until they were white. It seemed to last an age. 'Well then.' He adopted the tone of an intelligent man beset by fools. 'Very well. May I take a score with me to the station? I understand that there may be some waiting around.'

Sarah looked at Lee. 'Could you help Mr Stephenson find the score he wants to take with him?'

Stephenson asked Lee to find a jacket for him to throw over his shoulders to cover the cuffs. They sealed the door and went to the car.

They sat him in the back passenger seat. Elaine wriggled in beside him, huffing and puffing and saying, 'Shove up, would you?'

Sarah wondered if she was doing it on purpose. Lee was staring forward giving every impression of stifling a giggle and Sarah too found she had to resist the temptation to look at her two passengers in the rear-view mirror.

Elaine and Sarah left Lee arranging for Stephenson to see his lawyer and drove the forty minutes west to Katherine Herringham's house.

Katherine opened the door. She was in shorts and a cropped top. She looked lean and fit and bad-tempered.

'You should have telephoned first. I'm going for a run.'

Sarah said, 'Can we come in?'

Katherine leaned her hand on the door frame. 'No, you can't. This is the third time one or other of you has been here. You gave me your card. If I had had anything more to tell you, I'd have rung.'

'We've got news.'

Katherine's face changed: there, in an instant, was that blankness of expression that the death message sometimes brings. Without speaking she moved through to the sitting room, sat down and waited, her hands folded in her lap.

Sarah sat opposite her. She said, 'We've found a body. We're still awaiting official confirmation, but we're confident it's Tania.'

First Katherine said, 'I just don't know.' Then, after a pause, 'I'd always hoped she was still alive.'

Elaine said, 'We can call someone for you.'

Katherine shook her head. There was silence.

Elaine said, 'Can I make you tea? Coffee?'

'No.' She gazed around the room blankly. 'Do you know how she died?'

Sarah said, 'We're working on that now. We need your help.'

Katherine nodded. She looked slack, defeated.

Sarah continued softly. 'Would you allow Elaine to make you that cup of tea?'

'Yes, all right, tea.'

Elaine filled the kettle, found cups. The water hissed its way to boiling.

Sarah said, 'Do you remember last time I was here I said I wanted you to feel you could talk to me about anything?'

Katherine nodded but did not speak.

Elaine put the sugar bowl and cups on the table. She sat too. Katherine looked warily between the two police officers.

Elaine said, 'Tania was unlawfully buried. Do you understand what that means?'

Katherine shook her head.

'That means someone hid her burial. We were never meant to find her.'

Sarah watched Katherine who appeared to be listening with an extreme attentiveness.

Elaine continued. 'Tania had suffered a fracture to the C2 vertebra in her neck. We're working on the basis that she was killed.'

Suddenly Katherine pressed her hands hard against her eyes. Both Sarah and Elaine waited but she did not speak.

Elaine said, 'Richard Stephenson says he spent the day with you the day she disappeared.'

Katherine took her hands away from her eyes. She looked at Elaine and nodded.

Elaine said, 'Is that a yes?'

'I was with him, yes.'

Elaine said, 'My guess is that you've got your reasons for not talking over all these years.'

Katherine assented with the tiniest dip of her nose.

Elaine said, 'But you need to talk to us now.'

There was a silence. Katherine took a swig of her tea. She rubbed her collar bone.

They drove Katherine to the interview suite. Elaine conducted the interview and Sarah watched on the screen in the control room.

The view offered by the camera was impersonal but in spite of the fixed indifferent eye Sarah saw well enough the nature of the thing in Katherine's faltering gestures – a hand on the face, a downward cast of the eyes, a running of the nail under the teeth. It was there too in the hesitant speech, the occasional sudden angry bluntness.

Painstakingly Elaine started to split what had happened into words and syllables, the first breach of the secrets Katherine had never told.

16 October 1987, the morning after the storm, and the phone had rung in Katherine's house. She'd been on her own in the garden, smoking, waiting for Tania to arrive. Those had been the last of the bored teenage days where every ring of the phone seemed to promise, if nothing else, then at least a break from tedium. She left her cigarette burning on the wall, ran inside, snatched the phone off its cradle before whoever it was hung up. When she realized who it was she blushed, was uncertain, pleased. Usually so aloof, he sounded friendly. He'd got Katherine's telephone number from the school's files, he said. He hoped she didn't mind him calling her at home?

'Uh, no, sir.'

There was a kindly chuckle on the other end of the line. 'Not sir any more, surely we know each other better than that?'

'Mr Stephenson, it's fine you calling, really.'

'*Richard.*'

'Yeah, OK then – Richard.'

While her own mind raced, he moved on breezily. He'd sensed recently with her playing that she was ready to go to the next level. All she needed was a bit of help, someone to show her the little things that would make all the difference. Today they'd both been given a bit of enforced idleness. He could come round? If she was on for it, that is . . . For the first time she heard a note of severity. He warned her he didn't like to work with people who weren't committed.

She dashed upstairs to change and put make-up on. She was a prey to spots in those days and she tried to cover them with her concealer stick. She'd forgotten briefly that Tania was coming too. Then she remembered but it was too late to ring and put her off. She was suddenly annoyed with Tania: they'd hardly been speaking. How come she suddenly wanted to be friends again?

Mr Stephenson was at the door in no time. He kissed her on the cheek at the doorway, just as if she were an adult. They went into the sitting room. He asked her to get her violin out. At first he sat and watched her playing. Then he got up and put an arm round her to show her the exact technique, the martelé bowing she had been struggling with. The door sounded. Stephenson stepped away from her.

He said, 'I thought you said you were free for a lesson.'

Katherine blushed. 'I am. It's only Tania. I'll tell her to come back later.'

'I'll wait here then.'

Tania was at the front door in her short skirt, with frizzy hair and her bag and violin case. Katherine didn't know why she lied to her. Perhaps because – as Mr Stephenson said to her later – she'd known all along what was going on. Sarah watched the adult Katherine on the monitor.

'I did know, in a way, but I didn't know. Not really. Does that make sense?'

Elaine nodded but did not speak.

Katherine said, 'So I said to Tania, "Sorry but I'd forgotten I'd promised my mum I'd go shopping."'

And Tania said, 'Oh Katherine! I've walked all the way here.'

'I'm sorry!'

'I can come in for a minute until you're ready to go –'

'No really. I'm not ready and Mum will be cross. She'll be back in a min.'

Tania hesitated. Then she shrugged. 'See you later then.'

The door shut. Katherine was nervous now, unsure this was such a good idea after all. She went back into the sitting room. Mr Stephenson was sitting, legs wide apart, hands on his knees. 'Everything all right?' he asked with what seemed an irritated smile.

She said, 'Should I start playing again?'

But then there was hammering on the door, shouting through the letterbox. 'I know he's in there! I can see the car!'

Katherine took the violin from under her chin and rested it on her arm. She didn't know what to do.

Stephenson said, 'I'll speak to her.'

He went to the hallway. At first she couldn't hear anything clearly, just a hushed insistent voice. She put her violin on the sofa, stepped from behind the door and watched from the end of the hall. Any view of Tania was obscured by Stephenson's back at the door. She heard him say, 'If you can't talk nicely I'll have to close the door.'

But then Tania leaned past him and saw Katherine and she started shouting, 'Katherine, Katherine!'

It was only a matter of seconds. Stephenson had already shut the door. The shouting stopped.

Katherine suddenly felt very, very sorry. She wanted to run out to Tania but Stephenson was in the doorway so she ran instead up to the first floor window of her parents' bedroom and watched her friend walking away, hunched over, looking at the pavement.

She wanted to go out, to say she was sorry and let's just be good friends again, like we've been for years. But Stephenson was there behind her. He put his arm around her.

He said kindly, 'You haven't done anything wrong.'

He kissed her softly on the cheek, whispered into her ear. *Come on, you know she was just jealous*. He put his hand on her cheek, turned his face to hers. *I really like you*. The words were nice but she was alarmed. She had been jealous of Tania but she hadn't meant this. The emptiness of the house was no longer a blessing. His teeth were hard against her own. His enormous tongue was in her mouth. She pulled away.

Come on, you know why I'm here.

His hand was on her breast. He'd hurt her. Later she'd seen a bruise. She tried to laugh it off but he wasn't laughing.

Come on. You want it too. Why else have you dressed like that?

This was surely nothing more than a misunderstanding. He would understand.

No, really, Mr Stephenson.

Richard.

Richard, I don't want—

But his hand was already between her legs, firmly pulling her pants to one side. It was very quick. She was on her back, noticing how there were cobwebs in the corner of the ceiling, and he was pushing her head against the wall repeatedly as he banged her on the floor of her parents' bedroom. It had hurt, but that was fine in a way because it wasn't her body it was happening to.

Afterwards she didn't know what to do. She thought he'd leave but he didn't. She wanted to be on her own but he stood in the doorway to the bathroom while she took a shower. He said she was lovely and that he wanted to treat her specially, like a lady, like she deserved. He helped her choose her outfit. He took her out in his big green car with the leather seats. She didn't want to go but she didn't know how to get rid of him. They weaved past fallen trees and had the roads almost to themselves. He bought her a meal in a pub, encouraged her to drink wine, told her she was special.

Elaine was completely still as she listened.

Katherine was still too, looking away to her left, speaking without inflection. Sarah made notes, being professional, assessing the account, trying to watch it all through the filter of evidence. But she could see the quiet country pub, the glimmering wine in the glass, Katherine being offered a menu and encouraged to choose. She was out of her depth, in shock, both elevated and betrayed by her predator's method.

On the way back, he pulled the car over into a country lane.

That car, the early autumn darkness already drawing in. The adult man with the appetite. The child in the seat next to him.

He slid his seat back away from the steering wheel.

Sarah wanted to interrupt the act. Here were his words, the inevitable words, the words that were no more than a method.

You are fantastically beautiful.

It's your fault. I can't resist you. It's not fair for you to lead me on like this.

It's a special thing you can do for me. I'll like it and you'll like it too.

No actions as he sat in the car increasingly impatient; no tender caresses, no kisses, just the steps necessary to have the thing he wanted.

He undid his flies. 'Come on, put it in your mouth.'

And here was Katherine, the child, resisting, protesting, fighting her corner.

I said I was frightened. I wanted to go home. I said I didn't know what to do. Before today I'd never done anything like this, only kissed a boy my own age a couple of times.

And then here was the devil, tired of waiting.

Don't be such a baby!

Tania loves doing this. Is there something wrong with you?

Stop – being – so – pathetic.

And finally, the violence.

He put his two hands on the back of my head and forced me down so hard I gagged.

Fifteen-year-old Katherine in the car, her face in his lap, his hands on the back of her head. Revolted, frightened, horrified.

I couldn't believe it when he came in my mouth. It was so dirty. I wasn't even sure what had happened.

Katherine getting out of the car, leaving the passenger door open in her haste, puking and puking over and over in the hedgerow. And Stephenson sitting in the car, feeling nothing but impatience with the demands of this object so boringly necessary to him, waiting for her to return, to stop the messy tiresome business of her suffering.

When I got back in the car he said I was a good girl and that he loved me. This was what love was like. I would come to like it. I was just inexperienced. All girls found it hard to start off with. I started crying. He said, don't cry. After all, you wanted it really, didn't you? Why else did you send Tania away? He gave me his handkerchief and waited. He turned the key in the ignition.

It was like I'd dreamed it. Could it really have been so awful?

He drove me home. All the time he was talking. Not only did he love me but also I was a good violinist, really good in fact, exceptional. He was going to make me famous. He dropped me round the corner from my house and I walked home.

At about ten o'clock the police came round and said Tania was missing and asked if I'd seen her.

I didn't know what to say. My last sight of Tania was her walking down the road, looking at the pavement. I'd taken Mr Stephenson from her and it had turned out I didn't want him. There's nothing worse than wishing with all your heart you hadn't done something.

I wanted to see her so badly, to say I was sorry, to talk to her. Did you hate it, like I do? Did you love him? I thought, she's probably dead. She's killed herself. I wanted to kill myself too. I woke up that night and puked and puked. I couldn't tell anyone what had happened. I was so ashamed. Until today I've never told anyone. But he couldn't have killed Tania because he was with me all day on the sixteenth of October.

They paused the interview. Stephenson's custody clock was ticking away towards the time when he would have to be charged or released. Establishing the detail of Katherine's account was a work of precision that would take all day. Sarah needed to free herself to deal with Stephenson. There was lots to do. His detention would need to be extended. He'd have to be re-interviewed. She didn't like to admit to herself that returning to this aspect of the investigation would also be an escape from Katherine's story.

She made a few calls and then spoke with Fedden.

'Stephenson has an alibi until at least early evening. But the burial is still linked to him so perhaps he killed her later, when he got home. I don't know, to be honest. I can't work it out. I've sent Lee to do a door-to-door at his former address. We're looking for anything anyone remembers out of the ordinary. It was the day after the great storm. That might jog people's memories. Can you task someone to take over from me here with Elaine? I'll go back to custody and interview Stephenson. Steve Bradshaw has said he's free to assist me.'

Steve let Sarah in through the back door of the nick as they'd agreed.

'We're good to go,' he said. He tapped his shirt pocket. 'You need a cigarette before we start?'

She shook her head. 'No, better crack on.' Briefly their eyes met, seeking out how things were between them nowadays. Steve broke out his crumpled smile that creased the tired lines at the edges of his eyes. It seemed to reveal something kinder than mere happiness but Sarah had long since come to suspect that it might be no more than a useful shorthand for getting on with people.

She said, 'Thanks for helping me out.'

'No worries. Sounds like a good job. I'm grateful to be asked to work on it.'

Sarah's first cynical impulse was *because he's one of the proper bad guys, the ones you approve of catching*, but then she thought of Lizzie lying unconscious in hospital. It was an unsettling image and the worry crossed her mind again that perhaps Steve had been right about Lizzie and she wrong.

She said, 'Yes, well, it's great to have you.'

They picked up the lawyer from where she was waiting in the front office and walked through into custody together.

Stephenson was sitting on the plastic mattress in his cell, annotating with a pencil the score he had brought with him. The fingers of his left hand tapped out a complex rhythm as he read the manuscript through the lenses of his rimless glasses. His jacket was laid out neatly at the bottom of the hard concrete shelf that formed the bed.

His lawyer was not the tired, scruffy type one usually saw in custody. She was in her forties, elegant, with shoulder-length steel-grey hair and an austere face that needed no make-up. She was slim, wore a dark pinstripe skirted suit over a light-grey silk blouse. She took a single step towards her client and said, 'Richard.'

Stephenson looked up and removed his glasses, as if the people standing in his cell were students interrupting his work, coming in for a lesson perhaps. He made eye contact solely with his lawyer as if she was the only one who held any relevance. 'Ah, Marion,' he said standing up and pulling on his jacket. He glanced at his watch. 'I've been in here eight hours already and nothing appears to be happening.'

The lawyer's voice was low. 'I'll be looking into all that in due course, but the officers are ready to interview now.'

The interview room was small and stuffy in the afternoon heat and smelled horribly of some earlier occupant. They discussed propping the door open but decided against: Mr Stephenson wished to maintain his privacy as far as possible.

'In that case,' he said, 'I hope you won't mind if I remove my jacket.'

Sarah said, 'Of course not.'

As he stood up, took off his jacket and hung it on the back of the chair, Sarah's eyes briefly met those of his lawyer. For a moment Marion seemed to leak an irritated impatience with Stephenson's overworked formality, but – if that had even been so – she quickly mastered herself, composing her face into a calm expression that revealed nothing whatsoever of what she might be thinking.

They had agreed that Steve would lead the interview, and Sarah sat back, making notes, as he went through the formalities and made the further arrests.

'The first allegation is that on the sixteenth of October 1987 between 0930 and 1100 hours you raped Katherine Herringham in her home; the second that on the same date between 1300 and 1800 hours you sexually assaulted Katherine in your green Jaguar car on a country road. This sexual assault was by way of orally raping Katherine. By today's legislation it would be arrested and charged as rape.'

Stephenson immediately began an affronted protest. Katherine was lying! He had never imagined how his dedication could be used against him. He had given his life to music! The whole thing was a witch-hunt!

Sarah summarized it all in a three-word note: *denies the offence.*

After that, she tuned out the protest: it had no evidential content. Historical sex-abuse cases were always difficult. It was always his word, her word. In this case she was confident not only that Katherine was telling the truth but also that Stephenson would be charged. Katherine's account chimed so finely with that of the other victims, who knew nothing of each other's experiences. One, a girl at a private school in Leicestershire, had been orally raped in the car in the exact same way and also, strikingly, like Katherine, after a pub lunch during which she'd been encouraged to drink. The challenge in this investigation would not be to get a charge but rather, later on, to persuade the court to join the charges against the multiple victims so that the jury knew the extent and similarity of Stephenson's offences.

Stephenson had perhaps picked up on her inattention, because he turned on her with some theatricality.

'Do you know about the way children were used to falsely accuse adults during the Chinese Cultural Revolution?'

Sarah suppressed a smile. She was familiar enough with these outraged reactions, but likening her to a member of a Maoist cadre was a better class of hyperbole.

Steve intervened with that patient kindness that seemed to suggest sympathy. 'Thank you, Mr Stephenson. Let's take it slowly. We'll begin with you telling me exactly what happened on the sixteenth of October.'

Sarah listened carefully while Stephenson narrated a day similar to the one Katherine had described but minus the sexual acts. In this telling the day and the man were of course entirely different:

Stephenson was a generous teacher who went more than the extra mile to encourage his pupils. He was, in fact, a victim of his own kindness.

'So,' he said as he came to the conclusion of his account, 'I dropped Katherine at home and that was that. Who'd have thought such a banal day would ever have ended up being discussed in a police station? Any teacher nowadays will have to be very careful.' He repeated that slowly, with the emphasis of an implicit threat. '*Very careful* about being friendly with his students.' He leaned back in his chair. 'Katherine at least rules me out of the murder inquiry. I can't have killed Tania because I was with her all day.' Then he put his well-kept hands flat on the table as if to say, *There, do your worst.*

Steve said, 'Well, Mr Stephenson, your link to the burial remains very strong, and the fact that Katherine states she believes you were sexually abusing Tania won't help your case.'

The lawyer made a note in her book but said nothing. Stephenson looked crossly between Steve and Sarah. 'Link to the burial? I had access to the car park. So what? So did hundreds of people.'

Steve said, 'You're stating categorically that you had nothing to do with the illegal burial of Tania's body? I want you to think carefully before you answer that.'

Marion raised her hand from the table as if to slow things down but Stephenson was already answering. 'I don't need to *think carefully* because I had nothing to do with Tania being there.'

Sarah produced three photographs and put them on the table without comment.

Stephenson's eyes flickered over them.

Sarah said, 'The lab has been looking at the carpet Tania was wrapped in.' She tapped the photograph on the left. 'Exhibit JMR/1: an image of the soiled carpet as recovered from the grave.' She tapped the next photo. 'JMR/2: a sample of that same carpet, cut away and cleaned by the forensic team. It's still discoloured and worn. Nevertheless there's enough there for the lab to provide evidence that it's a woollen carpet and that in significant details and proportions the pattern corresponds to that shown in JMR/3.' She tapped the final photo: a design of red flowers, winding stems and leaves against a pale green background. 'This carpet was manufactured by the Axminster company during the 1980s. Your former landlord provides a statement that it was in your flat when he rented it to you at the time of Tania's disappearance, and that when he took back possession of the flat the carpet had been removed without his permission.'

She looked across at Stephenson. His face had become still.

'Do you still deny that you had anything to do with the illegal burial of Tania Mills?'

Stephenson nodded. 'I see how you've done it. You've shown that carpet to my ex-landlord and then asked him if it's the right one. Not surprising he's said it is. He didn't like me.'

'No, Mr Stephenson. Your ex-landlord provided us with a description long before we found Tania or researched carpet designs. Today we showed him several possible samples of carpets. He picked this one out without hesitation. Turns out he'd put it in several of his properties. We're way beyond coincidence here.'

They left Stephenson and his lawyer in consultation in the interview room. Lee was in the main custody area, sitting on the bench playing on his phone. He stood up eagerly when he saw them.

'I've been waiting for you! Guess where I've been?'

Sarah shrugged. 'Dunno, Lee. Last time I saw you you were going on a door-to-door.'

'Bristol!'

'Bristol?'

He brandished a handwritten statement in a transparent folder. 'Call me Sherlock.'

Steve smiled. 'Why's that then? Are you taking cocaine?'

'What?'

Sarah laughed. 'Never mind. What have you got?'

Lee sucked his teeth. 'OK, so I found Stephenson's former downstairs neighbour. Not bad, eh? Nice bloke. His wife died of breast cancer when she was only thirty and he raised their boy on his own. He's only just moved out and gone to live with the son in Bristol. The new owner is still forwarding the post. Lucky to find him alive, to be honest. The old boy looks like a pelican. And not a healthy pelican either.'

Steve said, 'And the upshot is?'

'Stephenson was always a miserable bugger. Didn't like children playing outside. Complained if they got up early or arrived home late – he was a ceiling banger. But October sixteenth, he's Mr Friendly. Our witness remembers it because it's the day after the storm and a tree has fallen in the garden. Plus his son's had to have the day off school and he's taken him out with his mate. Bit of a treat – bowling and then fish and chips. Anyway they've come home and they're watching some chat show – *Wogan*, that's it. There's a knock. It's Mr Stephenson. Can't get into his flat. Front door's jammed or something. Doesn't want help with the front door. Just wants to borrow the ladder. Our friend the pelican foots the ladder and Mr S goes through the sash window. Doesn't come downstairs, just waves from the window. "Thanks a lot. Everything's fine now."' Lee grinned. 'I've taken a statement.'

Sarah said, 'What do you think it means?'

Lee shrugged. 'Search me, but it's a bit odd, don't you think?'

Steve said, 'Are you sure you're Sherlock, Lee, and not Watson?'

44

Lizzie didn't know where she was; only that she was in a lot of pain. There was a woman beside her and Lizzie saw her face as if it was in a gallery where everything else was unlit: dark black, sculpted, wide eyes, close-cut hair. The woman had a syringe in her right hand and she crooked Lizzie's arm and slid the needle in. In an amazingly short time Lizzie felt better, much better. Golden, in fact. She said, 'Thank you. Everyone's so lovely here! Where am I?'

The nurse smiled widely. 'You're in recovery, and my professional opinion is that you're off your face.'

She was being wheeled along a corridor. She could see the back of the porter: a short white man with a shaved head. Was it possible that Brannon was doing community service, working in the hospital? The thought was no more than disconcerting. The morphine had bestowed a trusting calm. She said, 'Mark?' and he turned, but it wasn't Brannon, just some old bloke with broken capillaries, in his fifties maybe, and he said, 'No, darling, I'm Sean.' She nodded in agreement and concentrated on the speckled ceiling tiles and the round white lights that were passing by evenly overhead. The lift doors opened and shut and opened.

A fat nurse with short, straight orange hair that looked like nylon took charge of her at the door to the ward. She began to wheel her through, to her side room.

'There's someone here. He's been waiting for you.'

Through the doors she saw the outline of Kieran standing, looking out of the window. She shut her eyes immediately. The bed came to a halt and the brakes went on, squeezing the wheels.

The nurse said, 'She's had a lot of pain relief. She'll be in and out of consciousness.'

She sensed him moving to the end of the bed. An oily reservoir of complication and difficulty was spreading across the floor. She opened her eyes and was on the edge of telling him their news but he smiled at seeing her conscious and she was silenced by his enthusiasm. He took her hand.

'I asked you not to take risks.'

I'm pregnant.

She closed her eyes again and tried to retreat into the haze of morphine, but he kept talking.

'I love you.'

She opened her eyes. 'No.'

He misunderstood her, smiled and said, 'I do love you.'

She wished he wouldn't talk, not while the precious morphine lasted. It was calm here and pain-free.

45

They were back in the interview room. Sarah met Stephenson's eyes for a moment, but he immediately looked away from her towards the corner of the room, as if she was no more than an annoying irrelevance.

Steve said, 'Can you just confirm this is your statement, Mr Stephenson.'

Stephenson said, 'Yes, that is my statement.' His lips twitched and he looked away again towards the corner of the room.

His lawyer began reading.

'On the sixteenth of October 1987, I returned home from my day with Katherine Herringham in the early evening to find that it was impossible to open the front door to my flat. I knocked but got no reply. I went around the back of the property and used the external fire stairs to climb to the door, but my wife, Abigail, had locked it from the inside. I banged on the door but she didn't answer. I knew the lock on the sash window at the front was broken so I went to the downstairs neighbour and asked to borrow his ladder. I climbed into the sitting room and went straight to the stairs down to the front door to see why it wouldn't open. Tania was there, dead, at the bottom of the stairs, blocking the doorway. My wife had locked that door from the inside. That was why I couldn't get in.

'Abigail was lying on the bed in the bedroom. She had drunk herself into a stupor. I sat in the sitting room trying to decide what to do. I should have called the police but I couldn't send my own wife to prison. She was pregnant. It was terrible but I decided to dispose of Tania's body. I pulled up the carpet from the stairs because it was stained. Later it was useful to wrap the body in.

'I deny any other involvement in Tania's death.

'On the advice of my lawyer, I shall answer no comment to any further questions.'

Sarah had no doubt that it would be pointless but Steve still had to ask the questions. Stephenson answered without ever looking away from the corner of the room, which seemed to hold his fixed attention.

'Were you having a sexual relationship with Tania?'

'No comment.'

'Did you rape Tania?'

'No comment.'

'What was Tania doing in your house?'

'No comment.'

No comment, no comment, no comment.

They put Stephenson back in his cell. Sarah called Elaine.

'How are you getting on?'

'We've finished. I've dropped Katherine home. There's just the two rapes to charge. After Tania went missing, Stephenson told Katherine he couldn't continue the relationship, as he called it. He felt too bad about Tania. He was bricking it, of course. Didn't dare push his luck.'

'You going off duty then?'

'Yes.'

There was a pause.

'Fucking hell, Sarah. What the hell is it now?'

'We need to arrest Stephenson's ex-wife and I'd really like to interview with you, if you could make it.'

46

As Sarah and Steve drew into Primrose Hill, Sarah had the familiar police sensation – the feeling of moving through a different element to the people around her. Even at this late hour people were milling around and the metal tables of the cafés were filled with late-night coffee drinkers.

The lights were on behind the glass pane of the hardwood door of Abigail Levy's house. She came to the door in a red beaded evening dress and frowned at the sight of Sarah and Steve, warrant cards in hands.

'It's ten o'clock at night! I've got friends here. Can't you come back later?'

Sarah shook her head. 'I'm sorry. We can't. We need to come in. You'll have to explain that something's cropped up and your friends need to leave.'

Abigail looked beyond Sarah to Steve and smiled with the charm of someone who had once been attractive. 'And if I don't want to do that?'

Sarah thought the sympathy in Steve's smile might be real this time. 'I'm sorry, Miss Levy. There is no "I don't want to" right now.'

The electric lights were off and candles were burning on the table and the mantelpiece. On the white tablecloth were empty coffee cups, a fancy-looking chocolate box with quite a few chocolates missing, a bottle of Sauternes, wine glasses. The guests – three men and two women – looked confused but quickly gathered themselves together, located handbags, pulled on jackets. One of the women draped a pashmina around her shoulders.

'Bye then, Abigail.'

There was a general kissing of cheeks but still the odd ungoverned glance at the two people who had arrived in suits and who were waiting patiently, never leaving Abigail alone for a second.

'Lovely to see you.'

'The risotto was delicious.'

When the front door finally shut, Steve made the arrest.

Abigail, running her index finger up and down the middle finger of the other hand, said, 'What happens now?'

Sarah said, 'We'll take you to custody where you'll be interviewed. We can get you a lawyer or, if you already have a lawyer, we can ring them for you. I'll have to put you in handcuffs, I'm afraid. Just for the journey. Just to keep everyone safe. We'll bring the car right to your door. No one need see.' She paused, considered the red dress. 'Would you like to change before we take you to the station?'

'I don't know. I've never been to . . .' Abigail hesitated. 'To *custody* before. What do you recommend?'

Recommend! As if it were a skiing trip or a day's hill walking.

'I'd put on something practical. I'll have to be in the room with you, but I'll turn my back while you change.'

Abigail stood five foot two at the height measure. For the custody images she sat nervously on the high chair, her slim ankles crossed and her knees to the side, turning her head obediently when she was told and offering a placatory smile to the camera as though these were studio shots. She had changed into blue pedal pushers, a grey T-shirt and a blue boxy jacket. She looked as if she was ready for a long day on her feet, perhaps volunteering in an organizing capacity for the National Trust. She stood, slightly on tiptoe, at the live-scan machine while the detention officer, a burly white man with a shaved head, rolled her fingers on the screen and clicked the foot pedal with practised ease. She was silent, studying the fingerprints emerging against the red light.

'So you don't use ink any more then?' she asked, and the detention officer said, 'No, love. This is much better. Computerized.'

She nodded as if she was on a tour of the facilities. 'Yes, that makes sense.'

Afterwards she sat in the consulting room with her lawyer. Sarah had drafted a summary of the evidence against her but still she beckoned her in.

'Before we begin, can I ask something?'

'If your lawyer's happy, then of course.'

'Has he said I did it?'

'He has. He says he came home and found Tania dead. She was blocking the doorway. Your downstairs neighbour corroborates his account to some extent.'

There was a pause.

'And I can sit now and talk to my lawyer for a bit?'

'You can, yes.'

Sarah went out into the yard to have a smoke with Steve. There was the usual ebb and flow of police cars and vans. Two armed-response vehicles pulled in and their occupants parked up and shot the breeze, standing together in the warm night. Car headlights flashed from beyond the gate and one of the AFOs walked over and let the car in. It was Elaine. She spotted Sarah and Steve and gave a little wave. Then there was a lot of sorting things out, reaching into the passenger seat, getting her capacious bag out of the back of the car.

Steve said, 'I can stay on and interview, if you'd like.'

Elaine was walking over, a bag of chips resting in her upturned right hand.

Sarah said, 'No. But thanks all the same.' She felt a moment's regret at sending Steve away. 'I think Abigail would be better interviewed by two women.'

Steve threw his cigarette on the floor and ground it out with his foot. 'You're probably right.'

'Thanks for your help with Stephenson.'

'You're welcome.'

Elaine offered the chips. 'Anyone want one?' she said. 'They're nice and hot. I drove like the clappers. Lots of salt. There's a good place on Lisson Grove.'

Steve said, 'No thanks. I'm off home.'

Sarah helped herself.

Elaine lifted her right foot and scratched her ankle. 'I've been bitten all over by mosquitoes, bloody things.'

Steve offered his hand. 'I'm Steve, by the way.'

There was a moment where Elaine wondered whether to offer her greasy hand. They both laughed and decided against.

'I'm Elaine,' she said, taking another chip. 'Fat Elaine, that is. You may have heard of me.'

He nodded and smiled. 'Yeah, I've heard of you.' He palmed his car keys. 'I'll leave you to it.' There was a pause. 'Good to work with you again, Sarah.'

She nodded. 'Yes. You too.'

Abigail sat neatly in the interview room. A plastic cup of water was on the table in front of her and she took regular sips. Her nails were perfectly manicured with grey polish. Everything about her was neat, and her lawyer, the duty brief, looked like he'd been provided as contrast – he was a young man with day-old stubble, wearing jeans and trainers.

Elaine was leading the interview. After the preliminaries, she said, 'Abigail, your lawyer has told us you want to tell us what happened.'

Abigail looked around the small room as though she wondered who Elaine was talking to, but then, as if finding no one else with the same name, she smiled emptily and said, 'Yes, that's right.'

Elaine placed one palm on top of the other hand and gave an encouraging smile. No one spoke, and after a little silence Abigail began.

'It was afternoon.'

She hesitated and looked across at her lawyer. He said quietly, 'I think you should continue. Like we discussed.'

She put her hand flat on her breastbone and made a little hum as if there was a pain there that she couldn't quite place. She looked up, took another sip of water.

'So. I lived in the top floor of a subdivided Victorian cottage with the man who was then my husband, Richard Stephenson. We'd only just got married and I'd moved down from Manchester – the first time I'd been away from home. I didn't know many people. I was pregnant.'

She stopped speaking and looked around at the other three people at the table, who all waited attentively. She resumed, almost as if she was telling a little anecdote that she was surprised to see held so much interest for everyone.

'The school where Richard worked had telephoned that morning to say they were closing for the day. Richard had told me he still needed to go out. There were things he had to do. I knew better than to ask. It just made him impatient. How things were was becoming plainer.'

Another pause, a self-deprecatory little smile that seemed to suggest the anecdote was perhaps tedious.

'I'd been watching daytime TV and I'd opened a bottle of wine. I'd started to do that. I'd found that a couple of glasses helped get me through the day. I was quite unhappy, to be honest. There was a Hollywood film on. *Love Is a Many-Splendored Thing.* I was enjoying it, actually. There was a knock. I switched the television off, put the glass in the kitchen. I went down to the front door and opened it and, well, there she was.'

Elaine prompted gently. 'Tania?'

Abigail nodded. 'Well, yes, I assume so, although she never told me her name.'

'How did she look?'

'She had a short skirt on, long frizzy hair, dark kohl eyeliner, big colourful glass earrings. She was carrying a violin case and a bag.

'I knew immediately who she was. I don't mean her name, of course, but one look and I knew everything else about her. She asked me if Mr Stephenson was in and I said no, and she was about to go away – how I wish I'd let her. But I asked her in. I don't know why I did that. It was . . .'

She faltered and Elaine prompted. 'Yes?'

'It was like I wanted company! Ridiculous, isn't it?'

Her face suddenly had a crumpled look about it, but she put her hand on her breastbone again, patted it a couple of times as if in encouragement and moved on briskly, her neat surface restored.

'They'd made an entrance to the flat from the ground floor, but it was a bad conversion and we had to climb steep, narrow stairs to get to the living area. Upstairs it was different.' She smiled as though she was saying something funny. 'It was a kind of Tardis. As soon as you stepped into the living room it was as if we lived in a big house, not a tiny one-bedroom flat. Richard always made a big show. In the front room we had a baby grand. We'd had to take the window out to get it in. Richard's violin was on top of it. There were flowers too, lilies. Richard always insisted on flowers.'

She stopped as though that was the end of the story.

Elaine said, 'So Tania was in your living room. Then what happened?'

'Well, nothing! Absolutely nothing. She just stood there! Looked around her like she was in a stately home or something.

'I wanted her to say what she was there for, but she didn't speak. I thought, *Well, say it then. Say what you've come to say.* It was one thing to come to my house and another to then just stand there and say nothing. I was kind of *furious* . . .'

'You were furious?'

'And upset too, of course. And also, well, ashamed.' She laughed as though she had said something a bit silly. 'All of that at the same time! Is that possible?' She looked directly at Elaine. 'I had had quite a lot to drink, you see.' She moved on briskly. 'Anyway, whatever was going on, however miserable it all was, I thought, *I'm still the wife and she shouldn't have come to my home.*' She rubbed her forehead. 'Pathetic, isn't it? As if her coming to my home really mattered! That was the least of my problems.' She looked at them all then with a suddenly amazed expression, as if surprising even herself. 'Until it wasn't, that is.'

She nodded as if expecting some sort of assent from the three people gathered around the table, and then, when the only reaction she got was a kind of desperate listening, she flicked her hands quickly as if embarrassed. She resumed, speaking quickly, as though she just needed to get to the end of the story.

'The girl didn't say anything, so in the end I spoke. I said, "Richard's your teacher?" and she nodded and I said, "Would you like to play for me?"

'She hesitated about playing. I remember that. Then she went to get her violin out of its case and I said, "Play his. It's a Joseph Rocca."'

Abigail looked at her lawyer and rubbed the knuckle of her ring finger compulsively. 'That was a kind of joke, do you see, because he loved that violin and he would never have let her play it.'

She looked around with a disappointed expression, as if no one had understood the joke.

'So she picked up his violin and tuned it against the piano. Then she started to play. It was a cantabile by Paganini. Richard had insisted I learn it too. The first three bars are easy, but pretty soon there's a tricky bit – sudden awkward fingerings and accidentals. Tania's fingers didn't move quickly enough or with sufficient confidence. You could feel her working, and that was counter to the whole point of the composition. It's a virtuoso piece, you see. It's supposed to feel effortless, but her fingers were like a stiff clockwork mechanism. I thought, *Poor thing. She isn't even very good.*

'She stopped playing, rested the violin on her knee. She said, "I can't really play it."

'I did feel sorry for her but I also wanted to slap her. I didn't know what to do. I was still waiting for her to say why she was here. And then, in a way, I couldn't be bothered. I just wanted her to go so I could catch the end of the film.

'I said, "Perhaps you'd better go now."

'She said, "Yes, I'd better," and she put the violin back in its case on the piano. Then she said, "I'm sorry. I shouldn't have come." That made me absolutely furious again! She was so pathetic and vulnerable. She'd been so used. She moved towards the stairs and I got up and followed her, as if I was showing her the way out, but then an impulse seized me. A moment of pure rage. I pushed her hard, very hard, in the back between the shoulder blades. It took her completely by surprise. She had her violin case in her hand and she fell headlong, couldn't catch herself. The stairs were very steep, remember. I could see straight away from the angle of her head that it was all wrong. And she made this sort of gasping sound. I ran down to her.

'There was a smell of shit: that absolutely horrified me. Why had that happened? This was all out of control. I couldn't keep up with what was happening. I didn't even know her name to call to her, but it didn't matter. She didn't seem conscious at all. She was floppy and her eyes were rolling back. Her lips had gone blue. There was a horrible sound, a kind of gasp. It seemed that almost immediately she had stopped breathing.

'I didn't know what to do. I was in a complete panic. I think I shouted, "Help! Help!" But no one came. I ran outside and knocked on the downstairs neighbour's door. There was no reply. I went back in, felt for a pulse, put my face against her mouth. There was nothing. I went upstairs and sat on the sofa. I thought of calling an ambulance, but what was the point? She was clearly dead.

'I went into the kitchen. I filled my glass again, downed it, filled it. I took another bottle through to the sitting room and watched the end of the film, kind of stared at it. All the time I was thinking, *It's not my fault! It's not my fault!*

'I went downstairs and looked at her again. I locked the front door and I locked the door to the fire escape. I kept drinking and I took some sleeping pills too. I got so pissed that I had to lie down. By the time Richard came back, I was asleep. I didn't even hear him come in. It was dark and he was shaking me awake. He was saying, "How many have you taken?" I said, "I don't know." And he sort of dragged me to the toilet and stuck his fingers down my throat. I was throwing up repeatedly. He didn't say anything, not a thing. I remember that really well. I remember being afraid of him and then just not caring about anything. I thought, he's really angry with me but I don't care what happens. He put me back to bed.

'In the morning he woke me and told me to have a bath and sort myself out. He made me coffee.

'That's when I asked him where she was, but he said, "Don't ask me anything."

'I said, "I'd better call the police."

'And he said, "We're not calling the police."'

Abigail stopped talking. She stared ahead of her as if no one else was there. Then she said, 'I want to say that I'm very sorry. Very sorry.'

After a pause, Elaine said, 'When you pushed her, did you mean to harm her?'

'I don't know what I meant. I was angry. I just pushed her.'

'Do you know what happened to her body?'

'I think Richard put her in the shed in the back garden to begin with. I must have been asleep when he did it. But where else could she have been? We had the back garden and the neighbour had the front. You could drive down a little alley and park the car there. No one else had a reason to go round there. After that, I don't know. He called a decorating company and I heard him saying how he had always hated the carpet and how there was a fine old floor underneath, just needed polishing up, and could they come and quote.'

'And you, what were you doing?'

'I let him take charge. There were all these appeals for Tania. It got harder and harder to tell. I felt I was in more and more serious trouble. The only thing I knew clearly was that I had to leave him. On the Monday morning he was back at work. I went to the doctor and arranged to have an abortion. I didn't tell Richard. Then, after I'd had the termination, I rang my dad and said things weren't working out, Richard had hit me and I had to come home. He picked me up when Richard was at work. I said I'd lost the baby and I didn't want to talk about it and he called me his little girl. Richard called me and told me to come home, and I said, "If you try to make me, I'll tell."'

There was the hand on the breastbone again, moving from side to side as if to ease some pain.

'You see that was the dreadful thing: Tania helped me get rid of him.'

There was silence.

The lawyer raised his hand slightly from the table as if asking permission to speak, and Elaine said, 'Yes?'

The lawyer said, 'Abigail, you need to tell the officers about how you were at that point. Mentally, I mean.'

She nodded as if she'd forgotten some minor detail. 'Oh yes. About three months later, I tried to kill myself.'

Elaine said, 'You tried to kill yourself? How did you do that?'

She pulled up the sleeves of her jacket and showed two deep white scars running along the length of her left wrist. 'And I took pills too, of course.'

Elaine said, 'And then?'

Abigail shrugged. 'I don't know. I was in hospital for a while. Then I decided to live.'

There was a long silence.

Sarah said, 'I don't understand why you asked her to play the violin.'

'I can't really explain it . . . It was sort of like I needed to hurt myself.' Abigail frowned and meshed her hands in a kind of cat's cradle. 'I'd really loved the violin, you see.'

Sarah scanned her notes thoughtfully. 'Tania said she was sorry, and that made you really angry because she looked ...' She placed her finger beneath each adjective as she spoke it. 'Pathetic. Vulnerable. Used.' She looked up 'Why did those things make you so angry? Why didn't you just feel sorry for her?'

Abigail said something inaudible.

Sarah prompted gently. 'I'm sorry, what was that?'

Abigail looked up, stared Sarah full in the face, spoke loudly. 'I said, *because she was me.*'

'She was you?'

'Yes, she was me! And so I hated her.'

Sarah tried to make sense of what she felt as she sat looking at Abigail in her too neat little outfit and her too precise little body.

Abigail was speaking about how she had loved to play the violin and Sarah saw her: at fourteen someone completely different. A pretty girl in a pretty dress who'd liked to amaze the adults by her ability to play Ysaÿe. She'd been proud, a bit of a show-off – she admitted that – and very good indeed at the violin. She had been the girl all the other girls wanted to be. She was going to have a musical career and marry well. And she'd been in awe of her teacher, who already knew famous people.

Stephenson had known his prey very well, known how to use her weaknesses. He'd flattered her, made promises, told her how impressed he was.

To really play, he'd told her, she needed to become a woman. And that was how he had started, first by putting his hands on her breasts and then between her legs and then finally pushing her down to her knees in front of him.

She hadn't even known this was rape. She had thought, as he had told her, that she had wanted it, needed it even. At just fourteen she had felt as if she'd rowed herself out far away from the land with its glittering shore lights into a dark ocean from which there was no return. How could she tell people the dirty things she'd done? How could she explain that she was no longer the precocious girl in the pretty dress but had become instead someone who was now secretly washing herself so much that her skin was red raw? Who could she possibly tell? Who could she admit this to?

She was approaching her seventeenth birthday and he was beginning to tire of her. He'd already moved away to take up his new teaching post. But he popped up just once to collect his stuff and he said he had to see her, one last time. 'Bored probably,' she said, both aghast and disconnected, as though she was talking about someone else. And he'd raped her, pushing her face into the carpet with the heel of his hand, and the condom had broken and that was that. She was pregnant.

That was the first time, she said, that she considered suicide. For what other options were there? At first Richard was angry, but then he'd suddenly got all enthusiastic. 'We'll get married then!' Her father had agreed. He'd been surprised, yes, angry even, but these things happened and Richard had wanted to do the right thing. His daughter was seventeen by then, so it wasn't such a shocking thing and Richard wasn't such a bad match. It was a low-key affair at a registry office. She'd worn a little pink suit and within a week she was watching daytime television in his flat in London.

Seventeen, Abigail said, was already too old for Richard, of course.

'I was – what do homosexuals call it? – I was his *beard*. With his young, pregnant wife he was beyond reproach. I'd moved into that house but he didn't even touch me any more. I hated music now. It gave me a headache. I was pregnant with his baby and I couldn't see my life at all. How was I ever going to escape and begin again?

'And then on the sixteenth of October there was this girl suddenly standing in my sitting room and I did that thing. I pushed her. And then I drank and I took pills but I was no good at it. And it wouldn't have suited Richard, you see, me dying, because he was doing so well and he was getting away with so much. He wasn't going to let this interfere with his wonderful life. It was my mistake, after all, not his. Why should he pay for these messy, irritating females? A girl going to the headmaster; that didn't happen much, and when it did, it was never really much of a problem. Perhaps there was a chat in a nice office, uncomfortable for everyone, admittedly. Used to put him in a bad mood. Perhaps he lost a pupil, had to move schools. But Tania dying, or me dying, that would have been too much, even for him, do you see that? Even Richard could never have recovered from that.

'I should have told and I should have paid but instead he took charge of everything and I moved out, and then, eventually, I decided to live. The only way I could do that was by never contacting Richard again, never thinking about the news I'd hear about him from time to time. I knew what opportunities he was making for himself – working on musicals and classical pop, involving himself in charities that encouraged disadvantaged young people to play an instrument. He had his own Wiki page. There was a piece in the paper about his MBE. And I knew I should tell so that he would be made to stop, but I didn't.'

47

E laine had followed Sarah out to the yard. 'Sorry, Sarah, I can tell you want to be left alone, but I need some bloody company after that.'

Sarah lit her cigarette. 'That's all right.'

For a while she just smoked in silence.

Then Elaine said, 'What do you think she'll get? Manslaughter or murder?'

Sarah sighed. 'Manslaughter, I think. There's an intent to harm maybe, but probably not enough for murder. It'll be complicated . . .'

'Any bet on what she'll serve?'

'No idea. The abuse will be mitigation, of course, but then she never told: the judge won't like that. I'd say two to five years. But you never know. It could even be suspended.'

'Do you agree with that?'

'I don't bloody know! My last job, I remember saying . . . to Steve, it was, you know the DC who was here earlier? We disagreed about something. Anyway I told him then: sentencing, mitigation, the bigger picture, that stuff: it's not our job. The law, that's what we do. Our job's just to find out what happened and to put them in front of the judge.'

Elaine said, 'You're way beyond me there.'

Sarah shrugged. 'Do you know what? I don't even know whether I'm right any more. Nothing brings Tania back anyway.' She threw her cigarette on the ground and lit another. 'I know I wish it was Stephenson who'd killed her.'

'Yep. Me too.'

They watched the gates open and a car arrive, and an officer leading a young man in handcuffs out of the back seat and towards the doors of custody.

Elaine said, 'Do you feel sorry for Abigail?'

'No. I don't.' And then, after a pause, 'Well, I don't know.'

'Imagine finding yourself married to him.'

'I can't. Not at all.'

'But still . . . I don't get it. Why did no one stand up to those creeps?'

'It was a different time then. Nobody was honest about anything.'

'Yeah, I guess so.' Elaine looked at Sarah thoughtfully. 'Hard for you too, was it? Being gay, I mean?'

Sarah laughed. 'Well, yes. I guess it was.' She shifted her weight, scratched the back of her neck. There was still a lot to do. 'Don't you need to go off duty?'

Elaine laughed now. 'Haven't you noticed? It's two o'clock in the morning. Gavin's on nights. Who on earth do you think's looking after the kids?'

'I don't know. Who is?'

'I called my mum. She's staying the night. I'm here for the duration.'

Sarah smiled. 'Good. Thanks for that. You were brilliant interviewing Katherine, by the way. I'm going to draft the charging advice for Abigail. Could you call the constabularies where the other women have made historic complaints against Stephenson, see if they want to send someone down to arrest him while he's in custody. I'll call Fedden. Someone needs to update the next of kins before this gets in the press, and it can't be you or me, sadly.'

Elaine nodded. Then she said, 'Maybe he'll serve more time than she does in the end. And there's the added bonus that he's got so much more to lose. That Wiki page she mentioned is going to be updated soon, and a whole lot of different stuff's going to come up when you google him.'

Sarah stubbed her second cigarette out.

'I know you don't care, but you've done a good job, Elaine. You're a good cop.'

'Thank you.' Then, after a moment's silence, 'Don't tell anyone, particularly not the boss, but I have to admit to a feeling of satisfaction that we've got the bastard.'

Sarah left Elaine to charge Stephenson and Abigail. They would both be remanded in custody to appear before the magistrates. Abigail's rape allegations against Stephenson would have to be investigated too, but they'd need advice on how to proceed. In the meantime, Tania's death would begin its way through the courts.

Sarah had offered to do the charging herself, but Elaine said no: she was horribly late now anyway, and it would be a pleasure. But no one should expect her in early the following day, if *at all*. And she'd be taking the time back in lieu, not as money – just in case anyone thought recent experiences had made her go soft on the job. She still hated the bastards. All of them.

Sarah smiled and kissed her on the cheek.

Elaine pulled a face. 'Admit it. You fancy me something rotten, don't you?'

And Sarah laughed and said, 'Yep, I do.'

Before she went off duty, Sarah watched Stephenson on the custody CCTV. He was sitting on the plastic mattress, wearing his reading glasses, still studying the score he had brought with him.

It was nearly five in the morning by the time she got home. The house was silent. She couldn't sleep. She put on a recording of

Sibelius' violin concerto. She closed her eyes and gave herself up to that first note, so tenderly dissonant. For a long time she sat like that, following the line of the violin, allowing herself to concentrate on its solitary voice sometimes holding firm and sometimes overwhelmed by the growing swell of the orchestra.

EPILOGUE

48

Friday 1 August 2014

Tania's funeral was held in the late morning. The church was full of people in their forties: Tania's old school friends and the young musicians who had played with her in the local youth orchestra.

A young cellist and a pianist from the Royal College of Music had volunteered to play and the congregation listened to Gluck's melody from *Orfeo ed Euridice*. The piano ran like water while Tania's life played in images on a screen. Tania playing netball, Tania in a paddling pool, Tania with her arms round her friend Katherine. Then the congregation stood and somehow managed to belt out together 'Lord of all Hopefulness'.

Katherine was in the church, next to Tania's mother. Claire had allowed her to come in spite of those years of silence. In fact, she'd welcomed her. She'd been able to understand that Katherine was a victim too and perhaps someone from whom she could draw comfort. Sarah looked at their two backs, side by side in the front pew, and remembered that plate of Penguin biscuits, waiting for Tania to come home. For the first time she felt a pang of regret: finding Tania had been an end to hope. Here was the irredeemable present.

A recording of a single piano was beginning, and Mahalia Jackson's voice soared. *There is a balm in Gilead to make the wounded whole.*

The undertakers turned the coffin and Claire filed out behind it with her ex-husband and Tania's old friends, now all grown up: fat or thin, married or single, successful or disappointed, whatever it was they had made of their uninterrupted lives.

The cemetery was a drive away – a natural burial ground – and at the grave mouth there were fewer people. Sarah, standing back, recognized Claire of course, holding long-stemmed white roses, and Tania's father with his third wife and their two teenage children.

Retired Detective Inspector Peter Stokes was there, like Sarah standing respectfully back from the family. He'd taken Sarah aside before the service and shaken her hand and said he was a man of his word and that there was a case of bubbly waiting for her in the boot of his car. Sarah had said, 'I'll have to split it with Elaine.' Stokes had raised his eyebrows and said, 'Fat Elaine?' and Sarah had said, 'That's right. Couldn't have done it without her.'

So Elaine was there too, and Robert McCarthy, with Ewan who was there to help Robert and had clearly borrowed the suit he was wearing. It was burgundy and too short in the sleeves. And there was Katherine, Tania's friend, who had watched her walking away on 16 October 1987.

It was a light brown coffin and it held Tania's name on its lid on a bronze plate. The undertakers put the straps underneath and lowered it into the ground.

At least Tania was known now. At least there was a grave to visit, and looking around, Sarah was pleased to see there were already trees: birches and ash.

She thought of Tania, fifteen years old, poised at the pivot between child and woman. Her imaginings of her were limited – she saw her on the netball court, an aggressive little wing attack; practising her violin in her school uniform; frizzing her hair and struggling into her jeans. She had been at that moment in her life when the world should have sung for her in all its glory. She should have made harmless mistakes, and agonized about teenage love, and adults should have shaken their heads at her behaviour; and she should have done both well and badly and, in the end, survived it all to become older and wiser.

Claire had chosen Psalm 98 for a graveside reading, and the undertakers handed out photocopied sheets. They read it together.

Make a joyful noise unto the LORD, all the earth: make a loud noise, and rejoice, and sing praise.

Sing unto the LORD with the harp; with the harp, and the voice of a psalm.

With trumpets and sound of cornet make a joyful noise before the LORD, the King.

Let the sea roar, and the fullness thereof; the world, and they that dwell therein.

Claire hesitated by the grave. The undertaker offered her the tray of soil but she declined to throw earth on her daughter. Instead she went down on her hands and knees and dropped the roses in.

49

E very day more reality.

They had moved her to another ward and Lizzie felt the demotion from critical to stable. The nurses maintained their professional cheerfulness but they were busier with more patients under their care. Lizzie imagined that they were tiring of her, as if she were a guest who had outstayed her welcome. She was tiring of hospital too. The drama of the intervention and then, later, the golden bliss of the morphine was resolving slowly into the frustration of rehabilitation. Gradually, more hours awake. Pain when she moved. The inglorious use of a bedpan, and then her first, slow walk to the toilet, wheeling her friend the trolley with the pack of fluids beside her.

'No, I'm fine, Mum. I can do it by myself.'

She had pulled up her nightie and looked at the dressing on her side and the spreading bruise across her shoulder and arm. Hard to believe that this was a body that had once run long-distance; that had competed in cross-country and acquitted itself pretty well. She wondered if the runner's high was lost to her forever. The wonderful power of it, the ease of her lungs, the strength in her feet – it was like remembering someone completely different. But it wasn't just the physical aspect. It felt to her as though she was saying goodbye to some other, younger person who had seen the world through different eyes. She knew she had to turn herself around, a reluctant sailor tacking close-hauled into the wind. The doctor wanted to see her to find out what she was thinking about that matter they'd discussed. She was going to have to make a decision.

Julie had asked permission to visit, and she popped her head round the door cautiously. 'All right for me to come in, Lizzie?'

She was carrying a plastic bag, and she sat down and lifted out a white box of fancy chocolates. 'I googled them,' she said. 'Hope you like truffles.' A hand-knitted cardigan followed. She held it up, and Lizzie saw finely blended moorland colours in herringbone with six thin red stripes zigzagging across the arms and chest.

Julie said, 'I nicked the pattern from something I saw in *Vogue*. Pretty sure I got your size right.'

She handed it to Lizzie. The wool was soft.

Julie said quietly, 'Wool-cashmere mix.'

'It's beautiful, but I'm sure I'm not allowed to accept it.'

'Rubbish.' Julie quickly folded it up with deft movements and put it in the locker beside the bed. 'There, look, you've *always* had it. Your mum brought it in from home.'

'Well, thank you. It's really lovely.'

'Don't be silly. Skye and me wound the yarn together.' Julie was back in the carrier bag, which seemed empty to Lizzie. 'One other thing.' She held out a loom band, bright pink and electric-blue. 'Skye wanted you to have this. Not sure about the colours.'

Lizzie took it and slipped it on her wrist, next to the plastic hospital identity bracelet. 'I wonder what happened to the other one she gave me.'

'Maybe the medics cut it off when they brought you in?'

Lizzie lay back. Just the thought of it, those bright lights and the kerfuffle around her when they'd lifted her from the ambulance, made her feel suddenly very tired. She wondered if she'd ever have the energy for life again.

Julie said, 'Well, I won't stay long.' She rubbed her hands together as if she was starting a fire in a survival movie. 'Before I go, I wanted to say . . .' She had tears in her eyes. 'Thank you.'

Lizzie interrupted with a wave of her hand. 'No, Julie. No. There's no reason.'

'There *is* a reason!' And then Julie was crying full on and getting up in a fluster and saying, 'I'd better go. They told me not to tire you.' She paused by the bed. 'Can I kiss you? Would you mind?'

Lizzie shook her head. 'No, I'd like that.'

When Julie had gone, Lizzie stared blindly at the ceiling. What struck her was how, for all her grief, all her loss, Julie was nothing but pleased to have another child to raise.

The doctor would be here shortly.

The obvious decision, the right decision, the rational decision was the one she had made before she'd gone into her house and seen Skye handcuffed to the radiator. She hated herself for not being able to make it. She wanted to be free and irresponsible, and more than anything, she hated the sensation that even though she was still in her twenties, she would no longer be young.

But she couldn't do it. It was as if, the way things had worked out, she couldn't give herself the choice. She and that tiny heartbeat had survived Brannon twice.

She got out of bed, struggled to the toilet with the trolley, struggled to pee. She didn't believe in signs and portents. She didn't want to make her life more difficult!

But what could she do? Time was moving on and the decision had to be made. Out of all this misery there was still this extra heartbeat inside her, and she couldn't bring herself to stop it.

50

It was early evening. Sarah stood in her bedroom, despairing at her decision to meet Caroline and despairing equally at the choice of an outfit.

All the constituents of clothing – the details of stitching, the flare of a trouser leg, how colours were combined, their shades and qualities – all this seemed to Sarah to speak a language that was both incomprehensible and annoying. When was a colour bold? Was bold a good thing? The issue of the cut of a shirt, the stitching of a pocket seemed to lay a claim to her attention that every part of her wanted to refute.

Work clothes were easy. She had a formula: smart dark suits, good white shirts, smart flat shoes. These were clothes that she identified without much thought as a kind of respectful nothing. Function was the arbiter and the only meaning she wished to convey was 'I am doing my job. You can trust me to concentrate on that and not on what I am wearing.' This was a message, she felt, that stated her position accurately.

But now, with only twenty minutes left before Caroline arrived, clothes presented themselves suddenly – and unavoidably – as an altogether more compelling matter. Each choice carried possible intimations, intimations that were alarming but that she realized she needed to dare to reveal. A disclosure of longing might perhaps be made by the height of a waist or the fabric of a shirt.

She would not allow herself even to think that underwear might be important, but she broke out, as disinterestedly as possible, brand-new cotton pants from unblemished cellophane. They sat flatly inviting across her hips – *this is here*, they seemed to say, *if you want it* – and left a plateau of unmarked skin between their straight hemline and her plain bra.

Then, in spite of her best intentions, she found herself speeding up, impulsively spinning her wardrobe and drawers as thoroughly as any search team, trying on outfits and discarding them onto a groaning pile on the bed. Stretch trousers – a glance in the mirror: too desperate. A linen dress – too frumpy. A short dark cotton skirt with a side-buttoned stripy jacket – God, no, what on earth had she been thinking when she bought that? Finally, old jeans with a wide brown leather belt, a light-blue shirt with a snowflake print and shell buttons.

It was a lovely shirt, even she could see that. She had bought it on a rare expedition to the fancy shops near Covent Garden. The assistant, a gay man, had pooh-poohed her protests and held different fabrics against her face, pulled shirts and trousers from shelves and hangers, entered the changing room with no embarrassment at all at finding her in bra and pants. He'd insisted on the shirt and she'd swiped her plastic obediently but also with secret pleasure. It was ridiculously expensive. On the way out of the shop she had looked over her shoulder, and he had caught her eye and winked.

Sarah paused and looked at herself.

Well, maybe.

Maybe even pretty good.

She looked again and confirmed her first impression. She agonized for several minutes over a detail, buttoning and unbuttoning the shirt at the neck, and then, when she had finally settled on two buttons undone, revealing just a hint of her breasts beneath, she worried that with her fussing she had softened the expensive, crisp fabric.

Shoes? Five pairs on and off while the dog watched balefully from the bedroom chair. Trainers: too boring. Flat pumps: too boring. Heels: no, she couldn't possibly . . . Finally, yes, *perhaps* – dark leather biker-style boots. She looked at Daisy.

'Well, what do you think?'

The dog lifted her head from the chair where she was lying and made a stab at wagging her tail.

'You don't think a bit dykey perhaps?'

She looked and looked again in the mirror, swung her hips to one side.

'But dykey in a good way, maybe?'

She glanced back to the spaniel, who responded by pushing her ears back in that expression that seemed to be a smile. Sarah returned to her reflection.

'Hell, you're right, Daisy girl. Why not?'

She smeared some red lipstick, applied some mascara. Not a lot of make-up, just enough to suggest she did this all the time and hadn't dedicated her life to the job. Of course she didn't spend her rest days in jogging trousers and old T-shirts. Only a fool would think that! She hoped the message was fine-tuned: she wasn't *trying* . . .

There was a knocking at the door, Daisy running down the stairs and barking in the hallway. She sat on the bed. The dog barked again. After a minute, another tentative knock. Caroline saying her name. An impulse passed through her like a cold tide – let the dog bark, wait for Caroline to leave – and so, before she could give in to it, she opened the door to her bedroom and walked downstairs.

Daisy immediately began jumping up at her leg. Sarah remembered an old joke about the dyke on a blind date being the one with the removal van. Having Daisy there made it worse: not a removal van but a surrogate child, for God's sake. It all felt so desperate. And she wasn't desperate. That was the truth. She was fine on her own. Better even. Daisy looked up at her and wagged her tail. Sarah opened the door.

At first she couldn't take in the fact of Caroline, could only feel the simple wash of excitement at her being there. Quickly, she made a nervous assessment of what Caroline had chosen to wear. Nothing that seemed to have been much of an effort: a light-blue scoop-neck T-shirt, low-cut jeans.

'Hey,' Caroline said and smiled. 'You look great.'

'You too.'

And she did, but she didn't look as though she'd spent ages trying on different outfits. She seemed so in control, so *normal*.

Daisy was weaving around between them in endless figures of eight, like a happy blessing with a wagging tail. Caroline picked the dog up and stroked her behind the ears. Daisy tried to lick her face.

Sarah had an acute sensation of need, of urgency. She imagined in a rush her lips on Caroline's mouth, her body against her. It made her cross and embarrassed, this longing. She felt a fool. She had a reckless urge to dispense with all this politeness and the meal that was in the oven. She wanted to show her hand, be rejected or accepted, put an end to her discomfort.

Caroline, still holding Daisy, smiled at her kindly. 'What a lovely dog.'

It was a good meal. They talked about this and that – teaching, policing – and avoided the subjects that interested them: Farah's death, Patti, sex.

Finally Sarah resorted to the bland question that had been lurking behind her talk of cuts in the policing service and the pressure on teachers in inner-city schools.

'How's Patti?'

Caroline paused with her spoon of chocolate mousse. 'She's still with her family in St Lucia.'

It was hard to think of a swift follow-up. She wanted to show a generous interest.

'You two been together long?'

Caroline grinned. 'You're really not very good at this, are you?'

It was Caroline, of course, who bridged the gap, getting up and tracing a tender smear of chocolate mousse on Sarah's lips, then licking it off with a slow and intending tongue. Sarah, still seated, nervously pulled away.

Caroline drew back and looked at her with a smile. 'You do want this, don't you?'

Although she was blushing, almost on the point of screaming with embarrassment, Sarah said hoarsely, 'Yes. Christ, yes, of course I do.'

And so Daisy was shut away somewhere upstairs and Caroline returned. She kissed Sarah again, first on the mouth and then moving down her neck. Sarah stood and pressed her body into Caroline's. It was easy after all: you just did at last what you had longed so badly to do. She kissed her on the mouth and then moved her hands down her back, beginning to kiss down her neck. Each touch was so perfect, so exhilarating. Suddenly they were both impatient. They began to struggle out of their clothes, laughing at their own desperation. There was a hiatus: the buttons on the new shirt were awkward. The impulse was to rip them off but instead Sarah stood still and solemn while Caroline carefully and slowly unbuttoned her fancy shirt and then moved deliberately down her body.

When it was done, they lay together in Sarah's bed. Sarah, hungry again, stroked her finger slowly down Caroline's belly towards the V of her legs.

'With my body I thee worship,' she said.

Caroline kissed her and laughed. 'Don't give me that! If it had been left to you, we would never have got here.'

Sarah's mobile was ringing.

Caroline said, 'Are you going to switch the damn thing off, or do you need to answer it?'

Sarah stroked Caroline's hair away from her face.

'I'm going to switch the damn thing off.'

ACKNOWLEDGEMENTS

For their creative help, support and kindness in the writing of this novel thank you to Margaret Stead, Sara O'Keeffe, Anne-Marie Doulton. The team at Corvus are always helpful and friendly but a particular thank you to Louise Cullen, who has had to endure the fiddly bits. Thanks also to everyone at Sly Fox Productions – Linda James, Tim Vaughan and Savannah James-Bayley.

Many people have generously shared their knowledge with me. Where there are errors, they are my own. Thank you to Dr Carolyn Millar, Dr Sergei Grachev, Dr Jamie K. Pringle, Jeffry and Claire Wilcox, David Walker, Sarah Walker and Avril Johnson.

As always I remain indebted to and inspired by my former colleagues.

Many people have helped throughout the writing of this book. I am horribly in debt to Uri Roodner. A good man is hard to find but I found one. Thanks too to Yoni and Daveed Roodner, Jane Robinson, Mark Attridge, Paul Needley, Paul Lindsell, Muriel and Fabrice Guine, Hemi and Keren Rudner, Kerry Edwards and Luke Philpotts. Special thanks and love to my sister, Ann Sutcliffe. She knows why. And enduring love to my dear sister Felicity Wood, who encouraged me and everyone around her and who always filled a room with laughter.